Fruitcake and Fraud

Fraud

Book 3 of the Small Town Girl Mysteries

Jann Franklin

CONTENTS

Also By Me

Find my books at jannfranklin.com and your favorite online retailers

Small Town Girl Series

Jen's life isn't perfect, but it's beautiful. A beautiful mess.

Jen was living her best big city life, until her husband Mike uproots them to small town Louisiana. Life throws you curveballs, but you've got to keep swinging.

This heartwarming series resonates with joyful, almost nostalgic feelings of encouragement. Readers living in big cities will feel the quaint, small-town Southern charm leaping off the pages, and experience a yearning to visit their very own Graisseville. And readers from small towns will see versions of themselves and their own community in these characters, nodding and laughing along with Jen and her family. There is something for everyone to relate to and thoughtfully consider.

Trading Bright Lights for Lightning Bugs
Shining Stars and Mason Jars
Cheese Grits and Hissy Fits

Small Town Girl Mystery Series

Why is murder so much fun?

Evangeline Delafose found Graisseville, Louisiana just as she remembered—boring and uneventful. Until she solved a murder. Now she's hooked.

Follow Ev as she takes on each mystery, with her frustrating but loveable private investigator by her side. And, of course, a bit of insider info from the quirky residents of her small town.

You'll laugh, cry and roll your eyes at the antics of this charming small-town Southern sleuth and her exasperating private investigator.

Muffalettas and Murder
Boudin and Bloodshed
Fruitcake and Fraud
Mardi Gras and Mayhem
Sweet Tea and Suspects

How Did I Get Here?

How did it happen? How did I end up back in my hometown of only 298 people? My kids played a major role, urging me to move closer to family after they went off to college. Not closer to them, of course.

"Mom, that would be weird. Our mother, living in the same town? We're college students! No, you should live closer to Uncle Nate and Aunt Bonnie. Grandpa too. You need to make some changes."

I'd been in Graisseville for three months—my brother Nate and my father maintaining watchful eyes over me. Despite their urging, I'd avoided the decorations committee at church, knitting group, and book club. Nate had become increasingly worried about my emotional state, so he found something for me to do.

"Ev, I'm working on a case that's officially inactive. We're at a dead end, but I can't let it go! The sheriff has read your books and he's a fan. We'd like you to look at the case through fresh eyes. Hopefully find something we missed. Would you do that for us?"

In the past, I'd written a series of crime fiction novels featuring New Orleans police detective Lou Bergeron. With Doug gone, I had no desire to visit Lou down at the police station, to flesh out his cases and celebrate his successes. I wasn't sure I would ever write again. But after three years of surviving without my husband, someone found me useful. The Michael Cook case became my reason to stop surviving and start living.

Before I'd realized it, I'd also gained a private investigator. Shorty Cormier had come back from the Gulf War with a purple heart and a prosthetic leg. Our fathers had been the best of friends, spending many afternoons at the Cormier farm. The man drove me crazy, but I counted him as one of my oldest and dearest friends.

When Shorty discovered my new project, he jumped in and used his private investigator skills to help me solve the case. Even my brother was impressed that a Gulf War veteran with a prosthetic leg and a woman who wrote mystery novels cracked a case that had stumped the entire sheriff's department.

A few months later, we solved the murder of Remy Robichaux and collected a reward from the victim's family. We impressed the sheriff even more, and hoped we'd earned the opportunity for another case.

Let's not forget my nickname. Shorty had called me Doc ever since my graduation from LSU with a PhD in English Literature. My parents bragged to everyone, including the entire village of Graisseville. Their daughter was a doctor! The word spread, a normal occurrence in small towns, and soon the story transformed. Skeeter and Muriel Bergeron's daughter Evangeline graduated from LSU medical school!

Doug and I visited my parents after graduation, and puzzled over people greeting me as *Doc*. My parents corrected no one, but eventually people figured it out. Shorty's family continued calling me *Doc*. They enjoyed having a doctor in their adopted family, even if it was a doctor of books. Why no one called my father, the veterinarian, *Doc*, was still a mystery.

As Shorty and I waited for our next case, I began dating his cousin Cayenne Cormier. Strange name but great guy—all his brothers and sisters were named after spices. Cay was preparing to take over the family restaurant and catering business, which left little time for dating. But we made it work...sort of.

Winter became spring, then summer. I added a Creative Writing class to my summer schedule. Shorty continued his private investigator business, in the supply closet at the Graisseville Gas n' More. The rent was cheap and the traffic flow was high. Summer turned to fall, and God blessed me with four classes at LSU. Shorty and I were happy, don't get me wrong. But we were itching for another case to solve.

Through the Victim's Eyes

Ronald reclined in his chair, surveying his kingdom. He'd stolen over $100,000 from Sid's company, and no one had a clue. Sure, Sid had asked a few questions, demanded a few extra reports for verification. But he was just in the early stages of suspicion. Ronald knew the stages well, because New Horizons was his seventh company to take to the cleaners. By the third company he'd figured out just the right words to say during the interview, just the perfect references to give. And he definitely knew just the right time to leave, which meant it was time to plan his exit strategy. Gauging Sid's knowledge of accounting, Ronald had a week, maybe less, before Sid figured it all out. Yeah, better start gathering all the evidence and head for the next victim...uh, place of employment.

What was that sound? Ronald had kept an eye on the parking lot all Friday afternoon. The last car shot out of the lot at exactly 3:30 p.m., and his car was the only one left. He touched his toes to the floor and pushed himself backwards toward the window. A quarter turn of his swivel chair and he could see through the open blinds. No, his car was the only one. Maybe the cleaning people came early? He glanced at his phone—5:12 p.m. Mike and his crew always parked out front. They wouldn't pay any attention to New Horizons' star employee tidying up his desk before the weekend. Hey, they might even tell the clueless owners he stuffed his briefcase full of work for the weekend.

"Hello, Ronald. You didn't expect to see me this evening, did you?"

Huh? His eyes swung towards the door, taking the rest of his face with them. It couldn't be!

"Um...well, no. I sure didn't. It's not that I don't enjoy your company. But whatever it is, can't it wait? I'm trying to get out of here to start the weekend."

To start the weekend on a plane out of East Baton Rouge Parish, for sure. He already had interviews with three other companies, each more flush with cash than this one.

"Oh, it won't take long. I just need to get a few things off my chest, so to speak. I know you've been skimming cash from every company that's employed you for the last few years, and I know how you're doing it. I finally figured it out. You're headed out this door, but I know you've already selected the next company to swindle. And I want in, or else I'm going to the police."

Oh geez, why hadn't he seen this coming? "Well, I appreciate your offer, but I'm going to decline. My operation is a one man show."

Ronald opened the bottom drawer of his desk, grabbing at papers and shoving them into the briefcase. He'd better hurry the exit process along, or it could get ugly.

"Funny, I thought you'd say that. But I'm not taking no for an answer. You stole from me, and I want my money...with interest!"

Oh, boy! Ronald was all too familiar with that look. If he could just make it to the door, he had a fighting chance.

"Calm down, okay? We can work something out. We're both reasonable people, and we can come to some sort of agreement."

Ronald stood up and closed his briefcase. He estimated two steps to get out from behind the desk, then five to hit the doorway.

"How about we talk about this over a cup of coffee tomorrow? You take the evening to put together what you want, and we'll hammer out the details tomorrow. There's a great coffee shop near the LSU campus—I can send you the address and we'll meet tomorrow."

Maybe a hand on the shoulder would emphasize his sincerity? But the unwanted visitor sidestepped the gesture.

"Wow! You think I'm that stupid? We both know you're on a plane out of here in just a few hours. No, we're settling this tonight."

Ronald gauged the distance again—only a couple of steps. He ran five miles a day, so if he could make it to the door, then he'd be home free.

"Now, why in the world would you think that? I've got a lot to do this weekend! I can't afford to get on a plane and go anywhere. Look at this briefcase, it's jammed full of work I'm taking home. Now I can squeeze you in early tomorrow for this little chat. But I want to get home. I'll text you the address of that coffee shop, okay?"

As he brushed past, he felt pain. He put a hand to his neck and felt a sticky dampness. Was that...

"What have you done?" Ronald faced his killer with puppy dog eyes. Out of all the people he'd wronged, he couldn't believe he was going to die for it.

"And really? You used *that* to kill me? Well, I have to hand it to you...it's original. And meaningful to both of us."

"**M**erry early Christmas, Doc! How's yore shoppin' comin' along?"

My second Christmas in Graisseville, and it was feeling more and more like home. "Pretty good. I've still got my dad and you. The two hardest people to shop for on my list. Any ideas for my dad?"

Even through the phone I could hear Shorty's brain cells sizzling. Since Annabelle entered his life, he took gift giving seriously. "Well, he's been complainin' he needs a new ratchet. An' he was thinkin' o'puttin' out some fertilizer on his front yard this spring."

Okay, maybe not as seriously as I had thought. "Those are great ideas, don't get me wrong. But I was thinking more along the lines of a new shirt, or some pillows for his couch."

Cue the horse snort. "See, that's why women jus' don't get it! We don't want somethin' on our couch we gotta move jus' t'sit! But if yer gonna get 'im a shirt, ya' should get 'im a work shirt. Think about it, Doc. The good Lord wants us t'work six days an' rest on Sunday. We need six times as many work shirts as we do Sunday go-tuh-meetin' shirts."

He made an excellent point, as always. "What if I got him a gift card to Big Ed's Parts n' More? Then he could buy a work shirt, a ratchet, or fertilizer? Whatever his heart desires, as long as it costs fifty dollars."

My friend and my father were cut from the same cloth—they bought their clothes and their fertilizer at the same store. It did make my shopping that much easier.

"Now that we got yore shoppin' all taken care of, I need yore opinion on somethin'. Do ya' have a few minutes?"

Another change from dating Annabelle–Shorty asked permission to interrupt my life. Most times, anyway. "Of course, any chance to give my opinion is welcome. Fire away!"

"Uh, well I'm tryin' t'come up with a gift for Annabelle. We've been datin' over a year, an' I already gave her all the flowers an' candles an' jewelry that she needs. She's tryin' t'watch her weight, so no food. Besides, it needs t'be more special than chocolate or flowers, anyway. Doc, this is the longest I ever dated a woman."

It certainly was, and the whole village knew it. Many a woman had tried to capture Shorty's heart, but failed. That was probably why Annabelle had succeeded...because she never tried. She continued to be her practically perfect self, letting Shorty know the kind of person she was from the beginning. My friend fell hook, line, and sinker for her refreshing honesty.

"Tell you what—I'm due for a coffee and chat with Annabelle, anyway. Let me talk to her and see what she's getting you. That should give me some ideas."

Part of me wanted to suggest an engagement ring. But marriage was a commitment two people needed to decide upon themselves. Well-meaning friends needed to stay out of it.

"Whatcha gettin' my *cuzzin'* for Christmas? Now, I don't know exactly what he got for ya', but I bet yer gonna like it! It's gotta be good, cuz every time I ask 'im about it, he gets real quiet."

Shopping for Cayenne—or Cay, as we all called him–had been easy. And hard. Truthfully, I couldn't put into words what it had been. Officially, we'd been dating for almost eleven months. In practice, we'd been on maybe eight dates. Cay's parents had retired, leaving him to manage the Hoot n' Holler restaurant and catering all on his own. He'd been flying solo for a while, anyway. But once folks found out Auntie Bell wasn't cooking, all H-E-Double hockey sticks broke loose.

"Auntie Bell's crab cakes were thicker than these. Send 'em back!"

"My etouffee had at least a dozen more shrimp in it when Auntie Bell was cooking—send it back and put more shrimp in it!"

The complaints and demands rained down on poor Cay like a thunderstorm—quick and painful, with no end in sight.

December traditionally was the most profitable month for the restaurant, with Christmas parties hosted and catered. Cay had already prepared me.

"I'm really sorry, Ev. You're not going to see or hear from me until after New Year's. Then, of course, it's Mardi Gras season...we'll be swimming in gumbo and King cake. But after that, for sure."

My gift to Cay was to break up with him. He'd be free to focus on the restaurant. And I'd be free from halfhearted excuses why we couldn't see each other. My heart hurt for what could have been. But the restaurant was the love of Cay's life, and I'd never even be a close second.

"Cay got me a gift? Last I heard, I wasn't going to see him until after Mardi Gras."

"Uh, well, I don't know about that, Doc. Look, forget I said anythin'. Anyway, What're ya' gettin' 'im?"

Someone had spilled the beans and was frantically shoving them back into the can. Or trying to.

"Probably a gift card to Big Ed's. Sounds like that's what the men in my life enjoy."

Another snort—some things never changed. "Nah, Cay's not gonna like that. How 'bout a nice new wallet? Or some o'that good smellin' men's cologne he wears?"

Was I really going to take gifting advice from Shorty? I couldn't tell him the truth—he'd take the breakup worse than Cay.

"The cologne sounds nice, Shorty. Thank you for the suggestion. Anything else on your mind?"

Much as I loved my friend, I knew he was calling for a reason other than to check the status of my Christmas shopping.

"Uh, yeah, now that ya' mention it. Iffin yer too busy with yore classes an' all, that's okay. But I've got a case I'd like some help on. Nothin' big, like a murder or a bank robbery. The sheriff an' his crew always get those big cases. Course that don't make any sense tuh me. Seems like we oughta have a crack at 'em."

"You know, you're right—that does seem unfair. Why should the people sworn to uphold the law get to catch the ones breaking those laws? Maybe you should talk to your cousin Hugh, see if he'll run an article in the *Gazette* about the injustice."

Shorty had learned to ignore my sarcasm. "Yeah, yeah, I'll do that. Anyways, I've got a robbery...well, sorta. I'd like ya' t'work with me an' figure it out."

"Here in Graisseville? A robbery? You mean one of the 298 people got robbed? Well, that narrows our suspect pool to the other 297. Actually, less than that if you eliminate us, my dad, my brother and his wife, ..."

A crackle of irritation sizzled through my phone. "Now hold on, Doc! No need t'be so sarcastic. An' it could be someone outside o'Graisseville. That number 298 is jus' the people livin' inside the village limits. I ain't part o'that number. So take off yore sarcastic hat an' put on yore detectin' hat, okay? I'm pullin' into yore driveway, so be sure an' have that detectin' hat on yore head when ya' answer the door. An' don't tell Zy, but I got another box o'treats for 'im."

Shorty's cousin Cletus owned Brown Dog Bakery, an up-scale dog treat company. He specialized in creating high end dog treat recipes and selling them to a national manufac-turer. Off the Chain Chewies, featuring my dog's face, had paid for Cletus' new fishing boat. Zy's payment for the use of his face was a monthly box of treats. Shorty insisted they arrive at his house, so he could bring them over and film Zy's reaction as we unboxed them. Zy probably needed to renegotiate his contract, but it was low on my to do list.

After the filming of the unboxing, we settled down to business. I'd learned to keep a stash of *Zapp's* Crawtator chips in my pantry, and orange soda in my refrigerator. I was on the downhill of losing the last stubborn ten pounds, so the rest of my kitchen featured what Shorty called *slim pickings*. As he made his way to the pantry, he slipped into PI mode.

"Pearlie Rabalais called me a few days ago. She's the lady who hands out fruitcakes durin' the Christmas holidays."

"Oh, yes...Pearlie. She makes one for every founding family in Graisseville, plus all the sheriff's deputies, firefighters, and EMT's. I heard she wanted to widen the circle to employees of the Graisseville school system, but the teacher's union stepped in. Something about the fruitcake violated union policy. I think it had something to do with bribery."

"Yeah, it's more like a *vie-oh-lay-shun* o'human decency! That fruitcake's dry as a cotton field in August. Fact is, I'd rather eat the dirt in my backyard than try t'put away one o'Miss Pearlie's fruitcakes."

Thankfully, I'd avoided Pearlie's questionable creations for quite some time. Mother had initially thanked Pearlie every year for her delivery, then dumped the crumbly loaf into the trash. When Nate was seven, Daddy deemed him old enough to answer the door and telephone. My father underestimated my brother's loyalty to the truth.

"Why hello there, Nathan! You may not remember me, but I'm Mrs. Rabalais. I've stopped by to deliver your family a delicious fruitcake that I've created from scratch. It's a closely guarded family recipe, handed down from my great great grandmother. Is your mama home? I'd love to chat with her."

As Pearlie squinted into the cool recesses of our hallway, Nate set her straight.

"No, ma'am. My mama isn't home, but I can save you some trouble. The second you leave our front porch, I'll just throw your fruitcake into the trash. That's what my mama does every year, and I've seen no evidence her behavior will change. So as soon as you leave, I'll just take care of that job for her."

Then, remembering the manners Mother and Daddy had poured into him, he finished with, "Now you have a nice day, Mrs. Rabalais. And stop by any time."

When Mother returned from the store, Nate stood at attention, giving her an official report on the phone call from Mrs. Willis and the visit from Pearlie Rabalais. Mother nodded at the phone call, but almost fainted at Nate's report on Miss Pearlie.

When Daddy got home, he patted Nate on the back and pronounced him the official door and phone keeper. Mother declared Nate would never come within five feet of either while living under her roof. In the end, it was a combination of both. Mother made me or my sister Mad handle outside communication when she wasn't home. When Daddy was in charge, he promoted Nate to keeper of doors and telephones.

Shorty was well aware of Nate's encounter with Pearlie and her fruitcake. "I guess she don't bring ya' one o'her grit cakes since ya' moved back. Seein' as how yore mama threw them out all those years."

"Nope, and I really should thank the good Lord for that blessing tonight when I say my prayers. But what about you? You're not part of a founding family, or a first responder—you don't get any of those frightful fruitcakes."

"Yeah? Ya'd think so. But when I come back from the Gulf War, an' the village threw that parade for me, it sealed my fate. Ol' Miss Pearlie, she brought me a fruitcake the next Christmas. T'thank me for my service, she said. Doc, the MRE's we got in Kuwait were better than that dang dry as a bone cake!"

Poor Shorty! He lost his right leg from the knee down in the Gulf War, a sacrifice well deserving of a reward. But not a reward best suited for compost in a garden.

"Anyways, this year Miss Pearlie had all her fruitcakes coolin' on her screened-in back porch. It wasn't locked or nothin'. I mean, who'd steal fruitcakes? But they did! Some-one stole eighty-two loaves of fruitcake, God bless 'em."

By then, my cup of jasmine tea was a perfect 180 degrees. As I sipped, I mulled over the story. "So, no leads, then?"

Shorty shook his head once, taking the bare minimum of time. He needed to get back to his chips and soda.

"Well, you've got to determine why someone would steal the fruitcake. That's going to give you a list of suspects."

My PI choked down his chips, eager to correct me. "Ain't that obvious? They stole 'em so they wouldn't have t'be all fake an' such, an' thank Miss Pearlie for her terrible fruit-cake!"

"No, that's not it. Think about it, Shorty. What's easier: thanking Miss Pearlie, who really is a sweet and kind lady, and throwing her fruitcake in the trash? Or pulling up your truck and throwing eighty-two fruitcakes into it, then find-ing somewhere to get rid of them? No, there's another reason someone stole them. And we've got to figure out why."

At last, a case! It had been over ten months since we'd solved the Remy Robichaux murder. Teaching crime fiction and creative writing paid the bills, but solving crime stirred my soul. Finding the fruitcake thief didn't rank as high on the fun scale as solving a murder, but desperate times called for desperate measures.

I did have one burning question, though. "How much is Miss Pearlie paying you? I'm not asking you to share the fee—I'm just curious."

Shorty wiped his mouth. "Uh, well, she wanted t'pay me in baked goods. Now, I ain't ever had anythin' other than her fruitcake. But I didn't wanna take no chances. I told her $200 a day plus expenses."

Of course! Shorty was a fan of *The Rockford Files*, so it made sense he'd quote Jim Rockford's fee structure. No matter it was from the late 1970's.

He took the last swig of orange soda and crunched the can. "Miss Pearlie said that was fine, but she could only afford two days, maybe three. Truth be told, I been missin' my PI time, solvin' cases an' all. So, I said I'd do it for a new set o'tires. The ones on muh truck are lookin' pretty bald."

As always, I knew this story had a logical thread in there somewhere. I just had to ask the right question. "Why would you ask Miss Pearlie to pay you with truck tires?"

Shorty stood up and tossed the soda can into my trash, then rolled the open end of the chip bag and clipped it. The words *neat freak* scrolled across my brain. "Geez,

Doc...don'tcha know? The Rabalais family owns Graisseville Tires n' More. Miss Pearlie's father-in-law opened the doors back in 1957. Or was it 1955? Anyway, her son runs it now. Yeah, she can get me some top o'the line tires."

Ah, small town connections! "That's right, I remember. And new tires are more than adequate payment. Okay, I'm in! It'll be fun to work with you again, anyway. So, where do we start?"

As if on cue, the theme song from *Murder, She Wrote* blared from my phone.

"Now, who could that be?" The only people who called me were family and friends—and they all had special ringtones.

"Evangeline? This is Jack Hebert. I bet you don't remember me."

Oh, but I did. I could barely remember what I'd eaten for breakfast, much less what happened in high school. And I'd had my nose in a book all four years. But Jack Hebert stuck out in my head. He'd tried his charms on me, but that wasn't the part I remembered. At the time I'd been too naïve to notice.

One afternoon in the library, I'd been killing time, waiting for middle school to let out. One of the tradeoffs for getting my license was to pick up my sister Mad every day. Her given name was Madeline, but Nate nicknamed her *Mad* for her temper. Unfortunately for Mad, it stuck.

Jack popped into the library, an unusual action for the school quarterback.

"Hey! Evangeline, isn't it? Say, would you like to go to The Burger Shack and get a shake? Most of the football team's already there—they're saving us seats."

As usual, I found books more intriguing than boys. "Oh, I don't know any football players. Besides, I've got to pick up my sister in another twenty minutes. Thanks anyway."

Jack was relentless. "We can bring her along. C'mon, it'll be fun! I'll introduce you to everybody. You two will get a real kick out of the whole experience."

Mad probably would. My sister had always been more concerned with fashion and popularity than I'd ever been. I'd never get her out of The Burger Shack.

"Oh, that's okay. We both need to get home and help my mother with supper. But I appreciate your invitation. Maybe another time."

Was Jack determined to mooch a milkshake off me? Or was he fascinated by a girl he couldn't impress? As I stuck my nose back into *Little Women*, I saw an index finger curl over the top of the book.

"Whatcha reading there? It can't be more interesting than me." My eyes traveled from the finger to the baby blues framed by the longest eyelashes I'd ever seen—especially on a boy. He pulled the book down to reveal his crooked grin. No doubt Jack had flashed that smile at enough women to fill our football stadium. The guy had been doing this his whole life. But he'd never met a girl like me.

"Actually, it is more interesting than you. I'm at the part where Beth gets scarlet fever and gets so sick, they don't think she's going to make it through the night."

Up went my book, blocking baby blues, inch long eyelashes, and a mouth open wide enough to swallow a burger from The Burger Shack.

Our little meeting in the library changed my relationship with Jack Hebert. The guy spoke to me in the hallways, even holding doors open for me. He continued to accumulate free movie tickets and food from his adoring masses, but he put me in a different category altogether.

In my senior yearbook he wrote, "To Evangeline—the one that got away." He headed off to LSU, then law school, settling into the Louisiana Attorney General's office. From there he took a turn toward politics, or so I'd heard. I never attended any high school class reunions, so I never knew where he landed.

Imagine my surprise a few years ago when I spotted a postcard in my mailbox. "Jackson Hebert: The Choice For Change." Jack's baby blues and crooked grin stared back at me, thirty plus years older, but just as handsome. Maybe a little wiser?

When I'd gone to the polls, I'd voted for him. He'd won by a landslide, and I'd considered reaching out. Then life got busy, Doug passed, and the kids needed their remaining parent more than ever. I'd heard through my father that Jack's wife died of ovarian cancer, but I wasn't sure what to say. "Hey, Jack! Welcome to the dead spouse club. It totally stinks, but you get a lot of sympathy food."

I'd wondered if he'd forgotten me. The voice on the other end answered that question.

"Jack? Of course, I remember you! Why, you're my United States senator. I voted for you, by the way."

Shorty's eyes squinted in that familiar slant I'd learned to recognize. Next would be the frantic hand gestures. I really should get with him sometime and learn what they all meant. I always felt like I was playing a round of Charades...and losing every time.

What did two hands facing palms up mean, anyway? Shorty didn't know something? Well, that was normal. But why was he telling me?

"Oh, well, thank you. I do appreciate your vote. I don't know if you've heard, but my uncle Sid Hebert has been arrested for murder. Of course, he didn't do it! My entire family is rallying around him."

Jack Hebert was calling me! *Senator* Jack Hebert was calling me. The last important political figure who'd contacted me was Roby Melancon. He'd decided to run for police chief of Graisseville. We didn't even have a police force, but Roby wanted the position, anyway. He thought people would respect him more with a title. Poor Roby didn't get enough signatures to even get on the ballot, which was a blessing. He'd made so many promises to get his petition signed, he would have spent his entire term trying to fulfill them. Jack definitely trumped Roby on the political ladder.

"Oh, no! I hadn't heard. I'm so sorry, Jack—I know you're close to your uncle. What can I do to help?"

"Thank you, Evangeline. I appreciate your sentiments. And you're right—Uncle Sid and I are close. His business dealings throughout the years have not always been on the up and up. But he'd never kill anyone. Anyway, I understand you and Shorty Cormier have some sort of investigation business. You've solved a couple of cases for the sheriff, I've heard. Is that right?"

Wow! Senator Jack Hebert knew about our crime fighting. Maybe he'd authorize some sort of signal, similar to the one Commissioner Gordon flashed in the sky for Batman? Then, when anyone needed us, they could call Jack and he could flash the signal. But what would it look like?

"Uh, Ev...are you there?"

Whoops! "Yes, Jack...I mean, Senator. Sorry, what was the question?"

A soft chuckle floated through my phone. "You can call me Jack. Is it true you've solved some cases for the sheriff?"

"Oh, yes! We've solved two murders, actually. And we're working on a robbery case right now."

Should I have mentioned the case of the missing fruit-cakes? Technically, it was my third investigation, which improved my statistics. At least, I thought it did. Honestly, I'd dropped my statistics class after failing the first test.

"Oh, hey, that's impressive. Uncle Sid's being held without bond at the jail in Baton Rouge. I'd like to hire you to find the real killer. When could you get here and talk to him? And his lawyer, I'm sure. He wants to be present for every single meeting, so he can bill more hours."

Interesting comment, considering Jack had practiced law for many years. Of course, he'd been a prosecutor. They worked for pennies but slept with a clear conscience.

"Let me talk to Shorty and I'll give you a call back. Or should I just talk to Sid's lawyer?"

Another chuckle drifted into my ear. "No, I'm calling the shots. In case you didn't know, the founding families have a slush fund of sorts. It helps with legal expenses for family members on the wrong side of the law. Sid isn't the first founding family member to utilize the fund. But everything's running through me—the expenses, the legal strategy...all of it. I want to make sure my uncle has access to every available resource."

"Of course. Give me five minutes and I'll call you right back."

Maybe I could have put Shorty on speaker phone, and we would have sorted out the details. But did I trust my PI to be professional and refrain from sarcastic comments? Not a chance.

"Was that the not-so-honorable Senator Jackson Hebert? Well, butter my behind and call me a biscuit! What's that guy want?"

"I'd rather not...butter your posterior, that is. Or anywhere on your person, for that matter. Goodness, I'm never going to get that image out of my mind! Senator Hebert wants us to meet with his uncle Sid at the jail in Baton Rouge. He's been charged with murder, and the senator would like us to find the real killer."

Ah, the all too familiar horse snort. "Well, of course he's sittin' in jail. Those Heberts are nothin' but a bunch o'thieves anyway. Not a far jump t'murderin', that's for sure."

Shorty didn't have much compassion for any of the founding families, except the Bergerons of course. Even though my ancestors were one of the five families to settle Graisseville, we didn't think much of it.

My dad would always say, "I betcha a Dunbar or a Cormier opened the door for ol' great great granddaddy Clement Bergeron, as he stepped into the clerk of court's office. Yes sir, ol' Clement was the fifth person to register his property in Graisseville. But if Bergerons were as polite as those Dunbars and Cormiers, why Clement would have been sixth or seventh in line. We Bergerons don't always have the best manners."

My father and Shorty's dad had been the best of friends, not caring who was and who wasn't a so-called founding family. "*Evangeline, God loves all of us, and He doesn't care when we* moved to Graisseville. Or Louisiana, for that matter. But I'll tell you one thing..."

Dad would always lean closer, like he was revealing an important secret. "It might not say so in the Bible, but I have it on good authority that the good Lord cheers for LSU on His day of rest."

Nate actually believed that bit of nonsense well into high school. All that to say, the other founding families could be a bit uppity at times.

"Okay, I'll call the senator back and tell him we'd rather chase a fruitcake thief than a murderer. After all, you do need new truck tires."

A low growl echoed in my kitchen. If my PI hadn't consumed half a bag of Crawtators and a can of soda, I'd think his stomach was complaining. But it was the sound of a man admitting I was right.

We crowded around the square metal table—two investigators, a defense lawyer, a suspect, and a senator. Jack definitely wasn't billing his uncle, but the rest of us were costing the founding family fund. "Good afternoon, Mr. Hebert. My name is Evangeline Delafose, but my maiden name is Bergeron. We attended several founding family events together. You may not remember me—that was several years ago."

Uncle Sid had to be at least seventy, because Jack was fifty-three. His tanned skin showed barely a wrinkle, and his dark hair revealed a hint of gray. Maybe Sid had been just a kid when Jack was born?

"Evangeline, I may be seventy-two years old, but I'm not senile. Of course, I remember you. And Mr. Cormier, it's indeed a pleasure to meet you. Tell me what you need from me."

Well, that answered my first question. "We'd like to hear your version of what happened, and anyone you think we should investigate. But let's start with what happened the night Ronald Reynolds was murdered."

Sid reclined in the metal chair, his five-foot seven-inch frame fitting easily into its back. He crossed his legs and placed his hands in his lap, fingers laced together. Those hands hadn't seen a day of hard labor. Despite his orange jumpsuit, he lounged as if wearing chinos and a button-down shirt. This man would not fare well in prison.

"Before we go any further, I want it on the record I'm against hiring you two. I've done a little digging into your history, and I'm not impressed. I've already given Jack and Sid my opinion of your expertise, and they've chosen to ignore me. But don't be surprised when my defense doesn't include anything from your so-called investigation."

Sid's lawyer, Holliman Fisher, spat his opinion into our conversation. My father always said don't trust lawyers, and don't trust anyone with two last names. With two strikes against him, Mr. Fisher wasn't winning friends or influencing people.

"An' who are you?" Shorty didn't take kindly to people looking down on him. He'd never been able to walk away from snide remarks.

"If you don't know who I am, then you have no business being in this interview. You've got one hour of my time, and the clock is ticking."

Sid lifted one hand, waving off his lawyer. But his eyes remained on me. "Don't you mind Holliman. He bills $650 an hour, so he's compelled to prove he's worth every dollar. Now where were we? Oh yes, my version of what happened the night Ronald was killed. Or what I like to call, the truth."

His joke, though small, made us all smile. "But first, let me give you a little background. I own New Horizons with Jerry Little. Jerry and I each own fifty percent, but I handle the day-to-day operations. Jerry comes in one Friday a month, picks up the financials from Ronald, and we head to lunch and an afternoon round of squash. On paper New Horizons looks green and growing, a healthy company with lots of potential. Jerry's been happy, and I let him win at squash now and again to make him downright giddy about his investment."

I couldn't help but like Sid. As I scribbled notes, I took a sideways glance at my PI. Shorty never took notes, and no food or drinks were allowed in the interview room. The poor guy didn't have much to do except stare at Sid. For an adult with ADHD, he was doing a fantastic job of looking alert and interested. My instincts told me he found Sid likable as well.

"New Horizons is a real estate development company, which means we buy land, put in the utilities and streets, then sell to home builders. One day Ronald was on another line, so my assistant put through a call from our bank. That's when I found out New Horizons is in deep trouble."

Sid unlaced and re-laced his fingers, his brow furrowed in thought. "It's my fault. I shouldn't have placed so much faith in Ronald. Instead of taking two-hour lunches, I should have been going over the finances with a fine-toothed comb. But Ronald came so highly recommended!"

More finger fiddling. My limited experience warned me he could be polishing his lies. "At first, I believed Ronald had made some mistakes. But as I dug into our bank accounts, I realized there was more to it. The financials Ronald gave Jerry and me every month were false. He'd just typed them up on his computer. When I pulled the transactions from our bank accounts, I couldn't tie any of the numbers back to our so-called profit and loss reports from Ronald. The day Ronald was killed, I left early, about 3:30 p.m. I had an appointment with an attorney, to see if I had a legal leg to stand on. He advised me that I didn't, because I had approved every single cash withdrawal. Ronald had convinced me of the necessity for each one, and I'd believed him. I was ruined!"

Sid uncrossed his legs and leaned across the table. "Evangeline, Mr. Cormier...you've got to believe me! Yes, I was angry, but not angry enough to kill Ronald. Why would I do that? With Ronald dead, I'm on the hook for the outstanding loans and missing cash. It would be in my best interest to keep him alive!"

Shorty shifted his weight, and the noise reminded me he was just eight inches away. "Mr. Hebert, why'd ya' go back tuh yore office? Seems like ya' shoulda reported whatcha knew tuh the police anyways."

Sid's shoulders drooped, and his chin wavered just a bit. His eyes reminded me of my father's, one day thirty-five years ago. The day my father told his family the veterinary practice might shut its doors. His eyes reflected a mixture of shame and anger, tinged with fear.

"That's an excellent question, Mr. Cormier...excellent. I'm not sure I have an answer. Pride, I guess. My pride prevented me from going to the police and admitting I'd been swindled by a kid. He's only thirty-three! Was...thirty-three. Anyway, my plan was to stop by the office, see if I could gather more evidence. But when I drove by the parking lot, I saw Ronald's car. Instead of driving into the lot, I pulled around the corner. I'd hoped to surprise Ronald, confront him and demand he go to the police. But when I stormed into his office, I didn't get far. He was lying on the floor. There was blood everywhere, so I pulled out my cell phone to call 9-1-1. That's when I heard the sirens."

During Sid's monologue Holliman glanced at his watch no less than twelve times. My guess was he'd calculated his bill rate per minute and was performing some mental calculations on his fees. I stole a look at my phone—Holliman had earned $86.67. *Earned* was a loose term for what he'd achieved in eight minutes. Shorty and I were in the wrong business.

"I gather the police received a tip about a dead body, and arrived to find you hovering over it? That's not much evidence to arrest you. What else do they have?"

Holliman tossed a manila folder across the table. For almost $11 a minute, the guy could have handed it to me.

"I'll save my client some money. Here's the police report—you can read, can't you? He shouldn't have to relive any more of that regrettable evening."

"Well, *cown-suh-lure*, seems yore client's relivin' that *ruh-gret-tuh-bull* evenin' ev'ry day he's wearin' those orange *puh-jaw-muz*. Mebbe ya' should be more friendly tuh the people who's gonna spring 'im from this place."

Jack had remained silent, but even he had to chuckle at Shorty's rebuttal. Yes, my PI barely graduated high school, but he could hold his own and then some. Holliman's eyes widened and he opened his mouth to get in the last word.

Jack ended the battle of wits. Or was it wills? "That's enough, Holliman. Mr. Cormier's correct—you've not done anything to get Sid out of here. Why don't you take your cue and leave? Sid and I can finish up."

Holliman closed his mouth, but his eyes broadcast that the argument had only been postponed. He knew who paid his fees, and he knew when to leave.

"Sorry about that—Holliman Fisher wasn't our first choice. Wouldn't you agree, Sid? His firm has represented the founding families in all our legal matters, and he's the one they sent. I'll do my best to keep interaction with him to a minimum."

Holliman's absence triggered a change in the room. All of us took a breath as we leaned into our chairs.

"Evangeline, you asked about the evidence against me. When I heard the sirens, I bent down to see if Ronald had a pulse. He had a gaping wound on his neck, so I pulled out my handkerchief and tried to stop the bleeding. When the police found me, I was drenched in blood and babbling like an idiot. Honestly, I was in shock from seeing a dead body. But the police determined the shock was caused from killing Ronald. They can't find the murder weapon, but that has worked against me. Apparently, I managed to dispose of it somehow."

That did seem strange. If Sid had just killed the victim, the police should find the weapon somewhere nearby. I made a note that Shorty and I should conduct our own search.

"Well, Mr. Hebert, ya' sure do have motive an' opportunity. The police prob'ly think it's jus' a matter o'time 'til they find the knife. Then they got it all wrapped up, jus' like a Christmas present."

"Oh, no, Mr. Cormier. It wasn't a knife that stabbed Ronald. The police aren't sure what the weapon could be, but whatever it is they can't find it."

I opened the file and turned to the coroner's report. Someday I wanted to meet Dr. Milton Gautreaux, because he took the most detailed notes I'd ever encountered. The man didn't just document a death. He crafted meticulous paragraphs, giving the reader a detailed picture of the body. I only looked at his photos if the report encouraged me to do so. Milt was the Longfellow of coroner reports. Well, maybe Edgar Allan Poe was a more accurate metaphor, since we were talking about death.

"The victim's carotid artery was punctured by a blunt metal weapon, eight inches in length. The tip of the object is square, one inch long before it broadens out to a wider mass. The current database of weapons includes nothing that would create this type of wound. Victim would have died anywhere from thirty seconds to a minute after the wound was inflicted."

The four of us sat around the rectangle table, pondering my words. My PI spoke first, always the voice of reason.

"Well, ain't that somethin'? I reckon we got our work cut out for us, Doc. Mr. Hebert, an' Senator, ya'll know about anyone that'd wanna do ol' Ronald Reynolds harm?"

Jack leaned forward, his palms resting on the table. "You should look at his ex-wife, Judy Reynolds. Officially, it was an amicable divorce. But my thought is, she knew about Ronald's habit of stealing. He pays child support, but I wouldn't be surprised if Judy wanted her hands on all his money."

Sid nodded. "Yes, that's a good idea. Another person you should look at is Moe Randall. Ronald was doing his books as well, and they're good friends. But if he was stealing from me and Jerry, I'm sure he was stealing from Moe."

My teal pen scribbled furiously. Why did this part always give me such a thrill?

"Good, good—anyone else?"

Sid snapped his fingers—did people still do that? "Melinda Davis! She's Ronald's former employer, before he came to work at New Horizons. She gave Ronald a glowing recommendation, and claimed he left on good terms. But now that I've discovered the fraud, I'm wondering how truthful she was."

Jack caught his uncle's eye. "Sid, you won't like this suggestion, but I'm going to give it, anyway." He turned his head in my direction. "You two should look at Sid's partner, Jerry Little. I know he stays out of the day-to-day business, but he may have caught on to the fraudulent activity. My uncle's future is on the line, maybe even his life. We need to look at every possibility."

Sid's lips pushed together, forming a thin line. Just like my mother's clothesline on a windy day, before she hung out the wash. His words were dancing a jig just behind those lips, but he wouldn't let them out on the dance floor. The guard's knock signaled our hour had vanished.

We thanked our client for his time, but was that really necessary? What else did this man have going on that afternoon? Jack asked for daily updates, and I agreed.

Shorty climbed into my Bronco, a gift from Bobbie Robichaux for solving her son's murder. Much as my PI hated to say, he preferred for me to drive. There was some part of him that enjoyed being chauffeured around by a woman.

"What's first on our list, Shorty? It's Monday afternoon, and most of the businesses are open. Where are we headed?"

Shorty stared out the window, eyes squinting. Not from the sun, but from my question.

"The first thing we do is introduce ourselves tuh the detective workin' Sid's case. He ain't gonna be happy about us pokin' around, so we might as well get it over with."

Should I ask? If speaking with the detective was our first stop, then why were we in the car? Just five minutes before, we'd probably been within twenty feet of our destination.

"Now, before we go back in, I jus' wanna offer my services. Ya' know, cuz yer gonna help me with a Christmas gift for Annabelle an' all. Jus' say the word, an' I'll do the same. I know, I know. Ya' said ya' settled on cologne an' all. But I bet if we put our heads together, we could come up with an even better gift for my cuzzin."

Well, I had my answer. Honestly, I'd rather be in the police station dealing with a hostile detective, than discussing my love life with Shorty. My plan had been to break up with Cay first, out of respect. Shorty wasn't going to make that possible. "We'd better talk about that. I really like your cousin, but I've got to be honest. In the eleven months we've been dating, I think we've been on less than ten dates. The restaurant takes up most of his waking hours."

My eyes focused on the police station in front of me. I couldn't even look at Shorty. "Since Big Jim and Auntie Bella's retirement, he spends his time convincing people the food quality is still the same. Cay's already told me he won't have any free time until after Mardi Gras. That's two months from now."

Sadness filled the Bronco, making the air stifling and sticky. My lungs could hardly take a breath. "It's better for Cay if we break up, anyway. He can focus on the restaurant. And I won't sit on my couch every evening, wondering when he'll have a moment for me."

No more hollow excuses from my so-called boyfriend either, but I'd keep that to myself. "Shorty, my heart is hurting—I wish we could have made a go of it. You and I both know the restaurant is his first love, like a child he's been given to nurture. But it's not my child, and not my love. Big Jim and Auntie Bella have an amazing marriage because they both put the restaurant first. Cay needs a woman who loves the restaurant as much as he does."

Tears pricked my eyes, stinging like a hard rain. I'd married my first real boyfriend, so I had no experience at breakups. Only a cold-hearted person could be on the giving end of a breakup without feeling like a jerk.

A sob darted to the front of my lips, bursting into the air before I could catch it. Cue the waterworks.

"Awww, Doc, please don't cry. Yer gonna make me cry, too. Look, I love my *cuzzin'*, but I know a lady needs to be first in a man's life. An' yer right—the Hoot n' Holler's always gonna be first in *Kie's* heart. Now don't worry—yer not the first woman t'break up with 'im over the restaurant. He'll understand. In fact, Annabelle an' I were surprised ya'll lasted this long."

He cleared his throat and handed me his frayed bandana. "Besides, ya' need a man who puts ya' first. Someone who enjoys solvin' mysteries like ya' do. Now, that Sheriff Dupre, he's a good man. An' he's still holdin' a candle for ya'—I can see it in his eyes. Jus' think! Iffen yer datin' the sheriff, why we'd get more cases than we could shake a stick at!"

Leave it to Shorty to point out the benefits for him. But he wasn't wrong. Mitch understood my love of puzzles, unraveling the clues to find the answers. And he didn't try to cover me in bubble wrap, like my brother. He'd even encouraged me to get my private investigator's license and apply to be an official consultant with the parish.

"Well, I'm glad we got that outta the way. Dry yore tears. Do ya' got some lipstick? Yer lookin' a little pale, like one o'the cadavers in the morgue. Do ya' got some o'that *roo-juh*? Ya' know, t'make yore cheeks kinda red an' such?"

Like a temperamental Louisiana winter, Shorty's warmth morphed into cold practicality. Advice on makeup...seriously? Eh...who was I kidding? He'd given me at least two minutes of undivided attention, which might be a record for our relationship.

"I've got some lipstick, but no rouge. We'd find that in my mother's purse, which is back in the 1960's. I'll run a brush through my hair—will that suffice?"

Hanging out with Shorty trained me to keep a stash of beauty tools close at hand. Why did a man who bought clothes and fertilizer at the same store care so much about my appearance? Something to ask the good Lord when I reached the pearly gates.

"Okay, Doc, let's talk about our meetin' with the detective. Now, I'm gonna let ya' do all the talkin'. See, I'm not feelin' real *chair-it-tuh-bull* today, so I'd best keep my trap shut."

Had we turned a corner? In ten minutes, Shorty had expressed concern, given solid advice (on relationships, not makeup), and offered to keep quiet. *Thank You, Lord, for small favors.*

We climbed the stairs to the precinct to stand before the desk sergeant. We'd never worked with the Baton Rouge police, only the sheriff. We had low expectations for the meeting.

"My name is Evangeline Delafose, and this is my colleague, Shorty Cormier. We have been hired by Sid Hebert as part of his defense team, so we'd like to introduce ourselves to the detective handling the case. Is he or she available?"

The sergeant's eyes never strayed from the computer screen. Southern etiquette dictated I wait for a greeting or even a nod before continuing. *Dear Lord, could You distract my mother for a few moments? She doesn't need to look down from Heaven and see her child commit such an atrocious breach of manners.*

"Excuse me? Sergeant? Is the detective handling Mr. Hebert's case available?"

My hands pushed forward until my elbows rested on the desk. The trick was to hover right around *annoying* but not cross the threshold of *irritation*. Any point past *irritation* and he'd call an officer to show us the door. In the South, a smile can work wonders. I flashed my teeth, trying not to resemble the Cheshire cat from *Alice in Wonderland*. That cat was downright creepy.

"'Scuse us, Sergeant. Senator Jack Hebert asked us t'stop in, see how the case against his uncle's goin'. I'd hate t'tell him at supper this evenin' that the detective couldn't find time for us."

Of course, dropping the right name can work just as well. The sergeant squared off with Shorty. My PI had cruised well past *irritating*, and the officer made sure he knew it. Shorty flashed his pearly whites, reminding me of the posters in my dentist's office. Maybe I should show Dr. Leblanc a picture of Shorty, so he could add him to the collection.

The sergeant never graced us with a sound, but he picked up the desk phone. "Detective, there's a couple of characters up here to see you. They say they're with Sidney Hebert's defense team. Whaddya want me to do with 'em?"

Way to make a lady feel special, officer. My PI maintained his winning smile. Yes, I should snap a photo and send it to Dr. Leblanc. Maybe I'd get a commission if Shorty made the wall of smiles.

No less than ten minutes later, a woman opened the door marked restricted access. Her black Oxfords barely squeaked as she crossed the waiting room. "Good afternoon. My name is Detective Lydia Barton. I'm handling the Sidney Hebert case. How can I help you?"

She offered a hand, and I shook it. So far so good. "Hello, Detective. I'm Dr. Delafose and this is Mr. Cormier. We are working with Holliman Fisher and Senator Jack Hebert on Sid's defense. We just wanted to introduce ourselves, since we may cross paths. We've received a copy of the police report, just so you know. If you have anything else to share, we'd appreciate it. Of course, if we find anything, we'll pass it along to you."

Would Detective Barton share with us, the defense? Probably not any more than we'd share with her. But it sounded professional and civil, which was the vibe I was trying to convey.

Lydia Barton met my look and held it. She wasn't more than thirty, so she was probably a fairly new detective. Her ring finger was bare. Being a detective meant late nights and often weekends. But her brown eyes shone, telling me she loved her job.

"I'd appreciate that, Dr. Delafose. Hopefully, we all want justice for Ronald Reynolds. I don't have anything to add to the police file yet. But you should stop in the morgue and speak with Dr. Gautreaux. In fact, I'm headed there myself if you'd like to join me."

We followed Detective Lydia as she punched in the code and led us to the elevator. What was the appropriate conversation with a detective intent on sending your client to prison?

"Jus' a few more days 'til Christmas, ain't it Detective? How's yore shoppin' comin' along?"

Well...discussions on gift purchases were probably safe. Shorty's choice of small talk worked well.

"Why, yes it is, Mr. Cormier. My boyfriend and I are hoping to finish our Christmas shopping this week."

Who was this man, and what had he done with my private investigator? As my companions chatted up the pros and cons of Amazon vs shopping in person, the doors mercifully opened.

"Watch your step and head to the left—Milt's office is just down the hall."

Detective Barton knocked on the door as she opened it, and a slightly balding man in his sixties greeted us. The words *Santa Claus* popped into my head, because Dr. Gautreaux sported a full white beard. The word *jolly* didn't even begin to describe the man.

"Well, hello, and welcome to my humble universe. I'm Milton Gautreaux. Lydia, I recognize, but you two are new friends. It's so nice to meet you!"

We made the round of introductions. I half expected Milt to pull out a handful of candy canes and ask us what we wanted for Christmas. I couldn't help but adore the man.

"Milt, could you give Dr. Delafose and Mr. Cormier a copy of your report on Ronald Reynolds? And if they have any questions, please help them find the answers."

"Of course, of course! Hey, we're all working toward the same goal, right? Justice for the victims. Now, all our files are computerized—just give me your email address, and I can send you a copy. But here's a paper file, if you'd like to go over it together right now. That way, I can answer any questions you have in person."

M ilt might be Edgar Allan Poe on paper, but he was P.T. Barnum in person. Before that afternoon, no one could have convinced me the morgue held the opportunity for education and enlightenment. But Milt changed my mind. Death wasn't amusing, but it could be interesting.

"The victim, Ronald Reynolds, was thirty-three years old. To say this guy was in good shape is an understatement! Why, I'd kill for those abs!"

Milt caught himself. "Sorry, folks...that was inappropriate. Let's just say that if anyone discovers Mr. Reynolds' exercise and nutrition regimen during your investigation, please let me know. I'd like to try it. Man, you could bounce a rock off that man's biceps!"

I exchanged my chuckle for a cough—after all, murder was serious business. Yet, my mind drifted to Milt, standing three feet or so from the victim, bouncing rocks off Ronald's arm muscles. Maybe even his abs too.

"Ya' okay there, Doc? Sounds like ya' got somethin' stuck in yore throat."

Mostly laughter stuck down there, but I couldn't say that. "Oh, thank you, Shorty. I'll be fine."

Shorty's concern interrupted Milt's monologue, but he worked it into the act. "Let me get you some water, Dr. Delafose. While I take a break, we'll have the stellar Miss Barton take us through her working theory. Mr. Cormier, would you be the suspect? Wonderful, wonderful—just stand right there. Perfect!"

Milt stepped back a foot or two, like a director checking the blocking on his stage. Satisfied with his work, he folded his arms. "Lydia, take it away!"

All eyes on the detective while Milt shuffled to the fridge just a few feet away. As he retrieved a bottle of water, Lydia cued up her presentation.

"Thank you, Milt. Police received a 9-1-1 call at 5:13 p. m. According to the recording, the caller claimed to hear fighting inside the New Horizons building. The dispatcher sent a squad car to the scene, which arrived at 5:25 p.m. Unfortunately, if the dispatcher had known someone was being murdered, she would have alerted the officers. And of course, they would have responded in a timelier fashion. But a pair of raised voices just doesn't justify officers turning on sirens and speeding through traffic lights."

The crime rate in Baton Rouge was 141% higher than the national average. With officers responding to all sorts of major crimes, I was impressed that a yelling match rated a ten-minute response.

"The following information is contained in the arrest report, and you are welcome to interview the officers if you like. But according to the report, the officers approached the building and found the front door unlocked. They entered the building and identified themselves, but no one responded. Officer Rodriguez took the hallway to his right, and Officer Day took the hallway to her left. It was Rodriguez who spotted the suspect, Sidney Hebert, crouched over the victim. He drew his gun and told the suspect to stand up and raise his arms. Rodriguez cuffed the suspect, then called in the arrest to dispatch and asked for backup. Officer Day finished clearing the building, then returned to her partner to assist. Both officers reported the suspect was covered in blood. They took a statement from him that he had been attempting to revive the victim. Mr. Hebert was taken into custody and put into the back of the squad car. Another patrol car arrived, and those two officers along with Day searched the inside of the building for the weapon. Rodriguez remained with the suspect. A second patrol car arrived, and the officers joined the others in canvassing the area to search for the murder weapon. They did not recover it."

By then I'd gulped half the water bottle from Milt. The facts were circumstantial, but an above average D.A. could convince a jury otherwise. "What's your theory, Detective?"

Lydia stood five feet from Shorty. "We know the victim was stealing from the suspect's company, New Horizons. Mr. Hebert admitted he came back to the office last Friday afternoon, spotted the victim's car, and decided to confront him. My theory is: the victim was standing behind his desk, most likely stuffing papers into his briefcase so he could make his 7:30 p.m. flight out of BTR Airport. The suspect spotted him, stepping into his office."

We waited, but our actor didn't move. "Mr. Cormier, step into my office."

"Huh? Oh, sorry." Shorty shuffled forward two feet.

"Wonderful! You are a marvelous actor, Mr. Cormier. Now, I believe the victim came out from behind his desk, about two steps. He would then need to take five more to reach the doorway. Except the suspect was in his way."

As Lydia spoke the words *two steps*, her feet made the motions. She and Shorty stood just a couple of steps apart.

"The suspect accused Ronald of stealing, and demanded his money back. Maybe he even wanted a cut of the profits. At any rate, the victim made a few empty promises, but Mr. Hebert didn't let him pass. Ronald only needed a couple of steps to get to the hallway and make a break for it. According to Mr. Reynolds' girlfriend, he ran five miles a day. Mr. Hebert was much older and not in as good of shape. The victim knew if he could make it to the door, he could outrun the suspect. Ronald decided to take that chance."

Lydia stepped forward, so that she was side by side with Shorty. "Now move your right arm, Mr. Cormier, and stab me in the carotid artery." She stood patiently, waiting to be stabbed.

"The *what* now?" Our murderer hadn't read the coroner's report and didn't know a carotid artery from a bronchial one. He probably didn't know a carotid from a carrot.

"Right here, Mr. Cormier." Lydia took his wrist, folded his fingers into a fist, and guided his hand to her neck. "The victim fell to the floor, dying."

Lydia bent her knees and sat on the floor, then pushed her legs out and leaned her head back until it rested on the linoleum tile. She turned her head towards the autopsy table so her ponytail wouldn't dig into her neck. She even widened her eyes and dropped her jaw an inch, to mimic a dead person. Well, except for when she finished her narration.

"The suspect kneeled over him, to make sure he was dead. The police arrived and arrested him." Our victim returned to dead body status, eyes open and mouth agape. A chug of water saved me from laughing. Murder shouldn't be so much fun.

Milt and I waited for our suspect to imitate our victim's theory. Or was it the detective's theory, who was just playing the victim?

"Shorty, kneel over the dead body."

"Doc, I think we all get the *pick-sher*. No need t'roll around on the floor."

Detective Barton hopped off the floor and adjusted her ponytail. "And now...Dr. Milton Gautreaux, coroner extraordinaire!"

Milt stepped forward, like the headliner who'd just been introduced by the opening act. "Ahem, thank you, Detective. The three-inch wound above the victim's right collarbone cut the carotid artery and punctured the right lung. Fun fact: the carotid artery is the artery typically used on the neck to take a person's pulse."

He rested his first two fingers of his right hand on Lydia's neck, looking at the watch on his left hand. "Seventy-two, Detective. Your personal trainer is taking good care of you."

Milt stepped back on his right foot, as if addressing a room full of students. "During the autopsy, I found a large amount of blood in the chest cavity, indicating Mr. Reynolds' heart had been beating for quite a while after he'd been stabbed. With an injury to the carotid artery, the victim suffered a great deal of blood loss. As they say on *Blue Bloods*, Ronald Reynolds bled out."

Milt watched my favorite show? Could this afternoon get any better?

"Now, I can't tell you with certainty how long the victim would have been alive after being stabbed. But given his excellent health, I'd guess it took thirty seconds to a minute for him to die. I'd say the killer had no concept of the brutality involved in severing the carotid artery. Why, stabbing someone at the base of the neck and severing the spinal cord is much more humane. But maybe the killer did know the length of suffering the victim would endure. Which means he or she is on Santa's naughty list for sure."

I pictured Santa going through his list, checking it twice. His quilled pen would hover just above the killer's name, then Santa would nod his head. "Ho, ho, hmmm...yes, on the naughty list. No mistake there." He'd scratch his head and make a note. "Yes, let's give this one an extra helping of coal for the stocking. In fact, if the reindeer lighten their load before we get to the house, I'm going to dump the contents of the pooper scooper down the chimney too. Just to get my point across—this one has been especially naughty this year."

By then, the killer should be behind bars. Did Santa deliver coal and reindeer poop to prisoners? How would that work exactly...

"Dr. Delafose? Did you hear me? I said we're moving on to the weapon, if there aren't any questions."

"Huh? Oh, no, I don't have any." No way was I vocalizing my thoughts on Santa visiting the prison. Maybe I should ask if Shorty and I would get extra gifts for catching such a naughty person? No, best not ask that question either.

"All right, then. As I've stated in my report, "The victim's carotid artery was punctured by a blunt metal weapon eight inches. The tip of the object is square, one inch long before it broadens out to a wider mass. I've had my assistant scour our database of weapons. But she couldn't find anything that would create this type of wound. Detective Barton, am I correct in stating the police could not locate the weapon?"

Lydia shook her head. "Not yet. But we're still digging through dumpsters and looking in storm drains. We're confident it will turn up soon. I've talked to Leah Guthrie, the ADA assigned to the case. While she always loves to have the murder weapon, she believes our case is solid enough to take to the grand jury. She's thinking she can get it on the docket in the next couple of weeks, maybe less."

Shorty and I exchanged a glance. In our vast experience of two cases, we'd never had a time constraint. Just unknown killers wanting us dead. This presented a new challenge.

"Detective Barton, did you look at any other suspects?"

Lydia turned her gray-green eyes on me. "There were a few names tossed around, but they all have alibis. The ex-wife, Judy Reynolds, was home with her housekeeper. One of the victim's clients, Moe Randall, was home with his wife. The other partner of New Horizons, where the victim and suspect work, is Jerry Little. He was out with his son. And the victim's former employer, Melinda Davis, was home with her husband. Besides, none of those people have nearly the motive Mr. Hebert does."

"Ya' got any ideas, Detective, why that murder weapon's missin'? Mebbe the killer took it with 'im. Or her."

Lydia shrugged. "That's a good route for you two to take, since you need to convince a jury your client didn't kill Ronald Reynolds. Me, I'm sticking with the theory that he's stashed it somewhere. It'll turn up, I'm confident of that."

Shorty turned to Milt. "Doc, ya' got any ideas on what the weapon could be?"

The doctor glanced at Lydia and received the okay. "Being in an office, my first thought was an award or trophy. When my kids were young, they had all kinds of trophies and awards in their rooms. Or had, rather. My wife caught my boys having a sword fight...trophy fight? Anyway, they'd each grabbed the base of a trophy and were waving the pointed tops at each other. She sent them outside and grabbed a cardboard box. When I got home, she had me take them all up into our attic. They're still there, I think."

Lydia crossed her arms in front of her chest. "In case you're wondering, I've had our forensics team bag all the trophies and awards that could cause that wound. They bagged anything in the building that could be used as a weapon, in fact. Which was more than I'd ever imagined. We're pretty backlogged, so it's going to take some time for them to swab and test all the surfaces for blood. We won't have the results in time for the grand jury, but I'm okay with that."

I didn't have to look at my PI to know he got it. We had to solve this case before Sid could be indicted by the grand jury. Even if he went to trial and the jury found him *not guilty*, his reputation would be ruined. Sid and the Hebert family image had already been tarnished by the splash on the cover of *The Advocate*, Baton Rouge's primary newspaper. Out of respect for Sid, his arrest had jumped back to page seven of *The Graisseville Gazette*. But a trip to the coffee shop could clear his name quick as a cricket. Unfortunately, Baton Rouge didn't offer a one stop shop for proving a person's innocence. We had to clear Sid's name *lickety-split*. Actually, that wasn't true. The definition of that word meant to do something right away without hesitation and as quickly as possible. It also meant going headlong at full speed and not asking for instructions. That definitely was not the way to solve this case. Maybe we should try half *lickety-split*? Three-fourths even?

"*Dock-ter*, Detective, thank ya' for yore assistance. I'd better get my *uh-so-see-uht* home. She's pretty wore out—it's been a hard day. We'll keep in touch."

As we slammed the doors to my Bronco, I panicked a bit. "Shorty, I have to tell you I'm worried. We've got to figure all this out before Sid goes before the grand jury. Any ideas on where to start?"

My PI rested his elbow on the open window, staring down the setting sun. "We gotta find some reasonable doubt, if we wanna prayer o'keepin' ol' Sid outta the slammer. So, we start with the suspects he gave us. But I gotta tell ya', Doc. I think the detective's barkin' up the wrong tree. Know what I think? I think that murder weapon meant somethin' tuh the killer. Mebbe tuh both o'them. That's why the killer brought it tuh the crime scene. Yep, he brought it, killed Ronald with it, an' took it home with 'im. Or her. Anyway, if we can find that murder weapon, we'd understand the killer's motive. So, when we interview these suspects, we gotta be on the lookout for the weapon."

"How in the world is that going to work? 'Excuse me, but we'd like to ask you some questions. In your home, if you don't mind. You know, so we can snoop around and look for the murder weapon.'"

"Well, Miss Smarty Pants, I didn't say I had the whole thing worked out yet. Mebbe ya' could lend a hand, an' figure out that part. It's time ya' pulled yore weight in this relationship.

Oh, an' be sure an' turn in yore miles tuh the senator. Finally, we got a client with some deep pockets! An' with yore family bein' a foundin' family an' all, why we better get all the cases for those folks!"

We spent the rest of the ride home arguing about how many founding family members had been in trouble with the law. The point of contention was the definition of *in trouble*.

"That wasn't a crime, Shorty! It was a misunderstanding. Quincy Bergeron honestly thought your uncle Mitchell lent him the car. It wasn't his fault your uncle was hard of hearing and thought he was borrowing a horse."

Mitchell Cormier owned the funeral home in Zachary twenty years ago. My cousin Quincy thought it would be fun one Halloween to borrow the sedan and take his friends riding around. He'd asked Mitchell to borrow the *hearse*. Except that Mitchell was deaf in his right ear and thought Quincy asked to borrow his *horse*. Everyone knew about Mitchell being hard of hearing, and we made a point to stand on his left side. Either Quincy forgot, or didn't realize how important that decision could be.

Either way, Shorty's uncle called the sheriff because he thought someone had stolen his hearse. My cousin was arrested and charged. The judge had married a Cormier woman, and he ruled that Quincy had to pay Mitchell twelve dollars for gas and fifty dollars for not standing on the correct side of Shorty's uncle.

My father argued with Shorty's dad for a solid two years after the incident. It became a source of contention, with each defending his relative to the point of shouting. Several times their wives made them go outside. It almost ruined their friendship.

"All I know is that everyone, I mean *everyone*, knew t'stand on Uncle Mitchell's left side. Yore *cuzzin'* knew that too. He's always been full o'mischief."

"Fine! Let's just move on, okay? Could we just agree that the founding families have had several run-ins with the law in the past, but not within the last twenty years? That's all I'm saying. We shouldn't pin our hopes on cases paid from the slush fund."

"Okay, yer prob'ly right. But let me enjoy this one, okay? An' we gotta find some time t'solve the case o'the missin' fruitcakes. Now I got some ideas on that case."

We pulled into my driveway, and Shorty followed me inside. No surprise there, since it was almost supper time.

"First on my list is Joe McMillan. Y'know, the hog farm off Highway 64. I've got it on good authority that every year he goes around collectin' Miss Pearlie's fruitcakes from his neighbors. His hogs love her fruitcakes, cuz they can knock 'em around a while before eatin' 'em. The outside's all hard as a brick, so they make good playthings for them hogs. Then, when they get all good an' hungry, they gnaw on those things. My buddy Monty said he's been out there an' seen those hogs take a good twenty minutes jus' t'get 'em all wet an' slobbery enough t'bite off a piece."

Why did conversations with my PI make me nauseous? "Okay, well, thanks for the graphic description. So, you're thinking Farmer Joe stole the fruitcakes for his hogs?"

"Huh?" Shorty had made a sharp left turn for my pantry and was deep inside. He emerged with a bag of Crawtators.

"Oh, yeah, yeah. An' I heard his kids are in 4H, an' that means big bucks for winners. Iffen he can get even one o' his kids a winnin' hog, why that'll pay for college. Mebbe not

LSU or that fancy college in New Orleans. But it'd pay for community college, an' mebbe even Louisiana Tech."

"That fancy college? Do you mean Loyola or Tulane? They're both in New Orleans." I'd taught at Loyola, and Shorty was right. It was a fancy school—they both were.

"Don't matter—they're both *fancy schmancy*. Point is Joe's got motive." *Pop!* Crawtators never strayed far from orange soda...in my house, anyway. I reached for a glass and filled it with water. I didn't have the metabolism of a twenty-year-old like my PI.

"What about opportunity and means?" Was I hungry? Watching Shorty chow down on potato chips made me feel hungry. No, I'd stick with water and start supper.

"Well, he's got four kids, an' two o'them drive. Not t'mention his wife. Any o' those people coulda worked as a team. Y'know, a couple kids distract Miss Pearlie while the others back up a minivan an' steal the fruitcake right from under the poor woman's nose. Yeah, I bet it took a whole team o'McMillans t'haul off that much fruitcake!"

My brain shifted to Joe and Bev McMillan and their four children, dressed in black hoodies and ski masks. As Miss Bev backed up her green minivan, the two youngest jumped out and circled to the front of Miss Pearlie's home. While they kept watch over the neighbors and the front door, Joe and the two oldest McMillan kids opened the back porch screen door. Forming a line and passing the loaves to each other they created a makeshift bucket brigade and shoved all eighty-two fruitcakes into the Bev's van. It had worked for firemen before the invention of fire engines—why couldn't a bucket brigade work for loaves of fruitcake?

"Yes, we should interview the McMillans. Anyone else? Oh, and are you staying for supper? If so, will Annabelle be joining us?"

"Thanks for the invite, Doc, but Annabelle an' I are goin' carolin'. 'Member she works with the young ladies at her church? They're singin' Christmas carols in the park t'night, an' they invited some young men t'join 'em. Annabelle thought I'd be a good influence, so she asked me t'go too. Then we'll go back tuh her house an' have some hot chocolate. Iffen ya' wanna join us, ya' can."

Shorty singing Christmas carols? In public? Then drinking something other than orange soda? Part of me desperately needed to witness this Christmas miracle, perhaps the first of the season. But I had finals in a week, and I had nothing to hand out yet.

"Although I can't think of a better way to spend my evening, I need to prepare for finals next week. But please have Annabelle take some pictures, because I don't think I've ever seen you sing. Or drink hot chocolate."

"Now that ain't true, Doc! Why, I sang at yore mama's funeral. I sang *Amazin' Grace* with everyone else just as pretty as ya' please. Now I don't know about drinkin' the hot chocolate this evenin'—it's gonna be seventy-two degrees. But Annabelle says I can have orange soda, if I put a candy cane in it."

The edges of Shorty's lips stretched across his face, and a sparkle made his brown eyes shine. A candy cane in his beloved orange drink? Yeah, only love makes us do such crazy things.

"Now, don't make a big deal outta this, but I'm gonna go tuh church with Annabelle on Sunday." Shorty took a step back. Was it to gauge my reaction, or to make sure I didn't hug him?

Those two had been dating for over a year, but he'd made it clear he had no interest in church. His mother Madie had been a faithful member of Graisseville Methodist until her death. Shorty attended as a child, but stopped in high school. I asked Mother about it, but she shook her head.

"Evangeline, sometimes people decide that church isn't for them. Maybe they expected too much from mere humans, but more often than not the church failed them. Let's just keep praying that Shorty changes his mind."

One time I mentioned something to Shorty about church not being a place for gossip and got an earful.

"Why, Doc, church people gossip jus' as much as the rest o' us. They jus' hide it as prayin'. They call ya' up an' say they wanna' pray for ya', but they jus' want ya' t'tell 'em yore secrets. Then they tell everybody else on the prayer chain." Shorty inserted air quotes around *prayer chain*. "How do y'think everyone found out my daddy almost lost our farm? Some lady at the church called my mama 'bout prayer requests. She broke down cryin' that we was about to be kicked offa' our farm."

Mother was right—sometimes the church fails its people. But I'd been faithful in my prayers, including a request that Shorty find a way back. God doesn't answer all our requests, and certainly not as fast as we'd like. Hopefully He was working on this one.

Which case to work on first? In one corner I had the fruitcake mystery and interviewing hog farmer Joe McMillan and crew. In the other corner sat our four suspects, also needing to be interviewed. While Shorty sang his little heart out and drank hot chocolate, I completed my professorial duties. Exams prepared and filed, I turned to my to do list. As I brewed a pot of tea, I pondered my next task.

Jack had texted me the contact information for Judy, Moe, Jerry, and Melinda. Why not set up interviews while my water boiled?

"Good evening, Mrs. Reynolds. My name is Evangeline Delafose, and I'm helping Sidney Hebert with his defense. When would be a good time for us to talk?"

"Miz."

Huh? "Uh, pardon me? I didn't understand what you said."

"It's Ms. Reynolds, not Mrs. Reynolds. Ronald and I divorced several years ago. I just kept his name for the sake of the children."

Once again, I managed to offend a potential suspect. Why didn't Shorty ever have these issues? Why hadn't I just let him schedule interviews? He always charmed the ladies and connected with the men, while I just stumbled and stuttered.

"Ms. Reynolds, I do apologize. I also become upset when people call me by the wrong name."

"Oh? What do they call you that's upsetting?"

Oh boy...the conversation had started with a wrong turn and continued barreling down the road. Pretty soon I'd hit the guardrails and tumble over a cliff, probably exploding upon impact, my conversation burned beyond recognition.

"Well, I have a doctorate. Often people call me Mrs. instead of Dr. Or sometimes they mispronounce Delafose."

"That's not really the same thing, is it?"

Just cut your losses, Ev. "No, it's really not. I'm sorry we got off on the wrong foot, Ms. Reynolds. I hope you'll still agree to meet with me."

Was that a sigh on the other end, or did a gust of wind blow through my phone?

"Well, I suppose so. I'm not a suspect, am I?"

Yep, just cleared the guardrails. "Oh, no ma'am. I mean, Ms. Reynolds. Of course not. We're talking to several people who worked with the victim...uh, Mr. Reynolds. But we'd also like to get a better feel of his personal life."

"Ha! His personal life? Lady, that man made it a point to keep his personal life as far away from me and the kids as he possibly could. He only paid child support because New Horizons garnished his wages. As for the rest of his income, the kids and I never saw a penny! You should talk to his girlfriend, Daisy Jane Mayfield. She tends bar at The Dirty Pelican almost every evening, when she's not spending Ronald's money. Guess she'll be finding another sucker to pay her bills."

Of course, it wouldn't be a case without a nod to the lowliest dive bar in East Baton Rouge Parish. A mere twenty minutes from Baton Rouge and just outside the Zachary city limits, it attracted degenerates from every walk of life. Shorty used to frequent the establishment until Annabelle got a hold of him. Yet another reason to love that girl.

"Ah, okay. Well, thank you for your time."

Was that...? Yes, the smell of gasoline and smoke as I went up in flames. Shorty was going to have to call Judy Reynolds back and get us an interview. I'd add Daisy Jane to the list too. My PI would have both women offering to deliver baked goods by the end of his call, if history repeated itself, anyway. My teapot had started its chorus, which was my cue to quit while I was behind. Except that...I needed to break up with Cay. Why not do it now? My mood couldn't get much worse.

My call went straight to voicemail, just like all the other calls I'd made to my so-called boyfriend in the last six months. Yeah, the first eight weeks of our relationship had been great. The third time my call went to voicemail I saw the writing on the wall.

"Cay, give me a call. We need to talk."

On a more pleasant note, I sent Shorty the contact information from Jack and asked him to schedule the interviews. I threw in Daisy Jane too—no doubt Shorty could figure out how to get in touch with her. Besides, Zydeco had been waiting long enough—I had a date with my dog and a good book.

"Good mornin', Doc! I got a hold of all the people on yore list. We're meetin' Jerry Little Saturday mornin' at the Zachary country club, after he gets off the golf course. Have ya' ever been tuh the country club? This is gonna be my first time. What should I wear?"

Shorty's night of singing and Christmas caroling was strange enough. But to be concerned about his clothes? To my knowledge, my friend had never cared what other people thought about his fashion statements.

"Uh, well dress pants, if you have them. And a collared shirt would be a nice touch. Do you have any loafers?"

I jerked my phone away from my ear, completely prepared to receive a dissertation on why real men didn't wear loafers. It would be something to the effect that wearing a shoe named after laziness was downright un-American.

"Yeah, yeah...I got some o'those loafer shoes. An' I jus' bought a pair o'khaki's. Now, I've got a dark green collared shirt an' a burgundy one—which one do ya' think I should wear?"

Burgundy? My PI actually knew a color other than the primary ones?

"Definitely the burgundy—it goes well with your brown eyes."

I was having the strangest conversation I'd ever had with my PI—and that included the one about the Blushing Bubbly

candle with citrus and pink champagne and muddled rasp-
berries.

"Yes, that sounds good, Shorty. Do we have any interviews
today?"

"Nah, everybody's busy. But tomorrow we got Ms. Judy
Reynolds, after supper. Speakin' o'which...I don't know why
you had so much trouble with her. That lady's as sweet as
my mama's iced tea. Why, she's even gonna bake a Louisiana
crunch cake for us t'munch on. My plan is t'keep her occupied with my line o'questionin', an' you can 'scuse yoreself t'go
tuh the bathroom. Then you can snoop around the house,
see if ya' can find the murder weapon."

"Sounds wonderful! She's not putting me on her Christmas
card list this season anyway, that's for sure."

A light chuckle drifted through my phone. "On Thursday
we got Moe Randall. Now try as I might, I couldn't get the
guy t'meet us at his house. Somethin' about his wife has a
del-lic-kuht con-stit-too-shun so she can't have no company.
Doc, how can ya' live in the South an' not be up for company?
That jus' ain't right."

"Agreed. But maybe this delicate constitution makes her,
well...delicate? And being so, uh, delicate..uh, prevents her
from receiving guests."

My PI's all too familiar snort smacked against my eardrum.
It used to annoy me, but I'd grown to accept it. Wasn't that
part of friendship, loving people for their positive *and* nega-
tive qualities?

"Weak constitution my Aunt Fanny! I called my favorite
librarian, an' she told me what it means. Annabelle says it
describes someone who lacks energy and struggles with
their health. Doc, I've seen Mrs. Randall. *Delicate* is not a

word I'd use t'describe the woman. She could hold her own in the women's mud wrestlin' down at The Dirty Pelican."

Someday I'd write down all the strange conversations I'd had with Shorty, to go back and read when I needed a good laugh. The conversation about delicate constitutions, however, wasn't the one to use as the starting point.

"Okay, well, we can figure out some other way to get into the Randalls' house. Who's next?"

"We got Melinda Davis on Friday. I turned on my charm an' she invited us tuh her house—she gets home 'bout five o'clock. She promised t'have somethin' for us t'snack on. What'd she call it? *Goo-duh*, I think. An' somethin' else called...what was it? *ozzy-uh-go*. Oh yeah, an' another somethin' called *grew-year*. Or somethin' like that."

Okay, that might just be the first story in my book. What would I call it? *Conversations with my Private Investigator*, maybe?

"Uh, Shorty, I think she's going to serve us cheese: Gouda, Asiago, and Gruyere, to be exact. My guess is Melinda will also have some assorted crackers and nuts to go with the cheese. It's called a charcuterie board."

"Well, what the hel...hello Dolly is that? What am I s'posed t'do with a piece o'wood? How big is it? An' what kinda wood is that? Didja say *shar-coot-ree*? Is that a type o'pine tree?"

Yes, this was definitely going to be the first story in my book. The names would be changed to protect...well, me.

"Charcuterie. It's French for cooked meat. But not all charcuterie boards are served with meat. In fact, they can have any or all kinds of meat, cheese, fruit, nuts, crackers, and dips. Although I've seen breakfast charcuterie boards with pancakes and eggs on them. At The Market Basket last week..."

"Okay, Doc, I get it. Well, I don't get it, cuz ya' jus' said this board is French for meat, but Mrs. Davis didn't mention no meat. All I know is I'm gonna be eatin' a snack before we head over there. I ain't ever heard o'any *rez-peck-tuh-bull* Southern woman servin' no cheese an' crackers tuh guests. What's this world comin' to?"

"Oh, Shorty, I just don't know. When did Southerners stop serving pecan pie and chocolate sheet cake to their guests? It's just all kinds of wrong."

"Yeah, some days I'm glad my mama ain't around t'see this world an' the way it treats people. She'd be mighty upset."

We lamented for a bit about the world and the continuing lack of good manners. Then Shorty's ADHD kicked in.

"An' we'll wrap up on Sunday by swingin' by Daisy Jane's apartment around six—she don't go t'work 'til eight, so we'll have plenty o'time t'talk. You should snoop around too, Doc. Sid didn't mention her, but she's a suspect all right. Or at least a person o'interest."

"Agreed. But what shall we do for the rest of the day? I'm assuming you've had your three cups of coffee, and scrambled eggs with boudin sausage—right? Have you checked both your email and your phone messages? I wouldn't want to get you off your routine."

"Yeah, yeah, I've done all that. I even been out t'feed the cattle an' hogs, an' I fixed the fence in the South pasture. What've *you* done today, Doc?"

"Uh, I've made my bed, thrown a load of laundry into the washer, and fed Zydeco. So yes, you've got me beat by a mile."

"An' my work ain't done yet. I've gotta go over tuh Nate's house an' fix his screen door. Yore brother said he'd throw in a dozen meat pies from Lasyon's iffen I'd do it today. He said Sydney's rabbit got out that door, an' they almost didn't find her. The rabbit that is...not Syd."

My niece Sydney loved animals, and her rabbit was the latest pet. My brother must have been in a bind—Lasyon's was in Natchitoches, three hours away. Whenever Nate got within twenty miles of there, he'd stock up on meat pies. To give away a dozen was akin to giving away one of his children.

"Hmmm...is that all he promised, to bump him to the top of the list?"

Getting on Shorty's list was the simple part. It lived on the first seven pages, front and back, of a spiral bound notebook. Getting to the top of the list was the trick. To achieve that feat, bribery came into play. Some families prepared entire meals to entice Shorty to their home.

"Oh, it wasn't easy. Ava Guidry promised me a Creole tamale pie, an Ooey Gooey cake, an' three dozen Cane syrup cookies t'get tuh Walt's tractor today. T'bump Ava, yore brother had t'promise a dozen meat pies today, an' a pot o'Bonnie's gumbo every week for two months."

Everyone knew my sister-in-law placed second in the state fair for her culinary perfection.

"But I got it all covered. I'm headed tuh the Guidry farm after we hang up. I'll take a look at Walt's tractor an' figure out what parts I need. While Walt skedaddles tuh Big Ed's t'get his parts, I'll swing by Nate's an' fix that screen door. See, Doc, ya' always gotta have a plan. The Army taught me that."

The Army taught my friend a lot of lessons, and he was a better person because of it. "Yes sir, I'll remember that—always have a plan."

"One more thing, then I gotta head out. So, this *shar-coot-ree* board...iffen we eat all the food on it, do we get t'take it home?"

Without my colleague, I felt a little lost. When life feels uncertain, head for the nearest comfort zone. For me, that was Maggie's Coffee Shop.

"Skinny chai tea latte and a piece of avocado toast, please!"

Maggie gave me her look, the one that told me she already knew exactly what I wanted. Mmmm...everyone should have a drink dealer like Maggie.

"I'm giving you some grace, since you just got the case yesterday. But girl! If you hadn't come by today to give me an update, I might have cut you off."

"Okay, first of all...rude! And perhaps against the law. I'd have a talk with the mayor if you refused to serve me. Even though you and Acadian are business partners, I think he'd side with me on this one."

Maggie snorted, almost as loud as Shorty's horse imitations. "Doubtful. As soon as you update me, I have to run over to his store and repeat what you told me. Oh, and Hugh wants you to stop by, if you have anything newsworthy. Something about his cousin of all people should be keeping him in the loop. Apparently, you're the next best thing."

Hugh and Shorty's fathers were brothers, making them first cousins. But in small towns, if your grandmother's sister dated your neighbor's grandfather's cousin, that somehow made you related. I'd stopped tracing family roots a long time ago.

"Bring the mayor over! Being a Fontenot and a founding family member, Acadian should be involved in the slush fund expenditures."

Honestly, I just wanted to spend time with Acadian. He fascinated me. As the oldest male Fontenot in his family, he stood in line to inherit...well, a heck of a lot of money. He could have continued to float along, the black sheep of the family but still in the will. Except he didn't.

Acadian founded Blissfully Balanced, an herbal medicine and holistic health store in bustling downtown Graisseville. An extremely successful health store—even my father Skeeter dropped in to pick up a special turmeric concoction for his arthritis. Bonnie and I agreed it definitely made him less grouchy.

But Acadian went one step further. He ran for mayor and won. Okay, he ran three times before he won. But we all agreed he was an amazing mayor. Then he got married, to the absolute love of his life. Their love story should have been captured in majestic movie fashion and played for the generations. I'd have paid $15 to watch it on the big screen.

Gracie Fontenot (okay, originally Dunbar, then because of a husband-turned-ex it became St. Clair, and then thanks to marrying the love of her life, Fontenot) made the perfect leading lady—beautiful but beautifully human. Their love story touched all of us.

"Uh, Ev? You kinda zoned out there. Acadian's pretty busy in the morning. But I could steal him away to join us for lunch. How about the Shining Stars Café? Since his wife owns the place and all."

What? How did I always lose focus? "Yes! Let's all do lunch. How about 1 p.m.? The café should be quiet."

After chai tea and toast, I hustled over to the *Gazette* to give Hugh my woefully sparse update. Then I promised to give him an exclusive, once we solved the case.

"Hello! Welcome to the Shining Stars Café! Why don't you take this table right here?"

To the owner's credit, she made a point of greeting all her guests and showing them a table. Our hostess was at least in her second trimester, maybe early third? Oh, who were we kidding? Gracie Fontenot was about to pop out a baby Fontenot any second. Thank You, Lord, that Shorty wasn't in the café to spout commentary.

"Uh, yes, this table is fine. And congratulations on your bundle of joy. I'm sure you and Acadian are beyond excited." Yes, good...stick with safe words.

"Ummm...hello? Have you met my husband? He's been two seconds from freaking out since I showed him the pregnancy stick. You know, the stick I peed on that proved he's going to be a father?"

Gracie shuffled...yes, shuffled from her right foot to her left. "Me? This is my fourth. Beyond excited? Yeah, that happened...like, never. Because for the first three, their father was not that great. Yep, thanks for that, Dave St. Clair. Anyway, Acadian's a wonderful stepfather, and he's going to be an amazing father. We just have to get him through the pregnancy, and the birth...oh, yeah, and high school graduation."

I couldn't help but like Gracie...I mean, who couldn't? She was five foot six inches of pure fire. Her blondish brown hair and hazel eyes spoke years of *don't mess with me.* Who was I to offer advice on pregnancy?

"Amen to that, sister! Thank you for the table—we'll just sit and wait for your husband, who's joining us. And let's be honest...the man's in a foreign land! He should be cowering in a corner somewhere! Instead, he's having lunch with two women *at* his wife's café. He's braving the field, coming toe to toe with all these strong women. I give him kudos for that, for sure."

Our precious little pregnant hostess took her hormones and shifted them aside. "Ah, Miss Ev...that's why people respect you. Because you breathe logic into a mess of emotions."

Okay...well, I'd take that.

"My poor, sweet husband! He's taken on three kids, and fixes breakfast every morning like a boss! Parents' Night? Yes, he's the one hustling me out the door, parking the car and getting us there on time. He's amazing, and I've waited over twenty years to get here. Thanks for reminding me."

Ah, sweet Acadian. Or lucky Acadian, as many men would say—even in her third trimester Gracie was a looker.

When our mayor's Skechers hit the entry of the Shining Stars Café, his wife threw herself into his arms...or, she would have, if his arms had been spread out in front of him. They were actually by his side, which made her greeting a little awkward. But still super sweet...at least by my rom-com movie standards. Acadian made it to the table within five minutes, after prying off his adoring wife.

"Uh, sorry for that, ladies. I'm sure I know nothing about pregnancy, but it does seem to involve a constant outpouring of emotions. We're getting through it, all right. But I am questioning my desire to have a second baby."

Our mayor pushed back his lank of blond hair, blue eyes gazing towards us. Yes, if I didn't already have a stray at home named Zydeco, I'd scoop up this young man and put him in the car. And keep him until the baby was born...maybe until the kid reached kindergarten. Graduation?

"Yeah...I'm thinking one is just wonderful. Yep, three amazing step kids and one more...just enough. Uh, if we can get through the pregnancy, that is."

My thoughts floated back to my two pregnancies. Poor Doug. Was I that crazy during my trimesters? No...maybe? Possibly? Uh...not something I wanted to think about.

Maggie jumped in. "Hormones during pregnancy are crazy! Don't worry, Acadian...Gracie doesn't mean any of what she says. You guys are meant for each other. Just be patient...it will all work out."

Our mayor looked at me, and I smiled my best smile. Did it look too much like the Cheshire cat? Judging from his face, it didn't.

"All right, ladies! Let's have our orders ready when the server arrives. The last thing we want is to be *those* customers. You know, the customers who can't get their act together."

Looking at our mayor's wild blue eyes, I realized he'd heard more than one story about customers without orders ready to go on a moment's notice. He would move Heaven and earth to keep from being associated with *those* customers.

Maggie spoke up first. "Yes! Well, I want water with lemon and the grilled chicken salad with Ranch dressing. Ev?"

Oh my goodness! Was I having lunch, or enduring an interrogation? "Uh, well, um...the same, I guess..."

Our mayor took over. "Wonderful! Amelia, hey! Yes, we'll all have water with lemon and grilled chicken salad with Ranch dressing. Great! Fantastic. Thank you."

Except that...

"Uh, Acadian, aren't you a vegetarian?"

Hello, elephant in the room.

Our mayor smiled...or was that a grimace of constipation? "Not during this trimester I'm not. If my wife serves me a salad with meat on it, so be it. If she remembers I'm a vegetarian and leaves it off, then praise God from Whom all blessings flow."

Dear Lord, please tell me I wasn't this ridiculous and scary during my pregnancies! Okay, well, if I was...then thank You for helping Doug to show me grace. An abundance of grace!

Maggie, in her infinite wisdom, changed the subject. "And so, dear Ev, please tell us about your latest case. I believe it involves Sid Hebert—yes?"

"Yes! The case! Evangeline, please tell us about your latest case." Sweet, dear Acadian. The poor soul needed a distraction.

"It's Ev to my friends. And I consider you a friend, Mr. Mayor. We know very little at the moment. I mean, obviously we've been hired to prove Sid Hebert's not guilty. And, assuming that's the case, we don't know much else. Honestly,

I've gathered you here to find out what you know. Do you mind if I ask you some questions?"

"Fire away, Miss Ev. I've got an extremely pregnant wife who's going to burst at any minute. If you have any way of distracting me... I mean, if there's any way I can help...then please let me know." Oh, bless his heart!

Maggie's hazel eyes darkened with concentration. She tugged at the clasp capturing her ponytail, releasing it. Her straight brown hair tumbled down from its prison and rejoiced at being sprung by the warden. The happiness shone through, sticking up all over Maggie's head. She ran her fingers through both sides, combing the strands into submission. No doubt she performed this ritual every day.

"Yes, well...Sid Hebert faints at the sight of blood. He came into the coffee shop one day, and Avery cut her finger on the espresso machine. Poor guy dropped to the floor as soon as he caught sight of the gushing."

Amelia had delivered our waters and disappeared into the kitchen. Maggie stopped to take a sip, and Acadian jumped in. "Well, I teach a yoga class at one of the community centers in Baton Rouge. Ronald Reynolds's ex-wife Judy takes it, so I know her. That woman's way too short to stab anyone really tall! Why, she's only about five foot five! How tall is...was Ronald?"

"If I remember the coroner's report correctly, he was six-foot three inches. So, yeah, that would be difficult. I'll have to check with Milt, to see if he can estimate the killer's height."

Acadian grinned, thrilled he provided such an important piece of evidence. "Oh, I shouldn't be so happy, should I? That didn't help Sid's case." Yet the man couldn't stop smiling.

Acadian's happiness made my mouth curve upward as well—I wasn't the only one who found murder so much fun. Well, solving a murder anyway.

Maggie's eyes lightened a little as she grinned. "This is fun, isn't it? Now, I don't know Sid's partner Jerry Little or the former employer Melinda Davis. But Moe Randall has family down here, with a farm. I heard something about him the other day...what was it?"

Her eyes shifted back to dark mode as Amelia served our salads. We all glanced at Acadian's, chock full of grilled chicken.

Amelia stepped back and eyed our mayor's salad. "I reminded her not to put chicken on it, but she forgot. Anyway, Miss Gracie says *hi* to everyone, and she loves you. But I think that second comment was just for you, Acadian. I sent her a link this morning on seven ways to naturally induce labor. That woman needs to have her baby, and put us all out of our misery!"

With a flip of her hair, she disappeared into the back. Acadian yelled after her, "Send me that link too, Amelia!"

Maggie and I exchanged a glance—no need to comment on the exchange with our server. My favorite barista found a new topic.

"I remember now! Moe was down here last week, helping his brother on the farm. He was in a bad car accident years ago and his right arm's never been the same. Yeah, his brother told me Moe does everything with his left hand—writing, eating. He couldn't have stabbed anyone with his right hand."

D ang fruitcake mystery! It was sucking time away from our murder investigation. But Shorty needed new tires, as he reminded me constantly. After he'd finished his jobs with Walt and my brother, he called me.

"Doc, we gotta go see ol' Joe McMillan tomorrow. He said come by anytime. What's yore schedule look like?"

"Uh, well, I'm in the middle of switching wet clothes to the dryer. My calendar's in the other room. Give me a minute."

I jogged the six feet from the laundry room to my office, mentally patting myself on the back for not dying. Why, I wasn't even out of breath!

"Let's see...tomorrow's Wednesday. I have book club at ten, and we're interviewing Judy Reynolds at seven. How about after lunch?"

Lila Trahan's book club served as the hot spot for village gossip. Normally I steered clear of hen parties, but the club had served a useful purpose in our investigations. Shorty encouraged me to attend, because I usually returned with at least one odd job or private investigation case for him. Yes, the book club had treated us well.

"Yeah, that works. Say, have ya' talked tuh my *cuzzin* yet? Are ya' broke up? Cuz Annabelle's got a new librarian workin' for her, an' this lady's a looker! She loves food an' wants t'own a restaurant herself. I thought she'd be a pretty good match for *Kie*. But Annabelle says we have t'wait for you two t'break up before I can introduce them."

A lesser person would be offended that Shorty was already trying to fix up my soon to be ex-boyfriend. The first thought that popped into my head was maybe that would make the breakup easier on Cay. "He's supposed to call me back. I'll tell you what—go ahead and give me this woman's phone number. After I break up with your cousin, I'll give it to him."

"Say, that'd be mighty nice o'you, Doc! An' I got a *pick-sher* too, that I can give ya'. Do ya' got a piece o'paper?"

My PI didn't believe in sharing contacts—something about the government might intercept the information. He had all his important numbers memorized, and carried a notepad in his truck console for all the others. Nate said I should convince Shorty of his misinformation. But I said some things were better left alone.

"Uh, yes. Although, I was kind of kidding. Don't you think it would be awkward for me to break up with Cay, then give him another woman's phone number? Honestly, I think that would be best coming from you."

Silence on the other end as Shorty pondered the dilemma. "Yeah, yeah, yer right. Tell ya' what—when ya' break up with *Kie*, call me an' let me know. Then I can call the poor guy, tell 'im I'm real sorry, an' give him Marla's number. Yeah, that'll work out real nice. Good idea, Doc."

Yet another conversation with my PI that turned strange and a little awkward. Maybe that was just the norm with us.

"Oh, that's Cay calling. Let me let you go. I'll call you when it's done, okay?"

I clicked over before Shorty's response. But what else could he do except agree?

As with most breakups, the conversation was mercifully short.

"Listen, Ev, I'm sorry I didn't get back to you until now. Look, I'm not much good at this, so I'm just going to say it. I think we should break up."

Well, that was unexpected! Should I be relieved or annoyed? "Uh, okay. Actually, I was calling to break up with you. So that really worked out well."

A rush of breath on the other end reminded me that breakups are never easy for anybody. "Well, that makes me feel better. I've been so out of pocket the last six months or so, and I'm sorry for that. Taking over the restaurant has been a lot more work than I'd realized. Most days I don't know if I'm coming or going. This is for the best. You're free to putter around and solve your cute little cases. And I can focus on the restaurant. I hope we can be friends, though, and you'll still come to Breaux Bridge and eat at the restaurant. The Hoot n' Holler's always open for you."

Cute little cases? My lungs filled with air, trapping angry words inside my mouth. Part of me hadn't been quite ready to admit defeat with the relationship. But after that remark I was all in.

"Of course, of course. That's some of the best food I've ever had. And with you and Shorty being cousins and all, there's no room for hard feelings. You take care."

Shorty was next on my call list, and for once he had little to say.

"Ya' know, I'm real sorry ya'll two didn't work out. But yore daddy an' I were hopin' ya'd end up with Sheriff Dupre an' all. Ya' might give 'im a call tonight."

"While I appreciate your sympathy and your romantic advice, I'm going to focus on our two cases for now. Matty and Ellie are due in town in just another week, and I've got to get ready for them."

"Yeah, sure, sure. O'course. It'd prob'ly be better iffen ya' called the sheriff tomorrow, anyway. We don't want the guy thinkin' yer *dess-pruht* or anythin'. Nah, that never wears good on a woman. Well, I'll give ol' *Kie* a ring an' cheer 'im up a bit. He might wanna give Miss Marla a call tonight, before the sports comes on."

My PI called back not fifteen minutes later, stammering with anger.

"I can't believe it! I jus' can't believe it! What a dirty, no good, donkey's behind! Doc, I'm real sorry I ever gotcha involved with that *cuzzin'* o'mine. Why, he's the sorriest man that ever wore a shirt!"

Harsh words, especially for family. The only other time I'd heard Shorty use that insult was on our first case. He referred to a drug dealer in that same way.

"What's going on? What'd Cay do to you?"

More stammering and sputtering, reminding me of my old tea kettle. The whistle broke early on, and when the kettle reached the boiling point, it would sputter steam and hot water from the opening. Shorty sounded similar.

"Ya' know what he told me? He told me he didn't want Marla's number, cuz he was already datin' someone else! Can ya' believe it?"

Such sweet sentiment from Shorty brought a lump to my throat. "Well, that was quick. And I appreciate your loyalty, getting all upset because Cay's been stepping out on me."

"Huh? Oh, yeah, that's true. No, I jus' can't believe he didn't want Marla's number! Now who'm I gonna fix her up with? Why, I guaranteed her a date for New Year's, told her she could double date with me an' Annabelle. Say, Doc...iffen ya' ain't gonna get with the sheriff until after Christmas, is it all right if I fix 'im up with Marla? She's a real sweet girl, and I promised Annabelle."

Normally, I taught class on Wednesday mornings at LSU, but I'd given my students the week off before finals. The women of the Graisseville Ladies' Book Club were dedicated, I'd give them that. Rain or shine, in sickness and in health, the ladies gathered with covered dishes and iced tea to discuss one of the classics. At least that was the cover story.

"Welcome, ladies! Please take a seat. As you know, our book this month is Jane Austen's *Sense and Sensibility*. Who would like to begin?"

Honestly, I was probably the only one who ever read the assigned book. The other ladies came for the food and the gossip. The crowd seemed larger than normal, which didn't surprise me. Word traveled fast in small towns—no doubt the crowd wanted to hear about Sid Hebert's case.

Anna Dunbar raised her hand. "Evangeline, could you please update us on Sid Hebert's case? Sid's wife Miriam is such a dear friend, and she's just worried sick!"

Anna was married to my mother's brother Miles Dunbar, making her my aunt. She'd only recently discovered our family roots, about the same time as I started solving murders. Funny how crime solving had made me a hot ticket in the village. Everyone was suddenly my new best friend.

"Of course, Anna, I'm happy to oblige. Please remember, I'm limited in what I can reveal, since it is an ongoing investigation."

Much head nodding from the peanut gallery. Really, they made it all too easy. I'd give them some general information, and they would take it and run. I'd gathered several key bits of information from the club.

"Shorty Cormier and I have been hired by Senator Jack Hebert to prove Sid's innocence. The police found Sid kneeling over the victim's body, so they have motive. But they haven't found the murder weapon, which is the means. The victim, Ronald Reynolds, was stealing from Sid's company. And that is the motive. We've spoken with the lead detective, and she isn't bothered by the lack of weapon."

Anna interrupted me. "Excuse me, Evangeline. How could Sid have disposed of the murder weapon that quickly? Miriam feels that's an important point for the defense."

This was what happened when people watch crime television and read books about investigations. Soon, they feel empowered to spout legal advice and police procedures.

"You know, Anna, I'm not a lawyer, so I can't really speak on Sid's defense. What you're saying does make sense, and I'm sure his lawyer will include that bit of strategy."

For $650 an hour he'd better include any and every strategy known to man.

Lila leaned forward, not a silver hair out of place despite the ceiling fan. Although December, we all felt the eighty-four-degree heat and humidity. Yet Lila's face revealed not a drop of discomfort.

"Evangeline, do you think Sid's innocent?" A gasp made its way around the room, like a small wildfire. But it was Lila, the founder and hostess, who'd asked the question. The gasp was quiet, like a hiccup.

"Lila, that's a fair question. Shorty and I don't determine someone's innocence or guilt, then work to prove ourselves right. Our approach is much simpler—we dig up all the clues we can find, then fit them together. If Sid's innocent, then our investigation will prove that. And if he's not, we'll prove that too."

I put my hands on my knees and moved my torso closer to the edge of my seat. Just a slight lean, as if I was coming in for something important to say. I even dropped my voice.

"But I will tell you this, ladies. Shorty and I have earned a reputation for being honest and persistent. Sid shouldn't have hired us if he's guilty."

Slowly, I reclined in my wingback and picked up my teacup. Lila kept jasmine tea in her cabinet, just for me, and always had a pot of water boiling when I arrived. My speech had allowed just the right amount of time for my tea to steep and cool to the perfect 180 degrees.

Had Shorty joined our hen party? Where was that horse snort coming from?

"My understanding is you've had two cases, Evangeline. I wasn't aware one could earn such a stellar reputation from only two. Maybe Graisseville's standards have slipped?"

Who was that? Oh, great! When did my other aunt show up? Normally she skipped the book club gatherings, because they were *nothing but dens of iniquity and gossip*. She was spot on with the gossip, but the den of iniquity always puzzled me. Since when did lemon squares and iced tea with mint become immoral or illegal?

Lila defended me. "Ruby Bergeron! That was rude, even for you. And to your own niece, at that!"

Yep, that was my aunt. She had been our mayor at one time, before I'd moved back. But she'd stepped down after draining the village bank account. A podcast called *Small Town Tales* contacted her about doing an episode. Ruby used her mayoral power to add village improvements before the interview. When her grandson Ethan figured out exactly what *Small Town Tales* was, he had to break the news to his grandmother. He explained that podcasts were audio only, so all the park benches and tree chandeliers didn't make a bit of difference. Ruby resigned in disgrace, and all the Bergerons took a hit in respectability. But family is family and we'd forgiven and forgotten.

"Lila, it's okay. Ruby, you're right. Personally, I've only had two cases. But Shorty has had at least seven more. We've satisfied all our clients, and put two murderers behind bars. In fact, Sheriff Dupre has spoken with me about consulting with the sheriff's office regularly. Maybe I misspoke—maybe I should have just said that we will do our best to find the killer and expose the truth."

Ruby settled down after my apology, but I'd lost momentum. Normally at that point, people would feed me information I could use to pursue leads. After Ruby's dig at my reputation, a few women remembered prior commitments and fled the meeting.

Many brave souls stayed to gossip about husbands staying out late and women buying hair coloring at the grocery store. But none of the revelations brought me closer to solving the case, even the fact that Moe Gladstone wore a toupee.

An hour later the main part of my brain screamed *cut your losses, Ev!* But I'd hung back, to catch up with Lila and scrounge some scraps of gossip. Unfortunately Ruby had the same idea. After discussing the new paint stripes for the downtown parking, I headed for the door.

"Ladies, it's been a real pleasure, but I've got to meet Shorty about one of our cases. If you'll excuse me, I'll pick up my fruit tray and head out the door."

Lila put a hand on my knee. "Please wait a moment, Evangeline. Ruby has something to say."

Ruby turned to me, her gray eyes framing tears. "Evangeline, I was too hard on you earlier. For that I am deeply sorry. This situation with Sid has me beside myself. I hope you can forgive me."

My mother's voice rang through my head. *"Evangeline, family is a beautiful gift God gave us. And there's a special place in Heaven for those who forgive."*

Her words were meant to soothe my anger. Mad had stolen my favorite red lipstick and drew large clown lips on the dog. Then she brushed his hair with my hairbrush. However, Mother's words applied to this situation as well.

"Of course, Aunt Ruby. I don't know Sid very well, but I know you and Uncle Al play bridge with him and Miriam. If there's anything I can do, please let me know."

Ruby poured another cup of coffee. "Find the real killer, that's all I ask. We've been on vacation with Sid and Miriam—there's no way he killed anyone."

Maybe this morning could be salvaged. "Sid's given me some potential suspects to investigate. If I read off their names, could you ladies tell me what you know about them?"

Both ladies nodded their heads. "Oh, yes, Evangeline! Anything to help you."

"Wonderful! The first suspect is Ronald Reynolds' ex-wife, Judy. Do either of you know her? Or have you heard anything about her?"

Two sets of eyebrows furrowed in thought, then two heads twisted back and forth. "No, that name doesn't sound familiar."

"That's okay. How about Moe Randall? His brother lives here, on a farm. Moe comes down sometimes and helps out."

Ruby's eyes glimmered. "Al plays dominos with a Randall, I think. Maybe he's the brother? Let me talk to Al, see if he knows anything. What specifically am I trying to find out?"

"From the coroner's report, it looks like the killer used his right hand to stab the victim. I've heard that Moe was in a car accident, and he can't use his right arm. In fact, I've heard Moe uses his left hand for writing and eating. I need to find out if he could have used his right hand to stab the victim."

Ruby nodded, and even managed a smile. "Yes, I can do that! Al is just as worried as I am. He wants to clear Sid's name too. Don't worry, Evangeline—I'm on it!"

"Great! On to suspect number three—Sid's partner, Jerry Little. Can either of you tell me anything about Jerry?"

Ruby lost her smile. "Oh, dear. Well, Jerry's left-handed. So, I guess he couldn't have done it. From what Miriam says, that man's not the most ethical person. She and Sid have argued throughout the years about his business ventures with Jerry. But at first glance it doesn't look like he could have stabbed someone with his right hand."

Lila poured another cup of tea for me, and I thanked her. "I'm left-handed and I do everything with that hand. I don't think I could stab someone with my right hand. But you never know."

I'd been bringing a low-calorie snack for those of us watching our weight. Who was I kidding? I was the only one who enjoyed it. I'd found it was easier to bring something that I could eat, instead of stressing about finding something low calorie among the tasty Southern treats. I reached for one of my strawberries and chewed thoughtfully.

"That leaves us with Melinda Davis, the victim's previous employer. Sid tells me she gave a glowing recommendation, but now he's wondering about it. If Ronald Reynolds was stealing from Sid, most likely he was stealing from Melinda as well. The question is...did she know about it? Did she write the recommendation because she truly thought Ronald was a good employee? Or was she just trying to get rid of him before he stole even more?"

The strawberry left a sweet taste in my mouth, but Ruby's brownies looked much better. Better have another strawberry.

Ruby glanced at the strawberries, then settled on a brownie. "Maybe she discovered the theft after Ronald had left? She was so angry that he'd stolen from her, and that she'd written a marvelous recommendation. Maybe she decided to come to his new place of employment and confront him."

Ruby took one bite and threw the rest away. Who did that?

Lila stuck with coffee. "Wait a minute! Did you say Melinda Davis?" She plopped down her coffee cup and scurried to the living room. Reappearing a few minutes later, she slammed the newspaper down on the kitchen table.

"This is last Thursday's edition of *The Advocate*. Look at page seven!"

Lila didn't wait for us to look—she grabbed the paper and turned the pages.

"See! Right there, in the picture. That woman is named Melinda Davis, and her right arm is in a sling."

We stared at the words *Baton Rouge Rotary Club donates $5,000 To Animal Shelter*. The question was...would the correct Melinda Davis please stand up?

Shorty picked me up after lunch and we headed to Joe McMillan's farm. The smell of Crawtators filled the cab like a car freshener gone wrong. For once I left it alone.

"Well, I spoke with the sheriff, an' he said he's not interested in Marla. So, I'm fixin' her up with my buddy Curt."

"The one who works at Graisseville Tires n' More? And who thought I was a medical doctor and asked me to examine his mole in the coffee shop? Yes, that sounds like a match made in Heaven."

The now familiar horse snort. "Well, it ain't like I got many options, Doc. Once ya' get past forty, the choices are slim tuh none. An' Slim jus' left town."

I had to chuckle. After all, that was pretty funny. "What about your cousin Cletus? Why, he's an entrepreneur! You know, Brown Dog Bakery is up and coming."

We turned down the road to Joe's farm. "Yeah, I thought about 'im. Trouble is, he ain't interested in a woman who don't like t'fish. Now that he's got this new boat, he's on it ev'ry chance he gets. He ain't got time for any woman that don't know a catfish from a crappie."

"Have you talked to Nate? Maybe he knows some single deputies in their forties. And every woman loves a man in uniform."

"Say now, Doc! That's a pretty good idea. Yeah, I shoulda asked the sheriff while I had 'im on the phone."

"Shorty, I don't think the sheriff would feel comfortable fixing up the people who work for him. Nate, on the other hand, works with these guys and isn't their boss. He'd have a better feel for who could use a date on New Year's Eve."

"Yeah, yeah...yer right. Except I kinda already mentioned it to Curt, an' he got real excited. Somethin' 'bout not havin' a date in a really long time...since Obama was in office, I think? When was that?"

"Uh, well he left office in 2017. So, Curt's been flying solo for quite some time. He might scare poor Marla with his...how shall we say it? He might scare her with his *eagerness*. What about your ex, Candy Cahill? Or one of the servers at The Dirty Pelican?"

Shorty shifted in his seat as we turned into Joe's gravel driveway. Mentioning Candy's name made him jittery.

"Candy's still with her Greyhound bus driver, seein' the world. Or at least most major cities south of the Mason-Dixon line. As long as that woman's not in the same state as me, my life is a whole lot easier. An' ya' know I don't hang out in The Dirty Pelican anymore—I promised Annabelle I only go there when I'm on a case."

He shut off the engine and pulled the key. "Hey, but I'm on two cases now, ain't I? Now, the ladies at the Pelican...they're all pretty young. But Curt's got a steady job an' a new Chevy Silverado. It's got all-weather floor liners an' elevated cross rails!"

We stepped out of Shorty's truck—Joe waved to us from the barn. "Yes, every girl goes crazy for floor liners and cross rails. Did you say elevated? Wow!"

Or did every girl go crazy for a sharp dressed man? Yeah, ZZ Top probably had it right.

"Hello, there! Good to see ya', Shorty. And is that Evangeline Bergeron? Why, I haven't seen you since you were a little girl in pigtails, hidin' behind yore daddy when he'd worm my hogs. Yeah, ya' used t'tell me yore daddy came tuh *unworm* my hogs. I always got a real kick outta that."

And there it was...yet another reason to love a small town. The people here had known me since I was a young'un. I'd tagged along with my dad when he visited his farm patients, always eager to spend time with the animals—and him. We lived in town, so visiting a farm was pretty interesting. While Dad shot the breeze with his client, I wandered around the barn and the pens. As I got older, I'd help my father out. Unfortunately, none of my employers cared that my essential job skills included worming a hog or vaccinating a steer.

"Yes, sir, my dad got a kick out of that too. In a lot of ways, I think he misses his visits out to the local farms. I know I do. Thank you for meeting with us."

Joe wiped his hands on his overalls before extending his right one to shake. "Sorry 'bout the dirt, but ya' came at muckin' time. See, while the horses get their exercise out in the paddock, it's a good time to clean out their stalls. If it's okay with ya'll, I'll keep workin' an' ya'll can ask yore questions."

Poor Shorty! He'd gotten used to sitting on a comfy living room couch, conducting interviews over iced tea and baked goods. I should have brought him a to-go box from the book club.

"That's fine, Joe. I'm not sure you've heard, but Pearlie Rabalais had eighty-two fruitcakes stolen off her back porch. She's hired us to find them, so we're just asking around. Have you heard anything?"

Joe kept his back to us as he mucked, so we couldn't read his facial expressions. Maybe this interview format wasn't the best option?

"Uh, no, I haven't. But if you ask me, they did everyone a favor. My mama's maiden name is Trahan, an' my cousins used t'bring Miss Pearlie's fruitcakes with 'em for Christmas. But my grandaddy put a stop tuh that. He said being a founding family has its burdens. An' one o'them is Miss Pearlie's fruitcakes. Trahans don't give away their burdens—they bear 'em with dignity an' humility. He told everyone t'keep their fruitcakes at home an' bring somethin' nice tuh Christmas supper."

I nterviewing Joe McMillan's backside just wasn't working for me. By the look of Shorty's face, which resembled my brother's when he tasted his first horseradish pickle, he wasn't feeling productive either. Or was it because Joe hadn't offered us chocolate sheet cake and coffee?

"Uh, Joe, do you think you could take a break? We promise not to take more than fifteen minutes of your time."

Joe's scowl told me, No he *couldn't* stop for a quarter of an hour. But he channeled his mama's good Southern manners and rested his hands on the pitchfork. We'd never interviewed someone holding a weapon before. Potential weapon? The day was only getting better.

"Now, Joe, the way I heard it, yore hogs sure like Miss Pearlie's fruitcakes. People have been known t'drop their unwanted cakes on yore front porch, in fact. Now, is it possible that mebbe ya' might've decided if a dozen or so fruitcakes were good for the hogs, then eighty-two would be even better? Save the village from Miss Pearlie's unwanted gifts an' get some treats for yore animals?"

The channel for Joe's Southern manners had lost its reception. "Listen here, Shorty Cormier! Don'tcha be accusin' me o'stealin' from no widow lady! My mama taught me better'n that. You two best hightail it outta here, before I use this pitchfork for somethin' other'n muckin' my horse stalls. Now ya'll have a good day, ya' hear!"

Joe grabbed his pitchfork and made a motion, as if he was shoveling...uh, well, muck, out of a stall. But he made his motion towards us, and we took our cue to skedaddle.

"Joe's mama raised him well—he wished us a good day as he threatened us with bodily harm. No one but a good Southerner does that anymore."

My joke fell flat on my PI's ears. "Who does that Joe McMillan think he is? Yeah, I'm gonna be talkin' to yore daddy 'bout that whole *sit-choo-ay-shun*. He ain't gonna take too kindly tuh his ol' client threatenin' his daughter. Yeah, ol' Skeeter's gonna hear about this!"

"Are you going to mention that you accused Joe of stealing eighty-two fruitcakes? Really, you should, because it changes the perspective on the threat just a hair."

My PI didn't move a muscle as he pulled onto Highway 64.

"C'mon, Shorty! Even *you* would have been offended if someone accused you of stealing. It's offensive if Joe's an honest man. And if he's not...well, he wouldn't have admitted to the crime."

Should I mention it's never a good idea to accuse someone of a crime while they're holding a pitchfork? Wasn't that obvious, especially to another farmer?

Shorty pulled onto a dirt road leading up to a gate.

"Hey, you're not kicking me out of the truck, are you? Because I made some valid points. But if you're that upset..."

My PI shoved the gearshift into park. "Stay here an' leave the engine runnin'. That's Teddy's truck—he works for Joe. If a bunch o'fruitcakes showed up on Joe's farm, I bet he'd know somethin' about it."

Shorty hopped out of the truck and hobbled over to the gate. He unclipped the latch, opening the gate just enough to slip through. After closing the gate and latch, he made a beeline for Teddy, who was spraying fertilizer. As the two men talked, I checked my phone.

Milt's report sat in my inbox, but I'd never opened it. Since he'd provided me with a paper copy, I didn't have a need. But it was either Milt's report or Facebook. What kind of person was I, choosing to read about a murder instead of looking at my friends' photos of their vacations and grandchildren? Best not to put much thought into that question.

After learning who was left-handed or had injured right arms, I knew I had to go back to the report. Learning the killer's height was crucial as well—maybe Judy Reynolds *could* have killed her ex-husband? What if she'd been wearing heels? More than one petite lady chose to wear stilt-like heels to even the playing field.

I scrolled through the report, looking for anything related to the height of the killer. There it was!

"The wound was made from a stabbing motion at an upward angle. This indicates the person holding the weapon was at least five inches shorter than the victim."

Why hadn't someone informed me that solving crimes involved so much math? There were twelve inches in a foot, times six feet...oh good grief! Where was the calculator app thingy on my phone?

Shorty opened his door right in the middle of my scramble through the twelve screens on my phone, looking at app icons. Okay, maybe not twelve, but at least three.

"Quick! If Ronald Reynolds was...how tall was Ronald Reynolds?"

He slid into the seat and shut the door. "Could we focus on one case atta time, Doc? Makes it easier to keep things straight."

Why was my PI trying to confuse me with logic? "Yes, but first help me figure out how tall the killer was. Now, the coroner's report says that the victim is...was five inches taller than the killer. So, if we carry the two..."

"The killer's five foot ten inches, Doc. Can we focus on the fruitcakes now?"

"How...? Never mind. Yes, I'm ready to focus on the fruit-cakes."

But first I scribbled that handy bit of information in my notebook. Shorty had already put the truck into drive and pulled onto the highway.

"Teddy wasn't real eager t'talk tuh me at first—he didn't wanna get his boss in trouble or nothin'. But he had some interestin' information t'share."

Shorty pulled an orange soda from the cooler behind me. Of course! It was time for his mid-afternoon snack.

Pop! The sound used to jar my soul—now it soothed my soul. Well, maybe not soothed, but my soul didn't leap out of my body at the sound anymore.

"Teddy said Joe told 'im t'cut out early, the day before Miss Pearlie's discovered her fruitcakes missin'. Didn't give no reason why. Then, when Teddy was gettin' ready for bed, he 'membered he forgot t'lock the tool shed. He knew ol' Joe'd be real upset iffen he found the unlocked shed first, so he hightailed it back tuh the farm t'shut it."

Shorty took two quick gulps and swallowed. "Teddy slowed down an' turned in Joe's driveway. That's when he saw Mrs. McMillan's minivan comin' towards him. He slowed down, so he could roll down his window an' explain why he was comin' back so late at night. But the minivan kept goin.'"

Two more gulps and a swallow. "Well Teddy, he drove on in an' parked, an' locked the tool shed. Then he knocked on the door tuh the McMillan's house. Ya' know, t'tell ol' Joe what was goin' on. Nobody answered, an' all the lights in the house were out."

Next came the bag of Crawtators. No wonder the cab smelled like kettle fried potato chips. "Teddy said with four kids, there's always someone home t'answer the door. But not that night. An' then, the next mornin, the mornin' Miss Pearlie noticed her fruitcakes missin', he told Joe that he'd come back the night before t'lock the shed. Now Teddy's a real honest kid, he's got that goin' for 'im. Not so much in the brains department, but he's a good kid. He wanted t'admit his mistake an' let his boss know he made it right."

Could Shorty open a bag of chips while keeping his truck on the highway? Of course he could. "An' Joe told 'im no problem, an' thanked him for comin' back t'lock the shed. So, Teddy asked, 'hey, where was Mrs. McMillan goin' so late last night, an' how come no one answered the door?'"

Shorty doled out that part of the story while driving one handed and opening the Crawtators. I'd learned not to offer help.

"Teddy said Joe got a mean look on his face, an' told him, 'Listen, son, if ya' like workin' on this farm, then ya'd best mind yore own business, not mine.' Then he told Teddy t'stop jabberin' an' go muck out the horse stalls. An' Teddy did what he was told."

All that with a mouth full of kettle fried goodness. Then two more gulps of orange soda. "Now, Doc, don'tcha think that sounds mighty strange?"

"Yes, I do. But I think we wore out our welcome with Mr. McMillan. What about Teddy? Would he be willing to do some spying for us?"

More crunching. Nope, that still annoyed me. No soothing of my soul in those noises.

"Yeah, yeah, I think he might. Like I said, he's an honest kid. An' he's fascinated with me, since I'm an Army vet an' I got this artificial leg. Yeah, I bet if I told 'im it's his *pay-tree-ah-tick* duty, an' offered t'take off my leg an' show it tuh him, he'd do some recon for us."

Ahh…the things we do for justice.

Shorty dropped me at my house, even waited for me to open my front door. He was getting better. Zydeco greeted me with a bark and a nuzzle. Thank goodness for dogs, the most loyal companions on earth. My phone rang, the theme song from *Blue Bloods*. Why was the sheriff calling me?

"Ev, why is Shorty trying to fix me up with some librarian in Zachary?"

Ah…that was why. "Uh, well, it's a long story. You see, I broke up with that guy I'd been seeing, Shorty's cousin. And he promised this librarian he'd fix her up with someone for

New Year's Eve, so they could double date with Shorty and his girlfriend."

Good grief, was I back in high school? No, my love life had never been this complicated. "But it seems my now ex-boyfriend has already moved on, so..."

"Stop! You had me at the words *ex-boyfriend*. So, you're single, then?"

Oh boy. I'd hoped to have this conversation after I'd solved both cases and muddled through Christmas. The last thing I needed was another present on my list. Unless he liked gift cards to Big Ed's.

"Ev? Did you hear me? I'm asking you out on a proper date."

"Uh, could we make it after Christmas? My kids are coming in, and I've got these two cases to solve."

A chuckle on the other end. "Wait, two cases? Now, I heard about the one with Sid Hebert. But what's this other case?"

"Officially, it's Shorty's case, and his fees will be paid in new truck tires. I'm helping him investigate the mysterious disappearance of eighty-two loaves of fruitcake. So far, our primary suspect is a hog farmer. We think he stole them to feed to his hogs. That would help his kids to win money in 4-H for college."

Was it divine intervention that the man wasn't laughing hysterically? "Shorty's going to talk to his hired hand, a kid named Teddy, who's fascinated with his prosthetic leg. My PI thinks if he takes off his artificial limb, and lets Teddy handle it, he'll be willing to spy on his boss, the hog farmer."

Now that I'd described the case out loud, even I had to laugh. Yet Mitch remained silent.

"Well, I was in 4H as a kid, and I gotta tell you...the competition is fierce. This hog farmer sounds like a viable suspect to me. And that's a great idea, using the hired hand as an informant. Tell you what! We'll have our date after Christmas...how about New Year's Eve? But before then, let's have supper, and you can tell me all about both cases. It's a working supper, not a date. Because I wouldn't want to twist your arm and take you out before you're ready."

"Really? Just a working meal then? So, why not lunch? I'll be in Baton Rouge next week for finals at LSU."

"Oh, I'm the sheriff of East Baton Rouge Parish—I don't have time for lunch. You can ask my assistant! She orders my food in. No, it'll have to be in the evening."

Who did he think he was fooling? "Well, that's an interesting change of pace. Because I'm pretty positive that we had a business lunch several months ago, when I was working on the Remy Robichaux case."

Another chuckle—I was beginning to get used to those deep laughs. "Oh, Ev, that was a lifetime ago! Things change. Now, I'm taking you to supper—the question is when and where?"

Mitch and I agreed on supper for Saturday night. He lived in Baton Rouge and insisted on picking me up, so I chose Señor Sombrero's in Zachary. It didn't make sense for us to drive all the way back to Baton Rouge to eat. Mitch said it was good for him to make appearances around the parish anyway, so people didn't think he was too good to eat anywhere but in the big city.

My sudden increase in social activities delayed my progress on the case...uh, cases. My next call was to Ethan Bergeron, my go-to for all things on the world wide web.

"Hey, Ev! I wondered when you'd be calling. Mom told me yesterday about Sid Hebert, and that you're on the case. What can I do to help?"

"Thanks Ethan, I appreciate that. I'll text you a list of suspects to run down. Now, you're right in the middle of finals—how are you going to handle this? Because we've got a time crunch with this case. We need to solve it before it goes to the grand jury."

"Don't worry, I'm going to farm out the work this time. We've all got finals next week, but if each of my friends takes a name, this will go fast. Today is Wednesday, right? To be honest, I've been so busy with projects, I haven't had time to come up for air."

"Yes, it's Wednesday. How soon can you have the list? It's five people—I'm going to include Sid on it."

A seven second pause as Ethan made some calculations. "How about Monday?"

"How about Friday instead?"

"Uh, gee, Ev...I don't know. That's a day and a half."

"Let's split the difference and say Saturday. Morning."

At that moment, if I had looked up the word *hesitation* in the dictionary, I'd probably see Ethan's face. Oh, that's right...no one looks up words in a dictionary anymore.

"Ummm...okay...I'll do my best. But I'm not promising any-thing."

"Ethan, I really need you to get this done. Do it for your grandmother. She's worried sick about Sid and Miriam."

Ethan's face probably resembled the phrase *between a rock in a hard place*. Was that in the dictionary?

"Okay, I'll get it done. But only because it's for Grandma B."

Thank goodness Ruby had such a strong relationship with her grandson! Shorty, however, wasn't as pleased.

"Whatcha mean ya' didn't include ol' Joe? Doc, ya' keep forgettin' we got two...count 'em...two cases! Poor Miss Pearlie's jus' beside herself with grief over them fruitcakes!"

"Shorty, you don't fool me. You're counting on those truck tires—that's all this case is about. So don't even act like you're concerned about Miss Pearlie and her fruitcakes."

Silence on the other end, wrapping itself around our conversation like a scratchy blanket. My PI knew he'd been caught.

"Yeah, well, anyways I've got a few more suspects. Now, don't get me wrong, I think ol' Joe's our guy. But my buddy Curt turned me on tuh some other likely candidates."

Should I ask? Well, of course I should. "Why were you talking to Curt?"

Not exactly a horse snort, more of a...what was that? "Well, it's a long story. See, I took yore advice an' asked Nate if he knows any single deputies. Turns out he does, an' he gave me some names an' numbers. I been spendin' most o'the afternoon callin' aroun', tryin' t'find Marla a date. An' Doc, I hit pay dirt! This guy checks all the boxes. He an' Marla are gonna go out Friday night, an' hopefully things'll click an' they go out New Year's."

"That's wonderful, Shorty. So then you had to break the news to poor Curt, I guess. Is that why you were talking to him?"

"Oh, yeah, but turns out some lady come in tuh the shop, an' bought some new tires for her *Cad-eel-lack*. She an' Curt got t'talkin', an' they have a lot in common."

Yeah, I had to ask. "Like what? What do they have in common?"

"Well, they're both single, an' neither uh them got a date for New Year's."

"Shorty, by those standards, most of us have a lot in common with your friend Curt. Was there anything else?"

"Okay, Miss Smarty Pants, there was! They was both born in the hospital in Zachary."

"Again, a lot of us have those things in common. What else?"

Why was it so much fun to irritate my PI? "They both like crawfish an' they both hate standin' in line. Is that enough for ya'?"

The fun was starting to wane. "Yes, you're right. Curt and this fine woman are a match made in Heaven. Please continue."

The crackle of irritation coming through the phone slowed to just a bit of static. "Anyway, Curt said this lady's gonna be better suited for 'im. He said he don't know what t'say tuh librarians. An' he had a bad experience with one, when he was a kid. He lost a book, an' she charged him six bucks! Yeah, everythin's workin' out great. Oh, how was yore call with the sheriff?"

How the... "How'd you know Sheriff Dupre called?"

Now that was definitely a horse snort. "Doc, didja really think I called the sheriff t'fix 'im up with Marla? Nah, that was jus' an excuse, so I could let 'im know you an' *Kie*'d broken up."

Although I couldn't see Shorty's toothy grin, I could feel the glow of that smile through my phone. "So? Did it work? Did the sheriff ask ya' out?"

There were no secrets with this one. "Yes, he did. But I told him I didn't have time for dating until after we've solved these cases...both cases. But before you argue with me, we are having supper this Saturday night, and it's a working meal. We're going to discuss the cases."

Was that silence on the other end, or had my PI hung up in frustration?

"Shorty? Are you there?"

"Yeah, yeah, I'm here, Doc. I'm jus' goin' through yore wardrobe in my mind, tryin' t'figure out what ya' should wear on yore first date. Now, I'd go with that red blouse, with the shiny buttons..."

After settling on a wardrobe with my would-be fashion consultant (never thought I'd ever say those words), I called Milt. I'd done some searching on the internet, and my findings made me question the coroner's report.

"Hello, Dr. Delafose! To what do I owe this pleasure?"

Although Milt was the only coroner I'd ever met, he had to be the nicest—in Louisiana, at least. "Forgive me if I caught you walking out the door, Dr. Gautreaux. I just had a quick question."

A hearty laugh from the other end—did he just say *ho, ho, ho*? No, it couldn't be!

"Oh, no rest this time of year! I've already called the missus, and told her I'm ordering in. My assistant and I will be here most of tonight, and through the weekend. Now, what can I do for you?"

"I've been going over your report, especially the part about estimating the killer's height. It says the wound indicates that the person holding the weapon was approximately five inches shorter than the victim. Correct?"

"Let me pull up the report—you must think a lot of me, if you imagine I've got them all memorized. Let's see...ah, yes. Correct—I estimated the killer was approximately five inches shorter than the victim, who stood at six foot three inches. Give or take."

"Well, I've been doing some research on the internet. Dangerous, I know, but I found an article that said one can determine an attacker's height by the angle of the stab wound. It said you can do that with a good deal of accuracy. I'm wondering why you used the word *approximately* in your report. In fact, you just said *give or take*. What's that about?"

Another laugh...maybe a *ho ho*? "That's an excellent question, Dr. Delafose. Yes, one can determine the attacker's height from the angle. But what kind of shoes was the attacker wearing? Was he standing on a curb, or maybe a stool? If the killer was a woman and wearing heels, how tall were her heels? And did you know that the soles for men's shoes vary as well? Why, just the other day my wife showed me a website that makes shoes with soles ranging from two to four inches in height."

"Ugh! Okay, so all we really know is that the killer stood at five foot ten inches when he...or she stabbed the victim. Well, Sid Hebert's five foot seven, so if he was barefoot, then he couldn't have stabbed Ronald. But if the soles of his shoes were three inches thick, then..."

The possibilities of shoes and the difficulty in determining which ones the killer had been wearing blew my mind. It was like those algebra problems back in high school...if a train leaves the station going fifty miles an hour, and another train leaves the station one hour later going seventy miles an hour, how long would it take before Ev fled the room crying hysterically? I used to wake up in the middle of the night, screaming about trains.

"Yes, you might want to focus on another part of the case, like the murder weapon. Detective Barton and I had lunch today—we like to meet occasionally and discuss LSU football stats and politics. Lydia told me the police still haven't found the murder weapon. Between you and me, Lydia's beginning to have doubts that Mr. Hebert is the killer. How could he have killed Mr. Reynolds and disposed of the weapon in such a short amount of time?"

"Agreed. And, speaking of time, we're running out of it. Do you think Detective Barton might pursue another suspect?"

"She can't, Dr. Delafose. She's getting pressure from the higher ups to tie a pretty red bow on this case and deliver it to the district attorney's office as an early Christmas present. Until another suspect climbs down the chimney, I think she has to keep going down the path she's started."

Poor Sid! He just might be spending the holidays in the slammer. I never did check the internet and find out if Santa visits the inmates at the Baton Rouge jail. Or Angola state prison, for that matter...

"...so I think you might want to check that lead. But don't use my name if you do."

"Huh? What lead? Sorry, I was wondering if Santa visits people in jail."

A definite *ho ho ho* from the other end. "Oh, Santa's reputation has been exaggerated over the last hundred years or so. That naughty and nice list is more of a guideline. In fact, Santa visits people behind bars, if they've repented for their crimes and are trying to stay on the straight and narrow path. Especially if they leave sugar cookies out on Christmas Eve. You know, the ones with buttercream frosting? Of course, it's hard to find freshly baked cookies in prison. So, I always recommend purchasing the cookies from NoLa Cookie Co., in New Orleans. They even ship to the North Pole."

How in the world did Milt know about Santa's favorite cookies, and where to buy them? Hmmm...my favorite coroner did have a broad face and a round little belly. Did it shake when he laughed...like a bowl full of jelly?

"Uh, okay, thanks for clearing that up, Milt. Now what's this about a lead?"

My would-be Santa slipped back into professional mode. "Oh, yes. My wife Reba knows Judy Reynolds pretty well. She once told Reba that Ronald wasn't reporting all the money he made, and Judy was pretty sure he was stealing it from his employers. She also thought he might be taking money under the table, so to speak, so he didn't have to pay child support on it."

"That doesn't surprise me. Now Judy's only five foot five, or so. Does she wear heels? How tall are they?"

"Funny you should ask. We were discussing that just last night. According to Reba, they're a couple of inches. Which would put Judy at...what? Five foot seven? But she could have taller ones—that's just the heels she wears normally. With the right height, Judy could have stabbed Ronald."

"Thanks, Milt. May I call you *Milt*?"

Or would *Kris Kringle* be more appropriate?

"Of course! And may I call you Evangeline?"

"Certainly, but I'm *Ev* to my friends. And you're becoming a friend."

If I could have seen Milt's face, it would have been flushed with happiness.

"Thank you, Ev! Oh, one more thing. Since you're defending Sid, you should know...I have it on good authority that Sid has ties to the mob. So, if you don't get him off, you may have bigger problems on your hands. Oh, that's Reba—I've got to go. Have a great weekend!"

"**A**re we going Christmas shopping together or not? Okay, who are we kidding? I don't care about that at all—that's why we have the internet. We both know I want to hear about your cases. Especially the fruitcake mystery. I lie awake at night wondering if the thieves will break into my house to steal my peppermint divinity."My best friend...always able to make me laugh. Thank You, Lord, for bringing Elizabeth into my life.

"I've got to stop by Big Ed's and pick up gift cards for my father and Shorty. Then I'm done. Oh, question...I don't have to buy a gift for my date on New Year's Eve, do I?"

As I held the phone an arm's length from my body, I contemplated Elizabeth's answer. Did a high-pitched squeal mean *yes* or *no*?

"Okay, honey, I'm coming over right now—and I'm bringing my divinity with me! We can't have the Graisseville robbers striking twice this Christmas season."

Elizabeth lived just two minutes from my house. Small towns didn't have traffic or multiple neighborhoods. The choices were in the village or outside the village, and neither choice was a long distance. I'd just turned on the water to boil when Zydeco greeted our guest with a loving *woof!* He and Elizabeth were great friends.

"Okay, start with the date—that's the most important part! Murders and robberies are a distant second."

My bestie plopped down on the couch and opened the plastic container of peppermint divinity, holding it out toward me like a beacon. A beacon of peppermint goodness. Christmas was the worst time to lose weight!

"Just one, but when the kettle boils, I'm pouring us peppermint tea."

My friend nodded her head innocently, but left the container open on the coffee table. Zy walked up and sniffed, then curled up by my feet. He rarely strayed from my side.

"Mitch Dupre asked me out, and I told him my first opening was New Year's Eve."

Elizabeth leaned back a couple of inches, inspecting me for signs of insanity. "Sheriff McDreamy asked you out, and your social calendar is booked until the end of the year? Have you lost your mind? You can't wait that long to run your fingers through his sand-colored hair and gaze into his moss green eyes?"

"You always had a flair for the dramatic, even back in college. Christmas is right on the horizon, and the kids are coming home. Matty graduates in May, and he's interviewing in Dallas and Houston—even Orlando and New York City. Who knows where he'll end up? Then he'll meet some girl, get married, and they'll never come home for Christmas. The grandkids will come along, and I'll be lucky to see them on Groundhog Day. Yeah, they'll give me some random holiday like that one."

Elizabeth nibbled her divinity like a rabbit, her brown eyes studying me. "Ev, I realize I'm lucky that Cal is raising his family in my backyard. Most people move away from their parents, not towards them. But you and Matty have a wonderful relationship—that's not going to change. Moving to New York City won't make a bit of difference, and neither will getting married. He'll come visit you. And you can always go visit him."

She placed her half-eaten divinity on the side table and turned so her eyes fixed upon me. "Who knows? Maybe you and Sheriff McDreamy can take a trip to visit Matty? Make a vacation of it. Is that the tea kettle? I'll get it."

For fifty-three years old, she dodged my throw pillow like a pro. Zy looked at me, his dark eyes questioning why I was throwing something other than his ball. I stood up, grabbed the pillow, and laid it back on the couch.

"If this date with Mitch turns into a thing, you can't call him Sheriff McDreamy. That's embarrassing for you and me."

I stood in front of the cabinet, searching for our mugs, each lemon and cream with the sun peeping from the bottom. The beginnings of a sunrise, symbolizing the beginning of our lives as college graduates.

For Christmas our senior year, Elizabeth had bought us the matching mugs. The story was she'd searched Ruston far and wide, for just the perfect ones. Being poor college students, I suspected she'd walked in the local thrift store and picked them up. But I still loved them.

"You're marrying Doug and going off to grad school at LSU. And I'm following Cliff back to the hole in the wall you call Graisseville. But we've got to keep this friendship going! It's your fault I fell in love with that guy and he's dragging me away from the big city! Here, you get a mug and I get one. Whenever we talk on the phone, we'll drink tea out of our sunshine mugs. And when we're together, we'll do the same. It's going to be our thing, our connection."

And we had. We spoke at least once a month, often more. Over the years we'd bonded over husbands missing the laundry basket, newborns who wouldn't sleep through the night, and the trauma of sending our first-born children off to kindergarten...then college. Our mugs and our friendship got us through it all.

Elizabeth had driven to New Orleans when Doug passed, her mug wrapped in an old shirt and packed into a cardboard box. She'd strapped it into the back seat, much to the amusement of her husband. Elizabeth spent a week with me, helping with the funeral arrangements and all that came with it. We ended every evening, mugs filled with chamomile tea, crying and coping. I couldn't have survived Doug's death without her.

Once I'd moved back to Graisseville, Elizabeth gifted me with her mug. "We both know I'm going to be over here all the time, and we'll only talk on the phone to say I'm coming over. So, you'll be the official keeper of the mugs." It was an important job, but I was up for the task.

"Well? If you promise to call him Mitch, then I promise to stop whining about Matty...and tell you about my business meal with the sheriff this Saturday evening."

Elizabeth took the mugs from me and placed the tea bags inside. "Okay, that's a deal. Now, where are you going on your business meal? And look! I didn't even use air quotes. You should be so proud."

She poured the boiling water from the kettle, and we took our brewing tea into the living room. From experience I grabbed some napkins. "We're going to Señor Sombrero's. Mitch is coming from Baton Rouge and insists on picking me up. He likes to show his face in Zachary, and let's face it–the Sombrero makes the best chips and queso in the parish."

We reclined in our favorite corners of my couch, sharing my gray fleece blanket. Zy repositioned himself at my feet, nose touching Elizabeth's shoe. I suspected his heart rejoiced at his two favorite people within three feet of each other.

Our tea was still hot to the touch and I didn't need any more divinity, but I had to occupy my mouth. "Shorty thinks I should wear my red blouse, with the butterfly sleeves. Oh, and the shiny buttons. What do you think? "Elizabeth stared at me as she blew into her mug. "Normally I wouldn't recommend taking fashion advice from Shorty Cormier. But in this case, he's right. Maybe he consulted with Annabelle? And you should wear a skirt and some heels. Nothing too high—we don't want you falling over during this event. He's pretty tall, isn't he? Maybe a two-inch heel? Oh, those black knee-high boots would be perfect!"

"Yes, they would be perfect. Thanks, El. Speaking of heels though, let me run something past you."

As I outlined Judy Reynolds and her heels, my friend nodded in agreement. "Some women have all kinds of heels in their closet, with varying sizes. I don't know this Judy personally, but I have a friend that's about Judy's height. And she loves her heels! Mindy has some that are almost five inches tall, that she wears to galas and black-tie occasions. Goodness knows how the woman walks in them without breaking an ankle! Not to mention, if Judy went to her ex-husband's office with the notion to kill him, she might have worn super high heels to help her get the job done."

My eyes turned towards the wall as I imagined trying to stab someone in five-inch heels. "Yeah, if I did that, I'd lose my balance and fall on my victim. For me, a gun would work much better."

Elizabeth studied me again—was she contemplating my sanity for the second time that evening? Then she laughed, the tone matching the wind chimes on my front porch. "Why is it, when I'm with you, we have the *best* conversations?"

I pulled my mug towards my mouth, testing the temperature. "Just lucky, I guess. And my tea is finished brewing—how's yours?"

A nod from my bestie signaled perfection.

"El, I think Milt's right—I'm going to have to put the question of the killer's height aside, and focus on finding the murder weapon. Do you have any opinions on that? Shorty thinks the killer brought it with him, and that it has some sort of significance to both Ronald and the killer."

We both sipped as we brainstormed. Elizabeth spoke up first, almost spitting out her tea in excitement. She put down her mug and wiped her mouth. Yes, napkins were a must with my bestie and me.

"Hey! What about a wedding gift? If it's Judy, I mean. Cliff's great aunt got us this awful wooden statue, claimed it came from her great great grandfather. I wanted to throw it in the trash, but my husband took his aunt's side. He tried to tell me it's a valuable antique, passed down from his ancestors when they came over from England. Ev, I found one just like it on eBay! It was made in China, and the starting bid was two dollars!"

Her hand snaked toward the divinity, then pulled back. She was still trying to lose some weight from her anniversary cruise back in May. Peppermint tea definitely had fewer calories, so her fingers cupped the mug with determination. "Yeah, if I was going to kill Cliff, I'd use that. Then I'd wipe off the blood and fingerprints, and put it back in the china cabinet. I'd stare at that statue from time to time, letting it remind me of the justice I'd doled out."

"Who are you, and what have you done with my best friend? Since when did you start planning the demise of my favorite veterinarian?"

Elizabeth tossed her silver hair—she had embraced her age with open arms. "I didn't say I was going to kill him...I only said *if* I killed him. Big difference." She stared at her mug and made a sour face. "Peppermint divinity is so much better than peppermint tea! Losing weight stinks!" She reached towards the coffee table and retrieved two pieces of sugared goodness.

"I'm not eating this by myself, girlfriend. But these two pieces will be it. I'll put the lid back on the divinity and we won't eat any more—out of sight, out of mind."

"Fine! Let's hope Sheriff McDreamy likes his women a little chunky." We nibbled on our candy. "I like your idea about the wedding gift, though. Or it could be a vacation souvenir. Doug brought home a South American fertility statue from our honeymoon in Mexico. He put it on the coffee table, so I had to stare at it every evening. Funny thing though...every time I dusted in the living room, the darn thing disappeared. But Doug managed to find it, even when I stuck it in the trash."

My jaw chewed slowly, letting my tongue savor the candy cane taste. "You know, it could even be something Ronald brought into the marriage. If ugly shirts could be used as weapons, Doug's closet would have been full of opportunities. Until I snuck all the offenses on fashion out the door."

We both shuddered. "Ev, remember that conversation we had, just after we both got married? You know, the one about ugly shirts and bath towels? Both of our husbands brought some horrendous items into our marriage. Thank goodness we conspired to get those hideous things into the thrift store bag!"

My turn to spill tea as I laughed. "Yes! Doug asked about that orange and blue shirt for a good six months after I got rid of it. But he never asked about the mud-colored serving platter from his Aunt Madge. Even *he* realized how ugly it was."

I cherished these conversations with my best friend—they made life worth living.

"But back to the murder case. I heard a rumor that Sid is involved with the mob. Have you heard anything like that?"

Elizabeth popped the lid on the divinity, smiling at the *snap*. "If only we could contain all our temptations like this one, huh, Ev?"

"Yes, it would be nice. Have you heard any rumors about Sid Hebert and the mob? Does Louisiana even have a mob?"

My friend leaned her shoulder blades into the back of my couch, trying to become a part of my favorite piece of furniture.

"El? Are you going to answer me?"

My shoulders sank into the back cushions as well, and I shifted my right leg so I could square off against my friend. I even crossed my arms for effect.

At last Elizabeth broke the silence. "Did you know Sid banks at the First Bank of Zachary? Or he used to. That's the bank where Cal works. About six months ago our son came to Cliff, said he needed some advice. They took a walk down the street, so I didn't hear their conversation. But Cliff told me later."

She picked up her mug again, noticed the lukewarm tea, and set it down. "Sid approached Cal about a business deal, something that the bank board of directors wouldn't approve of. He needed a loan, and asked Cal to falsify some papers. You know, to make the loan application look more legitimate. Sid told him that he'd make it worth his while. And if Cal didn't fudge the application, Sid would pull all his money from the bank."

Elizabeth picked up her mug again, then set it back down. "Cal told his father that Sid's eyes were wild, like he was afraid of something. Or someone. He kept telling Cal that he really needed this loan, and he needed it fast. He said that it was in the best interest of Cal's family to push the paperwork through. Ev, he threatened my grandbabies!"

She took a breath to steady herself. "Cal knew what he was going to do, he just needed his father to help plan out his answer. My son's an honest man. He'd already decided not to help Sid. But he told Cliff he hesitated when Sid made the comments about his family. I'm going to get some more tea."

Zy and I followed her into the kitchen. Adrenaline rushed through my body as we emptied our tea into the sink. My brain struggled to process El's words, choosing to focus on the tea poured down the drain. That was a normal part of our get-togethers—we spent more time talking than drinking, and our tea suffered because of it. This new revelation was enormous, potentially game-changing. Was Sid actually guilty? Could Cal be in danger? What should I say?

"Ev, do you want another cup?" I nodded and put another bag into my mug. As Elizabeth poured the hot water I struggled to find my words.

"How did it all work out, El? With the bank, I mean? Did Cal get into trouble?"

She stirred her tea, even though she'd put nothing in it. "The board wasn't happy when Sid pulled his money. And Cal didn't want to speak against Sid, but he had to give a reason. He and Cliff decided honesty was the best policy, sort of. Cal told the board he and Sid tried but couldn't come up with a set of financials that would give Sid the terms he needed to do his deal. He found another institution to give him the loan on the terms he wanted. But the agreement included Sid moving all his money. So, he took his business elsewhere, and parted on good terms with Cal and the bank. Cal got a black mark on his record, but he didn't get fired. And we've managed to remain on civil terms with Sid and Miriam."

Elizabeth continued to stir her tea. "Ev, I don't know that Sid is involved in the mob, or mafia, or whatever it's called nowadays. Cliff's friend at the FBI insists there isn't any evidence those organizations still exist in Louisiana. But whatever Sid has his hands in, it's something highly illegal. Dangerous, even. It's good that you're trying to help Sid, not put him away. That will make you an ally, not an enemy."

As I put the mug to my lips, I felt a chill. The temperature in the house always stayed a toasty seventy-five degrees. The conversation, on the other hand, had migrated toward the frosty side.

"Let's head back to the couch, and I'll fill you in on my fruitcake case. Wow! Try saying that three times really fast!"

My joke shoved the tension to the back of our minds, and in no time, we sat in our favorite spots. "Okay, tell me about your fruitcake suspects—and are any of them involved with the mob?"

"Well, now that you mention it, there is a fruitcake mob in Baton Rouge. The FBI is keeping it under wraps, because they're doing the public such a service. You know, taking all the dry and crumbly cakes off the streets."

"Okay, but in all seriousness, who's on the suspect list? Oh, Cliff asked if you could refrain from solving this case. Miss Pearlie's fruitcakes give him constipation, and he's having a merrier Christmas without them."

"What? Why does Cliff eat the fruitcake? Everyone knows you're supposed to thank her and dump it in the trash. Or, if you have a garden, in the compost pile."

Garden! Shorty and I had better check all the people with large gardens. Word on the street was that Miss Pearlie's fruitcakes made wonderful compost.

"Because Miss Pearlie delivers her fruitcake to the vet clinic when she brings in her Yorkshire Terrier for his annual checkup. She even pulls a knife and some paper plates out of her handbag, and slices up big, thick servings for the entire staff. Poor Cliff has to choke it down with a smile and a thank you. He's learned to take a pint of milk with him the day of Miss Pearlie's appointment, and keep it in the clinic's refrigerator. He says the milk helps soften the slice so it slides down his throat more easily. We've never figured out how to solve the constipation problem. Ev, don't laugh so hard—you're going to spill your tea."

But I couldn't help it, as hard as I tried. A vision of poor Cliff choking down fruitcake with milk as Miss Pearlie watched him carefully walked into my brain and refused to leave, even when I pointed toward the door.

Elizabeth smiled and handed me a napkin.

"Now, Doc, I'll be over at six forty-five. I expect ya' t'be ready an' waitin' for me. We don't wanna be late tuh Miz Reynolds' house. That Louisiana crunch cake's callin' my name."

"You might want to come earlier than that. Elizabeth stopped by for a chat, and she left a container of peppermint divinity for you. We sampled a few pieces, for quality control purposes."

"Aww...she didn't have t'do that! What a sweetheart. Well, ya' tell her thank ya'. If her candy's half as good as her cakes, I can't wait t'have some!"

Shorty moved Elizabeth up to the front of his list regularly, as well as her son Cal and daughter-in-law Annelise, thanks to her Louisiana syrup cake. Made with Louisiana's own *Steen's* pure cane syrup, it resembled a spice cake taken to the next level. Sometimes Shorty would call my friend, asking if there was anything she needed him to do. He loved that cake.

As I told Shorty about my conversation with El, I realized I'd messed up by mentioning the divinity. "I had an interesting conversation. We were discussing the murder weapon and..."

"How big is this box?"

"Huh? What box?"

"The box o'divinity. How many pieces do ya' think it holds? An' how big are the pieces?"

"Shorty, I really don't know. Do you want me to open the box and count them?"

"Hey, that'd be great, Doc! I'll stay on the line."

Three times I reminded myself that Christmas was the season for peace and goodwill. I tried to hum *Silent Night*, but it made me lose count.

"Twenty-seven pieces of divinity. Are you happy now?"

"Uh-huh. An' how big would ya' say they are?"

What were the words to that song? Let there be peace on earth, and let it begin with me...

"Each piece is about an inch and a half, but there are some smaller pieces in the box."

"Uh-huh. An' 'bout how many would ya' say you an' Elizabeth ate?"

"We each had two. Do I owe you four pieces of divinity?"

"Nah, I ain't that way, an' ya' know it. Did she say if she's gonna be makin' any more?"

"No, she didn't. Could I bring you up to speed on the case?"

"Oh, I already know about Sid pullin' his money from Cal's bank cuz o'some shady deal. That's old news. An' I'm the one who said the weapon's somethin' personal between Ronald an' the killer. Ya' got anythin' else?"

Shorty was right—the divinity was the most important part of our conversation.

"I'm guessin' from yore silence that ya' ain't got anythin' else. Let's talk about our fruitcake suspects. I've got interviews set up with three other people, an' Teddy's gonna do some diggin', an' call me if he finds anythin'."

"Do you have any gardeners on your suspect list? People say Miss Pearlie's fruitcakes work wonders in the compost pile."

"No, but that's a great idea, Doc. Somebody'd hafta have a mighty big garden, if it's gonna need eighty-two fruitcakes t'compost it. But now that ya' got my brain a'goin', what about ol' Sam Kellerman? He owns that gardenin' company outside o'Zachary. Now, he could use a heap o'fruitcakes t'put in his specialty compost."

"What is the difference between compost and mulch, anyway?"

No horse snort at my ignorance? My PI had embraced the Christmas spirit.

"Compost goes t'work in the dirt, an' mulch works on top o'the dirt. Ya' have t'till the compost into the dirt, but ya' jus' spread mulch all over yore garden. Make sense?"

"Yes. So the fruitcakes could be used for either?"

"Yeah, but mulch has t'be used pretty quick, else it loses the nutrients. The longer mulch is stored, the more nutrients it loses. An' the best time t'mulch is spring and fall. Nah, if Sam's usin' the fruitcakes, it'd be for compost. I'll set up an interview. Anythin' else?"

"Not that I can think of."

"Good. I'm in yore driveway—I'll be at yore door in five seconds."

"To pick up the divinity, I assume."

"Of course. Why else would I be at yore house?"

After handing off the divinity to Shorty, Zy and I settled into the couch for another cup of tea (me) and a nap (the dog). I still had a couple of hours until my PI picked me up for our meeting with Judy Reynolds. Just as I grabbed Jane Austen (the book, not the author), my phone rang.

"Hello, Aunt Ruby. What can I do for you?"

When was the last time I spoke with my aunt, other than that morning? Try as I could, my brain couldn't recall.

"I've got you on speaker phone with Al. It turns out he *does* play dominoes with Moe Randall's brother, Marshall. He went over there this afternoon, to gather information. Al, tell Ev what you found out."

Clearly, Al did not go to Marshall's of his own accord. "Uh, well, I made up a story about my cousin being in a car accident and can't use his right arm. I wanted to know how Moe had handled the same situation. Marshall told me his brother can't really use his right arm at all, and he's not much help on the farm. But Ruby and I wondered if he could have used his left arm to stab Ronald Reynolds? Maybe hold the weapon in his left hand, and swing it over his body to stab him?"

"Well, yes, that might work. I'll talk to the coroner about that theory. Thanks Uncle Al."

"Oh, one more thing, Ev. Marshall brought up Sid's arrest and said he wasn't surprised Ronald had been murdered. He said Moe suspected Ronald had been cooking his books too. He'd hired a CPA firm to come in and take a look at everything. In fact, he met with them last Friday morning, to go over their findings. He said it was pretty bad—Moe's company was missing a lot of money. Ev, Moe got that report the same day that Ronald was murdered."

Honestly, I was a little nervous about our meeting with Judy Reynolds. Who was I kidding? I was terrified. We'd ended our first conversation on bad terms. She clearly didn't like me. And because of her dislike, Shorty was going to distract her with the interview while I searched her house. What if she found me looking through her house? Why had I started *Sense and Sensibility* again? Why hadn't I chosen an Agatha Christie or a Dorothy L. Sayers? How did one conduct an illegal search without getting caught? Yes, I definitely should have gone back and at least skimmed Kerry Greenwood's Corinna Chapman series, except the books always made me hungry. How could someone own a bakery and not be fat? Alas, too late—I'd have to wing it.

"Evenin', *Miz* Reynolds. Thank ya' for takin' some time an' talkin' with us. Ya' 'member Dr. Delafose, don'tcha?"

Judy Reynolds smiled, Christmas spirit radiating all around her. "Yes, yes! It's such a pleasure to speak with you in person, Doctor. Do come in. The kids are upstairs doing homework, so we should have a quiet visit. Let's head to the dining room—I've got dessert and coffee. Mr. Cormier, per your request, it's Louisiana crunch cake."

Per his request? When did my PI start ordering the snacks served during our interviews? Judging from the flirtatious smile dancing on Judy's lips, she didn't mind a bit.

"It's so nice to meet a man who knows what he wants. Mr. Cormier, how do you take your coffee?"

"Thank ya', ma'am. I take my coffee black—no cream or sugar."

A light giggle drifted from Judy's throat. "Of course! Strong and uncomplicated...just like you."

Seriously? If Judy was setting the tone for the evening, then I'd have to excuse myself for the bathroom soon. My stomach was already protesting the conversation.

"Why, thank ya', Miz Reynolds. But I'm spoken fer already. Her name's Annabelle, an' she's the head librarian at the branch in Zachary. I 'preciate the compliment, though."

Judy giggled again, though not as confidently. "Oh, well, all the good ones are taken. Aren't they, Doctor?"

Huh? Shorty's eyes told me to agree. "Uh, yes. They seem to be. Or locked up in prison for selling drugs."

Two pairs of eyes bored into my soul. One pair looking for the rest of that story, and the other pair threatening me with bodily harm if I disclosed details from our first case.

"Oh, I'm just kidding! In our line of work, our sense of humor can be a little...macabre."

Judy relaxed her gaze just a little, but she didn't buy my excuse for a minute. "Would you like cream or sugar with your coffee, Doctor?"

"Please call me 'Ev.' And a little cream would be nice, thank you."

Judy handed me a cup and saucer, white with a gold rim. "These cups are part of our formal china pattern, when

Ronald and I got married. I got the house and everything in it, and half of our bank accounts and investments. He got the twenty-year-old blonde. My friends tell me I had a good lawyer."

She leaned back in her chair and took a sip. "If I'd had a great lawyer, I'd have gotten half of the money in the Caymans. Now that Ronald's dead, the kids are entitled to everything. I've hired a private investigator to find that money overseas. I want my children to have it all."

Judy took another sip and stared into her coffee, a creamy color from all the...well, cream. "Oh, dear. I just made myself a suspect, didn't I? But that's why you're here, right? You need to throw suspicion on someone else. Reasonable doubt and all that good stuff." Another sip. "Yes, I watch television. So, how am I doing? Am I a pretty good suspect?"

Judy raised her eyes and smiled, her ruby lipstick framing a perfect smile. No lipstick stain on the cup, either. I needed to ask her what brand she used. Should I do that before or after I searched her house for the murder weapon? Probably before.

"Miz Reynolds, we're jus' lookin' for the truth. That's all. If yer innocent, then ya' got nothin' t'worry about. Can ya' tell us anythin' about Ronald's personal life? Did he have any enemies? Mebbe the kids talked about people in their dad's life? People he was afraid of?"

"Uh, excuse me. Where's your bathroom?"

Judy's eyes never strayed from Shorty's face. "Down the hall and to the right."

I left my PI to continue the awkward conversation with our suspect and took off down the hallway.

If I were a blunt metal object about eight inches, where would I be? Oh, with a square tip around one inch long. If Milt's theory was correct, the kids' rooms or a home office would be the places to find a trophy or award. But if El and I were right, then maybe the china cabinet? I'd already studied the living room and saw nothing.

Judy's office was just past the bathroom. Wow! Why didn't I bring my phone to take pictures? I'd love my office to look just like this one. Her desk was made from a white wooden door, topped with glass. Two white cabinets supported the door, and a rolling chair with rose-colored fabric tucked neatly under it. Two accent chairs nestled in the corners, with sculpted backs and rose-colored flannel with cream piping detail. Could they be as comfy as they looked? Yes, yes, they were! A lavender and fuchsia rug spread under my feet. There was no way I could get caught—I needed to find out where Judy bought her office furniture. Not to mention her lipstick.

I scanned the office, but nothing caught my eye. Wait a minute! Judy's office was all about her—nothing that re-motely resembled her marriage to Ronald. No, if the weapon meant something to both of them, it wouldn't be here. Or the children's bedrooms. Elizabeth's china cabinet theory was looking good.

"What are you doing in my mother's office?"

My legs reacted before my brain, propelling me to my feet. C'mon brain, think of an excuse. "Uh, hi. I was coming back from the bathroom and I wanted to take a closer look at your mother's office chairs. Do you know where she bought them?"

"Wayfair. Mom buys everything on that website. You'd better go—she gets really mad when people come into her office uninvited. Believe me, I know."

Maybe my search wouldn't be a total loss. "Do you know where she gets her lipstick?"

"So ya' mean t'tell me, while I was pullin' out all the stops, turnin' on all the charm, ya' were jus' sittin' in a chair feelin' its fabric?"

"Well, when you put it that way..." Judy's daughter Millie had followed me back to the living room, and we were greeted with laughter and a half-eaten Louisiana crunch cake.

To be fair, Millie didn't rat me out. "Mom, I need help with my homework—when are you going to wrap up your social hour?"

From the look on Judy's face, it wasn't any time soon. But Shorty took his cue and we headed for the door. With the pan of crunch cake tucked under Shorty's arm, of course.

Millie and I shared a moment over my intrusion into her mother's office, but that didn't impress my PI. Shorty wanted a play by play of my activities while absent from the living room. Since I couldn't come up with a better version of the truth, I had to come clean. And I didn't get any points for honesty either.

"Millie and I bonded over fabric and online shopping. I felt a real connection with her, and I think I can circle back and talk to her about a possible murder weapon."

"Whatcha gonna do? Ask her if her mama bought it on Wayfair?"

"Number one...that's impressive you remembered the name of the online shopping store. Number two...no. But I could ask her if there's anything around the house that held sentimental value for her mother. It's an innocent question, one that wouldn't raise any suspicions."

Shorty turned onto the highway and we headed back to Graisseville. "That's not a bad idea, Doc. Not bad at all. Question is, how ya' gonna get a chance t'talk tuh her?"

He had a point—I couldn't just show up at the junior high and ask for Millie Reynolds.

Shorty's eyes glanced in the rearview mirror, checking on his crunch cake. The man took his interest in food to a whole new level. "Lucky for you, I got some intel on Millie an' her brother, Ronald Jr. Millie goes tuh the junior high, an' she's stayin' after school everyday this week t'practice her clarinet for the Christmas concert. Miz Reynolds has an appointment Friday afternoon, an' Ronald Jr. has basketball practice. So, I offered t'pick up Millie an' drop her at home. Ya' can come with me, an' we'll talk tuh her together."

Shorty's arm snaked towards the back seat, pulling out an orange soda. The crunch cake had been digested and his stomach needed something to fill the hole. *Pop!* Cue the Crawtators, also in the back seat. My eyes scrunched tight, and I held my scream. My PI had no hands on the steering wheel for a good five seconds.

"Changing the subject...did you find out anything useful during your social hour with Judy?"

Thankfully, Shorty gulped down the contents of his mouth before answering. "I sure did. First of all, she thinks Moe

Randall killed her ex-husband, not Sid. She says Moe has a real shady past, which is why he an' Ronald worked great together. Birds of a feather, she called it. Before Ronald moved out, she heard him on the phone with Moe late at night, talkin' about movin' money around, creatin' dummy LLC's...all sorts o'stuff that's illegal. That wasn't Miz Reynolds' first clue her husband was into dishonest activities, but it was the first time she got a name."

"Okay, that's good. What's your theory?"

More crunching before I got an answer. "Sure, it was no problem when Moe an' Ronald were cheatin' Moe's business partners an' clients. But she thinks Ronald started stealin' from Moe, an' that's where things got ugly."

"Well, Al Bergeron confirmed that Moe suspected Ronald of cooking the books. And he'd hired a CPA firm to find out if he was right. I bet Moe was furious! That's a motive for murder."

I puzzled over our findings as Shorty finished off his bag of chips and soda. Solving crime created quite an appetite. For my PI, anyway.

"Hey, Doc. Can ya' reach in the back an' slice me off a piece o'crunch cake? Here, ya' can use my pocket knife."

"Shorty, I'm not going to hold an open blade in a moving vehicle doing, what? Ninety? Ninety-five?"

"Okay, fair enough. How 'bout if I slow down tuh eighty-five? Would that make ya' feel better?"

Was he serious? "I'm not crawling in the back of your truck at double digit speeds and wielding a knife. Forget it!"

"Okay, okay! I was jus' askin'. No need t'get all testy about it."

We drove along in silence. I opened my mouth to discuss Sid's possible connection to the mob. Mafia? Cartel? What should I call an organized body of criminals with a sketchy moral code?

"Couldja mebbe jus' break off a slice o'cake? Ya' know, with yore fingers? No knife or nothin'."

Would this ride never end? "How about you pull over on the shoulder? I'll get out of the truck, jump in the backseat, and slice you off a chunk."

The first horse snort of the ride—the snack had slowed him down. "Why ya' gotta make everythin' a big deal? All I'm askin' for is jus' one slice. I didn't ask ya' t'*bake* me a cake—jus' cut off a piece!"

It had been a while since we'd bickered. Honestly, we were overdue. "Shorty, I'm not going to risk life and limb so you can eat a piece of cake. Look, there's the Dairy Delight. Why don't you pull through the drive-thru and order something? A milkshake, or some fries? You know, something to tide you over the last twenty minutes of this ride."

Another horse snort. Yes, we were all caught up. "Doc, why would I waste good money on fast food when I got a perfectly good cake sittin' in my back seat? Didn't yore daddy teach ya' to manage yore money better n' that?"

We spent the last twenty minutes in silence, while Shorty mumbled under his breath about people who say they're a good friend but they're really not. No doubt he was talking about me, but I wasn't in the mood. That was definitely the longest twenty minutes of my life—and that included the time I was held at gunpoint by someone who'd already killed two other people. My Christmas spirit was in need of a boost.

The gravel in my driveway hit the tops of my boots, thanks to Shorty peeling out of my driveway. After he'd gotten out of the truck and grabbed his crunch cake, of course, taking his sweet time to buckle it into the front seat. I hoped Shorty and his new best friend had a pleasant drive back to the farm. Who was I kidding? That cake never made it to Highway 64.

Zy was happy to see me, and followed me into the backyard. As he went about his business, my phone rang.

"Hello, Lila. How are you?"

"Evangeline, dear, I'm so sorry to bother you at home. Do you have time to stop by tonight? I'll put on a pot of tea for us. I'd like to talk to you about your case. The one with the fruitcakes, not the one with the dead body."

"Of course, Lila. But I've been gone all evening. Could you come over? I hate to leave Zydeco again."

"Well, we've got our grandkids for the night. Why don't you bring him with you? The kids can take him out in the backyard and play while you and I have a visit."

"Let me grab my notebook and pen. We'll be there in five minutes."

Lila lived just around the corner, in the exclusive Historic District of Graisseville. She and her husband Arnold lived alone, but a steady stream of kids and grandkids kept the house full. It was no surprise that two visitors were on an extended stay.

Zy and I enjoyed the walk to Lila's and the balmy sixty-five degrees. We stepped up the wide wooden stairs and were greeted by two children, about ten and eight years old. Their greeting was sandwiched between rocking on the porch swing and taking bites out of frosted sugar cookies.

"Hello, Miss Ev. How are you tonight?"

In the South, we practiced a blend of courtesy and casualness. We didn't drop all appearances of formality, but we didn't embrace them either. Instead of calling someone older than us by their first name, we added a Miss or a Mr. to it. My parents' friends had always been Miss Mary and Mr. Joe, instead of Mr. and Mrs. Delacroix. We said yes ma'am and no sir a lot too, or risked getting the evil eye from our parents.

"I'm doing just fine tonight. You must be Miss Lila's grandchildren."

"Yes, ma'am, we are. I'm Ella-Mae, and this is my brother Gunner. Our granny's inside waiting for you. We're supposed to offer you a cookie too—would you like one?"

Double names were also common in the South. It was our way of honoring beloved family members. It was also a way to take a traditional name, like Mae, and tuck it into a more conventional or preferred name, to make it unique. If memory served, Lila's mother's name was Mae.

"No thank you, Ella-Mae. But I'll be sure and tell your granny that you offered. This is my dog, Zydeco."

Ella-Mae fixed her warm blue eyes on my companion, and Gunner buried his head in Zy's neck.

"Would he like a cookie, Miss Ev?"

Ella-Mae was growing up to be a fine Southern lady, even showing manners to my dog. "Why, yes, I think he would. How about the one shaped like a Christmas tree?"

The petite bobbed blonde picked up the cookie by its edges, carefully avoiding the icing. She laid it in her palm and waited patiently for Zy. The dog didn't even sniff his treat—somehow, he knew this sweet Southern hostess had his best interest at heart.

"Let's not tell your granny we fed the dog one of her famous vanilla-butter sugar cookies. I'm not sure she'd be happy about that."

Ella-Mae nodded her head, her hair bouncing in agreement. "Yes, ma'am, let's not do that. Gunner? Did you hear what Miss Ev said? Not a word about Zydeco's cookie."

Gunner shared his sister's blue eyes, but got his dark hair from a different part of the family. "Yes, ma'am. Could we take him in the backyard and play? Granny said it was okay, as long as we didn't come through the house."

Lila let her grandkids run all over her home, but she drew the line at visitors with fur. "Of course, here's his leash. I'll meet you in the backyard."

My last word was lost in the middle of squeals and barking, and feet leaping off the porch. My dog was going to sleep well, and so were Lila's grandchildren.

"Evangeline! It's so good to see you. Did Ella-Mae offer you a cookie?"

"Yes, ma'am she did. You've got some wonderful grandchildren. Whose are they?"

Lila ushered me into her kitchen, and I heard the kettle warming up its voice. "Maxwell's. He and Josette are spending a long weekend in Dallas, Christmas shopping. Oh! There goes the kettle."

Lila poured the water and I added the bags to the teapot, then moved to the cabinet for the sugar bowl. Lila already had her silver tray ready, and we stacked it with our necessities. Next was the ceremonial placing of the tea cozy, a gift from her mother-in-law many years before.

"I may need to get you a tea cart, Lila, like mine. This tray's a little overloaded, and I'd hate to stumble and drop it."

I set down the tray. "Seriously, though...I'll have to make two trips. What if we just take our cups outside? When we're ready for more tea, I'll bring out the teapot and the sugar bowl."

"Of course, Evangeline. I'm sorry I can't help you. My balance isn't what it used to be."

"Let me take both cups and you get the door. Where's Arnold, by the way?" Lila's husband rarely left his recliner, except to attend church and escape from Lila's book club.

"He's in the bedroom. The kids wanted to watch a movie, and he wanted to watch a western. Grandchildren always trump cowboys, so he changed rooms. We struck a deal: I invited you and your dog over here to wear out the children. In return, Arnold's going to bring them in at nine-thirty for bath and bedtime. They're on Christmas break, so their bedtime is later."

We settled into the lounge chairs on the deck. "Isn't it a bit early for break? LSU hasn't even had finals."

Lila kept a watchful eye on her guests. "They're home-schooled. I'm not sure how I feel about that personally, but we get to spend a lot more time with them than our other grandchildren. And that counts for a lot."

We both tested our tea and found it perfect. "And you're using me and Zy to wear out your guests?"

Lila smiled, the corners of her mouth spreading across her cheeks. Even at seventy-two she was beautiful. "Let's just say I'm using your dog. You are a bonus."

We cupped our hands around the tea, relishing the sounds of children and dogs. Did I have to break the spell?

"Was there something you wanted to discuss? You mentioned my fruitcake mystery."

Lila's eyelids fluttered as she returned to reality. "Yes, but I'm not sure if I should say anything. The Tibbs are dear friends—the elder Tibbs, that is. Curtis Senior and Janet. Curtis and Arnold played football together in high school, and he was the best man at our wedding."

Lila ran her finger around the rim. "And yet I want to do the right thing. Why, in our citizens' watch meeting last month, the deputy told us to report any suspicious activity."

She brought her cup to her lips and took a sip. "The Tibbs live directly behind us, on Thistleberry Street. Curtis' son, that is. Curtis Junior and his wife Bitsy. A couple of weeks ago Junior put in one of those storage sheds. You know, the kind you buy at Big Ed's. Arnold just had a fit! He said installing a prefabricated structure like that would bring down the value of all our homes. Arnold marched right over to Junior's and had it out with him."

Arnold vacated the recliner for something other than church or book club? That could be my second Christmas miracle.

"He returned home within ten minutes, and he was angrier than when he left. Junior told Arnold that he needed this shed for a project he's working on for the store."

"Lila, what store?" I set down my tea and picked up my notebook.

"Oh, I'm sorry. Let me back up a little. Curtis Senior started Tibbs King Cakes n' More about forty years ago. Junior runs it now. They started out selling king cakes but branched out to all kinds of Mardi Gras decorations and party supplies. Junior claims this storage shed is for something to do with the store. Arnold said he put in a window unit, to keep the area cool as a cucumber. Arnold sulked in his recliner for a week, but I got curious."

As if on cue, Arnold appeared. "Kids, time for baths and bed. Oh, hello, Evangeline. It's always a pleasure to see you."

Once an investment advisor in Baton Rouge, Arnold had embraced retirement with open arms. He took Lila on a cruise out of New Orleans once a year, but the rest of his retirement was spent reading investment magazines and watching westerns. The Trahans' golden years shone with financial security. Lila was content to spend all her time with her grandchildren and her friends while Arnold counted their money in the bank. They were well suited for each other.

After kisses for Granny and a promise to lead bedtime prayers, Lila returned to her story. "I baked some oatmeal cookies and took them over to Bitsy, when Junior was at the store. We chatted for a while, and I asked about the new building. I told her Maxwell's thinking of putting one in himself. Bitsy told me Junior's branching out into fruitcakes this year, and he's storing them in the building. Evangeline, that simply can't be true!"

Lila's fingers shook as she reached for her cup, so she leaned back and clasped them in her lap. Her eyes darkened with anger.

"Junior has a huge warehouse behind the store, with a heating and air conditioning system that he put in just a few years ago. Why would he need this storage shed at his home to store fruitcakes? I looked in Bitsy's eyes, and saw that the poor dear believes that ridiculous story! I don't think she has any idea what's really going on."

I picked up my cup, warming my hands as I puzzled over Lila's words. Bath time could take a good twenty minutes, if we were lucky. Knowing Arnold, he'd be eager to return to the recliner. Lila's prayer services would be required soon.

"Lila, I'm not following you. What does all this have to do with Miss Pearlie's fruitcakes?"

My friend reached for her tea, the shakes down to just a slight tremble. "People around here can't be seen purchasing fruitcakes during the Christmas season. A couple of years ago, Miss Pearlie's daughter and granddaughter started helping her with the baking and delivery. The extra help gave Miss Pearlie an idea. The ladies began baking extra cakes for the holidays—bonus cakes, she calls them. If she sees someone buying a fruitcake, someone who didn't receive one of hers, she makes them put it back and gives them one out of her back seat. Then she marks that person on her list, and she starts giving them a fruitcake at Christmas."

Oh, dear! Was no one safe from Miss Pearlie's inedible baked goods?

"And woe to someone who did receive a crumbly con-coction from Miss Pearlie! If she spots anyone purchasing a fruitcake after she gifted them one...well, she thinks that person scarfed hers down! She brings that poor soul *another* fruitcake, and marks on her list to give two the next year. Why, you have to sneak over to Mississippi or Texas to buy a decent fruitcake, if you want to escape the watchful eyes of Pearlie Rabalais."

"Okay, but I'm still confused." My notebook remained bare, because I couldn't figure out what to write.

"Well, I think Junior stole all Miss Pearlie's fruitcakes, so people can buy his without fear of retribution. They can enjoy a lovely loaf from Junior's store, and they won't be punished with Miss Pearlie handing them another brick of bitterness. It's brilliant. In fact, the village might give Junior a commendation for saving Christmas."

Zy and I began our trek home, which would have given me five minutes to ponder Junior Tibbs as a suspect. But I only got two minutes of fruitcake sleuthing before Shorty called.

"Doc, I hate t'bother ya', but I need ya' t'clear yore calendar tomorrow. Teddy called, an' he's got some information he wants t'share. Now, we can't meet the kid in person, or anything like that. We gotta meet Teddy someplace outta the way, so nobody sees us. I was thinkin' we could use that secret room in the coffee shop."

"That should work. I'll call Maggie tomorrow, after the morning rush. She's asleep right now, since she opens at 6 a.m. What time should I tell her?"

"How 'bout jus' around lunch? Say, 12 p.m.? An' can ya' ask her t'have my coffee an' a coupla boudin kolaches? Oh, and mebbe one o'those cream cheese danishes? No, make it two."

The man could put food away like nobody's business. "All those items you mentioned are gone by 8 a.m. You'll have to make it through the meeting without your afternoon snacks. Or bring your own."

"Don't worry about it! I'll jus' call Maggie in the mornin' an' ask her t'put those back for our meeting. She does that all the time for me."

Yeah, I should have seen that coming. At least he didn't expect me to make that request.

"Y'know, Doc, I gotta busy mornin' tomorrow, what with feedin' the cattle an' the hogs. Since yer callin' Maggie anyway, can't ya' jus' put in my order? Ya' have a good evenin'."

Thursday morning arrived, just like every day before it. But it was grocery day and that made it special. It was my day to go back in time and spend a few hours with my Grandmother Elliana, my daughter Ellie's namesake. And my heart warmed to the task.

As I flipped through the pages, my thoughts raced to the past. My grandmother's friends had called her Ellie, but we always called her Memaw E. I spent many summers cooking in her kitchen, hearing stories of her childhood while we baked. My father's mother, Memaw C, passed when I was only seven. My memories of her were just as sweet, but I had only a handful to cherish.

When it came time to name our daughter, Doug and I both agreed to name her after our favorite grandmothers. Her crooked smile came straight from Doug's grandma Seraphine. But that child's curious brown eyes still reminded me of Memaw E.

The woman's cookbooks even smelled like her kitchen! I brushed my fingers across the top of the pages, burying my nose into the center of the book. Cinnamon with a hint of clove greeted my senses, along with a wave of emotion. The recipes welcomed me with open arms. Come on, Ev! Follow us back to Memaw E's kitchen for a little bit of cooking and a whole lot of stories. Grocery day was my favorite day of the week.

Why was Shorty barging into my favorite day?

"Doc, did ya' call Maggie this morning, an' make sure she put back my snacks? I don't want her sellin' my boudin kolaches."

"Yes, I did, but I texted her. And if you're that concerned about my capabilities, you should have taken care of it yourself."

The all too familiar horse snort. "Hey, ya' don't gotta be all rude about it! I'm jus' tryin' t'be helpful, is all that is. You remind me o'stuff all the time. I don't take it so personal like."

"Oh, but you do. Every time I ask about a task you're supposed to take care of for me, you kindly remind me that I'm not your mother. You're a grown man and you don't need reminding. Well, I'm a grown woman—I don't need reminders either. That's why I have a to-do list. Your task was on it, and now it's crossed off. Rest assured your precious kolaches and cream cheese danishes have been set aside. Maggie put them behind a velvet rope with a *Reserved* sign prominently displayed. She even mentioned something about a bodyguard to scare off potential pastry thieves."

Yes, definitely a horse snort. "Ya' know, I told yore daddy that yore snarkiness was gettin' better. But this attitude o'yores is gonna make me go back an' tell 'im I was wrong. Where's yore Christmas spirit?"

"It's wearing an orange jumpsuit and sitting behind bars, just like Sid Hebert. Before we talk to Teddy, I'm going to give Milt a call. I want to know if the killer could have used his left arm and swung it across his body to stab Ronald. And don't forget that we're also talking to Moe Randall this afternoon, at 4 p.m. Are you ready for the interview?"

No sound from the other end of the conversation, snorting or otherwise.

"Shorty? Are you there?"

"Yeah, Doc, I'm here. Don't worry—I'll be ready."

"Oh, and I've got another fruitcake suspect, Junior Tibbs. He's started selling fruitcakes, and his timing's awfully suspicious."

"Sure. Whatcha doin' around 2 p.m.? Junior's always at the store around then, so's he can make a big show uh bein' there for his best customers."

Why had I agreed to take on two cases during the holidays? I could barely walk and chew gum at the same time. "Sure, that's fine. But after Teddy's interview, let's eat lunch at Señor Sombrero's. I love their chicken fajita salads."

That place was about as Mexican as my aunt Eula Mae Fontenot. But they made a darn good salad.

"Yeah, that sounds okay. But ya' can't piddle away the time, goin' on and on about how great yore salad is. We gotta get tuh the interview with Junior."

"Since when do I...? Oh, never mind. I'll meet you in the secret room at 12 noon exactly. Don't be late."

I hit the *end call* button before I got a dissertation on my PI's attention to timeliness.

My call with our jolly old saint of the coroner's office was brief and not as informative as I'd hoped. Milt found my crossbody-left hand-stab theory plausible, but needed to perform a few tests. With his current workload, that would take a while. No one was exempt from the Christmas rush, not even the morgue. Or, could Milt actually be Santa Claus?

That item crossed off my to-do list, I made my way to Maggie's Coffee Shop with eight minutes to spare. My palms pushed against the secret door and it answered with a *pop*. The door swung open, revealing Maggie's improvements since my last visit. She'd added a couple of floor lamps and a throw rug, which cozied up the dimly lit area. Judging from the wingback chair and side table, my favorite barista was using the secret room herself. I spotted a favorite Truman Capote book, with a napkin marking her place.

The narrow room was spotless, as were the table and three chairs placed in the center. My eyes spotted the steaming coffee pot, and a carafe of hot water for my tea. Without looking, I knew the dorm sized refrigerator contained light almond milk and heavy cream. And of course, she had included three mugs, my chai tea bags, sugar, and honey. They stood in a circle on the counter, waiting for their guests. As I poured the steaming water into my mug, I heard the door open, then my PI's voice.

"Hey, this is a nice place! Them speakeasy people sure knew how to keep a secret. I'm gonna have t'talk tuh Maggie, see if I can use this spot when I'm doin' all my thinkin'."

Should I go there? Sometimes I just couldn't help myself.

"All your thinking? What do you mean by that phrase?"

Shorty made himself comfortable in Maggie's wingback, glancing at the book. "Oh, ya' know, I gotta lot on my mind, Doc. We've got two cases, an' I had t'turn one down this week. Mabel Delacroix asked me t'tail her brother. He says he's workin' in Baton Rouge, but she's convinced he's steppin' out on his wife. An' what with her pregnant an' all. The wife, not Mabel..."

And yet, when I went there, I always wished I could take the next ride back. "Okay, I get it. You've got a lot on your mind. Anyway, Maggie's got your coffee over here. Chicory with cayenne pepper and five shots of espresso."

A third *pop* signaled Teddy's arrival, and I turned to greet our informant. "Hello, Teddy. Thank you for coming. Would you like some coffee?"

To compare Teddy's eyes to my mother's teacup saucers would be an understatement. They resembled her salad plates. Clearly, he'd never visited a secret room before.

"Please keep your knowledge of this room to yourself. Shorty and I use it in our investigations, when we need a private and secluded place. Can you do that?"

Our informant closed his mouth and nodded his head, still in shock that our beloved coffee shop had a secret room. My opinion of this kid's information started sliding down the useful scale.

"Yeah tuh the coffee, or yeah t'keeping this place under yore hat? Which one is it, son?"

Teddy gulped, still unable to talk.

"Uh, why don't I pour you a cup of coffee? Do you take cream or sugar? Both?" Best to start with something familiar and easy to answer.

"Yes, ma'am."

Maybe not familiar or easy enough. "Do you take sugar?"

"Yes, ma'am."

"How many spoons? Spoons of sugar."

"Uh, two. No, one! Just one, please. Ma'am."

Shorty's spoonful of patience must have dissolved in his coffee. "Dang it, Teddy! We don't got time t'mollycoddle ya! Take yore coffee mug an' sit at the table! Doc, you too. Let's get this show on the road."

I grabbed the almond milk out of the fridge and settled between the two. So far, our interview was going well.

"Now on the phone you were all fired up about somethin' ya' saw at ol' Joe's farm. While yore coffee's coolin', collect yore thoughts an' tell us what ya' saw."

Unfortunately, Teddy's thoughts were not in order. Judging from the long pause he took while collecting them, anyway. A memory of Matty's room, the day he came home from college, stumbled into my brain. After surveying the mess, I had accused my son's roommate of placing a bomb in Matty's suitcase. Obviously, it exploded and scattered the contents across the floor, the bed, and random places like the windowsill. What else could explain the socks on top of the lampshade? Maybe Teddy's thoughts resembled Matty's room.

"Son, either start talkin' or start headin' for the door. The doc an' I got things t'do. We don't got time t'deal with this."

Sometimes tough love is what a person needs. "I'm sorry, Mr. Shorty. I don't want to get Mr. Joe in trouble. He's been real good to me. But if he's breaking the law, then my mama says I have to tell somebody. My mama says you're real honest, and Mrs., uh, Dr. Delafose is real smart. She says I need to tell you everything."

Teddy stared at his mug, but there were no answers floating in the dark sugary goodness. He shrugged, then took a sip. Shorty's clenched fists rested on the table, displaying his irritation more clearly than any words could. Teddy might not be the brightest light on the Christmas tree, but even he could tell my PI was two steps from shoving him out the door. Maybe only one.

"I heard Mr. Joe on the phone yesterday when I went back in the barn to get the wheelbarrow. He was awfully mad, Mr. Joe was. He told whoever he was talking to that they'd better keep their end of the bargain. He said he was risking a lot by breaking the law. And not just him, but his whole family was involved. So this person better not get cold feet, an' he'd better find Mr. Joe some more supplies. He said he couldn't go back and get any more for a while, that he had to lay low cuz you two were on to him. He said he'd been promised some good stuff, and he needed it fast. He told whoever it was they'd better find him some real quick, or else Mr. Joe was going to pay them a visit. And he'd bring Beulah with him."

Shorty's fists relaxed and he pushed his palms flat on the table. His eyes told me his brain was working overtime. "Uh oh. That ain't good. Nobody messes with Joe an' Beulah."

But I was confused. "Okay, I don't get it. Who's Beulah?"

My mind conjured up a large middle-aged woman with multiple black belts in various forms of martial arts—none of whose names I could pronounce. She probably carried brass knuckles and a taser in her cross-body purse.

Shorty's eyes stayed vacant, his brain continuing to tumble theories around in his head. "Beulah's ol' Joe's Winchester 12-gauge pump shotgun."

Refraining from singing the praises of my salad proved more difficult than I'd imagined. What was the harm in discussing good food I didn't have to cook? But I didn't want to bicker with Shorty, I just wanted to discuss our case. Either case, I wasn't picky.

"Shall we start outlining the suspects? You know, motive, means, and opportunity? You pick which investigation you want to start with."

According to the shrug of his shoulders, my PI had no opinion. Had this ever happened in the forty plus years of our friendship?

"Okay, I'll start. I like the ex-wife, Judy Reynolds. She knows Ronald's stealing money from his clients, and he won't give any of it to her for child support. She could have worn really high heels to reach the victim's neck with the weapon. And you and I agree the killer used something personal to both of them. Marriage creates lots of memories and emotions, so those two are bound to have something that's personal and could kill. Judy's housekeeper is her alibi, but I bet we could find a hole in it. What do you think?"

"I think I'd like the waitress t'come over here and refill my sweet tea. Did she have t'go tuh the next parish t'get more tea an' sugar?"

His entire upper body swiveled, circling nearly 360 degrees in search of our server.

"Since when did sweet tea become more interesting than a murder investigation? Shorty, what's going on?"

"There she is, chattin' it up with her girlfriends...who are also neglectin' their tables. I tell ya', a person could die of thirst around here!"

Shorty stuck his right index finger and thumb into his open mouth, giving everyone in the restaurant a near heart attack with the resulting sound. I'd heard trains whistle more quietly than my PI.

Our server, and everyone else in the room for that matter, looked up at Shorty. She trotted over when she saw him wave, and the rest of the audience returned to their conversations.

"Yes sir? What can I do for you?"

The look in Shorty's eyes told me the young lady was about to be on the receiving end of a lecture. My friend was a firm believer in wait staff etiquette.

"Young lady, droppin' off our meal ain't the end of yore job. No ma'am, yore job is jus' beginnin'! Eatin' all this good food makes yore customers mighty thirsty, an' yore job is t'make sure we got enough t'drink. This here's my drink."

Shorty held up his glass at the young lady's eye level. "It's mighty pitiful, what with all that ice meltin' an' no tea t'mix with it. Now, what do ya' think you can do about it?"

Our server eyed him with one hand on her hip. Did she need the job more than she needed to flash some attitude?

Ten years ago, I'd have said the job was more necessary, but nowadays I wasn't as certain.

"Coming right up, sir. Sweet tea, right?" Shorty placed his right index finger on his nose, which signaled she'd gotten it right. He could have dialed down the attitude, but I understood his frustration. I just hoped she didn't spit into the tea pitcher before pouring the contents into his glass.

"Hey, Doc, I talked tuh my buddy Monty at the sheriff's station. Turns out he's related tuh Jerry Little on his mother's side. He told me Jerry's been tryin' t'get more involved in the business, but Sid's been givin' him a lot o'pushback. Jerry thinks Sid doesn't want him involved, an' that maybe he's tryin' t'hide somethin. He also told me that his cuzzin' Jerry may write with his left hand, but he's what ya' call *am-bruh-drex-us*."

"Do you mean *ambidextrous*?"

"Well, I've heard it both ways. Anyway, Monty says he can do some stuff with his right hand too."

"Possibly. I'm left-handed, but I use scissors with my right hand. And I open doors with my right hand too. But I couldn't stab someone with my right hand. Maybe I could, but I wouldn't do a very good job. What can Jerry do with his right hand?"

"Monty didn't know *exactly*, jus' said Jerry was braggin' about it at some family reunion. He told everybody they'd want him on their cornhole throwin' team, since he can pitch with both hands. Question is, if he can throw right-handed, then can he kill someone right-handed?"

Our server returned with a pitcher. "Here you go, sir. There we are! Nice and full. I brought a bowl of lemons too, because your wedge is looking a little sad."

Next, she turned her sights on me. "And ma'am? Would you like some more water?"

There was no way that girl was touching my glass! "No thank you, just the check. Put it all together, please. And thank you so much."

I watched our server sashay towards her friends, but Shorty focused on his brimming glass. "Shorty! You're not going to drink that, are you? There's no telling what she put in it."

My friend tipped back his head, draining the glass to half full. "Aw, y'know me, Doc. I like t'live jus' down the road from danger."

Despite Shorty's lesson on wait staff etiquette, we arrived at Junior's store in record time. My PI claimed it was because I reigned in my enthusiasm for my salad.

"Yeah, ya' did good, Doc! Most times we don't get outta Señor Sombrero's in under two hours. Why ya' gotta go on an' on about yore salad? It's jus' lettuce an' tomato, with some cucumber an' bacon bits thrown in. Rabbits eat that stuff every day, but ya' don't see 'em sittin' around chattin' about their food. No sir, they eat their meal all quick like, an' they move on. But not you! Ya' gotta talk about the presentation, an' how pretty it looks. Then ya' gotta describe all the stuff on yore plate, how bright the colors are an' how fresh everything is. Ya' even have t'talk about how Señor's jus' gotta have a garden out back, because all this good food jus' can't come off a truck. Doc, let me tell ya' somethin'! There ain't any garden out back o' Señor Sombrero's—trust me! There ain't anythin' back there except some empty boxes an' a bunch o'cigarette butts. Ya' don't wanna eat *nothin'* outta any garden planted behind Señor's, trust me."

Would this conversation ever end? Could it even be considered a conversation, since I'd had no opportunity to join in? What could I say, anyway? Shorty was right, I spent more time than I should talking about food. In my quest to lose weight, I'd looked for the good in eating smaller portions of healthy food. I'd discovered if I focused on how appealing my meal was, it distracted me from the fact it wasn't covered in gravy or fried in vegetable oil. It wasn't much, but it had helped me lose *some* weight.

Eating with other people was the hardest, especially people who could eat anything without gaining an ounce. During meals with Shorty, I'd tried to describe how wonderful my food was, hoping to convince myself I didn't care what he was eating. My friend might be inhaling a deep fried chimichanga with refried beans and rice, but I had a beautiful salad. No wonder Shorty hated eating with me.

"Okay, but usually my salad has grilled chicken or shrimp on it. Sometimes a couple of hard boiled eggs. Rabbits don't eat that."

Cue the horse snort. "What does that have to do with anything? Anyway, thanks for keepin' the Food Network chatter to a minimum. It's mighty appreciated."

"Glad I could make your day. What are we going to say to Junior Tibbs?"

We continued to sit in Shorty's truck, staring at the front of Tibbs King Cakes n' More. What was with this community?

We had Big Ed's Parts n' More, Graisseville Gas n' More, and Graisseville Tires n' More. For a village with few businesses, I'd think we could have been more creative. To be fair, these businesses were started by men. Our other stores included A Good Yarn, Bristle n' Blush, and Dolly's Delights, all owned by women. There was a conclusion to be drawn about men versus women, but I had two cases to solve. My brain put that puzzle to the back of my head for later.

"We really need to get into the shed sitting in Junior's backyard, don't you think? How is talking to him at the store going to help? If anything, it could blow up in our faces. You know, just like at Joe's farm, when you accused him of stealing Miss Pearlie's fruitcakes."

"That's not the way I remember that conversation. An' yore daddy's right—ya' exaggerate yore stories. Ol' Joe overreacted, that's all. He's always been a little high-strung, jus' like his horses. Junior's a good guy, real laid back an' such. We'll jus' stroll in, ask t'look at his fruitcake inventory, an' go from there."

Shorty opened his door, signaling the end of our conversation. I had to jump out of the truck and hop the curb to catch up.

"Afternoon, Miss Adele! How's yore arthritis actin' today? I sure hope it's doin' better."

Shorty always knew what was going on with people, their sorrows and their joys. And he always had a way with the ladies. Except for our waitress earlier, of course. We wouldn't be going back to Señor Sombrero's for a while.

"Afternoon, Shorty. Thank you for asking! Yes, it's better today. I stopped by the mayor's store, just like you suggested. Acadian fixed me right up with some wonderful herbal supplements. And that turmeric concoction he recommended is a godsend. You are such a dear!"

"Yer mighty welcome, Miss Adele. An' I hope ya' told our mayor that I sent ya' over there."

Adele giggled—had I ever heard a sixty plus year old woman giggle? Both Acadian and Shorty had that effect on women. Which one generated the giggle was unclear. Maybe both?

"Oh, yes sir, I did! He said to tell you thank you kindly. Now, Junior's waiting for you in Aisle 12, near the crawfish pinatas. Go on back."

Only in Louisiana do we take a fine Mexican tradition and try to inject it into our own customs. The result was mixed. Of all the Mardi Gras parties I'd attended, I'd never seen a pinata, much less one shaped like a crawfish. But fortune favors the bold.

"Since when have you tried to get in good with the mayor, Shorty? I thought you wanted nothing to do with any of the founding families."

My PI kept his eyes on the back of the store. "Doc, it ain't never hurt nobody t'have friends in high places."

"**S**horty! How ya' doin'? And who's this charming young lady?"

After hearing Lila's story, I walked into the store disliking Junior Tibbs. Meeting him did not improve my opinion. *Dear Lord, help me give grace. Help me remember we all could make some improvements in our lives, because none of us are perfect. Even though Junior's wearing a purple plaid suit with a gold tie, that doesn't make him a bad person. A bad dresser, yes. But not a bad person.*

"This here's my friend Evangeline Delafose. She's Skeeter Bergeron's daughter. Ya' remember ol' Skeeter? He used t'be the vet out on Highway 64."

Junior took my hand and I attempted to mold my grimace into a smile. The man had sweaty palms.

"Well, it's a pleasure to meet you, little lady. You're a sight for sore eyes."

My first impulse was to look around for the camera crew. Had I stepped right into the middle of a bad movie? The ones where the writers pull out their phones and type in search strings like *Southern sayings* or *Charming descriptions of Southern women*. Then we pay good money to watch the so-called movies about the South and walk out shaking our heads. No respectable Southerner talks that way, except in bad movies. Or if they're wearing an LSU themed suit.

"Thank you for taking time out of your busy schedule to meet with us. You have a lovely store."

As I gazed up and around Aisle 12, I realized LSU and Mardi Gras colors were the same. Well, we add green into the mix for Mardi Gras, whereas my alma mater simply used purple and gold. Maybe the n' More in Tibbs King Cakes n' More included the plaid suit Junior was modeling? Did that make it better or worse, that Junior might simply be displaying something from his inventory? Would my father like that suit for Christmas? No, I should stick with the Big Ed's gift card.

"My pleasure. Shorty said you're writing an article for the newspaper about my store? Let me show you around. Which paper is it, by the way? Oh, hey, where's your camera?"

I forced my eyes to remain on Junior, and my hands to remain at my side. But my body was begging me. *Please, Ev! Please let us glare at Shorty and shake a fist at him. We could even whisper a few words in his ear about how he continues to get us into these impossible situations. Please! No, don't take those deep breaths, just let us do our job. You'll thank us later...*

"Oh yeah, Miz Delafose works for The Times-Pick-cane. That's outta New Orleans. Yeah, she's puttin' together a real nice spread about yore expansion plan. She heard yer sellin' fruitcakes this year. Can ya' tell us more about that?"

Thank You, Lord, for keeping me calm, although Shorty butchering the name of the New Orleans newspaper didn't help. But whatever You did, please remember it. I'm betting You'll need to do it again soon.

"Why yes, I can! Now, of course, we can't compete with Miss Pearlie's fruitcakes. Hers are just...well, they're just special. But we all know the woman is in her eighties. Even with her daughter and granddaughter helping out, there's no way they can bake enough fruitcakes for everyone."

Junior led us towards the back and through black double doors. Fans twirled above, making his comb over scatter around his head like brown worms. He clamped his left hand over his head like a tarp while his right hand reached for something on a nearby hook. A dark purple felt cowboy hat with a gold band completed his look. No, I definitely didn't want my father wearing that blight on humanity.

"Dadgum ceiling fans mess up my hair every dang time I come back here! But it gets too hot to turn 'em off. Ladies and gents, this is where the magic happens!"

My guess was that Junior didn't get a lot of people interested in 'where the magic happened.' They just wanted their beads and King cakes. But I pulled out the face I'd used when Matty or Ellie would bring home yet another pencil holder made of clay.

"Why, yes, Mr. Tibbs! This is amazing. How do you do it?"

Junior wasn't my favorite person, but he had to be pretty successful. The homes in Lila's neighborhood started at $400,000, and Bitsy's only job was taking care of Junior.

"We bring in these King cakes from New Orleans, and store them in our state of the art refrigerated cooler. We have seven flavors—traditional, pralines and cream, strawberries and cream, maple bacon, cinnamon and pecan, cookie butter, and bananas foster."

My stomach rumbled, telling me my amazing chicken salad couldn't hold a candle to cookie butter King cake. Stay strong, Ev.

"Do ya' have any samples? Ya' know, so Miz Delafose could write that she tasted the cakes, an' they are some kinda good? It would make the story more genuine."

Oh, Shorty was *clever*! Other than our interview with Joe McMillan, my PI had finagled some kind of baked good out of every meeting. And they'd all been free.

"Uh, well, I guess so. Are you going to reimburse me? These cakes start at $30."

Hmmm...Miss Pearlie's rubbery loaves were looking pretty reasonable. Mother always said you get what you pay for, but don't pay for it unless you have a coupon.

"Mr. Tibbs...Junior...let's just skip the taste testing. You mentioned Miss Pearlie. How will her fruitcakes affect your sales? Since hers are free and yours are not."

Junior stretched out his arms, putting one around me and one around Shorty. "Folks, I have it on good authority that Miss Pearlie is out of business this year. You didn't hear it from me, but someone stole all her fruitcakes right off her screened in porch. What is this world coming to, when a person can't leave their baked goods in their own backyard? Well, it's a shame, that's what it is."

Junior shook his head, shaken and defeated by the world today. "Did I mention we deliver? For only $10 more, we can deliver your fruitcakes to your home. Yes sir, we've got a special van, it says Bubba's Flowers on it. We can deliver your order right to your door, and no one's the wiser. But I imagine Miss Pearlie will be hanging up her apron after this season."

"Doc, will ya' hand me those Crawtators?"

Surprisingly, my PI didn't want to twist his upper body 180 degrees so he could dig through the backseat himself. Was Shorty changing his ways?

"Sure. Here you go. What's your take on Junior Tibbs? His cryptic message makes me think he had something to do with stealing the fruitcake."

"Mebbe. But once he figured out ya' ain't a reporter, he shooed us out the door mighty quick. Couldn't ya' at least pretended ya' work for The Times *Pick-cane*? Why didn't ya' tell him that ya' use your phone for pictures?"

"First of all, it's pronounced *Pick-uh-yoon*. Second, how could I pretend to work at *The Times-Picayune*? I don't know anything about journalism. And he wasn't going to believe I take photos for the newspaper with my iPhone. Do you think that maybe, just maybe, we should have gone over our cover story? You know, *before* introducing me to Junior Tibbs as a reporter. And while we were going over the story, I could have told you how to pronounce the name of the newspaper. Anyone who's helping a reporter would know how to say the name of the paper."

"Well, I've heard it said both ways, Miss Smarty Pants! *Pick-cane*, *Pick-uh-yoon*—they sound pretty much the same."

I had a feeling Shorty wanted to continue bickering, but his hunger diverted his attention. The crunching kept us from finishing the argument, which was a good thing. And really, are any arguments ever finished? No doubt my PI would bring it up again, even if it was five years later.

"Yer right, Doc. We need t'get into Junior's storage shed. No way we can do it with him around. I've met his wife Bitsy—she's not the sharpest tool in Santa's workshop. I bet if you distract her, I can get into the shed. Put that on our list for Saturday, cuz that's the busiest day at Junior's store. He'll be out the door early, an' won't be comin' home for lunch."

"Oh, Saturday's such a busy day! We've got our interviews with Ronnie Joe Hopgood and Sam Kellerman. On the Sid Hebert case, we've got Jerry Little. And Ethan's going to call me with his findings from the internet."

Not to mention my date with Mitch that evening.

"Are you sure we can squeeze it all in?"

"No problem, Doc. We'll hit Junior's first thing Saturday, before we talk tuh Ronnie Joe. That just means ya' can't lounge around all morning in yore *puh-jaw-muz*."

Shorty needed to pick up some fertilizer at Big Ed's, before we started our day.

"Ya' don't mind, do ya', Doc? Big Ed's sells a lot more than just farm parts an' supplies."

"No, I don't mind. And yes, I do know that. It says so right in the name. You know, the *n' More* part. It tells me that there's so much more."

Shorty chose to ignore my sarcasm, which worked out well for both of us. My temper hadn't quite settled down from our argument about how to pronounce *Picayune*.

"So ya' wanna come in with me, or do ya' wanna stay in the truck? Ladies' choice."

"Oh, I'll come in. I'm sure I can always use more of *something*."

Big Ed didn't run Big Ed's anymore—he'd retired several years ago. His boys didn't want any part of it, probably because they spent most of their teenage years working in the store. My bet was that none of them cared to step foot in that place ever again. Big Ed sold it to Mike Guidry, who'd moved his wife and kids back to his hometown. He said he wanted his boys to have the same childhood he did, with small town values and community spirit.

Mike hired Jimmy Melancon to help out in the store, and he couldn't have asked for a better employee. Jimmy was about twenty-five, and had the mental reasoning of a sixth grader. But the kid had grown up in Big Ed's, coming every week with his father to pick up supplies. He knew the store as well as I knew my clothes closet, probably better. And he could use the cash register, which was more than I could do. Shorty preferred to ask Jimmy to pull his order, instead of wandering around the store, because Jimmy did it faster. Plus, Shorty enjoyed talking to the kid.

Jimmy's mother Amy also worked at Big Ed's, doing payroll and tracking inventory. They both went to my church, but I didn't know them very well.

"Jimmy! I need twelve bags o' fertilizer an' four bags o' chicken feed loaded in my truck. Ya' know the kind I like. An' keep my tab open, cuz I gotta grab some bug spray. Hey, Miss Amy. Can ya' show Doc to the fancy womanly stuff ya'll sell?"

Amy smiled and motioned me to Aisle 4. Shorty was right—they had some tasteful items for purchase.

"I've got to admit, Amy, I've never shopped here before. But I'm coming back."

Amy's smile grew wider, covering her face from cheek to cheek. Her love of her job shone through.

"Come back next week, Ev. All our Christmas clothes and decorations will be on sale. I convinced Mike to discount them before Christmas Eve. Doesn't it just drive you crazy when you have to wait until *after* Christmas to get the best deals? Then you've got to stuff them in a closet, and hope next year you remember where you put them."

"Definitely! Thanks for convincing Mike to do that. Then I guess I'll just wait for Shorty."

My PI appeared at the front with his buddy, and Jimmy rang him up. "Doc, let's bring the truck tuh the back o'the store. Jimmy needs t'load my fertilizer an' my chicken feed."

I waved goodbye to Amy. "See you at church on Sunday." Small towns provided many opportunities to see friends and neighbors. Mostly, that was a good thing.

As Jimmy loaded the truck, Shorty fiddled with the radio. "Ya' know, people don't realize how smart Jimmy is. They say things in front o'him they wouldn't say in front of anybody else."

Was there a point to this? With Shorty I never knew.

"Jimmy told me somethin' interestin'."

Okay, it could apply to one of our cases. Or it could be something unrelated. Again, I had no idea.

"Jimmy says Sid's lawyer, Holliman Fisher, has some land down here in Graisseville. Says he was in here a while back, talkin' on his phone while he made Jimmy push around the cart. Then he'd point at stuff on the shelves for Jimmy t'put in the cart—all the while, jus' talkin' on his phone. Jus' like the boy wasn't even there."

Jimmy's face appeared at Shorty's window. "Here ya' go, Mr. Shorty. I'll put all that on your account. Ya'll take care now, and have a good day."

Shorty waved at Jimmy and we drove off. I stared at the windshield, waiting for my PI to reach his destination. Not with his truck to my house, but the destination of our conversation. Impatience never worked with him—it just took us down a bickering rabbit trail.

"'Member how Sid told us he was gatherin' evidence against Ronald, but he jus' couldn't believe the guy was cheatin' him?"

Shorty saw my head nod out of the corner of his eye.

"Well, Jimmy says Fisher was talkin' tuh somebody about Sid's case. He said Sid had already gathered all the evidence he could find. An' he took it tuh Fisher, t'see if the police could use it. Fisher said there wasn't enough to arrest Ronald, an' Sid was basically up a creek without a paddle. He told Sid there wasn't a snowball's chance in a Louisiana summer he'd get his money back. Or get Ronald put in jail."

Our last stop on *the Thursday that would never end* was Moe Randall. Ronald worked full time for Sid and Jerry, but everyone had agreed he could continue to work for Moe in his personal time. We were both curious if Ronald had committed fraud with Moe, and if it had been discovered.

My PI had to grumble about our meeting place.

"*Dell-ick-uht con-stit-too-shun* my Aunt Fanny! She *has* t'be a Yankee, cuz no respectable Southern woman turns away company. It ain't right."

"Shorty, we've been over this. We need to give Mrs. Randall some grace. Maybe she's not feeling well, or just had surgery. It's really none of our business."

Horse snorts had become as familiar to our relationship as Crawtators and orange soda. "Well, all I know is it just ain't right!"

"Maybe so, but interviewing Moe at his place of business can't be any worse than interviewing Joe McMillan's back-side. And chances are Moe won't have a pitchfork in his office."

A grunt from my driver confirmed his agreement.

"Let's review. Judy Reynolds believes Moe's our killer, because of his shady past. She overheard a conversation between Ronald and Moe about moving money around and creating companies to hold the funds."

"An' Al Bergeron told us Moe's on tuh Ronald, even hired a big shot CPA firm t'look at the books. An' they found out he was right."

"Yes, let's ask Moe about that report—maybe he'll give us a copy. We also need to watch him carefully, see how he uses his right hand. Milt seems pretty sure the killer held the murder weapon in the right hand. But we should still keep an eye out."

"Yeah, an' we'll look around for a murder weapon. If the killer took the weapon, it's gotta be important. I bet it's so important that it's sittin' right in plain sight."

"Yes, we need to do that. And let's dig into Moe's alibi with his wife, see if he stays strong on that. Goodness, this is a lot of things to track! Good thing I wrote them all down."

"Ain't no need for that, Doc. I got a mind like a steel trap." Shorty touched the first two fingers of his right hand to his temple, in case I didn't understand what he was saying. I understood it all right...I just didn't believe it. My PI's steel trap was constructed out of wire mesh.

"Mr. Randall, thank you for meeting us. We appreciate it so much!"

"Yeah, but I sure would've liked t'see yore house, Moe. I'm thinkin' o'movin' tuh Baton Rouge, an' I was hopin' t'see it. Mebbe we could move our meetin' over tuh yore neck o'the woods?"

Moe stared at Shorty, his hazel eyes reflecting question marks. No doubt the men had shared a drawn out discussion about this topic already. The best strategy was to ignore my PI.

"Anyway, thank you again. What a beautiful office!" I spotted a trophy on the bookshelf and stepped closer for a better look. "Oh look, you won the...Company Culture award?"

My brain shifted into overdrive as I pondered the name. My PI came to the rescue.

"What in the blue blazes is that? I ain't ever heard o'no *cul-cher* trophy."

Well, maybe not to the rescue...but at least I didn't have to ask.

"It's a nationally recognized award for being the best workplace in the country. We've been able to attract the top recruits in the country because of it."

"Well, it looks pretty sharp on the top. Not real pointy, but I bet it'd do the trick. Ya' know, if ya' wanted t'hurt somebody. Or kill 'em."

Speaking of bluntness...

"Uh, I think what my PI is trying to say, Moe, is that it's a very nice award. And thankfully there are no small children working here. Otherwise, you'd need to put it on a higher shelf."

From the look on Moe's face, he regretted saying *yes* to the interview. And he definitely was glad he hadn't brought us home for his wife to experience.

Could I salvage this meeting? "I believe you have some ties to Graisseville. I'm not sure if you know this, but my father, Skeeter Bergeron, was the village veterinarian for several years. Maybe you met him?"

People loved my father—hopefully that love could rescue the interview.

Moe's face relaxed a bit—he didn't look like he'd swallowed a habanero pepper anymore. But his face did remind me of the time we gave my dad a jalapeño and told him it was a red pepper. Extremely irritated but not ready to kill.

"Oh yeah! Your dad was an amazing vet! We had a Pekinese named Princess Peewee. That beautiful creature enriched our lives for over fifteen years. Oh, we doted on that precious dog! P. P. and your dad had this incredible relationship..."

"I thought ya' said the dog's name was Peewee. Didn't ya' jus' say *Peepee*? As in a puddle o'dog pee? So, which one is it? An' while we're talkin', what's a *peekin-knees*?"

Someone remind me again...*why* had I brought Shorty along?

Moe took up the cause. "Uh, yes. Her registered name was Princess Peewee. But we called her by her initials, P.P. As for the breed, the Pekinese line originated in Peking, China. The dogs were bred especially for Chinese royalty. They are extremely sought after animals. Very affectionate and full of spirit."

"That ain't one o'those yappy breeds, is it? Ya' know, those dogs that jus' yip an' yap at yore ankles. They got more bark than bite, if ya' ask me."

No one was asking you, Shorty. And while we were at it...*Dear Lord, please show me how to get our interview back on track before Moe throws us out.*

"You know what, Moe? I do remember Dad talking about P.P. Yes, he looked forward to visits from your sweet dog, and would come home every night telling us about your visit."

"Oh, that's so wonderful to hear! Your father and P.P. had this remarkable relationship. He put his hand out to pet her, and she'd nip playfully at it with her teeth. You know, all sweet and cute and such."

Oh, dear! Yes, I did remember P.P.'s visits to his office. But not like Moe did.

Dad would come home from the clinic. "Well, Miz Princess Peepee an' her royalty crowd visited me today at the clinic. And let me tell you what that dang dog did! First of all, she growled at Missy, the very best receptionist I could ever hope to hire. Then she bit Janie, the very best vet tech I could ever hope to hire. Then..."

Yes, every employee my father had was, and I quote, "the very best (insert title) I could ever hope to hire."

Was I the very best daughter he ever hoped to hire? For some reason, I didn't want to know the answer. My saving grace was Mad, who was still single with no kids and still finding herself. None of us knew where Mad had lost herself, so we really couldn't help her with that task. But we thanked the good Lord every day she didn't have kids. If *we* couldn't find her, then what chance did they have?

In my mind, I'd fulfilled all my daughterly duties. I lived just two short minutes from my father-check! I also lived two minutes from my younger brother-check! And, I lived five minutes from my private investigator—but I didn't know if that counted for anything.

"Anyways, Moe, we'd like to get yore thoughts on Ronald Reynolds' murder. Do ya' think Sid did it?"

That was my PI—straight to the point. It wasn't the point I'd planned to pursue, but he did get right there.

"Oh, my money's on Melinda Davis. Did you know she fired Ronald? Yeah, he was always showing up late to work. Melinda got tired of it and finally let him go. Ronald just does...did...my books in his spare time, so he didn't have specific times to come and go at this office."

"But Melinda's right arm is in a sling, isn't it? How could she murder Ronald?" I had my theory, but I was curious about Moe's.

I'd never understood the phrase sideways grin until that moment. Moe's lips lifted towards his forehead just a quarter inch as he raised his eyebrows. His eyes looked away from me. But then he flashed a full-on smile and winked.

"Oh, I imagine anyone with a bum hand could kill someone if they really wanted to."

"Say, Moe, does yore wife have that irritatin' bowels disease? Is that why she don't want anyone t'visit?"

Moe's smile disappeared faster than a summer rain shower. "This meeting is over, folks. You can see yourself out."

"In what universe is it a good idea to inquire about someone's chronic illness? At the moment I can't think of a single one, except maybe some bizarre, backwards, no social etiquette allowed universe! And even then, you should at least get the name of the illness right. It's not *irritating bowels* disease. It's irritable bowel syndrome."

To say our return trip was merry and bright would be a gross misstatement.

"Well, I'm pretty sure ya' can say it either way. Cuz if my bowels were irritable, I'd find it pretty irritatin'. An' what's the difference between a disease an' a syndrome, anyway? Neither one o'those things is gonna be much fun."

Oh, the conversations I had with Shorty...nobody would believe them if I ever tried to repeat them. One of my dear friends had IBS, or Irritable Bowel Syndrome. It was a difficult disorder to have, and I had great sympathy for her. I had great sympathy for anyone that had to continually watch their diet and stress to avoid cramping, abdominal pain, etc. Against my better judgment, I continued the conversation.

"Look, it's an incredibly difficult problem to have. And it's not something a person should inquire about. IBS isn't like a broken arm or a bad tooth. It's a condition that's very personal and private. Whatever the reasons for Mrs. Randall's refusal to have guests, it's none of our business."

My PI kept his eyes on the road, his back stiff as a board and both hands holding the steering wheel like a vise. Maybe he had 'irritating bowel disease?' He was definitely irritated about something.

"Shorty, if the Randalls wanted us to know why they didn't have visitors to their home, Moe would have told us. Asking him directly about his wife's delicate condition isn't going to win us an invitation. But let's focus on what we learned."

What had we learned before being kicked out? It wasn't much. "What did you think about the award in Moe's office?"

Ah...we hadn't had a horse snort in quite a while. "I think that's about the most ridiculous award anyone could ever give! Ya' know what the Army says about that? The Army says 'we don't pay ya' t'feel good about yoreself...we pay ya' t'get yore job done!' Culture's for fancy rich people who've got too much money an' not enough o'the sense the Good Lord gave 'em. Yore paycheck's all the culture ya' need. Why, when I was back in The Gulf War..."

Oh, boy! Shorty had pulled out his soapbox and put one foot on the top. But maybe, just maybe, I could keep the other foot firmly on the ground. "Oh, yeah, don't I know it! But I was talking about the shape of the award. Do you think it could be the murder weapon?"

My PI placed his foot back on the ground. But I sensed the soapbox was still there, just in case he could use it down the road. "Uh, well, mebbe. It woulda been nice if Moe had let us measure it, mebbe even take it back to ol' Milt an' see if it matched. Say, Doc, do ya' think if I called an' asked, Moe'd let me come pick it up? I'd bring it right back, after Milt tested it t'see if it's the weapon that killed Ronald."

"Let me think about that for one second...uh, no. I'm pretty sure we've burned our bridges with Moe. But, maybe..." Ev, sometimes you were a genius!

"What? Whatcha got in mind, Doc?"

"What if we sent my dad over there? Yes, that could actually work. You heard Moe-he loves my father! Dad could tell Moe he's thinking of applying for the Corporate Culture award himself, and he wants to come by and chat about it."

"Hey, yeah, that's a great idea, Doc! An' he can ask t'borrow the trophy, t'see if it fits in his trophy case. Or wherever he puts all his trophies."

It really wasn't a trophy—trophies were for sports competitions. Weren't they? And did my father have a trophy case? Did he even have any trophies? Wait a minute, didn't he win a bowling trophy at some point in my childhood? How long ago was that? A memory drifted into my head.

Dad came home one Friday night when I was about fourteen, his face shining with pride. He'd won a bowling trophy! Mother declared it a special occasion and pulled out the ice cream. It wasn't just any day, she announced, that our father came home with such a special award. As we savored our creamy dessert, my father told us the story of how his team won the league championship that night. He'd described a long and terrible battle, full of twists and turns with every frame. But the best team prevailed and the players were crowned the kings of Zachary Bowling Center and Arcade. Nate had an important question.

"Dad, are you also the king of the arcade? And do we get free tokens?"

My father broke the bad news that no, we weren't getting any free tokens. Then he made an important declaration. He announced this trophy was too special to go in just any room. Oh, no! With joy in his eyes, our father informed us that he would be putting this special award in the living room, next to the photograph of him and Mother on their wedding day.

The kitchen got awfully quiet, just after Mother put down her spoon. Her voice became low, slightly above a whisper. Then she said something...what were her words exactly? "Hershel Bergeron...that will only happen over my dead body. There is no way on this earth that I will allow that trashy bowling trophy to set foot in my living room." We all wondered how a trophy without feet could set foot anywhere, but knew better than to ask.

Mother's words shooed the pride and joy out of Dad's eyes, but he held firm. "Well, that isn't my first choice, over your dead body. But if that's what has to happen, then so be it. I'll make sure we sing 'I'll Fly Away' at your funeral."

Then they sent all us kids to our rooms. Where *did* that trophy end up? Oh, that's right...in Dad's office at the clinic.

"Yeah, Doc, this is a good idea. I'll talk to yore daddy about it. We're havin' supper tonight at The Cajun Frog. Say, why don'tcha join us? I mean, our usual conversation is t'talk about ya'. But this'll be even better. We can talk about ya' right in front of ya', an' you'll be there t'answer any questions. We'll pick ya' up at 6:30 p.m."

In what universe was supper with Shorty and my father a good idea? Probably the same universe as the one where people inquire about someone's chronic illness. Yes, that bizarre, backwards, no social etiquette allowed universe.

"Now, this is real nice, two of my favorite people sitting at the same table with me. I sure wish your mama could be here, Evangeline. You know, Shorty held a special place in her heart."

Hmmm...that was actually true. Of course, special doesn't always mean *dear*.

"Skeeter! Why does that Shorty Cormier always have to hang out at our house every Saturday and Sunday afternoon? He has a whole house full of people to bother. Why does he feel the need to spread his annoyance to our family?"

"Now, Muriel! You know Shorty's daddy is my best friend. I'm over there all the time during the week working on their cattle and hogs. Madie always brings me a big hunk of cornbread and a tall glass of buttermilk to thank me for all my hard work. Good grief! The woman's a saint for living in that tiny house with six kids. Come on, Muriel, the least we can do is pay a little back, feed the boy and keep him outta his mama's hair for a few hours. Besides, Shorty's a good kid, and he's always willing to help me around the house. Until Nate starts pulling his weight around here, Shorty's the only help I got."

At that time, Nate was four years old. It was going to be awhile before he mowed the yard and raked the leaves. And Mother kept me and Mad pretty busy with all her sewing and baking and canning projects. Between that and school, we didn't have much time to help out our father.

"Now say what you will about Shorty, even at fourteen years old, he works harder than any grown man I know. Just name someone, Muriel! Just name someone who works harder than Shorty."

Mother knew she was beat—nobody worked harder than Shorty, except my father. She also knew Dad went over to the Cormiers to shoot the breeze more than to check up on the farm animals. Did he really think Mother believed the Cormiers could afford visits from their veterinarian every other day? But it made Dad happy, and kept him out of her hair. If Shorty and his never ending appetite was the price she had to pay, she'd do it. And he really was a sweet kid, extremely polite but overly curious. Mother left plates of food on the back porch, so she didn't have to deal with him. But he and Dad became fast friends.

"Right Evangeline? Child, you need to speak when spoken to."

"Huh? Oh, yes! Shorty always held a special place in Mother's heart. I've no doubt she's looking down from Heaven, so happy that we're all sitting here together"

That actually could be true. Mother was most likely ecstatic that she wasn't sitting at the table with us.

"Shorty tells me you two have a favor to ask me. What is it?"

Please, Lord, help this part of the meal go well. Because we've only ordered our drinks, so there's a long ways to go until it's over. And if Dad doesn't want to help us, Shorty might not appreciate that. And, well, You know how Shorty is, Lord. We both know the rest of the evening won't be pleasant at all. Amen.

"You know that we're investigating the murder of Ronald Reynolds. Moe Randall is one of our suspects, but our interview with him ended abruptly."

"Abruptly? What does that mean?"

Without looking at my PI, I could sense his shoulders droop toward the floor. He didn't like disappointing my father, who had spent a good deal of Shorty's youth lecturing him about minding his own business.

"Uh, as much as we tried, Moe didn't want to answer our questions. Shorty decided it was best to cut our losses and exit the interview. Now, Moe had an award in his office that resembled the murder weapon. We're hoping you could pay a visit to his office and ask to borrow it for us. Then we could take it to the coroner and see if it matches the wounds made by the murder weapon."

The waiter arrived to take our order, but my father was rendered mute, contemplating all that I'd shared. Shorty helped him out.

"Yeah, he'll have the ribeye, medium, with mixed vegetables. I'll have a bowl o'gumbo...not the cup, the bowl. An' I'll have the crawfish etouffee with two pieces o'cornbread. Doc, whatcha gettin'?"

"Uh, the grilled chicken salad with Ranch dressing on the side. Thank you."

The server took our menus and headed for the kitchen. Shorty and I waited for my father to regain his speech. He took a gulp of water, then another.

"Let me get this straight. You two want me to show up at Moe Randall's and ask to borrow some award he's got sitting on his desk? So you can have it tested as a possible murder weapon."

Shorty took a swig of sweet tea, reached up to wipe his mouth with his hand, thought better of it, and grabbed his napkin. "Well, yeah. Except the trophy, or award, or whatever ya' want t'call it's sittin' on Moe's bookshelf, not his desk. An' ya' oughta make an appointment with Moe's secretary. Ya' don't wanna jus' show up—that ain't good manners."

The rest of supper and the ride home was surprisingly pleasant. My father had been waiting for us to invite him to join our sleuthing escapades—who knew?

"Thanks again for letting me play detective with you. Nate never lets me do this!"

Mmmm...could that be because Nate was an actual detective, and he wasn't allowed to bring in random people to work with him? Still, I embraced the small dig at my brother. After all, wasn't it time for Nate to give up his coveted position as favorite child? Move over, little brother...your sister's catching up!

"Evangeline, I'll call Moe tomorrow, and tell him I'm looking really hard at this Corporate Culture award. I'll get him to meet with me in the afternoon to talk about it. In the meantime, I'll work on my story of why I need to borrow the trophy. Right now, I'm thinking I'll tell him I need it so I can put it alongside my other trophies. You know, so I can see how they'll all look together in my trophy case."

Yes, some might say it was a ridiculous plan, one that would never work. My father didn't own a trophy case. But then the potential weapon wasn't really a trophy. Besides, who was going to argue with an eighty-one-year-old retired veterinarian? I'd seen my father wrangle free and discounted items from most of the businesses in Graisseville and Zachary, because of his advanced age and wisdom. I'd put him up against Moe Randall any day of the week, and twice on Sundays. As Zydeco and I settled in for the night, I had complete faith in my father, the amateur sleuth.

As I sipped my second cup of tea, my phone rang. "Evangeline, this is your daddy speaking. I hope I didn't wake you up."

"Dad, it's 9 a.m. I've been up for over two hours. I've got a load of laundry in the washer, one in the dryer, and I'm on my second cup of tea."

"Oh, well, I never know with you. Anyway, I spoke with Moe a few minutes ago. He's agreed to meet me at his office at 2 p.m. Is there anything special I should wear for my interrogation?"

"Dad, it's not an interrogation, it's not even an interview. All you're doing is borrowing Moe's award so we can test it. Just wear something comfortable."

"Right. Should I bring something to transport the trophy? I was thinking one of those plastic grocery bags from The Market Basket. But then I thought of your mother's tote bag. You know the one? She used to take her books back and forth to the library in it."

"You still have that? Dad, Mother's been gone for five years."

"Evangeline, I'm well aware how long it's been since your mother passed. And yes I still have it—I thought it might come in handy someday. I think the trophy would fit nicely in the bag. Aren't you glad I kept it?"

Should I correct my father, remind him it was an award and not a trophy? Should I point out that finding a use for a tote bag after five years of storing it wasn't a good enough reason to continue storing it? No, I knew the right answer.

"Yes, Dad, I'm so glad you kept it."

"Good mornin', Doc. Hey, ain't that lucky that yore daddy kept that tote bag o'yore mama's? It sounds like it's gonna really do the trick. That trophy's gonna fit real nice in it."

No wonder those two were such great friends. "Yes, thank goodness he did. My father is some sort of storage genius. Now tell me about Vince Owens."

Shorty threw his truck into reverse and we flew into the middle of Pecan Street. How the man managed to live life without a scratch or dent on his truck was nothing short of amazing. He jerked it into drive and we were off.

"Like I said, Vince Owens is puttin' in a big patio in his backyard. Now, his wife Tilda's been naggin' him t'put one in for a long time. But bricks are pretty expensive, so Vince kept tellin' his wife it ain't gonna happen. But jus' after Miss Pearlie's fruitcakes disappeared, Tilda announced at the ladies' coffee she's gettin' her patio. Vince told her it was gonna be about seventy by forty feet. Wanna guess the length and width of eighty-two fruitcakes laid out like bricks?"

"Shorty, you know I'm horrible at math. How big?"

The clock on the dashboard showed 9:45 a.m. Time for my PI's mid-morning snack. He grabbed the bag of Crawtators between us. Annabelle had purchased an early Christmas gift—a storage bin that fastened to the truck console. She knew her boyfriend well.

"Sixty-eight by forty-one foot. Pretty darn close. An' I know Vince—he must've found a darn good deal t'build Tilda that patio. Cuz he's put her off for close tuh four years now, on account o'the price o'materials."

We pulled up to the Owens' residence, just across the street from my father. "Oh, yore daddy wanted t'come along on this interview too, since Vince an' Tilda are his neighbors. But I told 'im he had t'start off slow, work with us on jus' one case at a time. An' if he did a good job, we might let 'im help us with somethin' else. He's real excited about this, Doc. And it's real good for him t'have somethin' t'do besides readin' the paper an' playin' dominoes."

Shorty put the truck into park and turned off the engine. "Think about it this way. The more yore daddy has t'do, the less he'll be worryin' about you. Now, don'tcha think that's a good thing?"

Shorty and I avoided the front door and headed straight for the backyard. My first question was *what idiot would make a patio out of fruitcake?* But then I *met* Vince and it all made sense.

"Hey, ya'll! Come on back! I'm just back here digging a hole for our new patio."

A tall lanky man in his early forties walked over and offered a hand.

"Dang it, Vince! Ya' got mud all over yore hand. I ain't gonna shake it."

Vince squinted at Shorty, squinted at his hand, then wiped it on his pants and offered it again. "Sorry about that. How ya'll doing?"

Shorty's arms remained at his side. "It's *mud*, not dirt! Ya' can't jus' wipe mud off yore hand. Ya' gotta use soap an' water t'get it all off. Jus' never mind about the handshakin'."

Vince shrugged his shoulders and turned his attention on me.

"Vince, this here's Miz Delafose. We have a few questions t'ask ya'."

Our host pivoted thirty degrees and offered me his hand, then stared at it. "Oh, that's right...it's got mud on it. I guess you don't wanna shake it either?"

"No, Vince, she don't wanna shake yore muddy hand neither. Let's get down tuh business. We want t'take a look at the bricks for yore patio. Where are they?"

Shorty and I both turned a half circle, searching in vain for the bricks. "They ain't in the yard, Vince. Where are they?"

Our host also completed the half circle, as puzzled as we were about the missing bricks. "Huh! No, they sure ain't back here." Vince's jaw dropped a good inch, revealing crooked teeth stained with tobacco juice. He gasped and snapped his fingers, signaling he'd solved the mystery.

"Oh yeah! Now I remember! Uh, they're not at the house." He smiled, proud of his revelation.

I tried to catch Shorty's attention, but he focused his irritation on Vince. Shorty always seemed impatient with me, until I saw him interacting with other people. He actually had more patience dealing with me than a dogwood tree has blooms. And that's a lot!

"Dadgummit, Vince! It don't take a dang rocket scientist t'see the dad blasted bricks ain't here. Where in tarnation are they?"

Wow, that was the most I'd heard Shorty use...well, he wasn't using curse words. He was using what we call *Southern cuss words*. And that was the most I'd heard him string together in a sentence in a long time. He'd promised Annabelle to stop cursing last November, and had done a pretty good job. Still, his choice of words made me want to laugh. My chuckles died a quick death as I glanced at his eyes, which had turned coal black. The man was just this side of the phrase *madder than a box of frogs*.

And yet Vince wasn't catching on, reminding me of my earlier question: *what idiot would make a patio out of fruitcake?* Yes, Vince was checking all the boxes.

"Well, let's see...I got a really good deal on them. My brother-in-law, Gerald, told me that he knew someone who had a bunch of bricks and she wasn't even using them. He'd seen them in her backyard, just sitting out in rows. Yes sir, just sitting in this woman's backyard, as pretty as you please."

Shorty's eyes lightened, more like his usual muddy brown color. His temper had cooled, like an ooey gooey cake five minutes out of the oven. Mmm...my Memaw E used to make one every month for her bridge club. It had cream cheese frosting, and...

"Doc! Are ya' listenin' tuh this?"

"Sort of. I mean, yes, definitely. I am listening. What am I listening to again?" My hot tea and toast from two hours ago had disappeared, leaving a *vacancy* sign in front of my stomach.

Shorty's right hand cupped his face, the thumb and index finger resting on his temples. His patience had packed its bags and was standing by the door, arms crossed. No doubt one hand was reaching for the doorknob.

"Doc, Vince's brother-in-law knew some lady with a bunch o'bricks. A bunch o'bricks she wasn't usin'. Jus' a whole lotta bricks sittin' in a backyard, right there in neat rows. Don't that sound like a bunch o'fruitcake loaves coolin'?"

"Oh yes! Miss Pearlie's fruitcakes! Yes, Shorty, you're right." We faced our best suspect, arms folded against our chests. I pulled out the look I reserved for Zy when he wanted to go outside at 2 a.m. But my PI took the lead.

"Vince, who's this lady ya' got these bricks from? An' where are they now? Does yore brother-in-law have 'em?"

Poor Vince! His face reminded me of the deer I'd spotted in my headlights on Firetower Road. Which question should he answer first?

"Uh, well, maybe you should talk to Gerald. He's the one who found the bricks. And he's storing them in his garage until I got my hole dug."

Vince's goggly eyes...or were they googly? Anyway, Vince's bulging eyes relaxed as he returned to something familiar, like digging. "Yeah, I took off work today to dig this here hole. It's really something, isn't it? You see, I borrowed some rope from my uncle. You know, to measure the hole. Now, these bricks, they're two and a half inches thick. And I want my patio to stick half an inch above the ground. So I need to make this hole just..."

Shorty's patience had turned the doorknob and stuck one foot out the door. "Vince! I don't wanna hear about yore dadgum hole! We need t'see these bricks in Gerald's garage. Ya' gotta stop what yer doin' an' take us there. Understand?"

Vince had started to resemble the deer again, so I decided to try my luck. "Vince, is Gerald home right now?" Best to start with an easy question.

A gulp from our suspect, who wasn't looking like a suspect anymore. He was probably just a really clueless accomplice. "No, ma'am. Gerald's at work. You see, I took off work today, to dig this here hole. But Gerald didn't. I asked him to take off work and help me, cuz I thought two diggers would be better than one. But he said he couldn't, on account of his boss is out today. You see..."

"Okay, that's fine. If we come back this evening, say around six, could we pick you up and go visit Gerald?"

Vince grinned, his brown teeth poking out from his lips. "Oh, sure thing! I should be done with my hole by then. You see, I took off work today, to dig this here hole..."

S horty dropped me at home—our ten minute ride had no words. What could we say? My mind was still processing why the good Lord made someone so...naïve? Clueless? Obviously missing the frontal lobe of his brain?

"Say, Doc, I'm gonna meet Annabelle for lunch. Would ya' like t'join us? I know she'd love t'see ya.'"

"Oh, Shorty, that's awfully kind of you. But I've got leftovers in the fridge, and I need to let Zydeco outside for a while. That reminds me, though. She and I need to catch up—I'll text her and schedule something. I'll see you at four, when we pick up Judy Reynolds' daughter Millie from school."

While Zy was sniffing the grass and barking at the squirrels, I scheduled a coffee date with Annabelle for Sunday afternoon. It had been too long.

My dog and I headed back into the kitchen, and my stomach rumbled its appreciation. As I prepared my salad with tuna on top, I thanked God for my blessings. The good Lord understood that my stomach didn't want to take time at the table for prayers.

"Mmmm! Zy, this salad is amazing! The romaine is crisp and fresh, and these Roma tomatoes are plump and juicy. Oh, this tuna makes it even better! Yes, it's from a can, but I tell you, it tastes as fresh as the rest of my salad." My faithful companion wagged his tail in agreement. He didn't care how much I gushed over my lunch.

My brain begged for a reprieve—all the time spent with Vince had pushed it beyond capacity. Zy and I both knew that a pot of tea and a book on the front porch would soothe my aching head. I'd never met anyone who could literally give me a headache. Oh, his poor wife! Or maybe, she was just as exasperating? Honestly, I didn't want to risk another headache to find out.

My stomach announced it was still hungry, and I stepped inside to prepare a snack and refill my teapot. Zy ran into the back of my knees as I stopped to stare at the strategizing room.

The original owners had used it as a formal living room to greet visitors. When I moved in, I put my bookshelves and Zy's crate in it. A month or so ago, I sold the crate—he never slept in it, anyway. On our second case, Shorty dubbed it our *strat-uh-jize-in'* room.

"Doc, let's hang the white board in this room off the hallway. We could put a coupla chairs in here an' make this our *strat-uh-jize-in'* room. Whatcha think?"

My sixty by forty-eight-inch dry erase board hung on the far wall, facing two chairs and a snack table. My brother donated two club chairs from his bachelor days. To show her gratitude, his wife Bonnie reupholstered them in denim and painted a small table to sit between them. It was their way of congratulating me on my new career. My father had a sign made, *Cormier & Delafose Investigations*. He and I both knew Shorty would complain if his name wasn't first. And we both knew I didn't care if my name was listed at all. Our partnership worked perfectly.

"Evangeline, I want you to hang this sign in your strategizing room. As part of your Christmas, I'm going to pay for you to get your private investigator's license. Shorty and I've been talking, and we think it's time."

"That's wonderful, Dad. I appreciate it. And I promise, after Christmas, I'll start working on it."

Speaking of time, it was time to start working on the grid. But which case? Well, Ev, how about the one where someone actually died?

I jogged to the kitchen to grab an apple...okay, I didn't really jog. Strolled would be the more appropriate term. But at my age, I probably should be jogging. And a jog to the kitchen would be a good start. Maybe after the holidays...

My apple in my right hand and a green dry erase marker in my left, I printed the suspects down the left side of a grid. The three elements stared at me across the top: Motive (a reason to kill), Means (a way to kill), and Opportunity (a chance to kill). Then I picked up the red highlighter. Time to list the suspects with the strongest elements.

Sid's motive was strong—he knew Ronald had stolen from him, but his lawyer said it wasn't enough to take to the police. Sid was also found with the body. The fact that he fainted at the sight of blood was his only saving grace. Sid had two columns in red and one in green.

Judy had a strong motive as well, because she knew Ronald had more money than he was reporting for child support. Of course it was illegal money, but that didn't seem to bother Judy. She could have stabbed him if she'd been wearing high heels, but her housekeeper was vouching for her. Judy had a red, a yellow, and a green column on the grid. We needed to learn more about her alibi.

Moe's motive was strong too, because the CPA firm he'd hired proved that Ronald was stealing. But thanks to his injured right arm and wife as his alibi, he had one red column and two green.

Jerry's columns were all green, which meant our interview tomorrow was crucial. Same with Melinda Davis—all green for her, meaning we needed more information.

Completing the grid made me feel better, so I rewarded myself with another cup of tea. What should I do until my father returned?

My phone rang, *Thank you for being a friend! Traveled down a road and back again. Your heart is true—*

"Elizabeth! I was just trying to figure out how to spend an hour waiting for my father."

Low chuckles floated into my ear. "Why in the world are you waiting on your father?"

"Uh, well, he's on a case. Let's just say Shorty burned our bridges with one of our suspects, so we've got my dad going in to recover an award. We think the killer may have used it to stab Ronald Reynolds."

The low chuckles turned to peals of laughter. "Ev, you are the best friend a girl could ever have! You make my life so much better! Who else do I know that's sending in their eighty-one-year-old father to lift a potential murder weapon?"

"Dadgum, Evangeline! If this is the kind of detective work you're going to give me, I'm quitting right now!"

Not a *hi* or a *hello*, or even a *good afternoon*. The visit to Moe's must have been pretty terrible.

"Well, I had to hear all about Miz Princess Peepee! Dang it, Ev, that guy has the memory of a twenty-year-old. He could recollect every visit that yappy dog made to my office—and she lived to be seventeen!"

Dad followed me to the kitchen and took a stool. His eyes followed my hands as I opened the cabinet and pulled out a dessert plate.

"Seventeen years! That's a lot of visits to the clinic. That Moe Randall, he even remembered Missy and Janie. And he remembered that girl who filled in for Missy when she had her baby. Heck, I didn't even remember her name!"

His eyes never lost sight of my hands, reaching into the pantry for the cane syrup cookies I'd baked that morning. Somehow, I had a feeling my father would need them. Either that, or a healthy shot of Jameson whiskey. I'd opted for the cookies.

As my father munched on his treat, I poured a glass of lemonade. "How did Moe's dog end up at your clinic? I thought he lived in Baton Rouge?"

Dad swallowed. "He does. He and his wife were down here visiting family, and that dumb dog got caught in some barbed wire. Moe called the emergency number, which is really for the ranchers. Not for people who aren't smart enough to know fancy little yippy yappy dogs don't belong on a farm. Anyway, unfortunately for me, they loved how I treated their ball of fluff. They loved it so much they decided to switch vets. They spent the rest of that dang dog's life trekking down to Graisseville to bring her to me. You know, Janie almost quit after that rat dog bit her for the second time. Why, Janie was the very best vet tech I could ever hope to hire..."

Yes, best to steer this trip from Memory Lane back to Relevant Road. "Uh, Dad, so how did the rest of the visit go? Did you get the award?"

My father pushed his plate towards me, a definite sign he wanted a refill. I returned from the pantry with the cookie jar and set it in front of him. After all, he'd earned it.

"Yeah, yeah, I did. And let me tell you something..."

Oh? Had my father discovered a key piece of evidence?

"You should be thanking me that I kept your mother's tote bag all these years. I was right! It came in mighty handy today. Why, that trophy fit perfectly in the bag. Yes sir, I sure am glad I kept it. If your mother was here today, she'd agree."

"Dad, if Mother was here today, she wouldn't have let you saunter into a potential killer's office and try to finagle the murder weapon from him. And she certainly wouldn't have let you take her tote bag. Today is Friday. Mother would be using it to go to the library today."

My father munched his cookies in silence, trying to find a hole in my reasoning. "Well, anyway, I've got it in the car. Do you want me to bring it in?"

"No, Dad—you should leave it in the car. It would be much more useful in my driveway than in my house. In fact, why don't you just leave it there? We'll stare at it through the window as we puzzle over whether it's actually the murder weapon."

My father and I locked eyes. He suspected I'd added a good helping of sarcasm with my answer. On the other hand, he really hoped I would ask him to deliver the award to Milt. I broke eye contact first.

"Tell you what, Dad. Shorty and I have an appointment at four. Could you do me a favor and carry your tote bag over to the coroner's office? Just ask for Dr. Milt Gautreaux, and tell him it's from me. Ask him to call me with the results."

The look on my father's face told me Christmas had come early. "Do you mean it, Evangeline? I can really take the trophy over to the coroner's office?"

"Of course, Dad. I'd really appreciate it."

Hmmm...could this errand count as my father's Christmas gift? Gosh, that would really help with my finances.

Picking up a teenager was something new for Shorty. Why did I take great joy from my PI's discomfort?

"How ya' doin', Millie? Yore mama asked us t'pick ya' up from school today."

Judging from our passenger's eye roll, Shorty hadn't revealed anything earth-shattering.

"I was thinkin' we could stop somewhere an' get some ice cream. Whatcha think? Want some ice cream?"

Another eye roll. "I'm trying out for majorette in the spring, so I've got to watch my weight. But thanks anyway."

It was the perfect opportunity for Shorty to present his own eye roll with a generous helping of exasperated sighing. Time for the mother of a teenager to step in.

"Millie, before you put in your ear buds, I wanted to ask your opinion on something. My daughter Ellie's coming home for Christmas. Now, I've got her big gift already wrapped and under the tree—Doc Martens Quad Platform Chelsea Boots. But I'm wanting to get her some other, less expensive gifts. She's eighteen, a bit older than you...but I wondered if you have some ideas."

Want to impress a teenage girl? Let her know you have expensive taste and then ask her opinion. I strategically left out the part Ellie had begged for the boots, and I'd brought in my brother, sister, and father to pool our resources and pay for Ellie's most expensive Christmas gift to date. Poor Matty was getting socks and a gift card to Walmart.

"Oh wow! You're a great mom, Mrs. Delafose. My mom always gets me lame presents, like lip gloss or fuzzy socks. Yeah, I bet your daughter would like a mini perfume sampler from Sephora. Or some rectangle sunglasses—you can get them for less than twenty dollars at any major department store."

Oops! I'd given Ellie lip gloss and fuzzy socks on her last birthday. But Millie would never know.

"Thank you so much! Shorty, how about we stop for some coffee instead? Millie, where's your favorite coffee shop?"

Thirty minutes and two caffeinated drinks later (ice cream for Shorty), we'd gathered around a square metal table in the back. Millie hadn't issued an eye roll for quite some time.

My PI occupied himself by mixing his scoop of chocolate and scoop of peanut butter cookie dough ice cream into one squishy lump. He'd let the women talk.

"Millie, you know that Mr. Cormier and I are investigating the death of your father. We're very sorry for your loss."

My new friend lifted her shoulders up a few inches, then let them down. She would have achieved her goal, to convey an air of indifference, except I spotted the tears in the corners of her eyes.

"Millie, I've raised two kids myself, and something I've learned is that they know a lot more about what's going on than their parents think."

The hint of tears might have disappeared. I wouldn't know, because Millie had lowered her eyes. The tabletop had become incredibly fascinating. She lifted her right hand from her lap and traced the faux wood grain with her index finger.

"Honey, I'm not asking you to betray your mother. I'm just asking you to tell me what you know about the night your father was killed."

Millie's index finger never hesitated, continuing its task of tracing the swirls on the tabletop. My experience as a mother told me to let her choose the words and the moment. Shorty's bowl rested on the table, sticky with the last drips of his snack.

"I'm gonna find the bathroom."

My lungs protested, and I realized I'd been holding my breath. What did Millie know?

The index finger never wavered in its task. "Miss Trudy's her alibi. My mother's alibi. Miss Trudy's our housekeeper, and she comes in during the week to clean and make supper. I wasn't home that night, but Miss Trudy told the police

Mom came home about 4:30. She made supper and Mom ate around six. She told that lady detective that my mom never left the house."

The police found Sid with the body at 5:25, which meant Judy couldn't have killed her ex-husband.

"But I heard her on the phone—Miss Trudy, not my mother. She told whoever it was on the other end that Mom greeted Miss Trudy, put her purse on the hall table, and went upstairs to take a bath. Miss Trudy heard the water running, but she didn't see Mom again until she called her for supper at six."

Round and round the swirls...it was mesmerizing, really. At last Millie stopped, but she kept her eyes on the tabletop. "A few years ago, Mom and Dad had a stairway put in their bedroom. You know, in case there was a fire in the middle of the night. Our escape plan was to meet in the master bedroom and all go down the stairs together."

Shorty stopped at the table, noted my eyes, and moved past us to the counter. Was he seriously ordering another bowl of ice cream?

"It's possible my mom ran her bathwater, then snuck out the back stairs and took her car to Dad's office. Miss Trudy never told the police Mom's car was in the driveway that evening. She just told them that my mother was home all night."

Oh, poor child! To have her father murdered, then wonder if her mother was the killer. That was too much for a four-teen-year-old to shoulder. Or anyone, for that matter.

Millie's left hand appeared on the table, and she inter-twined her fingers. She straightened her shoulders, making her seem twice her age. "Whoever murdered my father, I want them behind bars. Even if it's my mother. Ronald

Reynolds wasn't the best father in the world—he didn't even qualify for the top fifty percent. But he was my father, and he deserves justice."

My hands covered her clasped fingers without a second thought. "Millie, I promise you, Mr. Cormier and I will do everything we can to find out who killed your father. Even if it's our client, we will uncover the truth. You have my word."

I slid my hands towards Millie, until they touched her wrists. "But I need something from you. We think the murder weapon meant something to both your father and his killer, because it's not a traditional weapon. We think it's an award, or some sort of souvenir. The coroner tells us that it's a blunt metal object about eight inches, with a square tip around one inch long. Is there anything in your home matching that description? Something that held sentimental value for your parents, maybe something they purchased on a vacation?"

Millie looked towards the wall, accessing her memory. "No, I can't think of anything at the moment. But I can look around the house, see if there's an object like that somewhere. But wouldn't the killer get rid of the murder weapon? Keeping it is such a reckless thing to do. And my mom's not reckless."

The girl at the counter was about sixteen or so. Shorty held a special charm for women of all ages, but even he couldn't carry on a conversation with a teenager for long periods of time. He returned to our table with a half-eaten bowl of ice cream.

"Our working theory is that this object holds such a strong memory, the killer doesn't want to get rid of it. He or she wants to keep it around, to look at and feel a certain satisfaction."

Millie's chocolate eyes mirrored the doubt that had crept into my thoughts. The theory had seemed sound when Shorty and I discussed it. After telling Millie, I wasn't so sure.

Next on our list was a visit with Melinda Davis. "Member of the Baton Rouge Rotary Club and former employer of Ronald Reynolds. Her right arm's in a sling, and she injured it before the murder. We know that thanks to the photo in the newspaper. Melinda told police she was home with her husband at the time of the murder. Now, what don't we know?"

Shorty's cup holder and hands were conspicuously empty. He'd mentioned eating a snack before our visit, on the off chance he wouldn't like Melinda's snacks. But my guess was he planned to save his appetite for Melinda's charcuterie board, and save the chips and soda for *Plan B*.

"Are ya' sure this *shar-coot-ree* board ain't gonna have any chocolate cake or pecan pie on it? Or even some Christmas cookies? We're jus' a coupla weeks from the birth of our Lord an' Savior—that miracle needs to be celebrated with somethin' besides cheese an' crackers!"

"Like I've said before, charcuterie boards are different things to different people. But it sounded like Melinda would be preparing a simple cheese board—Asiago, Gouda, and Gruyere. I'm sure there will be crackers, and maybe even some fruit. Possibly some nuts, like pecans and almonds."

My PI mumbled something under his breath, but I only caught the words *respectable Southerners.*

"Shorty, we're meeting at five o'clock—that's a little late to expect a full-blown table of snacks. We don't want to ruin our supper. Or I don't, anyway."

His shoulders straightened as a positive thought entered his brain. "Hey, mebbe the nuts will be served in some cookies. Whatcha think, Doc? It could happen. An' yer real sure we don't get t'take the board home? Y'know, like a souvenir?"

"I thought you had no idea what to do with one piece of wood. Why do you care about it now?"

"Because free is free. I ain't a fan o'oatmeal raisin cookies neither—rather have the ones with chocolate chips. But I'm not turnin' down no free cookies! If someone offered me the ones with raisins, I'd say thank ya' mighty kindly and go on my way. Well, it's the same with a free piece o'wood."

My brain raced to churn out a response, but sputtered and stalled. How could a person respond to this line of reasoning? "Stranger things have happened. Could we focus on the investigation?"

A grunt indicated we could. "I say let's forget about all that heels or no heels nonsense. Like ol' Milt said, unless we know what shoes the killer was wearin', there ain't a way t'tell his height. Or her height. An' until we do some kinda testin', t'see if a person can kill left-handed and it looks like they killed with their right, then we forget all about that too. Let's get back tuh the basics."

"I think you're right. So, what is our focus?"

"Glad ya' asked! My buddy told me that Sid an' Melinda know each other, through the Rotary Club. But they ain't big pals...can't stand each other, in fact. I say let's ask her about Sid."

"Shorty, why would we ask her about our client? We're trying to prove his innocence."

My PI turned into Melinda's driveway. "Because you promised Millie Reynolds justice for her father, even if it's our client. I heard ya' say it in the coffee shop. Ya' gave yore word."

He turned off the engine and opened his door. "Well, let's go—I jus' can't wait for my big bowl o'cheese an' nuts."

Melinda greeted us, her right arm captured in a sling made of purple fabric dotted with hibiscus. "Look, folks, my lawyer's advised me not to answer any questions about my relationship with Ronald. You're wasting your time by coming out here."

Melinda's home reflected her love of all things feline. She led us down a hallway filled with framed photographs and paintings of various breeds of cats.

"Oh my, Melinda. I'm guessing you love cats. I don't think I've seen such a...complete collection of the various breeds. At least not in the same location."

Melinda's gray eyes swelled with pride. "Oh, thank you! Yes, I've been collecting every painting, figurine, and fabric I can get my hands on since I was a little girl. Few people appreciate my passion. Thank you for the compliment."

For once, I'd made it to the dining room without offending my host. By my count that was the third Christmas miracle I'd witnessed.

We took our seats on Melinda's couch and I moved my eyes to the coffee table. The gasp of pleasure from my PI took me a good inch off the couch cushion. Melinda had outdone herself.

We stared at no less than seven kinds of gourmet cheeses, each paired with a different type of cracker. These delights only took up a third of the three-foot white marble slab. Christmas cookies piped in icing had been stacked in rows, along with petite pumpkin tarts and slices of lemon cake. Was that drool glistening on my PI's chin? No doubt I'd be flying solo during this interview. Shorty would be too busy with his food choices.

"Let's steer clear of Ronald entirely. What can you tell us about Sid Hebert?"

Melinda struggled to pour cups of coffee one-handed, then offered the carafe to me. I skipped the third cup and set down the black carafe. Shorty wouldn't have time for a drink, what with all the food to consume.

"What can I tell you about Sid? Oh, honey, how much time do you have? I know for a fact Sid knew Ronald was skimming all along, and confronted him. Ronald agreed to give Sid a piece of the action, in exchange for his silence. Sid wanted to cut Ronald out, but he couldn't figure out how the kid was doing it, and that made him hate Ronald. Sid can't stand people smarter than him. He knew Jerry was about to figure it all out, so he was going to have to get rid of Ronald."

Melinda took a sip of her cooling drink. "Sid got wind that Ronald was leaving town, and he went back to the office to confront him."

A jarring sound filled the air. "That's my phone. Can we cut this interview short? I'm trying to close a deal, and I've got to soothe my partner's egos. Why don't you take this food with you? I've got some plastic to go containers in the kitchen–bottom right, by the sink." She stood up, taking her drink with her. "Bill, calm down..."

Shorty had returned from the kitchen balancing multiple sizes of plastic storage units. Which did my PI enjoy more–solving the case or sampling the free food?

J umping back and forth between cases made me jumpy, myself. My fifty-something brain struggled to keep the suspects and the theories on track. My brain wasn't dealing well with the knowledge that our client might just be guilty. How would that play out with future clients?

"Yes, we were hired to prove our client was innocent. But we helped put him behind bars instead. Oh, no sir—I'm sure that wouldn't happen in *your* case!"

I'd promised Millie to find justice for her father, even if it meant putting my client away. Maybe that should be our tagline: We find justice, no matter the cost. Mmmm...it needed work.

"All right, Doc. We gotta go pick up Vince, then head over tuh Gerald's place. But first, ya' sure ya' don't want any of this great food Melinda sent home with us?"

My charming PI scored the entire charcuterie board, minus the board. "Once I saw it wasn't a board, I didn't want it, anyway. What would I do with a piece o'marble? But this cheese sure is good, Doc! Who'd've guessed I liked fancy cheese an' crackers?"

"Not me, not in a million years. After we take a look at these bricks in Gerald's garage, do you have time to stop by my house? We need to update our grid with the information Melinda gave us."

"Yeah, sure. I'll need t'let Annabelle know I might be late pickin' her up."

Shorty pulled into Vince's driveway. "Can ya' go up there an' get him? I don't think he's sittin' around waitin' for us. He's forgot we're pickin' him up. He's not the fastest reindeer in Santa's herd."

Shorty didn't know everything, but he knew people. On my third ring of the doorbell and two knocks that hurt my knuckles, Vince's wife Tilda opened the door.

"Hello. We already go to church, and we don't need any magazine subscriptions."

"I'm happy to hear you have a church and a decent supply of magazines. But I'm here for Vince."

Tilda blinked twice. "Vince?" She looked past my head into her front yard. "Where is he?"

A picture of Abbott and Costello and the words *Who's on First* flashed through my thoughts. "Mrs. Owens, I don't know where your husband is. My colleague, Shorty Cormier, and I agreed to meet him at his house and pick him up. We're headed to Gerald's house."

Abbott and Costello were shoved out of my head, replaced by the words *lightbulb moment.* "Oh yes! Vince is at Gerald's." Pleased as punch with her revelation, Tilda pushed the door forward to close it.

I opened the screen door and shoved my foot inside. "Could you tell me where Gerald lives?"

Tilda, still pleased with her intelligent answer, grinned. "Of course! He's my brother—of course I know where he lives. He lives next door to my parents."

Slam! Thankfully, Shorty knew where Gerald lived. "Oh yeah, I know where he lives. I jus' thought the visit would go better if we had Vince with us. Don'tcha worry, Doc. I'll get us there in no time. Can ya' hand me some more o'that *Good-uh* cheese? I think it's my favorite. An' put it on one o'those fancy crackers too, if ya' don't mind."

My PI was right—by the time he'd gulped down his Gouda cheese and fancy cracker, it was time to put his truck into park. "All right, we're here." I'd learned not to ask questions such as *how did you know where Gerald lived?* But I did wonder, being related and all, how Gerald's intelligence measured up to Vince and his wife. I was about to find out.

"Hey, Nadine—is Gerald home?" The short, squatty woman in plastic hair rollers and a house robe jerked her head behind her. So far, so good—this woman knew where her husband was.

"Hey, Shorty! Wanna beer?" Gerald rested his adult beverage in the middle of his stomach with one hand, while the other tapped the ashes off a cigarette.

"Naw, but thank ya' anyways. This here's my friend Evangeline Delafose. She's thinkin' about puttin' in a patio, an' wants t'see the bricks ya' got for Vince. Could ya' show 'em to us?"

Vince jumped up. "Oh sure, sure! Oh, hey, you were gonna come pick me up, weren't you? Hey, sorry about that—I forgot."

Not surprising. "That's okay, Vince. We're here now. So, if you don't mind, could you please take us into the garage and show us? I'd really like to see if they're the kind of bricks I want."

Gerald took a drag on his cigarette, his beer balancing expertly on his ample stomach. "Hold your horses there, missy. Who told ya' I got bricks in my garage?" He glanced sideways at Vince.

"Oh, yeah, I did. But they're my bricks! I can show 'em to whoever I want. Besides, while they're here, they can help me load 'em into the back of my truck." That actually was a pretty good plan.

Gerald looked me up and down as he blew smoke in my direction. I tried not to cough, but failed. "Why are you so interested in these bricks? Are you a cop, or something? Do you have a warrant? Cuz I ain't showing you nothing without a piece of paper that says I got to. So if you ain't got a warrant, then you can skedaddle." He punctuated his statement with another drag.

"Gerald Rouzan! Don't you be getting into trouble with the police again! You know Shorty's one of their investigators."

Gerald was on his feet before his wife had the words *don't you be* out of her mouth. His only hesitation was what the woman wanted from him.

"If you know what's good for you, you'll take these fine people to the garage and show 'em those bricks!"

Gerald crushed out his cigarette, set his beer square on a coaster, and headed towards the door. "You heard the woman! Right this way."

Thanks to Mrs. Rouzan, we crossed Vince off our suspect list. The bricks were stolen, all right, but not from Miss Pearlie.

"Gerald! If I'd known those bricks were stolen, I'd have turned you into the police myself. You and Vince best march yourselves over to Miles and Anna Dunbar's house and return those stolen goods. You do it right now, you hear? Vince, you better thank your lucky stars I'm not on the phone right now with *your* wife. Now git!"

You're welcome, Aunt Anna.

"Please stop laughing. It's not really...okay, well, it really is that funny. But please stop laughing or you're going to choke. And then I'd have to call 9-1-1 because I don't know CPR."

Sometimes I believed Elizabeth kept me around as comic relief. After supper she'd shooed Cliff to his study, which was code for man cave, then we adjourned to the sunroom off the back.

"Now I *really* have to meet these people, Vince and Gerald and their better halves. Or, in Vince's case, that might be a stretch. But Gerald's wife is keeping her husband on the straight and narrow."

I'd brought our matching mugs, tucked into a cardboard box with a bath towel. We sipped our tea while we mused over my fruitcake suspects.

"I'm sure your aunt will be pleased with you. After all, you solved another case. What shall we call that one? The Case of The Missing Bricks?"

"Call it whatever you want, it still won't win me any favor in Aunt Anna's eyes. She takes her cues from Lila, but she's jealous of my friendship with her. If she had her way, I'd still be on Lila's hit list from thirty years ago, when I toilet papered her magnolia trees."

Elizabeth did a spit take. "Oh, and not with the high-priced fancy toilet paper either! No, you had to go and use the cheap and tawdry kind that gas stations purchase. Why, Evangeline Delafose! I'm surprised your mother ever lived that down at bridge club."

I studied my steamy brew carefully. The mention of my mother's name always put a lump in my throat. "Yes, she moved me down the list, even after Mad, I'm sure. And it took a lot to be ranked lower than her."

"Ah, yes! How is Mad? Is she coming home for Christmas? Maybe that's why she can't find herself...because she left herself back in Graisseville." My friend took another sip, savoring the taste of her spiced Christmas tea.

"Uh, that would be a *no*. She's got a new boyfriend, her yoga instructor. They're headed to Arizona for some retreat. She's posted crazy pictures of them contriving all sorts of yoga poses. Thank goodness Dad doesn't have Instagram, or he'd be terribly embarrassed by his younger daughter."

Elizabeth fixed her caramel eyes on me. "Since when are you on Instagram? You barely do Facebook."

"I'm not, really. I mean, I have an account, but I can't ever figure out how to post anything on it. Post? Is that the right word? Anyway, Ellie's on there. She and Mad are friends. Or do they follow each other? Maybe they snap at each other?" I took another sip, trying to remember the terminology for each social media app.

"You *friend* people on Facebook, but you *follow* people on Instagram. Anyway, so Ellie's the one who found Mad's photos? Do you have any to show me?"

Being an only child, Elizabeth had developed a great fascination for my siblings. "Ooh! That yoga instructor's a real snack. No wonder Mad's going to Arizona for Christmas."

"A what? Did you just refer to Mad's boyfriend as a small meal?"

Elizabeth chuckled. "Sort of. I basically said the guy's attractive. Haven't you heard your kids say that?"

"Girl, my kids would never say that around me! Then I might know something personal about them, like who they like or what they're doing."

Another sip. "Hey, maybe I should ask Ellie if she has any snacks in her Biology class?"

More laughter from my bestie. "Ev, don't say it like that. She'll think you're talking about food. Don't worry about it—Cal never tells me anything. I get all my intel from his wife. Annelise is the best! Her weekly status reports are dope."

Sigh...how did my friend reach a level of coolness beyond me? "Her reports are what now?"

Elizabeth set down her mug and touched my arm. "Remember that I volunteer for the after-school program at the library. Those kids teach me all the trendy words. And since I'm not their mother, they don't mind that I'm basic. You know, I fit all the stereotypes of a white, slightly over middle-aged, middle-class woman. They call me Miss OG, because I'm the original version. Although I'm not sure of what." She picked up her mug, contemplating what version she might be.

We sat in silence for just a second. "Who are you interviewing tomorrow? More fruitcake suspects? Or the murdering kind?"

"Both actually. While I distract Bitsy Tibbs, Shorty's going to break into Junior's shed. We're hoping to find contraband fruitcake. If we're unsuccessful, we've got Ronnie Joe Hopgood to talk to next. He's a competitive bass fisherman, and rumor around the village is that Miss Pearlie's fruitcakes make wonderful bait. Shorty thinks Ronnie Joe could have stolen Miss Pearlie's loaves to use in the upcoming Big Bass Rodeo in New Orleans. We're also going to speak with Sam Kellerman, owner of Kellerman's Gardening Supplies n' More. We've heard that people use Miss Pearlie's fruitcakes in their gardens, as compost. Maybe Sam stole the eighty-two loaves to mix in with his specialty compost. Elizabeth, please stop laughing—you're spilling tea all over your shirt. And that's the one I got you for Christmas last year. I paid good money for that shirt."

As I handed my best friend several napkins, I reviewed my strategy. Yes, I should have started with the murder suspects.

"Good morning, Ethan! How are you this fine day?" I wasn't about to leave my cousin's report to chance. "I thought it would be easier if I called you. Did you finish your search?"

"Yes, with time to spare. A bunch of my friends helped out, so we pulled one big all-nighter and knocked it all out. But I'm afraid you'll be disappointed. I didn't find much."

"That's okay. Give me what you got."

A pause as Ethan pulled up his screen. "First thing, Melinda Davis. Her husband has a prescription to help him sleep. It's really strong stuff, and he takes them pretty much every night. Melinda posted a few things about doing some online shopping while her husband was passed out cold. He's also a big gamer—he spends a lot of time on the weekends holed up in his office playing online. One of my friends actually plays with him—his gamertag is *GhostFaceGangsta*. Mr. Davis, that is. Anyway, he bragged about how he works from home on Fridays, knocks off around four. Then he eats a snack, takes a couple of his pills, and he's knocked out until about nine or so. Then he stays up all night gaming."

Which was why we never saw Melinda's husband during her interview. "Ethan, that's wonderful information! Thank you. And thank your friends too."

"Sure thing, Ev. The only other thing I found out is about Sid. Of course, none of us would ever break into any government databases—we wouldn't even know how. Let's just say a confidential informant has disclosed that Sid's being investigated by the FBI."

"Oh boy! Well, we knew that our client isn't squeaky clean by any means. Why's he on their radar?"

Another pause as Ethan scrolled his screen. "Fraud. It looks like he's been taking his clients' money and promising to invest it in deals that can't fail. But he's really using the money to pay off some deals that have gone bad."

"Oh? Robbing Peter to pay Paul? Yeah, that's not good."

Ethan scanned his report. "Uh, I didn't mention any names. Who are Peter and Paul?"

"Goodness, I feel old! It means taking money from one person to pay someone else."

"Oh, okay. Yeah, that's what Sid's doing. Grandpa B says those Heberts have always chosen shortcuts over an honest day's work. Then Grandma B tells him to stop talking about people. But I think he's right, at least in this case."

"Yes, I do too. But committing fraud isn't the same as murder. Although it could provide a motive. What else do you know about the investigation? Did the FBI talk to Ronald? Maybe Sid killed Ronald to keep him from testifying."

"They're pretty early into the case, but Ronald's name is on the potential interview list. A few months ago, three of Sid's clients went to the local police to complain about Sid. The police turned it over to the FBI, and they are putting together a case. Since Ronald handled all the finances, he would be a good informant. But there's no record they'd talked to him yet."

"Ethan, did Sid know about the investigation?"

"Hard to say, Ev. You know his nephew Jack's one of our United States senators, with connections all across Washington, DC. And I'm sure there are Hebert connections involved in all the branches of the government—state and federal. It's not a stretch to believe Sid had the interview list, or even the entire file."

"Thanks, Ethan—you've been a tremendous help. And again, please tell your friends thanks as well. We've got deep pockets on this case, thanks to the founding family slush fund. I'm going to put in a request that you and your team get paid."

"Oh, that'd be great! But honestly, we didn't do it for the money. Although, it's always nice to get paid. Maybe you could get us a free meal...or two?"

"Of course! I'll talk to Jack and see what I can do."

"Thanks, Ev. Oh, I almost forgot. Shorty called me about this other case you're working on. Something about Miss Pearlie and her fruitcakes? Those loaves are the stuff nightmares are made of."

"Nice! Were you borrowing from Sam Spade in *The Maltese Falcon*, or Prospero in *The Tempest*? That's what you were doing, right? Taking the quote 'the stuff that dreams are made of', and changing it up a bit."

"Yes, I was! And it was Sam Spade. You know my dad's named after that character, right? Grandma and Grandpa B used to make us watch all the Humphrey Bogart movies. But *The Maltese Falcon* is my favorite."

"Mine too. So do you have anything on our other case? Oh, and you can take Vince Owens off the list—we cleared him."

"Great! Actually, Ev, I don't have anything. All those suspects stay off the world wide web. I mean, Junior Tibbs and Sam Kellerman have a lot of advertising for their business ventures, but they're not the ones posting. And I don't think Joe McMillan or Ronnie Joe Hopgood even have social media accounts. After finals, if you need me to dig deeper, I can do that. But we've all really got to focus on school this week. I'm a senior, you know—I've got to start looking for a job too, or Dad says I'll have to come back home. And there's no way I'm ever going back to that boring little village, except to visit."

Where had I heard those words before? Oh yes, *me*. I had said those words the day I left for college. Should I mention that to my cousin? Not a chance.

"I hear ya', kid. If you need a reference or letter of recommendation, I'm happy to write one for you. I can talk about how much you've helped me on my cases."

Ethan's deep chuckles hit my ear, making me jump. "Uh, that's okay. Most of what I did for you wasn't exactly legal. Merry Christmas, Ev."

Before my fifty-something brain forgot, I texted Jack Hebert. *I'd like to pay my technical team—they're students and have asked to be paid with food. Is that a problem?*

I got an answer faster than I'd expected. *That's fine. I'll authorize $800. In fact, I need to pay you for the work you've done so far. Let's meet for supper—how's tomorrow night?*

Should I mention my date with Mitch? No, that sounded unprofessional. *I already have plans. How about Monday evening?*

Perfect. The Senate's on holiday break, so I'm in Baton Rouge until after the first of the year.

Was that an invitation? Hopefully not—one suitor in my life was plenty. And after the fiasco with Cay, I had my doubts about trying again. Maybe Doug was my one great love, and I would be single for the rest of my life. How long would that be...thirty years? Unless I got hit by a truck, or taken out by one of the killers I was chasing.

I'll text you my address. I've got a new grill and you'll be my first guestLooking forward to catching up.

"Now, are ya' sure it ain't a date? Datin' a senator could be mighty helpful, Doc. Jack could get us on some federal cases! Maybe we could take a crack at catchin' that TBD killer! We'd be famous for sure."

"I think you mean BTK. And he was caught a long time ago—in the early 2000's, I'm pretty sure."

Shorty glared at me as he sat at my kitchen counter munching on the rest of Dad's syrup cookies. For some reason, he found me particularly irritating lately.

"Well, whatever! I bet there's a lot more o'them serial killers out there, jus' itchin' t'be caught. Why couldn't it be us findin' 'em all?"

"Oh, maybe because to date we've only caught two murderers. Now, I could be wrong, but I'm guessing the men and women searching for these criminals have caught a few more than us. But I'll tell you what. When I have supper with Jack, I'll bring it up. It couldn't hurt, right?"

Shorty searched my expression, trying to decide if I was using sarcasm or being sincere. I pulled the corners of my mouth up just a little farther. My smile felt tight, like a rubber band stretched across my face.

"Okay, I guess that'd work. An' while yer at it, talk tuh the sheriff tomorrow night too. See if he's got some more cases. Payin' ones! We're about t'wrap up this Sid Hebert case an' we'll need another one."

Had my PI lost his mind? "Shorty, in what scenario do we have Sid's case solved? We've got three suspects with solid motives, and three with no alibis. Judy Reynolds has solid motive and no alibi, and so does our client."

"Exactly! We go tuh Jack an' tell him it's Judy. We've got the motive an' opportunity. An' the woman takes yoga! She put on those stilettos o'hers an' used her yoga strength t'stab her ex. That gives Sid reasonable doubt! The jury finds him not guilty an' we move on tuh the next case."

"Actually, you might be onto something. Our job is to help our client's lawyer show reasonable doubt, not solve the murder. Except..."

"Except what? Let's collect our money. Then we can focus on Miss Pearlie's case, an' take on another one. We don't have time for *except*."

"But what if Sid really did kill Ronald? Shorty, I couldn't sleep at night knowing I helped a killer go free."

"Dang it, Doc! You an' yore ethics. Okay, well, if yer gonna be that way, then I'll go ahead an' tell ya' what I found out last night."

"Last night? I thought you had a date with Annabelle."

"Yeah, I did. We went tuh the same restaurant Jerry Little claims he was at with his son. Says they were there the whole time the murder happened."

"That was a great idea! What did you find out?"

Shorty loved to tell a story—hopefully this would put him in a better mood.

"My buddy's cousin works there, an' he told me who it was that served Jerry an' his kid that day: The guy's name is Ashton, an' he's workin' tonight, he says. So, Annabelle and I ask for his section. After we order, I slip it in that

I'm workin' on the Sid Hebert case. The kid gets all nervous like, but Annabelle turns on her charm—y'know, tells this kid that we jus' want the truth, an innocent man shouldn't go t'jail...y'know."

"The kid admits Jerry paid him $3,000 to help with his alibi. But what *really* happened is, Jerry's son sat down at the table around five, an' waited an' waited for his dad. The kid was gettin' real irritated, told Ashton his dad was supposed t'meet him at five o'clock, an' he couldn't get a hold of him. The son called Jerry's secretary, who told him Jerry left the office around 4:45, but she didn't know where he went. Ashton says Jerry finally showed up at about six."

As Shorty wiped the crumbs from his mouth I made a mental note to make my father more cookies.

"So Jerry could have headed over to New Horizons, killed Ronald, and rushed over to the restaurant."

"Yeah, it looks that way."

"We've got *four* suspects with no alibi."

Shorty's face took on a hangdog expression. You know, a dejected or guilty appearance. "Uh, well, it's closer to five. All five of our suspects are missin' alibis."

"Oh? Who's left? Let's see...Sid, Judy, Jerry, Melinda. Are you telling me that Moe Randall's alibi doesn't play out either?"

The hangdog look covered his face like a blanket. "Uh, well, yeah. Muh buddy Bill, his wife Janelle's best friends with Moe's wife Sheila. Janelle told Bill that Sheila loves t'blab on the phone with her sister every Friday. They each put on a pot o' coffee an' sit an' gab for a coupla hours, at least. Sheila told Janelle the Friday Ronald was killed wudn't any different. Sheila told Janelle she was on the phone with her sister for at least two hours. She has *no idea* when exac'ly it is that Moe came home from work that day. But she told the police her husband was home safe an' sound by five o'clock, so there's no way he could've killed Ronald. Doc, she lied to 'em."

N one of our suspects had an alibi, and our ability to prove means was looking pretty poor too. Not to mention, Sid, Judy, and Moe had plenty of motive—Jerry and Melinda probably did too, if we dug a little deeper. What should we do?"I'll ya' what we should do, Doc! We should jus' keep goin'. We're gonna talk tuh Jerry today, an' we'll work on our other case. Don't forget we're gonna look into Junior's shed. Oh, an' talk tuh Ronnie Joe too, an' Sam Kellerman. Somethin's gonna turn up."

"Of course...how could I forget that we're committing a felony this morning? I'm going to make sure and have a good breakfast—it could be my last. I hear prison food tastes pretty bad."

"There ya' go again, always exaggeratin'! Breakin' into Junior's shed is jus' a misdemeanor. Now, if I stole somethin', that'd be a felony. But I won't...unless I see one o'Miss Pearlie's fruitcakes. Then I'll take it...for evidence, y'know."

Shorty scratched his head. Was he thinking, or just itching?

"Ya' really need t'get yore private investigator's license, Doc. Ya' need t'know the differences with all these kinds o'things."

Nope, just scratching And by the way...how did my life come to this? At what point did it become essential to know the difference between a misdemeanor and a felony? Oh yes, about the same time my brother said I *have an idea*. About the same time I began investigating my first case. And now my father was involved. Hmmm...he should be learning the differences too. Note to self: encourage my father to also get his PI license. Then the whole family can be working for Shorty Cormier. Was my mother rolling in her grave right now? Yeah...best to just focus on the case at hand.

"Doc! Are ya' even listenin'? No, ya' ain't. Ya' know I can always tell cuz yore eyes get this weird look, like yer in some other place. I'll start over. I was talkin' about the plan. Yep, yer gonna ring the doorbell. When Bitsy answers, ask her if she's seen Zy. Then ya' gotta..."

"That plan won't work. We all know Zydeco would never get out—the dog never leaves my side! And when I'm not there, he sits in front of the door, waiting for me to come home."

Strange. Was there a wind tunnel in my kitchen? Was that a normal occurrence in East Baton Rouge Parish? No, my PI pushed all the air out of his lungs so he wouldn't yell at me.

"In case ya' forgot, Doc, Bitsy ain't that bright. She's sweet as pie—puttin' up with Junior she'd have t'be. But her bread puddin' ain't quite done in the middle, if ya' know what I mean. She ain't gonna know that Zy don't leave the house without ya'. An' she loves t'help people. If ya' ask her t'help you find yore dog, then she'll drop what she's doin' an' start lookin'. Trust me, Doc, this plan's gonna work."

"Okay, but how much jail time do I get for accessory to breaking and entering? And why are you clenching your hands like that? Are those fists?"

"Oh, hi, Ev. What can I do for you?" Bitsy swung her screen door wide open, revealing a long hallway with dark wood crown molding. Definitely not old money, but she had her fair share of it. Bitsy's strawberry blonde curls bobbed in her eagerness to display Southern hospitality. I was surprised she didn't offer me a glass of iced tea and a plate of cookies. But it was 9 a.m.

"I'm sorry to bother you, Bitsy. My dog's missing, and I wondered if you'd seen him."

Her eyes reminded me of Elizabeth's Persian cat, Persephone. Tropical blue, wide and clear. Persephone's eyes displayed more intelligence than Bitsy's, however.

"Dog? I didn't know you had a dog." She stared past me, towards the street. Was she looking for the dog in question?

"Uh, well you and Junior wave at me every evening from your front porch, when I'm walking him past your house. You know, the brown dog with the black muzzle? He wears a red collar with a matching leash."

Yes, there it was...the lightbulb moment. "Oh, yes! That's your dog? Oh, I thought you were picking up some extra money as a dog walker."

How does one respond to a comment like that? I chose to ignore it. "Anyway, he's missing. Have you seen him?"

Bitsy smiled, revealing a set of teeth that probably cost more than my Ford Bronco. "Now that you mention it, I have!"

What? Zy couldn't have gotten out—I'd locked the front and back doors. "When? When did you see him, Bitsy?"

My neighbor smiled. "Why, every evening when you walk him! Junior and I like to sit on the front porch, look up at the stars and drink my homemade lemonade. Have you ever tried it, Ev? I make it special, with lavender and vanilla. It's to die for! Oh, sometimes I think Junior married me just for my lemonade." Bitsy placed a hand over her mouth, to catch the escaping giggles.

Why hadn't I volunteered to commit the misdemeanor? Shorty had to be doing better than I was. But at least I was doing my part—Bitsy was definitely distracted. Of course, it didn't take much to do that. Time for a change in the plan.

"You know, I've never had your lemonade, Bitsy. Did you say it has lavender and vanilla in it? Oh, I love that flavor combination! Could I have a glass? Maybe we could sit on the front porch, get to know each other better."

My new friend clapped her hands and squealed, reminding me of my seven year old niece, Sydney. She hadn't squealed and clapped since she was five. Yes, Shorty was definitely getting the better end of this deal.

"Why don't you sit on the front porch while I get us a pitcher of lemonade and two glasses? The best thing about my specialty drink is that you can have it any time of the day!"

What *can't* we drink at any time of the day? No, don't ask.

"Of course! I'll sit in one of these lovely wicker chairs and enjoy the view of Thistleberry Street."

Or was it Thornberry Street? Elderberry maybe? Bitsy didn't correct me, so perhaps I got it right.

Less than thirty seconds later, Bitsy revisited the front porch, no lavender vanilla lemonade in sight. "What exactly is Shorty Cormier doing in my backyard?"

Bitsy had insisted on calling the sheriff's department. "If Shorty's helping you look for your dog, he should ask permission before he saunters into my fenced in backyard. And the gate was locked—how did he get in?"

Maybe Bitsy was smarter than I gave her credit for. "I'm sorry, Ev, but I've called the sheriff. If you two know what's good for you, you'll both stay put and answer the deputy's questions."

This time, my PI did know what was good for him. His face popped into view from the corner of the porch. "I'm real sorry t'scare ya' like that, Miss Bitsy. I was lookin' for Zy, Ev's dog."

"Hmph! Well, at least you two have your stories straight. We'll see what the deputy says about all this."

Shorty's face showed no concern, which made me think his buddy Monty was on duty. Monty and Shorty played poker every Saturday night, and he let Shorty go at least ten miles over the speed limit without flashing his lights. This friendship had allowed my PI to scare the living daylights out of me with his driving. Finally, it was my time to benefit from the forty plus years these two had known each other.

Monty took our statements separately. "Miss Ev, you had no idea Shorty was in Miss Bitsy's backyard, did ya'?" Monty wrote the words into his notepad, not waiting for me to agree with them. He spent even less time with his buddy, probably confirming poker night was still on and who was bringing the chips and drinks. His conversation with Bitsy lasted a good while longer.

"Corporal, you can't possibly believe these two are completely innocent! Shorty broke into my yard, and Ev obviously was trying to distract me."

"Bitsy, if Mrs. Delafose was distracting you, then why did she ask for lemonade? Surely she knew while you fetched it from the kitchen, you'd be in eyesight of your backyard."

Well, I guess I should have.

Bitsy's eyes narrowed as she processed Monty's logic. "Maybe. But Shorty did break into my yard—you can't argue with that."

"Yes, ma'am. Mr. Cormier's statement is that he was looking for Mrs. Delafose's dog. He thought he spotted the animal in your backyard. The gate was unlocked, so he entered your property. Mr. Cormier realized what he'd thought was a dog, was actually a large bush. He was about to exit the premises when you spotted him. Really, it sounds like a big misunderstanding to me. Nothing was taken, nothing was broken, so I suggest we all forget about this incident."

Bitsy's eyes continued their downward slant—the woman wasn't going to forget anything. Monty tried a different approach.

"Say, is your lavender vanilla lemonade as good as everybody says? My Aunt Bobbie tells me it's a little slice of heaven. And if a person has it with some of your sugar cookies, why, I hear it feels like winning the lottery!"

Bitsy relaxed her eyes and warmed up her face with a small smile. "Well, I don't know, Corporal. Why don't we find out?"

Those two headed inside, leaving me and Shorty on the front porch. My shoulders tensed, bracing for my PI's tirade. But none was forthcoming.

The silence surrounded us as we walked the four minutes to my house. "Shorty, would you like to come inside? I have some orange soda and Crawtators."

My PI stared at me. Had I grown an extra head after leaving Bitsy's?

"Didja ever stop t'think Bitsy might peek into her backyard while she was in the kitchen? In the kitchen pourin' *yore* lemonade? Didn't I make myself clear? Doc, ya' were there t'do a job, not sip drinks an' trade recipes,"

"Yes, Shorty, I realize that. But the woman wouldn't leave her house! Instead, she offered me lemonade. So I thought if we sat on the front porch drinking it, then she wouldn't be able to look in the backyard. I've never been in her house! How was I supposed to know the kitchen was in the back and faced the yard?"

We were overdue for a good old fashioned horse snort—thank goodness Shorty provided one. "How many houses have ya' been in that the kitchen *don't* have a window facin' the backyard? Huh? How many?"

"To be honest, I've never counted. But if you prefer, I can spend the next hour and go back fifty years to my childhood. You know, start with the home I grew up in, branch out to my friends' homes, work my way up to my current house." Which had two windows overlooking my backyard, but I wasn't going to voice that revelation.

Thank goodness the theme from 21 *Jump Street* blared from my pocket. "Ethan! What a lovely surprise!" Shorty charged into my house, or tried to. I stepped beside him to unlock my front door. Then he charged into my house. No matter how mad he was, that man would not refuse free food.

"Ev, I'm glad I caught you! Listen, one of my friends hadn't checked in when you called this morning. He found a couple of things that might interest you."

Anything to avoid talking to Shorty. "Great! Take all the time you need." Shorty already had the cookies and orange soda on the counter, sipping with one hand and feeding Zy a dog treat with the other.

"Sid Hebert has *two* partners in New Horizons. Up until a month ago, Joseph Dwyer owned just one percent and hadn't been involved in the business. But he recently increased his ownership by investing $500,000. We found the new partnership agreement, which states the money is to be used for a new project. Remember how you said Sid was taking clients' money to cover for the funds Ronald had stolen? I bet he's doing the same thing with Dwyer's money too. Maybe this guy figured it out, confronted Ronald, or Sid, or both? Maybe he killed Ronald and pinned it all on Sid."

"That's a good theory, Ethan. I'm writing it down." And I really was—I'd never remember that on my own.

"Oh, and we found some social media posts that tagged Ronald and Daisy Jane—but the tags were removed. Ronald started dating Daisy Jane Mayfield while he was still dating a woman named Natalie Wheeler. I guess Natalie followed him one evening, and saw him picking up Daisy Jane. They had a huge blow up in front of Daisy Jane's apartment and someone filmed the entire thing. Natalie took a baseball bat and bashed in Ronald's windshield. The cops showed up and arrested Natalie. I can send you the link to the video."

"Yes, Ethan, thank you! This is great stuff."

Shorty's temper settled as I relayed Ethan's news. The cookies and orange soda didn't hurt either. "I was wonderin' if we should add Daisy Jane tuh our list of suspects, but I figured we'd wait 'til we talk tuh her. But now I'm thinkin' this Natalie Wheeler needs t'go on the list now."

"What about Joseph Dwyer? He trusted his partners and sunk money in a dying company. He'll never get that money back! That's motive. And if he doesn't have an alibi, then we need to focus on him."

Another horse snort. "We got enough people on our list missin' an alibi, Doc. Sid's only savin' grace is he faints at blood. Otherwise, he'd be right up there too. Nah, we gotta dig deeper, find out where these people really were when Ronald was murdered. I'm hopin' after our talk with Jerry, mebbe we can cross him off our list."

A swipe of a paper towel across his mouth, and Shorty hopped off my kitchen stool. The man ate more than Zydeco, but at least he rinsed his dishes and put them in the dishwasher. As he loaded the plate and shut the door, his forehead wrinkled in thought.

"Let's focus on our fruitcake case for a while, since we got Ronnie Joe t'interview next." He tossed his soda can in the trash. "Now I did some research, an' I found out bass eat pretty much anythin' that's smaller than they are. My buddy Cal said a fish might take a real likin' tuh Miss Pearlie's fruitcake for bait, with it bein' all thick an' chunky."

"Who's Cal? Cal Trahan? Since when is Cal one of your buddies?" If that was true, Elizabeth would have definitely told me.

Shorty doubled down. "Of course he's my buddy! That's what I said, didn't I?"

"Oh? So you play poker together? Do you and Annabelle double date with Cal and his wife Annelise? Maybe you play tennis with him at the country club." The last remark gave me a chuckle, as I pictured Shorty in tennis shorts lobbing a ball over the net.

"Oh wait! Cal's an avid cyclist. Do you dress up in black spandex, don a helmet, and bike with Cal all over East Baton Rouge Parish?" Okay, that last one made me laugh out loud.

"No, Miss Smarty Pants, I don't play tennis, an' I don't put on no *pandex* neither. Cal's my banker, an' we get together once a month or so, an' shoot the breeze. But that don't make his information anythin' less than the truth."

Why did I always have to poke the bear? "You're right, Shorty. I'm sorry. And it is good information. When we talk to Ronnie Joe, what should we say?"

"Well, I already thought about that. I called Ronnie Joe an' told 'im I wanna start bass fishin', an' I wanna know what I need t'use as bait."

"Okay, but why am I coming with you? I'll never pass as a fishing expert."

Shorty's eyes stared at my tennis shoes and worked their way up to my forehead. "Nah, no one's gonna believe ya' fish.

Yer as pale as one o'those *'bino* deer my nephew showed me. Y'know, on Insta Tube?"

Don't laugh, don't laugh... "Yes, I've seen those videos of albino deer. But I think I saw them on YouTube."

My PI's shoulders lifted up and down. "Yeah, that stuff's all over the *inner net*. Anyway, yore skin ain't seen the light o'day in a coon's age."

His mouth stopped running as he pondered my cover ID. "Hey, the sheriff likes t'go bass fishin', don't he? We'll tell Ronnie Joe yer taggin' along cuz ya' need some ideas for Christmas."

"The sheriff and I haven't even been on a date yet, and I'm already shopping for his Christmas present? Doesn't that convey an air of desperation?"

Another shrug. "Yeah, well, ya' kinda do that anyway, even before ya' started datin' my cuzzin'. An' now that he's dumped ya' for someone else, ya' reek of desperation. Besides, it's for our case. Jus' go along with it."

"Thank ya' mighty kindly for meetin' with us today, Ronnie Joe. Like I said, I wanna start bass fishin', so I wanna talk to an expert. This here's my friend, Evangeline Delafose—she's Skeeter's daughter. She's shoppin' for Christmas, an' she's datin' a bass fisherman. I told her t'get 'im some bait, so why don't we start with that? Whatcha recommend?"

Admittedly, Ronnie Joe appeared more intelligent than our other suspects. Well, Joe McMillan seemed smart too, once we started interviewing his front side instead of his backside.

"Oh, sure! Bass are one of the most difficult fish to catch. Yeah, they'll eat 'most anything. But you've gotta know where to find them. The best place to fish for them is..."

Once again, Shorty's impatience got the best of him. "Dang it, Ronnie Joe! We wanna know about yore bait! Do bass like live bait or artificial?"

Ronnie's eyes widened—obviously he'd never incurred the wrath of Shorty. "Uh, sorry. My personal favorite is live bait—shiners, minnows, shad, and crawfish. You can buy a bucket at any bait shop. But I'd wait to buy them until closer to December 25. That smell under your tree ain't gonna make your Christmas very merry. In fact, you should cut out a picture of some bait, put it with some cash, and stick it in an envelope under the tree. That'd smell a whole lot better."

My turn to try. "Thank you, Ronnie Joe. What about bread, like maybe the heels from a loaf of bread? In fact, with it being so close to Christmas, what about fruitcake? Would that work?"

Ronnie Joe blinked twice. "Miz Delafose, I wouldn't use fruitcake for bait, if I were you. It'll just fall off the hook once it hits the water. Only an idiot would use fruitcake to catch a fish."

The question then became...was there such an idiot in East Baton Rouge Parish?

"That was Jerry on the phone. His golf game got cut short. He was playin' with one o'them baby doctors, an' the guy had t'go deliver one."

"One what? A baby?"

My PI's muddy brown eyes darkened to the color of black-jack dirt, dark and sticky. "Good grief, Evangeline! What else would a baby doctor be deliverin'?"

What was going on with Shorty? Yes, he lost his temper with me from time to time, but not on a daily basis. Was he really that stressed about finding a Christmas present for Annabelle?

"Shorty, Annabelle's coming over to my house tomorrow for coffee and a chat. I promise to figure out the best gift ever for her. Don't worry about it—I've got it covered."

But instead of soothing my friend's feelings, I angered him even more. "Don't you be talkin' tuh my girlfriend about that! I'm a grown man, I'll take care of it. I don't need yore advice."

The drive to the country club was only twenty minutes, but it felt like 200. My eyes fixed on the grass outside my window, and my brain willed back the tears. It took the entire ride to shove my emotions back inside my heart. Why did this bother me so much? But I had to focus on Jerry Little.

We parked in silence. Shorty beat me to the lobby by a good thirty seconds. By the time I arrived, the men were shaking hands. "Hello, I'm Jerry Little. You must be Evangeline Delafose. It's a pleasure to meet you. Let's head to the dining room for lunch—my treat."

No wonder Shorty hadn't protested over meeting our suspect outside of his house. We were getting an actual meal out of this interview. My stomach rumbled in appreciation, but my heart shushed it. At that moment, my heart didn't want to be anywhere near Shorty.

"I'm sure you two are trying to gather evidence to clear Sid's name. And I'm sorry to say I don't have any. In fact, I think he did it. Let me tell you a couple of things."

Jerry paused as our waiter, a twenty-something named Crawford, took our drink orders. While I trained my eyes on my menu instead of Shorty, our host continued.

"I stopped by the office last Friday, the day of the murder, trying to get in to see Sid. When we formed the partnership with Joseph Dwyer, we all agreed that Sid would do the heavy hitting. Joseph and I wanted to sit back and collect our share of the profits. Only, there are no profits to share. That's why I want to get more involved, see if there's something unethical going on or just bad luck. Or maybe it's poor management—Sid has collected a great deal of wealth from his past business ventures, but maybe he's slowing down in his old age."

Mmmm...grilled shrimp with steamed vegetables, or perhaps the chicken salad? My brain concentrated on my choices, because I'd cry if I thought of anything else.

"That receptionist tried to tell me Sid was busy, but I knew better. I knew he'd been dodging me. I took off down the hallway, toward Sid's office. That's when I heard the yelling."

Okay, wait a minute...this was getting interesting.

"Sid was standing right in front of his office," Jerry continued, "totally out of control. He was screaming at Ronald, even pushed him. The poor kid had his hands up, palms out, trying to calm Sid down. They both saw me and stopped. Sid quit screaming and Ronald put his hands down, then turned back toward his office. You know, that story about Sid fainting at the sight of blood is incomplete. The guy has some major anger issues. If he's mad enough, he can handle blood. In college I saw him get so worked up, he punched a guy in the nose for insulting his date. Blood everywhere! But Sid just kept hitting the kid. It took three of us to pull him off."

Crawford brought our drinks. Was that a family name, or did his mother just not like him? "Our special today is grilled Mahi in a pepper lime marinade with your choice of a baked potato or steamed vegetables. It comes with a side salad. Is everyone ready to order, or do you need a few minutes?"

"Yeah, I'll have the New York Strip, medium rare. Ya' got any o'those steak fries? Y'know, the thick French fries? I don't want none o'those skinny, wimpy fries. I like mine big an' juicy."

Our waiter paused his order taking, eyeing his customer over the notepad. "Yes sir, we have steak fries. Would you like those as a side?"

"Yeah, yeah that's fine. An' I want a baked potato with all the fixins. Y'know, butter, sour cream, a bunch o'those bits o'bacon. But not those green things—I don't like those."

Crawford's patience knew no limits. "Chives, sir. They're called chives. I'll tell the chef to leave them off your potato. Your steak comes with a side salad. What kind of dressing would you like?"

I didn't have to look up to know the answer. "Nah, I won't eat none of that. I see ya' got garlic mashed potatoes—can I have that instead?"

Crawford's eyes held steady as he wrote, never reflecting his opinions on three side orders of potatoes. The kid should try his hand at poker. "Very good, sir. Anything else?"

"Yeah, don't get too far away—I've got my eye on a coupla yore desserts."

Hopefully, Jerry brought his credit card.

The rest of the meal was a blur, and the ride home reeked of awkwardness. As far as our case was going, we couldn't cross Jerry off our list just yet. And our client was looking more and more guilty. Experience taught me we were getting close to the truth. In the past, as we started digging and asking questions, people hurled accusations like dodgeballs. Some of them were true and some were not. But they all pointed to one conclusion...people knew more than what they were telling us. And they were trying hard to point us away from them.

At this point my PI and I would discuss our theories and determine our next steps. Shorty didn't seem in the mood for an apology, and my feelings had been crushed into bits. All I wanted was to get out of Shorty's truck and into a hot bath.

Unfortunately, we still had to interview Sam Kellerman, landscaper extraordinaire. From my way of thinking, Vince was off the list—the man didn't realize he was stealing bricks, but he *did* realize they were bricks. And Ronnie Joe, at least in my mind, was telling the truth. Maybe there was an idiot who would use fruitcake for bait, but it wasn't him. Should I try to patch things up with Shorty, so we could get at least one case solved?

"What do you think about Ronnie Joe? Do you think we can cross him off the suspect list?"

"How much do ya' think it costs t'join that country club? What...a coupla hundred a month?"

Apparently, we wouldn't be discussing the case. "Uh, I'm really not sure. Cliff and Elizabeth are members—do you want me to ask them?"

"Yeah, that'd be great. Annabelle'd really like that place. Y'know, dressin' up and eatin' a bunch o'fancy food."

"I guess I didn't know that. She's always struck me as someone who prefers jeans over dresses, and cooking at home versus dressing up and going out. But you know her better than I do."

"When I booked that table at *Man Sures*, Annabelle couldn't get enough of it. She kept goin' on an' on about how great it was."

No, not going to mention it's pronounced MAN-*Sirs*. "I'm sure she did. But honestly, Shorty, I think she loved it because she was there with you. Don't get me wrong—Mansurs on the Boulevard is a wonderful restaurant. I just think she'd be happy with chicken spaghetti and a glass of iced tea, as long as she's sharing it with you."

Was that a grunt or a noise from the truck engine? No, it was a grunt. But did that mean he agreed with me? Probably not.

"Anyway, I'll be sure to ask Elizabeth about the country club. In the meantime, maybe we can focus on our next interview. What's our plan for Sam Kellerman?"

Another grunt. "Sam's been crazy about plants all his life. When his granddaddy died, Sam came into some money, so he bought a building an' opened up a garden supply store. He sells a lot o'garden stuff, includin' compost. He has his own special brand, an' he don't tell a soul what's in it. Now an expert gardener knows it takes a good while for the compost t'sit. My mama's compost sat for a good year before she'd use it."

This had been a strange conversation, even without the discussion on the country club. Shorty ate so much during our lunch with Jerry, he hadn't broken out the Crawtators and orange soda. My PI finished his entire train of thought without a *crunch* or a *gulp*. That was...what? My third Christmas miracle? As we pulled into the parking lot of Kellerman's Gardening Supplies n' More, I recounted. Shorty singing Christmas carols and drinking hot chocolate was the first one of the season. Arnold Trahan vacating his recliner to yell at Junior Tibbs was the second, because he only did that for church and to escape Lila's book club. Oh, wait! The third miracle of the season was that I made it to Melinda Davis' dining room without offending her. Normally I provoked suspects on the phone or on their front porch. Would Shorty's lack of appetite on the ride home qualify as a fourth Christmas miracle? Mmm...probably not. But we still had two weeks to go, so there could be more. *Dear Lord, please help us solve these two cases—I think we may need miracles four and five. Amen.*

Sam Kellerman met us in his store, just to the right of the poinsettias. "Hey man, it's good to see ya'! I'm bringing the guacamole tonight, right? I couldn't remember."

Shorty's Saturday night poker game was a big event around Graisseville. It was by invitation only and limited to three tables. Originally, Shorty's game took place at a friend's house. That is, until he lost control of the guest list.

"Yeah, I *know* we play at Ken Chapman's place. But I started the dadgum poker game! An' what I say goes! That so? Well, jus' for that, I'm *un-invitin'* ya! An' I may jus' *un-invite* Blake too, fer not keepin' his mouth shut!"

Shorty had a metal shed on the farm that his daddy used to store the overflow from the barn. My resourceful poker-loving friend made room in the barn for the overflow and converted the shed into a poker room. He cut a couple of holes in the sheet metal walls and installed box air conditioners for the hot Louisiana summers. He purchased floor heaters for the few but bitterly cold winter days. Shorty even put up a sixty-inch flat screen television and tapped into his home cable, so his guests wouldn't miss out on any sports events. According to Shorty, it was something his father always wished he could do, if his wife would have approved.

"Yeah, when Daddy heard 'bout those man caves, he got real excited. He even drew out a plan on the back o'the water bill, an' started lookin' into portable air conditioners. Me an' my brothers were gonna get 'im a nice television t'put out there.

But Mama put her foot down. She said the barn was Daddy's man cave, an' he spent enough time away from the house workin' in there."

When Shorty's father passed, the kids discovered his secret. Mack Cormier had taken one of the horse stalls and created his own man cave. When his wife Madie bought a new couch, Mack didn't take the old one to the landfill. Instead, he brought it to the barn. Shorty said my mother's old coffee table was out there too, which meant my father had a hand in creating the makeshift man cave. No wonder Dad spent all that time on the Cormier farm! It also explained why Dad announced several years ago that he and Mother needed a new television, which caused a huge fight.

"Hershel Bergeron! We don't need a new television. The one we have is perfectly fine." Mother only called my father Hershel when she meant business.

"Well, I'm getting one, anyway. They're on sale." Normally, Dad deferred to his wife on financial matters, so that was unusual. After several tense minutes my mother gave in. Perhaps she sensed it was important.

Why didn't Dad just buy a television and put it in Mack's barn? Because Mother watched the bank account like a hawk. No, he had to devise a workaround. I often wondered if the tears he shed at Mack's funeral were just for his friend, or also for the man cave?

"Doc! Ya' need t'stay focused. I can't have ya' lookin' all dreamy eyed—it ain't professional. Stay with me!"

I steered the conversation back to Relevant Road. "Yes, Sam, you should bring guacamole to the poker game. I have a great recipe if you want it."

Shorty's hands twitched toward me, but remained by his side. His eyes, however, were a different story. They held as much irritation and frustration as they could cram into their brown orbs, which startled me a bit. Perhaps I'd pushed my PI over the edge.

But he sucked in the largest amount of air his lungs would accept, then pushed it out with a *whoosh*. His eyes changed, becoming a color more like coffee lightened with cream.

"We've already got the guacamole discussion taken care of, thank ya' very much. Now we're talkin' about Sam's compost production. Would ya' like t'join in on this conversation, *Dock-ter*? Or do ya' wanna keep tradin' recipes? Mebbe ya' can share one o'Bitsy Tibbs' tasty treats from yore discussion on her front porch?"

Sam perked up, like my orchid, when I remembered to water it. "Oh? Do you have her lavender vanilla lemonade recipe? I've tried and tried, but the woman won't give it up."

Maybe I'd never made it to Relevant Road. I certainly wasn't on Memory Lane anymore. Was Crazy Town at the intersection of the two?

One glance at my PI confirmed that his patience had packed a suitcase and left the key on the table. Did it leave behind a Dear John letter too?

"Bitsy didn't give me her recipe, Sam. But I'll try to find someone who does have it. Let me see what I can do. In the meantime, could we tour the place where you make your famous compost? Every year I struggle with my garden, and I'm thinking I should add some of your magical mixture. But I'm particular with what I use, because of my allergies and all. I'd feel better if I could see what goes into your mixture."

Sam's smile walked out the door—maybe it joined Shorty's patience. "Miss Ev, you can read the ingredients on my compost bag. There shouldn't be anything in there that would cause an allergic reaction."

"Oh, I'm sure I can read about the ingredients. Like I said, I'm concerned about my allergies—I'd rather see how everything is put together."

"You're not getting into my back room, even if you hand me Miss Bitsy's lemonade recipe on a silver platter. That compost is my best seller! People come from two parishes over to buy it. It's a tried and true combination of several key ingredients, resting in compost bins for just the right amount of time. If anyone could duplicate it, why I'd be out of business."

"Sam, buddy, calm down. We're not gonna steal yore recipe. Now, I'll see ya' tonight at the game. An' I'll save ya' a seat across from the television. I've got the World Series of Poker recorded an' I'll get ya' the best seat in the house."

As we walked out of Kellerman's Gardening Supplies n' More I had to ask. "You guys watch poker while you're *playing* poker?"

Shorty kept an even pace towards the truck, never slowing his stride. "Well, sometimes we watch underwater boxing, or a hot dog-eating contest. My favorite, though, is the strong man tournaments. But I couldn't find any of those on ESPN this week. An' the world poker series isn't too bad—I get some real good tips from watchin' the pros play."

As I pondered the logic in watching people playing poker while playing poker, Shorty gave his two cents on Sam. "It was a longshot anyway, thinkin' Sam stole the fruitcake. I've known Sam since we were kids, an' he's got a good heart. An' his mama'd made sure he never got in much trouble neither. Why, if she caught him doin' somethin' wrong, she'd make 'im go out tuh the cypress tree in the backyard an' cut her a switch. Besides, Sam loves Miss Pearlie! She an' his mama are best friends—he'd never steal from her. But I had t'look that man in the eyes, jus' t'make sure I was right."

"Well, it sounds like his old family recipe has worked well for him up to now. I don't see him messing with the formula. We'd better cross him off the list. Out of Farmer Joe and Junior Tibbs, which one is the more likely suspect?"

Shorty pointed his car toward Highway 64. "My money's on ol' Joe. I'll get in touch with Teddy, see if he's seen anything else lookin' suspicious. Why don'tcha call Millie when ya' get home, see if she's learned anythin'? Tonight at the poker game, I'm gonna ask around an' see if anyone knows this Natalie Wheeler gal. I'll ask about Joseph Dwyer too, but chances are my buddies are gonna know more about a crazy ex-girlfriend than a guy who's got half a million dollars t'spend. Those kinds o'people don't hang out at The Dirty Pelican or the Gas n' More."

"Without a doubt."

"Hey, yore date with the sheriff's tonight, ain't it?"

Technically, it wasn't a date, but I kept silent. The fact Shorty mentioned it at all warmed my heart, like my mother's ooey gooey cake cooling on the stovetop. "It is tonight, thanks for remembering. Do you have any words of wisdom?"

Shorty pulled into my driveway. "Yeah. Don't wear yore happy bottoms."

"And this is why I'll never understand men! Why would they watch a game they're already playing? It doesn't make any sense."

As always, Elizabeth enjoyed hearing about my extracurricular activities, even if she couldn't understand them. I didn't either, which was why I needed her to keep me sane.

"Well, I don't understand why they watch it either. But for some reason I am extremely irritating to him, so I'm keeping my sarcasm under the radar."

"You're irritating? Has he looked in the mirror lately?"

"Oh, that reminds me, El. How much does it cost to join the country club? And what are the monthly dues?"

Just the briefest of pauses—nothing I said surprised her anymore. "What? You're joining the country club? Well, you'll need a sponsor—Cliff and I are happy to do that. Then you'll have to cough up $2,000 as a deposit. You'll get it back if you resign from the club, but not if you're kicked out. It's also used to cover any potential damage you might cause as a member. The monthly dues vary, depending on whether you use the pool or the golf course or the tennis courts. Cliff hates golf and tennis, so we have the social membership. When Scarlett and Jep came along we added the pool. You'll find out soon enough, Ev—grandchildren were born for spoiling! But the social membership alone is just $450 a month."

"Good grief! There's nothing country about that club. You should change the name to the rich people's club, it's more fitting."

"Are you thinking about joining? That's a lot of money, I know. And you can always come with me—each member can bring one guest."

"No thanks—my idea of fun is happy bottoms and a good book. No, Shorty asked me to look into joining. He mentioned something about how Annabelle likes to dress up and go to fancy restaurants."

Even through the phone I could feel Elizabeth's disbelief, like a wet blanket draped over my shoulders. "Obviously he knows her better than I do, but the few times I've met Annabelle I didn't get that vibe. I mean, she'd fit right into the country club with the right clothes. But my impression has always been she'd rather not."

"That's what I told Shorty! He took her to Mansurs on the Boulevard, said she gushed over it. But my guess is she knew how much it was costing him, and wanted to make it obvious she appreciated the date. And now he thinks she expects that, I guess."

We shared a moment of silence, unusual for our relationship. Elizabeth broke the peace. "Aren't you having her over for coffee tomorrow afternoon? Maybe you should tell her what Shorty said, that he wants you to look into what it takes to join the country club. We don't want him forking over all that money if that's not even what she wants."

"Maybe. I really don't want to get involved, though. Shorty's already on his last nerve when it comes to me. I just don't want to ruin our friendship beyond repair."

My best friend liked to insert logic into our conversations. "Ev, I get that. I really do. But above that, you don't want Shorty misunderstanding what Annabelle really wants. It could hurt their relationship. Why, the last time Shorty came over to repair something, he whistled the entire time. Now, it wasn't very good whistling—I couldn't even figure out the tune. But he's happy, Ev...so happy! We don't want him to do anything to change that."

Oh, why did she have to be right so often? "Okay, I'll talk to Annabelle tomorrow. But if she really wants to be all fancy and go to the country club, will you sponsor Shorty?"

"Uh, was that Cliff calling me? Yes, he's shouting at me from the bedroom. Sorry, honey, I've got to go. Let me know how it goes with Annabelle tomorrow."

The time 3:00 popped onto the face of my phone. Didn't Cliff take his grandkids fishing on Saturday afternoons?

I took Shorty's advice and gave Millie a call. Of course she didn't answer—did anyone under the age of forty answer their phones nowadays? I attempted a text, trying to sound light-hearted and cheery. *Hey, Millie! I hope you're having a great Saturday. I wondered if you'd had any luck in your task.*

No, that sounded weird. Assignment? No. Duty? Worse. What about...*Just wanted to check in and see how you're doing.* Yes, much better. As my kids would say, it ranked much lower on the lameness scale.

Fine. I haven't had much luck finding that thing you mentioned. But I do have some news. Could you meet me down the street from my house in twenty minutes?

Should I call Shorty? No, best to keep it between the women. Except that he had been so irritable recently. No, I should call him, after I text back. *Sounds great—will be there.*

"I took your advice and talked to Millie. She wants to meet in twenty minutes down the street from her home. Would you like to join me?"

"Nah, ya'll can handle it. Jus' keep me posted."

Honestly, relief washed over my body, warm and soothing. My stomach took a break from the flip flopping. A persistent nose nudged my leg. Zydeco was feeling neglected.

"C'mon, Zy! Let's go for a ride!" My dog definitely preferred women over men—hopefully Millie wouldn't be the exception.

"Awww...he's adorable! What's his name?" Zy warmed up to his new friend, licking her face in time with his tail wags. I'd stacked the odds by bringing a bag of his favorite dog treats, Off the Chain Chewies.

"Zydeco. Give him some more treats—he loves them. And see? Zy's face is right on the bag."

"What? How is that possible?"

"Remember Shorty? His cousin owns an upscale dog treat company called Brown Dog Bakery. He uses Zydeco's face on the treats. You should search social media for the compa-ny—Zy's all over their channels."

The conversation with Millie reminded me that I should probably be getting a lot more money for Zydeco's face. Maybe I should talk to a lawyer. Maybe Zy needed an agent.

"Thanks for meeting me, Miss Ev. I didn't find anything looking like the murder weapon you described. But I did find some other interesting things."

"Should we go somewhere else? We can take my car."

"No, Mom's in the house, she thinks I'm reading so she'll leave me alone for a while. But if she starts looking for me, and blows up my phone, I need to tell her I took a walk around the block."

"Okay, then let's take a walk around the block with Zy."

As our steps led us farther from the Reynolds' house, I wondered how far was far enough. How far away would we need to be for Millie to feel safe? My answer came at the next corner.

"Mom went out with her friends last night and my brother went to the basketball game. They left me home with some cash and told me to order pizza. Boy, that made me mad! We never spend time together as a family. And now with my dad gone, those two are the only family I have."

Millie clenched her hands into fists and increased her pace. Zydeco matched her easily, but I wondered how long I'd last. I really needed to start an exercise program!

"First, I started with Mom's bedroom. I figured she'd keep stuff in there she didn't want anyone to see. I looked in the closets and the drawers...nothing! I looked under the bed and in her shoeboxes. I couldn't find anything."

Her pace slowed as she prepared her words. Zy decreased his steps and I finally caught my breath. "Then I thought to myself, what is something in my mother's bedroom I'd never want to look at? And I went straight to her shoe closet and bingo!"

Millie's voice rose and she walked faster. Maybe this girl would be a good walking partner? Note to self: Ask Millie if she'd like to go walking with me regularly. My brain sent my thoughts to my heart, who sent a message back: *don't you dare!*

Something Millie wouldn't want to see? My first thought was some sort of feminine products or birth control. Both my children steered clear of anything labeled with those words. So had my husband.

"I pulled out a box labeled 'Baby Book' and there they were: financial statements from the Cayman Islands, with my father's name as the sole owner."

Yeah, that was true as well. My kids would never look in their baby books. Well played, Judy.

"I also found some invoices from a private investigator. It looks like Mom hired him to find Dad's missing money. And he was successful."

"Was there any correspondence in there, between the PI and your mom?"

Millie led us to the end of the block. She noticed my gasps for air and stopped at the corner. We were halfway. "No, and her computer's password protected so I can't get in her email. But if she knew the money was there, then she would want her fair share. Even if it was stolen money."

One block, turn the corner, then another block and we'd be back at our starting point. "I also found some letters to Dad from some lady named Melinda. They're definitely R-rated! It was really gross reading about how sexy she thinks my dad is. Or was. That's why this Melinda hired him, because she wanted him around the office. She said she was in love with him, and she was jealous of Mom because she had him all to herself. I mean, talk about yuck!"

"Millie, when did your parents divorce? Was it while he was working for Melinda?"

My new friend scrunched her nose as she thought. "It was two years ago, that's all I know. Is this woman Melinda Davis? As in, Mrs. Davis that Dad worked for before his job at New Horizons?"

"My guess is yes. From what you're saying, Melinda was in love with him, and he might have rejected her. If he turned her down and stole from her, that's definitely a motive for murder."

We finished the block and turned the last corner—not a lot of time left. "Millie, does your mother wear super tall heels? Like over four inches?"

More nose scrunching. "Yeah, Mom has several pairs. But her favorites are her Dolce & Gabbana stiletto booties. They're made from denim with a Swarovski crystal buckle. She won't ever let me borrow them—she said they cost $1,500!"

"Hmmm...how tall is the heel?"

"Oh, I don't know. But when she and Dad were married, she wore them on their date nights. She said she was as tall as Princess Diana, and twice as beautiful. Whatever that means."

We stopped at Millie's corner and I wheezed my goodbyes. My heart caught a break. I wouldn't be requesting a teenager to be my walking partner...not this one, anyway. Zy barked his goodbyes and jumped into my Bronco. Maybe Lila Trahan would be my partner?

I pulled out my phone to search for Princess Di's height. Five foot ten inches...I'd forgotten how tall she was. Milt said the killer was approximately five inches shorter than the victim, making them...five foot ten inches. Hmmm...Judy Reynolds, you've jumped to the top of my list.

J ust a business meal, Ev. Colleagues only, sharing a meal and discussing cases. What did one wear to a business meal? A dress or pants? What did Jessica Fletcher wear to these kinds of events? Angela Lansbury always made murder look so fashionable.

"Elizabeth, what do I wear tonight? What says business meal but also still fits?"

"I'm not sure. Why don't you unlock your front door and let me in? Then I can give a better answer."

Of course. Why wouldn't my best friend be standing on my front porch two hours before my business meal with Sheriff McDreamy?

"Thank goodness you're here! Is it okay to wear the same thing I did on my first date with Cay? Or should I save that for a real first date with Mitch? Or do I have to shove it to the back of the closet, because it's already been worn as a first date outfit?"

Elizabeth sailed past my panicked face and headed for the kitchen. Zy followed her—after all, she might be getting food.

"What are you doing? I don't store my clothes in there! And how can you hum 'O Come All Ye Faithful' at a time like this?"

And why was I screaming at my best friend from the hallway? The sound of opened cabinets and the clatter of my teapot beckoned me to the kitchen.

"You're making tea at a time like this? Have you lost your mind?"

No response, other than the second stanza of my friend's chosen song. Zy had settled at my feet, resting his chin on my foot.

"Elizabeth! Answer me."

A pair of caramel colored eyes surveyed my panicked state. "First, we make a pot of tea, then we drink it. We'll still have an hour and fifteen minutes to plan your dazzling outfit, makeup, and hair. But honey, first we've got to get you calmed down."

She was right, of course. I stepped over my dog and padded toward the cabinet with our special mugs. "All right. But as we're making our tea, could we discuss what I should wear?"

The humming resumed. "How many stanzas are there, anyway? And have you hummed them all yet?"

Another survey of my soul with her eyes. "There are only three, and yes, I'm done. Let's start with an easy question: what restaurant will you be dining at?"

"Well, he's picking me up, like a proper gentleman, and we're going to Señor Sombrero's. I'm thinking my black cardigan with the purple flowers, over a black dress."

"No, no cardigans. You're not a librarian, Ev. And we're not in the eighteenth century anymore—you can at least show the lower half of your arms. And some ankle too, maybe even your calves. Men like a glimpse of what's underneath—you know, to make sure they're not being tricked with push up bras and Spanx."

The kettle whistled for our attention. Elizabeth poured the boiling water into my teapot, the bags of Peppermint Cheer waiting inside. "I vote for your emerald green dress and your black knee high boots with the two-inch heel. McDreamy's pretty tall, so he'll still tower above you."

We carried our mugs and teapot to my tea cart. My heart didn't hurt quite as much at the sight of Doug's gift, and the reminder I was a widow. In fact, it warmed a little to the memory, like a fleece blanket keeping my heart snug and safe.

"El, have you been talking to Shorty? Because that sounds like something he'd say. Besides, I hate push up bras—they cut off the blood flow! And, while I should be wearing Spanx, I don't have any for tricking men. My only trick is to wear my shirts untucked. And men do that too, so who's tricking whom?"

Zydeco followed us to the living room, settling between the two of us. We let the tea steep a few more minutes as we finalized my outfit. "Okay, I'll take your suggestion, wear the dress and the boots. What about earrings? I'm thinking my gold hoops."

Elizabeth laid her hand on my arm. "Honey, I know you think those hoops are flattering. And they would be, if you'd stop fiddling with them. But you spend every moment reaching up to first one ear, then the other, untangling them from your hair. And what if you catch one on your ring again, and it flies out of your ear?"

"I'm never going to live that down, am I? Who knew a five-dollar pair of earrings was aerodynamic? Thank goodness it missed Miss Elsie, although just by a couple of inches."

A couple of months ago, I'd worn my thrift shop hoops to church. As we'd sung "Bringing in the Sheaves" before the sermon, I'd reached up to adjust my right earring and untangle it from my hair. Somehow, the hoop caught on my ring, and it shot out of my ear when I dropped my hand to my side. My plan had been to sneak up to the piano after church and retrieve it, and no one would have been the wiser. Unfortunately, it almost hit our pianist Elsie Hubbard.

"Oh, no, you're *never* living that down! You nearly gave Miss Elsie a heart attack! The woman just had to halt the entire service, convinced she'd seen a sign of the end times. She's always had a flair for the dramatic, though." Elizabeth prolonged my embarrassment by imitating our pianist, even laying the back of her hand against her forehead.

"My word! Did anyone see that? Why, it looked like one of those seven stars from the book of Revelation. You know, Brother Tom, those seven stars that represent the angels of the seven churches. I do declare, it must be a sign the Rapture is coming."

Part of me was annoyed, but the other part had to join in. I too had to put the back of my right hand on my forehead and force my voice up half an octave. "Why, yes, it must be a sign. Brother Tom, you'd best change your sermon and focus on getting us all ready to go up to Heaven. And you'd better hurry too—no telling how much time you've got to preach."

Elizabeth had always soothed my fears and calmed my nerves. Once again she performed her magic act and got me ready for my business meal. Oh, who were we kidding? It was a date.

Sheriff McDreamy, uh, Mitch, arrived with a bouquet that definitely didn't come from The Market Basket in Zachary. "I know we agreed this isn't a date, so these aren't those date kind of flowers. I got them from my neighbor."

Mitch followed me into the kitchen as I rummaged for a vase. "Well, since they aren't those date kind of flowers, could I put them in a mason jar? I couldn't tell you the last time I got flowers, so I'm not even sure I own a vase."

I filled the jar with water and arranged the flowers. "Hmmm...I didn't know we could grow roses and lilies here in Louisiana, in December. Your neighbor must be an exceptional gardener."

Mitch chuckled. "Well, he owns a flower shop, so that helps."

I'd locked Zydeco in my bedroom—sometimes he didn't react well to men. Honestly, it was most times. He'd definitely been abused by one or more men before he'd arrived on my front porch.

"The flowers look great in the jar. But they pale compared to you. Why, Evangeline Delafose, I don't believe I've ever seen you so dressed up before! I hope my clothes aren't too casual."

Mitch's long-sleeved deep blue shirt brightened his moss green eyes, while his dark jeans and Ariat boots made my heart jump. I'd always had a soft spot for men in jeans and cowboy boots.

"Oh no, not at all. We'll probably be the best dressed people in Señor Sombrero's. Now, you go ahead and walk out the door—I've got to let out my dog, and he's not too trusting of men."

"All right, but I'm staying on the front porch. My mama taught me to accompany a lady to and from her house."

If Zy had his way, I'd stay home all day long with him. And he'd had his way for quite some time—Cay had spent more time promising dates than actually taking me out on them. This man seemed like someone who'd like nothing better than to take me out on the town. I bet he also enjoyed an evening home, cooking supper and having interesting conversations.

"Okay, I've got Señor Sombrero's in my GPS. While we're headed there, tell me about your fruitcake mystery. That one sounds pretty interesting."

"Well it is, and it's probably the farthest along in discovering the criminal. We've narrowed our suspects down to two: Junior Tibbs and Joe McMillan."

The twenty minute ride felt like seconds as I laid out our case. The GPS, although helpful, kept interrupting me. Mitch shoved his gear stick into *park.* "Here we are, and I sure am glad! I don't know about you, but I was getting pretty tired of that bossy lady interrupting you. That's one heck of a mystery, Ev!"

Over chips and salsa I picked Mitch's brain. "What do you think? Who's your favorite suspect?"

My date eyed his iced tea, dropping in another lemon and stirring it with his spoon. "Based on what you've told me, my money's on Junior. Sure, Joe has motive, means, and opportunity. But he sounds like a good guy. Tibbs, on the other hand...well, you've described him as opportunistic and a little shady. But I gotta tell ya', Ev, I think I'm gonna have to go with Suspect Number Three."

"Huh? But I told you we're down to only two."

Mitch took a sip of his tea. "Oh, you know...the idiot in East Baton Rouge Parish that uses fruitcake to catch fish." Another sip. "And believe me, I've met more than my fair share."

All too soon our business meal came to a close. Mitch wanted to run to the office before church the next day, so he'd be up early. "Paperwork! The worst part of being sheriff." And I needed to mentally prepare myself for my weekly Bergeron Sunday lunch. Fortunately, church gave me the spiritual stamina required to handle my family.

"Thank you again, Ev, for a wonderful evening. I can't remember the last time I've laughed so hard, or pondered such a...well, such a unique case."

Mitch hesitated, his eyes becoming curiously fascinated with the boards on my front porch. "Uh, I know you said you're swamped right now with two cases and making plans for Christmas. But what about New Year's Eve? I've already asked you out for that evening, but you never answered me."

The porch lost its fascination and he brought his eyes level to mine. "So, how about it? Would you be my date on December 31st? I'll bring more flowers."

Laughter escaped my mouth before I could stop it. But why should I? "The kids will still be here, but I'm sure they'll have their own plans. Sure, that sounds fun. And bring the flowers—I bet my sister-in-law has a proper vase I could borrow."

A few beads of sweat slid down Mitch's temple. The poor guy was about as experienced with dating as I was. "Fantastic! I've got a couple of ideas, nothing too loud or crowded. I'm thinking, supper at a rooftop restaurant in Baton Rouge, where we can watch the fireworks at midnight. How does that sound?"

"It sounds like the perfect date—romantic, exciting, and special. Of course, this was a practically perfect date too. I mean, it's hard to top chips and queso from Señor Sombrero's."

Mitch took my hand. "Ev Delafose, I think you're practically perfect in every way."

What a compliment! And a quote from a childhood favorite, *Mary Poppins*. "You just keep thinking that Mister. So when my shoes don't match, or I trip over my own two feet, you can revisit that feeling."

Or when I almost whack an elderly pianist with an earring, causing rumors about the end of the world. Would Mitch still consider me practically perfect? *Dear Lord, please keep that story under wraps for as long as possible. Amen.*

"So? Did you kiss him? Because I came up with a new nickname if you did. How's Sheriff McSmoochy sound?"

"It sounds even worse than McDreamy. And no, we didn't kiss. Mitch seems to think the perfect setting for our first kiss is Red Stick Social, on the rooftop as the fireworks explode on New Year's Eve."

Hadn't I been talking to Elizabeth? Why did that sound like Shorty's horse snort on the other end?

"It sounds like the sheriff watches too many rom-coms. You know, a first kiss can be perfect amid the tortilla chips at Señor Sombrero's too. As long as the guy's a good kisser, the setting doesn't matter."

"Thank you for that. I wasn't aware you were Graisseville's expert on first kisses. And aren't you always complaining that couples take things way too fast these days? What's wrong with waiting to kiss? I think it's romantic."

No more snorting, just a sigh. "You're right, I'm sorry. Cliff's never been a romantic, and he's gotten worse through the years. The other night he was feeling amorous, so he got my attention by taking off a sock and throwing it at me. Yeah, now that I think about it, McSmoochy's doing it right."

"Thank you. But could you just call him Mitch? We're not twelve years old."

Yes, definitely a sigh. "Fine! If you insist. Did he say anything about you, or your outfit?"

"He said my flowers paled in comparison."

"Hmmm, well you might be right. This sheriff would fit right in on The Great American Family Channel. So when do I get to meet him?"

"Elizabeth! We've had one date and planned a second. There's no reason he should meet my friends until I know where this is headed."

Silence on the other end, which meant my bestie was planning something. "You know, I voted for Sheriff McSmoochy. As one of his constituents, I think it's my duty to visit the station, make sure he's doing a good job. Yes, I've got some time on Monday, I think I'll stop in and check up on him. Oh, that reminds me...when are you going to tell your brother that you're dating his boss?"

Elizabeth had been my haven, my refuge from the stresses in my life. Mostly, she kept me from losing my temper with my PI and my family. But if she continued to harass me about my love life, then I'd have to find another lifeline. Hmmm...I wonder if Millie was available? She wouldn't tease me about my love life.

As I sifted through my short list of friends, I realized everyone had stood for the benediction. *I'm so sorry, Lord! I didn't mean to let my petty issues distract me from the sermon. I promise to catch it on YouTube once it's posted. Or was it uploaded? When it was available.*

My sister-in-law caught me in the lobby. "Syd's been grounded for talking back to Nate. She'll probably try to con you into picking her up from school next week, so she can hit you up for a ride to a party on Friday. The party she's been grounded from. But don't succumb to her wiles, Ev. Stay strong and tell her that you're busy. Because we both know if she gets you alone in a car, you'll agree to pretty much anything."

She wasn't wrong. "No problem, Bonnie. And thanks for the heads up. I'll practice saying no on the way over to your house. Is there anything you need me to pick up at the store?"

My sister-in-law's eyes searched the lobby for her kids. At eleven, Jack pretended he had no parents. He'd tried to tell his friends he was a rich orphan, Bonnie was his maid, and Nate was his butler. In a small town that lie could never fly, and Nate had grounded his son for two weeks.

"No, but why didn't you warn me raising a male tween is so much harder than raising a little boy? Jack was never a problem until he discovered girls. Now it's all about being cool. Apparently, having parents does not fall within the current definition of *cool.*"

Her eyes rested on Syd and she raised her hand to motion the girl over. My niece stared past Bonnie, then turned to start yet another conversation on the best color of lip gloss.

Bonnie's shoulders lifted a good four inches, then dropped back down as she heaved a sigh. "And that one! She's seven going on seventeen, always with the attitude. Ev, she's bound and determined to finish out the year grounded more days than not! Hey!"

Bonnie tilted her head and put one hand on her hip. "Your kids are all grown. You've got all kinds of time now. How would you like to keep Syd a few days during Christmas break? You know, spend some good quality aunt time with your favorite niece?"

"That sounds like a lot of fun, Bonnie. But from the way you've been talking, it sounds like Syd will be grounded for most of Christmas break."

Bonnie tossed her head. "Oh, I'm sure I can convince Nate to exclude time with you from the grounding. Especially when I explain to him that she'll be out of the house, and we'll only have one impossible child to deal with."

My sister-in-law waved as she marched towards her daughter. What was it with kids these days? Even my sister would have scurried over to my mother, if she'd given Mad the same look Bonnie gave her daughter. Perhaps a few days with Aunt Ev and cousins Matty and Ellie would be good for Syd. Although I wasn't sure how good it would be for me.

"You know, that doesn't surprise me, ol' Junior Tibbs is a thief! His daddy isn't on a first name basis with the truth, that's for sure! And the apple doesn't fall too far from the tree."

"Gosh, Dad, could you throw in one more Southern saying into our conversation? And I didn't say Junior stole Miss Pearlie's fruitcakes. I only said he's a suspect."

My father ignored my jab at his love of Southern phrases. "I know! But you mark my words, Evangeline, that Junior Tibbs is a bad seed. A bad seed, I tell ya! He's just lucky he found a woman whose elevator doesn't go all the way to the top. She can't see he left his ethics under the bed when he moved out of his daddy's house."

And there it was...the third saying I'd requested. Then he turned to my fruitcake case. "Now, is there anything you want help with on Miss Pearlie's case? She's not paying you and Shorty with those heavy bricks of nastiness, is she? Cuz if she is, then I don't want any of those payments."

"No, Dad, she's not. And since when are you getting paid for helping us?"

My sister-in-law smoothed over the bickering. "Nate and I have a rule: no discussing cases at the table. It sounds like we need to extend that rule to include you two."

Nate glanced at the kids. "Children, your mother's right. And what you've heard so far will not be repeated. Understand?"

Jack stared at his plate, saying nothing. Or was he staring into the space between the table and his chest? My brother wasn't a decorated law enforcement officer for nothing.

"Jackson Bergeron! Do you have your phone at the table?"

Syd giggled at her brother's predicament But it didn't last. "Syd's got her tablet at the table too. If I'm getting punished for this stupid rule, then she should too." My niece's smile disappeared faster than a cold snap in Louisiana.

Nate leaped up, knocking his chair over with a *crash!* Syd and Jack's eyes widened at their father's anger. So did Bonnie's. My brother kept his emotions in check for most of his adult life. But parenting willful children had sprung Nate's anger from its cage. Dad and I settled in for the show. The look on my father's face told me he was enjoying our front row seats a little too much.

"Give me your electronics...now! You two are grounded until January first. You will go to school and church, and nothing else. No television, no computers except for schoolwork. Go to your rooms—your mother and I are right behind you."

As the quiet settled into the room, I glanced at my father. Was he about to proclaim some monumental parenting hack?

"And that Princess Peepee! Evangeline, did I ever tell you what a horrible dog that little ankle biter was? We all dreaded the days she and her royalty crowd traipsed in. Let me tell you what that dang dog did! First off, she growled at Missy, the very best receptionist I could ever hope to hire. Then she bit Janie, the very best vet tech I could ever hope to hire. Then..."

To my father's credit, he ended our conversation with his trip to the coroner's office. "And you know what? That's where they store all the dead bodies! Now, Milt wasn't supposed to let me go back and see them all. But since we're both doctors, he extended me what's called *professional courtesy*. Yes sir, ol' Milt took me back and let me see the autopsy room! Why, I even got to watch him cut up one a body."

Professional courtesy? Since when does a medical doctor extend professional courtesy to a veterinarian?

"Evangeline, I can't tell you when I've had a better day. Heck, it might have just been the best day I'd ever had."

"Oh? Not your wedding day, or the birth of any of your children?"

My father scoffed. "What? Nah, people get married and have kids all the time. But you know what people don't do all the time? They don't go into a room full of dead bodies! And they don't get to watch someone cut one open, and pull out all the organs. No sir, that's not something you see every day."

And thank the Good Lord for that.

During my escape back to the sanctity of my home, Aunt Ruby called. "Evangeline, how are you, dear? Al and I have been doing a bit of digging, uncharacteristic for us, as you know. We really don't like to pry into other people's business. But child, we had the best time! Al said we should add it to our date night rotation. You know, one month have supper in Baton Rouge, one month rent a movie, one month perform a *down deep* on a neighbor. Isn't that what you call it? A *down deep*?"

What had happened to my family? Even the extended branches of my family tree were enjoying private investigation way too much. "Actually, Aunt Ruby, it's called a *deep dive*. But go on."

"Oh, dear. Al insisted that didn't sound right, but I wouldn't believe him. Are you sure it's called a *deep dive*?"

"Yes, Aunt Ruby, I'm sure. But tell me what you've discovered on your date night."

Would Mitch enjoy a deep dive date night? Being an officer of the law, he probably couldn't take part.

"First of all, we discovered Ronald Reynolds had a business partner named Debbie Cooley. We're not really sure what happened exactly. All we know is Debbie called the police, but she never pressed charges. The business was dissolved and that was the end of it."

Hmmm...my aunt and uncle weren't very good at their new favorite activity. "Uh, okay. Well, thank you."

"Oh, but there's more! We found out Moe Randall hired a private investigator to look into Ronald. This investigator found some evidence that Ronald was stealing from other clients too. Sid wasn't the only victim, that's for sure. And Al got to talking to some of the other Randall family members. They claim Moe's arm is much stronger than he lets on. He milks that injury for all he can, because he's too lazy to work on the family farm. But Moe's family insists he's got a lot of strength in that right arm. Al and I think he could have stabbed Ronald."

"Oh, wow! You're right, Aunt Ruby, that's great information. Anything else?"

My aunt had been the mayor of Graisseville, and she still wielded power and influence. But I got the impression she was enjoying herself even more than when she'd been an elected official. "We discovered Melinda Davis has a personal trainer, and she takes Taekwondo. She's very strong. We think even with her sling, she could have stabbed Ronald. Oh, and there's one more thing."

Cue the dramatic pause—my aunt was having too much of a good time. "Al and I spoke with the occupants of the building next door to New Horizons. They'd noticed a mysterious man lurking around the parking lot the week of the murder, peeking through the car windows and digging through the dumpster. But when the police arrived, the man disappeared."

Was any of this helpful, other than to rekindle the romance between my aunt and uncle? "Thank you again, Aunt Ruby. Was there anything else you wanted to share?"

"Oh, yes, one more thing. Your neighbor, Linda Owen, told us a strange man came to your home last night, and you got into his car and drove away. And you didn't come back until well past eight o'clock. She said he looked familiar, but she couldn't place him. Evangeline, is there something you want to tell me?"

"That was smart, pretending your phone died. Hopefully, Aunt Ruby will drop that subject." Annabelle sipped her coffee, almost white from her generous dose of half and half. "And you didn't suffer through an interrogation with your meal, like most Bergeron family events." She worked overtime trying to salvage my afternoon.

"Yes, but watching my brother discipline his kids wasn't much better. After all that, I couldn't wait to escape and spend some time with you." I reached for my matching mug filled with chamomile tea and honey. Annabelle's presence soothed my soul, which needed an extra dose of soothing after my grilled pork chops and salad mixed with family drama.

"Ev, I feel for Nate and Bonnie, I really do. Thankfully, our kids are all grown! We have a different kind of worry, but our discipline days are over. My children do what they want, and they don't care to hear my opinions on their life choices. All I can do is cover them in a blanket of prayer."

"You're right, as usual, Annabelle. Now catch me up on your kids." We spent a good thirty minutes bragging on our children and confessing our concerns and worries. Annabelle was right—adult children required a king sized blanket of prayer.

"So, what are you getting Shorty for Christmas? I'm getting him a gift card to Big Ed's, but I expect you're going in more of a romantic direction."

Just a slight hesitation in Annabelle's eyes as she sipped her coffee. "I wanted to talk to you about that, Ev. He's been acting strange the last couple of weeks, ever since he spent Thanksgiving with my family. Don't get me wrong—my kids loved him! Even my parents agreed he was a step up from my ex-husband. I thought everything went easy as pie. But then..."

She took another sip, her eyes switching from uncertainty to thoughtfulness. "I'm not sure how to explain it. Honestly, it's more of a feeling than anything he's said or done. I feel like he's more distant now, maybe even pulling away. I wonder if he's going to break up with me."

A mist of tears washed over Annabelle's eyes, which beckoned my own eyes to follow. Then her tears vanished, leaving my eyes...well, confused, if that was even possible.

"Anyway, part of me wants to beat him to it, go ahead and break up. And that would save me a Christmas present to buy." She smiled, but it didn't reach her eyes.

"Oh, no, Annabelle! Don't do that. Shorty's not going to break up with you. In fact, he wants to join the country club, so you can enjoy dressing up and eating nice meals any time you want." Even in my head that didn't sound like Annabelle. Saying it out loud made it less believable.

"What? Why would I want to do that? My idea of a perfect date is a plate of Shorty's chicken spaghetti and a glass of iced tea." Annabelle paused to reflect on her perfect date scenario. "Mmmm, Shorty makes the best chicken spaghetti! And his iced tea's pretty good too." She swung her knees towards me and tucked one leg under the other, so that we sat on the couch eye to eye. "Ev, what's going on?"

"I'm not sure. He mentioned how much you loved your date at Mansurs, and that you enjoy dressing up and eating fancy meals."

Annabelle's eyes misted over again. "But that's not true! I mean, sure, Mansurs was amazing, don't get me wrong. But I had to suck in my stomach all night, so I didn't look pregnant in my dress. Not to mention, I wore three-inch heels for three hours straight! If I didn't know better, I'd think snapping turtles had locked onto my toes for the entire evening." Heaving a sigh, she reached for her coffee. We sipped a while in silence, pondering the situation.

"Oh, before I forget, I wanted to tell you something. Now, you know I don't get involved in gossip. But I heard something about Judy Reynolds. Her son, Ronald Junior, volunteers at the library ten hours a week after school."

"Oh, isn't that nice! I've never met him, just his sister. But he sounds like a great kid."

Was that an eye roll, or was Annabelle having a seizure? "Great kid, my Aunt Fanny! He's on probation for trying to steal a six-pack of beer from the liquor store. The idiot waltzed in the store, slapped a fake ID on the counter, and got tossed out...minus his card, of course. Then, the next day, he goes back in and tries to steal the six-pack. He's tall on looks but short on brains, that's for sure."

"Well, his sister Millie's a great kid—I know that for a fact. So tell me what you heard."

Annabelle sank her shoulders into the back of my couch and took a long drink, making a face. Her coffee had cooled during our chat session, which wasn't unusual.

"He's a good-looking young man, and since he's been serving time at my branch, we've had an influx of teenage girls. But not the ones who visit the library to improve their minds! No, the giggling, hair tossing, flirty kind, who only have eyes for Junior. Anyway, about a week ago, before Ronald Senior was murdered, his son Mr. Popular gathered his fangirls into the genealogy section of the library. It's pretty deserted back there, for the most part, so they had the area to themselves. Or so they thought."

My storyteller took another sip then fidgeted with her mug. "I was on the other side of the shelves, refiling some books after our monthly genealogy club meeting. But of course, the girls were all too busy flirting and hair tossing to notice me. I guess Junior was trying to impress his little entourage, because he told them he'd be coming into money pretty soon. His father had stashed a few million in the Cayman Islands, and he'd be getting his hands on it soon. He'd buy a yacht and hire...who's that singer that's only famous if you're under thirty?"

"Ha! I'm sure there's a handful. So, Junior claimed he's about to get a lion's share of his father's ill-gotten gains. How was that going to happen?"

Annabelle set her mug down next to mine—I'd long given up on my cold tea. "One of the girls...I guess one with a few more brain cells than the rest of the pack, asked that very question. She wanted to know, if Ronald Senior was still alive, how would Junior be getting his hands on the money? The kid just smiled, smirked really, and told them his mother was taking care of it."

My shoulders propelled forward from the back of my couch, so I could sit straight up in shock.

"What? Did he say what I think he said?"

Annabelle reached for her mug, remembered the temperature of its contents, and pulled her hand back. She clasped them both in her lap. "Well, he didn't come out and say it. But yes, I think he was saying that his mother had a plan to get rid of Ronald so her kids could get all the money. And since they're both minors, she'd have access to it too."

Annabelle left around four o'clock, leaving me two hours before our interview with Ronald's girlfriend, Daisy Jane. But I was still shell-shocked from Annabelle's news. Well, yes, thoughts on her relationship with Shorty had given me pause for thought. But mostly the Ronald Junior revelation consumed my frontal lobe. As my mind crossed back and forth, my phone sang the theme from *Murder, She Wrote*, which meant the caller didn't contact me often.

Millie! As much as I wanted to ask about her brother, I pushed the questions down into the pit of my stomach. The poor kid had enough going on. She didn't need to know what I knew. Shakespeare would have had a field day with this family! Or had he already covered that? No...Hamlet's uncle killed his father, Macbeth killed the king upon advice from his wife...good grief! How many dysfunctional families existed in the world back then? Or even now, for that matter? No, best to push those thoughts down into the pit of my stomach as well. My poor pit!

"Um, hello? Miss Ev? Are you there?"

And...back to Reality Road. "Yes! Millie! How are you?"

Just a small pause, which spoke volumes. "Miss Ev, I can't live here, thinking my mom killed my dad. I need you to come over and help me. We've got to clear her name or have her arrested—at this point, I don't care which one. Could you come over right now?"

Uh, less than two hours until my next interview. "Of course! I've got all the time you need. I'll be there in twenty minutes."

Millie met me at the door. "Let's just get this over with! I'm going to ask her point blank if she killed Dad, and you need to stand beside me and make her be honest. Let's go!"

Oh boy...this wasn't the best plan I'd heard. Although, thinking back, it definitely wasn't the worst.

"Mom! Mrs. Delafose is here because I need someone be-side me. I have to ask you some hard questions. I'll always love you, Mom, and I'll come visit you in Angola. RJ will too—I'll make sure he does. But I just need to know...did you kill my father?"

Okay, not the best way to start a conversation with your mother. What if Matty or Ellie talked to me in the same way? No, I was pretty sure I'd have the exact same look on my face as Judy had at that moment. Only she had the benefit of wishing death on me, instead of her daughter. Note to self: if my kids accused me of murder, make sure they brought along a total stranger, so I could stare daggers into their eyes instead of my own flesh and blood.

"Milla Lou! What are you saying?"

What? Was that even a name? Who would, of their own free will, record on a birth certificate the name *Milla Lou*? No wonder she went by *Millie*.

"Mom! I heard Miss Trudy on the phone telling someone that, on the night Dad was murdered, you went upstairs to take a bath. Miss Trudy said she heard the water running, but she didn't see you again until supper at six. And we all know about the escape plan."

Oh goodness! Judy's eyes reminded me of the time my father had to admit Doug was amazing and could replace him as the most important man in my life. Dad wasn't happy about the truth, and neither was Judy.

"Mom, you know? The escape plan? In case of a fire, we're supposed to meet in the master bedroom and all go down the stairs together."

Did Millie grow a couple of inches? No, but her eyes had lost their innocence. Before me stood two women squaring off, and I'd put my money on Millie. "The night my father died, I think you ran your bath, and slipped out the back stairs to get to your car. It's not far to Dad's office. I think you murdered him, and Miss Trudy never said a word."

Oh, that girl! "Faithful Miss Trudy...she told the police you were home all evening. Mom, look me in the eye and tell me what really happened that night."

Judy's face lost its hardened look, and she replaced it with...was that motherly love? "Millie, honey, I'm so sorry you've been carrying around this burden. I just can't imagine how painful that must be." She swiveled her neck a quarter turn in my direction. "Ev, thank you for being here with Millie. You're a good friend to both of us. And thank you for trying to convince my daughter I'm not a murderer."

Thank goodness Judy refocused her attention on her daughter and missed my jaw drop paired with a blank stare. "Honey, I did sneak out of the house that night, but it wasn't to kill your father. I went to a Pounds Off meeting, and I didn't want anyone to know. With my status in the community, I can't afford to gain any weight. But my scale is showing the effects of all this stress. And I can't let anyone see me hanging out with a bunch of fatties! I have a reputation to protect. Oh, Ev, let me send you the contact information of our leader, Janet."

"Thank you, Judy. That would be great. Then we can officially clear your name."

Judy's eyes never left her phone. "Oh, no, honey. I think you should come to our meetings. You've got quite a few pounds to lose yourself. But if anyone asks, I mistook the entrance to the meeting for a nail salon."

Before my brain could register resentment, Millie grabbed her mother in a death grip. Judy blinked, then reached around and patted her daughter once, then twice on the back. It wasn't an emotional display worthy of *Steel Magnolias*, but it was a start.

"Uh, well, let me leave you two alone, to sort out the rest of...well, the rest of your evening. I'll let myself out."

Thank goodness eliminating Judy as a murder suspect only took fifteen minutes—I still had almost an hour and a half until my interview with Daisy Jane. Plenty of time to get to

Baton Rouge, so Shorty couldn't fuss at me. It also meant my ride would be picking me up in just under thirty minutes. My church outfit doubled as my murder suspect interview wardrobe, which I'd never mentioned to my pastor. Somehow, I doubted Brother Tom would appreciate how well I utilized my clothes.

"Before I forget, I talked tuh Teddy this afternoon. He said ol' Joe's been actin' mighty strange. He told Teddy t'take off early last Friday, an' don't come back for nothin' until Monday. An' he said if Teddy sees you or me hangin' around his farm, let ol' Joe know ASAP. Teddy said Beulah don't leave Joe's side neither."

At least my PI was speaking to me. "What should we do? I have no interest in tangling with Beulah. Maybe I should ask Nate to go talk to him? Or maybe Mitch?"

Shorty waved at Monty as we broke at least three traffic laws. "Nah, I got a better idea. We're gonna take a peek into ol' Joe's barn tonight, after we meet with Daisy Jane. Teddy said the fence in the east pasture's got a loose spot, so we can crawl under it tonight."

"But I didn't bring my *commit a misdemeanor and/or felony* clothes! I've just got what I'm wearing—my *murder suspect interview* clothes. And they're too nice to wear while committing a crime."

"Well, look at it this way, Doc. If we get caught, you'll look mighty nice for yore mugshot."

Daisy Jane couldn't have been more than twenty-five. Did an eight-year age difference make Ronald a cradle robber? Most likely it made him the envy of his friends. Well, until he was murdered—no one was jealous of him anymore.

"I'm happy to help however I can, but I don't know anything. Ronald was just a fling—we had some laughs, and he spent a lot of money on me. But we weren't getting married or anything. I've never met his kids, or his ex-wife. Heck, I haven't met any of his friends or clients either."

Maybe it was her youth, but Daisy hadn't offered us a refreshment of any kind. Even the drug dealer I interviewed in my first case offered me a tepid glass of water in a red plastic cup. Daisy Jane's lack of Southern hospitality wasn't lost on my PI either.

"Do ya' got any cookies?" He glanced around the small apartment, willing the cookies to jump out of the pantry and dance into the living room.

"Uh, no. I get all my meals half price at The Dirty Pelican, and nonalcoholic drinks for free. Since I work there most every night, I just eat there. Plus, a lot of the customers buy me chips or jalapeno poppers. Especially since I'm a grieving girlfriend."

I studied the girl's face—from her smooth tanned forehead right down to the dimple on her chin, this girlfriend didn't exhibit any signs of grief. Well, maybe grief that the gravy train had come to a screeching halt. But nothing else.

"Do ya' got any crackers, mebbe? Those ones with the butter in 'em are my favorite. Mebbe ya' got some from work? Ya' know, those salad crackers."

Another head shake from our hostess. "No, not even those. But if you come in during my shift, I can get you twenty percent off your meal, if you enter the wet t-shirt contest." Daisy Jane glanced in my direction. "Probably not you, though."

Yeah, I really didn't care for this girl. "Did Ronald talk about anyone? Maybe he mentioned something that seemed innocent at the time, but could break the case."

Daisy glanced at her phone—obviously we were boring her. "Mmm...maybe. Give me a name."

I glanced at my PI but he'd headed toward the kitchen, no doubt verifying Daisy Jane's story that she had no cookies or crackers.

"Uh, what about Sid Hebert? Moe Randall? Melinda Davis? Joseph Dwyer? Natalie Wheeler?"

The last name generated a laugh. "Natalie? You've got to be kidding me! She's locked up in the parish jail awaiting trial. Ronald was lucky she only took a bat to his car. No, that girl's roof ain't nailed on tight. Her last boyfriend? She took a bat to *him*! She's not going nowhere for a good long time."

My teal pen scribbled as I crossed off Natalie Wheeler. Oh, and Judy Reynolds too. I'd called her Pounds Off leader Janet and confirmed Judy was learning how to think thin during the time of the murder.

Shorty appeared with a box of Triscuits. "Well, lookee what I found! Yeah, these will do just fine."

No way was I going to explain to my PI how disappointed his mouth would be in just a few seconds. I would pretend to be as surprised as he was. Oh, poor Shorty!

"What the hell...lo Dolly! These taste jus' like drywall!" He glared at the box. "These are the same people that make Oreos! Oh, why, Nabisco? Why would you trick me?"

So much for my PI. "Okay, thank you for clearing Natalie. What about Jerry Little?"

Daisy Jane took on a thoughtful look. "Hmmm, now that name does ring a bell. Ronald came over a few days before his death, all in a panic. Jerry's one of the owners where Ronald works...I mean, worked. He said Jerry had demanded the company financials. Jerry used to be a CPA, and he caught a few things that Sid Hebert missed. Ronald was panicking because Jerry had figured out he was stealing."

Could a twenty-five year old waitress who consumed chips and jalapeno poppers contemplate her boyfriend's murder? Possibly.

"You know, Ronald mentioned something else. He and Jerry played on the same softball team. Jerry claims he's left-handed, but he's really ambidextrous. He only writes with his left hand. But he throws both left and right-handed. He tries to keep that a secret, though."

Shorty had stormed off to the kitchen, presumably to find an acceptable substitute to drywall crackers. I was officially on my own. "Daisy Jane, if Jerry can throw with both hands, could he, say, use a knife to stab someone with his right hand?"

My hostess with the mostest met my gaze. "He definitely could. My cousin's ambidextrous, and she can use either hand to do whatever she needs to. From what Ronald said, Jerry can do the same. Jerry says it's handy, so he can surprise his opponent."

"First things first, we gotta go by the Dairy Delight! I still got the taste o'drywall in my mouth." Shorty had been spitting out the window since he started the truck, which drove my appetite back into the shadows of my stomach.

"Okay, but do I really have to crawl under a fence? And can I turn in my dry cleaning bill for reimbursement? That's a valid expense for this case, don't you think?"

Shorty was too busy yelling at the intercom to hear me. "What is it with these dang things? I can't understand what she's sayin', an' she can't understand me. How does this save me time, if my order's all messed up?" My head whacked the back window as we sailed forward.

"Look here, I can't understand a word yer sayin'. I want a Burger Delight with fries, an' uh, orange soda. Doc, ya' want anything?"

"Maybe an ice pack for the back of my head, and an unsweet tea." My PI placed my order, minus the ice pack. As we peeled out of the drive through line, our cashier waved. "Have a delightful evening!"

"Don't you think they take the *delight* thing just a little too far? The Dairy Delight has a Burger Delight, a Hot Dog Delight...even a Sundae Delight. And those poor employees are forced to tell everyone to have a delightful day."

Half of Shorty's hamburger was missing. Hopefully, it had ended up in his stomach. "Doc, it's all about marketing, an'

Earl's figured it out. Mebbe I could meet with 'im, see if he has any ideas t'market our investigation business."

"That's a great idea. Maybe we could start telling our clients to have a mysterious day. Or maybe a crime free day? No, then we'd have no cases. Maybe we should tell them to stay out of jail, but if they can't, then they should hire us."

"Nah, that's too long t'go on a billboard. I'll talk tuh Earl. He's a marketing genius."

To keep my PI happy, I reigned in my sarcasm. "Yes, I think you should do that. Please let me know what he says."

Shorty's burger had taken up residence in his stomach, along with his fries. His orange soda was still working on the move, and my iced tea was half gone. We drove by Joe's driveway, but couldn't make the turn. On account of all the deputies and federal agents blocking it with their cars.

"What in the Sam Hill…?" Was this another Christmas miracle…Shorty rendered speechless? It did fall under the category of *Things I've Never Seen Before*.

Nate jogged up to Shorty's truck and made the motion to roll down the window. "You two need to keep driving! We've got this under control."

"What's going on, Nate? Is Joe being arrested?"

My brother hesitated, but the look in his eyes told me he'd have to spill the story. "Teddy Pipkin's mother started getting worried, because Teddy's been coming home every evening all upset that Joe's doing something illegal. So she called her brother Frank, who's a retired deputy. Teddy told him everything, including that he heard Joe on the phone talking about explosives, and that he instructed Teddy to leave early on Friday. Frank called the sheriff, who got ATF involved."

My pulse quickened. "Wait! What's ATF, and why are they involved?"

Nate was so wound up, for once my questions didn't annoy him. "Alcohol, Tobacco, and Firearms. It's a federal agency, and they get pretty worked up by explosives. They'd heard some chatter about a terrorist cell down here, so they got a warrant. And here we are!"

Nate watched *Wheel of Fortune* every evening and had a secret crush on Vanna White. He demonstrated her key moves as he pointed to the flashing lights. How long had he been waiting to do that?

"Sweet Farmer Joe is a terrorist? How could we not know that?"

Nate's smile disappeared. "Oh, well, he's not. The actual words he used on the phone were *explosive situation*, referencing his mother-in-law's upcoming visit. Teddy was way off base on that one. But we did arrest him for buying hog feed that was stolen off a delivery truck. So that's something."

Nate's smile returned—apparently one man's misery was another man's happiness.

"Well, Doc, I guess we gotta cross off ol' Joe from our suspect list. If that don't beat all!" Hmmm...I guess one man's misery was another man's happiness and a third man's disappointment.

M onday morning I sipped my tea as Zy and I reviewed our cases. The elements board resembled a stop sign, the red writing almost blinding me. With Judy eliminated, all but Melinda had strong motive, means, and opportunity. The grand jury convened on Wednesday to hear the evidence against Sid. Oh, and our fruitcake mystery had one suspect left, but no evidence. Just typical cases for me and Shorty.

Milt had promised to test Moe Randall's award first thing, and call me with the results. My father spent the weekend bragging to anyone who'd listen that, as a professional courtesy, he would be assisting Milt with the testing. Nate and Dad were having a lot more fun with my cases than I was. And let's not forget I faced the unpleasant task of bringing Jack up to date on the investigation over supper.

Jack's enthusiasm flowed across the cell phone towers. "Ev, I appreciate you coming to my house tonight, and I promise you won't be disappointed. I hope you enjoy ribeyes and Caesar salad! One nice thing about the South is that you can grill all year round. Come hungry!"

I had my four finals on Tuesday, grades due on Saturday, then a nice long winter break. Well, it would be nice if I could solve my two cases. Matty and Ellie would be home after finals, and I wanted to focus on them instead of killers and fruitcake thieves.

My bestie's name popped up on my phone. "Ev, what time am I picking you up for our Christmas shopping today?"

Oh, yes...add that to my Monday list. "Well, I'm waiting for the coroner to call and tell me whether the potential murder weapon Dad borrowed from Moe Randall is a match. But I could take the call on the way, so pick me up at 10:00 a.m."

Her squeal pierced a hole in my eardrum. "Oh, if that happens, you've got to put him on speaker! I've never been on a call with a real live coroner before."

"Oh? Have you been on a call with a dead coroner before? Now that's a story worth telling."

"Shorty's right—you are a smart alec! Just for that, I'll pick you up at 9:30, causing you to drink one less cup of tea. Serves you right!"

The joke was on Elizabeth—I had a thirty ounce travel tumbler.

"Good morning, Milt. I have you on speaker with my friend Elizabeth Trahan. We're headed to Baton Rouge for some last minute Christmas shopping."

"Helping out Santa, are you? He definitely appreciates it! Well, I'm sorry to interrupt you, ladies. But Ev, I know you're eager to get the results."

How would he know what Santa appreciates? "Ev, are you there? Do you want me to tell you the results over the phone?"

My best friend and would-be sleuth spoke up. "Oh, she definitely wants to know right now! Tell us, Doctor, is Moe Randall spending Christmas in the slammer?"

"Good question, Elizabeth. From what I understand, he's on the naughty list this year, that's for sure. But his award didn't kill Ronald Reynolds. Is that all you needed, or should I email you the report?"

"No, that's all I needed, thank you, Milt. Wait! How do you know Moe's on the naughty list? And am I naughty or nice?"

My question was met with silence, because Milt had ended the call and moved on to other tasks.

"Elizabeth, don't you think it's strange that Milt knows Santa appreciates our shopping, and he's certain Moe's on the naughty list?"

"Oh, come on, Ev! He's just messing with you. We all know there's no such thing as Santa Claus. And even if there was, why would he moonlight as a coroner?"

"Well, the elves take care of the toys, and Mrs. Clause helps out a lot, I'm sure. There's probably not much for Santa to do for most of the year. So he uses his skills to perform autopsies and test potential murder weapons and...uh, all that other coroner type stuff."

My bestie tossed her silver hair, reminding me of Shorty's horse Festus. "Ev, the job skills for coroner and Santa Claus aren't anything alike. Your line of reasoning doesn't make sense. If you're going to pursue this logic that Santa has a side hustle, then look at someone like...your father! He's retired and has time on his hands, he's friendly and everyone loves him. Yeah, maybe ol' Skeeter Bergeron dons a red suit and flies a reindeer driven sleigh all over the world. Oh, and your dad's really good at keeping secrets, which is why we haven't figured it out yet. And he's an expert at reading people, which is how he completes the naughty and nice lists every year."

Elizabeth checked her rearview mirror, then the dashboard. "You should look in his garage when he goes to play dominos at the coffee shop tomorrow. I bet he has a barrel full of reindeer food and a red bag half full of presents."

"First of all, Dad wouldn't need reindeer food in his garage. It's eighty degrees outside! His reindeer would have to stay at the North Pole. Second, so would the presents and anything else that revealed his secret identity. He can't tell anyone he's Santa, so all evidence would reside in his second home up north. He couldn't tell me, and he certainly can't tell Nate—otherwise my own brother would have to arrest our father for breaking and entering."

El's right hand snaked toward the radio buttons. "Let's listen to some Christmas music, shall we?"

My phone played "We Are Family" by Sister Sledge. "Hello, dear sister-in-law! What's up?" Maybe my bestie was right, maybe our conversation needed to end. But the way she ended it hurt my feelings a little.

"You'd asked me for some Christmas gift ideas for Nate and the kids. Aren't you finishing up your shopping today? I wanted to make sure and text you the links so you could take care of my family."

"Elizabeth is driving us to Baton Rouge right now, so that would be great. We're almost to Bocage Village..."

Except we weren't. "Elizabeth, why aren't we headed to our favorite shopping center? You're driving us towards...the sheriff's office?"

No, this couldn't be happening. "Bonnie, I've got to go."

Oh, I knew that smile. It was the same one El wore when she dragged me out for pizza back in college, knowing we'd run into the cute guy I'd been stalking for six weeks.

"What are you doing? We're *not* going to see Mitch! He's at work, and this will embarrass him. And me. And pretty much anyone else that witnesses this...this...drop in disaster."

But I also knew that look that replaced the smile—jaw set, eyelids lowered just a tad. Cliff said when his wife wore that look, he headed to his workshop in the backyard.

Swoosh! Bonnie's gift links arrived safely among my text messages. But would I be using them any time soon?

"I just want to meet him, Ev. I think this guy is pretty special to you, and you're obviously special to him. So I just want to meet him."

Unfortunately, I didn't have a workshop to hide in. "Fine. But I'm waiting in the car."

The smile reappeared. "Okay, but if you're with me, I'm less likely to say anything embarrassing."

"Why, Ev! What a pleasant surprise. And this must be your best friend..." Mitch extended his right hand. "...coming to check up on me. Let's go into my office. Oh, Rebecca!"

Mitch's assistant glanced up from her computer screen. "Sheriff, let me guess. A pot of coffee and three mugs? But chamomile tea for Dr. Delafose. I'm on it!"

We each took a chair around the café table in Mitch's office. "I'm giving Rebecca $300 cash out of my own pocket for Christmas. Government workers don't get bonuses. But let me tell you, she deserves a bonus three times that size! Anyone who can handle the hectic pace of this office and keep me organized deserves a lot more than what I can afford."

As if on cue, Rebecca appeared with a tray. "You've got that meeting with the commissioner in thirty minutes—should I reschedule?"

Elizabeth smiled, but it didn't reach her eyes. "No, no! Sheriff, don't change up your day on our account. Ev and I were in the neighborhood, and I suggested we drop by. I've never been to any kind of law enforcement office, so I was curious. The only government building I've seen is the DMV. Oh, and the Social Security Administration building when I changed my last name to Trahan."

As Rebecca closed the door behind her, Elizabeth began the interrogation. She started by studying all of Mitch's features, from his sandy blond hair and moss green eyes to his black shiny shoes. Then she pounced. "You look tan. Do you spend a lot of time outdoors, or is your brown skin from a tanning salon?" She gazed at Mitch's fingers, looking for evidence of a manicure.

"Uh, I like to garden, actually. I have about half an acre in my backyard devoted to vegetables and fruits. A few flowers mixed in for color. And I love fishing, especially bass. I taught my neighbor's kids how to fish, and I've entered a few tournaments."

Elizabeth didn't try to disguise her intentions. "So you like kids then? How about college-age kids? What do you think of them?"

The sheriff blinked once, then twice. The phrase *nervous as a long tailed cat in a room full of rocking chairs* took up residence in my brain. "Ahem. Sorry, I needed to clear my throat. But to answer your question, yes I like college-age kids. My niece and nephew attend Tulane, and I make a trip to New Orleans once a month to see them. You know, take them out for pizza, go see the latest movie, slip them some spending money. But mostly to check on them, so their mama doesn't worry so much."

Mitch didn't notice it, but I did. Elizabeth's eyes softened as they widened just a little, and her jaw relaxed. If we were at her house, I'd tell Cliff it was safe to come out of the workshop.

My bestie leaned against the back of her chair, sipping her coffee while taking in the walls around us. "I see you graduated from Tulane. Ev taught at Loyola, but you probably know that."

Mitch's shoulders dropped an inch or two, pushing air out of his lungs. Or did he exhale, which brought his shoulders down? Either way, he knew he'd passed the test. "Yes, I did. I wish I could have gone to Loyola—it's a great school. But my parents thought it was for rich kids, and Tulane would offer me the same education but not make me too big for my britches, as Dad would say."

We all laughed. "Mom and Dad never went to college, and they sacrificed a great deal, so my twin brother Mike and I could go. On graduation day, they were pretty upset to learn they didn't get to walk across the stage too. I remember my father wrote a letter to the president of Tulane at the time. Mike and I were relieved we didn't have to come back in the fall, just in case the administration held a grudge."

It was my turn to relax my shoulders and tell the knot in my stomach to pack a bag and head out. This was nice, my best friend and my...well, whatever Mitch was...sitting together and getting to know each other.

Rebecca poked her head inside the office. "Sorry to bother you, Sheriff. Your meeting's in ten minutes, and you've got to get to the other side of the building. Are you sure you don't need me to reschedule?"

Mitch looked at Elizabeth, not me, for an answer. He received a smile that reached all the way to her eyes. "No, Sheriff, don't cancel for us. Ev and I need to hit the road...and the sales."

We said our goodbyes just outside Mitch's door. Elizabeth took the lead. "Sheriff...Mitch...thank you for taking the time to see us. We can see ourselves out."

Home free! We'd almost reached the exit sign and I'd not turned red from embarrassment. Maybe this was a good idea, even though I hadn't been a fan at the beginning.

Elizabeth put her hand on the doorknob and turned it a quarter, then stopped. That devious smile popped back on to her face.

"Oh, I'd just like to say...Sheriff, you really are as dreamy as you look on your campaign billboards. Wouldn't you agree, Ev?"

"I can't believe you! I mean, I'm speechless, literally. El, there are no words forming inside my brain to be delivered to my mouth."

Why couldn't Elizabeth stop chuckling? "Yes, honey, that's what *speechless* means. You cannot form words. But honey, you *are* forming words, so you're not literally speechless. And you should have turned around so you could see McDreamy's face! He looked like your dad just after he's eaten a piece of my carrot cake. You know, from the recipe I found in *Southern Living*? I think we made McDreamy's day."

Thank You, Lord, for making Elizabeth the driver on our little outing. Because if we had driven to Baton Rouge in my Bronco, only one of us would be in the car right now. Amen.

"Let's just change the subject, okay? Are we finally headed to Bocage Village? Because I've got a long list of gifts that doesn't match my small budget. We have to find some Christmas magic so I can finish my shopping without going into debt. Let's focus."

The rest of our day resembled one of those videos with time-lapse photography, or it did in my mind, anyway. My brain recorded us zipping into a blur of stores, scouring the clearance racks and bins, and digging into our phone apps for discounts and specials. We broke for lunch to fortify with food and caffeine, and review our battle plan.

"Let's see, I still need a few gifts for Matty. Poor kid can't wake up on Christmas Day to find just underwear and socks under the tree. Although, if my dad had his way..."

Elizabeth hunched her shoulders and squinted her eyes, then pointed her right index finger in the air. "Why, in my day we thanked the Good Lord for underwear and socks under the tree! Why, in my day we didn't even get new underwear and socks for Christmas. No sir, we did not. In my day our daddy got new underwear and socks, and the oldest child got Daddy's old undergarments. Then the next oldest got the oldest kid's hand me downs. And so on! No sir, in my day, only the man of the house got new things for Christmas. He was the only one bringing home the bacon!"

Of course I had to chime in. "Yes! Then Shorty would nod his head in agreement, like a bobblehead." My chin dropped to my chest then jumped back into the air, imitating my PI. "Mmm hmmm, yes sir, Skeeter! That's the way it was at my house too."

"Oh, Elizabeth, what a couple of hustlers! Why, I know for a fact Shorty and all his siblings got new clothes every Christmas. His mother worked out of her home as a seamstress, sewing beautiful party dresses, hemming clothes, and making alterations. And she sewed on all the patches for Boy Scout Troop 621, the one that met at Graisseville Baptist Church!"

I wound up for the finish. "Mother told me all Madie's money went to presents for her children. She also told me Dad's stories aren't on the up and up either. Mother says he got new clothes and toys for Christmas every year. I mean, it wasn't like kids today, that's for sure! But both those men had merrier Christmases than they let on."

My bestie brought it home "Oh, I'm sure! Ev, when have you known Shorty to ever tell a story without stretching it a little? Cliff remembers that guy telling the tallest tales in high school, ranging from, the hogs ate his homework to the bus came late so he had to ride a steer to school. Cliff said the kids looked forward to Shorty's colorful excuses every week. They'd even place bets on whether it would involve cattle or hogs, or both. It's no wonder your father's gotten caught up in Shorty's version of the truth. Those two spend way too much time together."

Why did remembering details of my childhood circle back to the loss of my mother? Because Muriel Bergeron was the primary creator of my childhood memories. "Oh, no, it's good they spend time together. Dad's best friend was Shorty's father, second only to my mother. Dad lost his two best friends, so he needs someone to spend time with. Besides, they have a lot of fun together—Shorty gets to hear stories about his father that he's never heard, and Dad has a best friend."

Elizabeth placed her hand on top of mine, covering it like a soft, warm blanket. "You're right, honey. And I'm sure glad you're my best friend. I can't imagine going through life without you. And please don't cry—you'll make me cry too. And my makeup's looking really good right now."

Just then my phone rang. "Millie! How are you?" Hopefully, my sniffles weren't loud enough to hear through cell phone towers.

"Miss Ev, I'm glad I caught you! Listen, Mom and I've been talking. We think Melinda Davis killed Dad."

Well, of course...she was the only one on the board not bleeding red. "Why exactly do you think that Millie,?"

I couldn't see Millie's face, but from the sucking of air on the other end I pictured her slowing down and composing herself. "First, Mom just told me that Melinda didn't fire my father for being late to work. Nope! Melinda fired him because he was stealing from her. So why didn't Melinda have him arrested, you might ask. It could have been because she was in love with him, or maybe there wasn't enough evidence. It doesn't really matter. Oh, and Melinda also discovered that my father had started his own real estate business, and was trying to take clients away from her. She mostly worked with people buying houses, but she had several clients that bought land and developed it for businesses and housing communities. Any of those situations could be her motive. But that's not the best part."

Why do people insist on creating cliff hangers? Why can't they just save us all the buildup and get to the ending?

Elizabeth examined my expression, looking for clues. What was the appropriate facial expression to convey *my informant's on the phone—she says the one suspect with no strong motive actually has one. Oh, and that's not even the best part.* No, there's really no way to make a person's face express that information.

"Okay, Millie, what's the best part?"

"The best part is that Mom's hairdresser also does Melinda's hair. She told Mom that Melinda's arm healed completely a few weeks ago. But she's enjoying the sympathy, so she keeps wearing the sling. Mom says people have already been whispering that if her arm was that injured, it'd be in a cast, not a sling. Oh, and she shouldn't wear a purple sling with hibiscus flowers on it—they're out of season, and the color is positively hideous."

I t was official—my elements board was 100% red. Every suspect checked the boxes. The boxes of "prime murder suspect," that is. Come suppertime, what kind of report could I tell Jack? If there was any kind of positive spin to be, well...spun, I couldn't see it.

"Good evening, Jack. Thanks for inviting me! My, you have a lovely home. Who is your decorator? I'd love to have the contact information. Case? What case? Oh, you mean your uncle's case. Why yes, Mr. Cormier and I have been working nonstop to clear Sid's name. Yes, we've been investigating our little hearts out, and we've made some progress. We actually have cleared Judy Reynolds, the ex-wife. Isn't that fantastic? Well, yes, I realize that doesn't really help Sid, but it is progress! Uh, what did you say? What other progress have we made? Um, well, the other suspects all have strong motive, means, and opportunity. That's pretty...uh, well, pretty good. We've got a lot of reasonable doubt, and I think you can present that to the jury and...what's that? Evidence? Hmmm, well, it's a funny thing about that..."

No, I wasn't looking forward to my supper, ribeyes or not. My phone played the theme from *The Rockford Files*.

"Hey, Doc! Are ya' ready for yore fancy meal tonight with the Senator? Say, I was thinkin' I should come along an' offer my professional opinions. Ya' know, I've got some insight I'd like t'share with ol' Jack. Yeah, my expertise'd be a big help tonight. What time should I pick ya' up?"

"Shorty...what's Annabelle doing tonight?"

"Uh, well, she's hostin' Christmas dinner, an' she's got a bunch o'family comin' in next week—includin' her kids. She's busy cleanin' an' stuff."

"Hmmm...that's what I thought. Look, I appreciate your enthusiasm, but I don't think it's a good idea for you to tag along. Jack only invited *me*, and it's not right to invite an extra guest. But I'll tell you what. Dad's making a pan of those meatballs you like so much, and some green beans with garlic too. He invited me over and I had to turn him down. I bet he'd love..."

Cell phones don't *click* when your caller hangs up on you. But the feeling is the same. I wasn't surprised Shorty cut the conversation short, but I was surprised we made it past the words *green beans*. My friend was becoming more patient.

Caller number two rang through. "Today was lots of fun, Ev. I hope you weren't too embarrassed that we crashed Sheriff McDreamy's place of work. I'm sure glad I voted for him—he's even cuter in person!"

"Elizabeth, has anyone explained the election process to you? As a registered voter, you're not supposed to vote for the best looking candidate. You're supposed to vote for the most qualified one, the person who best represents your values."

"Oh, honey! That man's values looked mighty fine to me. I don't have any problem with his values, and they line up just right with what I enjoy."

"Ok, stop. You're no longer embarrassing me, now you're just embarrassing yourself. Is this the only reason you called? Because I need to start getting ready for my appointment with Jack Hebert."

The woman was wound up, judging from her response. What was that word used to describe a loud and obnoxious laugh? Oh yes...*guffaw*. My best friend guffawed into my ear.

"Oh, is that what they're calling it nowadays? First a business meal with Sheriff McDreamy, now an appointment with Senator Sexy. Tell me what you're going to wear tonight."

"Elizabeth, what is going on? Have you started reading Harlequin romance novels again?" When we became roommates our freshman year, my new friend confessed her guilty pleasure was finishing off Harlequin novels late into the night. I'd started one, but couldn't get past the ridiculousness of the plot and the graphic descriptions of closed door activities. No, Jane Austen and the Brontë Sisters were more my style. Elizabeth met Cliff the next June at my dad's vet clinic, and right after her birthday in July she donated the Harlequins to the thrift shop. "Cliff convinced me I could do a lot better in the reading department. He gave me *Jane Eyre* by Charlotte Brontë. Oh, Ev, it's so romantic!"

We never told her, but Cliff had come to me the day before Elizabeth's birthday, desperate. "Ev, I have no idea what to give her! It's my first gift to her, and I want it to be special. Do you have any suggestions?"

Not only did I level up my best friend's reading list, but I earned a special place in Cliff's heart for bailing him out of a jam.

"Harlequin romances? Oh no, honey! I'm still a Brontë girl. It's just that Cliff's out of town—his brother's buying another racehorse and he wants Cliff to examine it. No, I guess I'm feeling a little lonely. I'm sorry! My comments were out of line. You don't have to tell me what you're wearing tonight."

"Okay, good. Because the way you just said it was kind of creepy. But I was thinking about my red cardigan with a black t-shirt underneath, jeans, and black flats. What do you think?"

"This isn't a date right? It really is just a platonic meal."

"Yes, Elizabeth. It's just me bringing my client up to speed."

"Then that sounds fine. He definitely won't be making any moves if you're wearing that outfit."

Caller number three rounded out my evening. "Hi, Dad, how are you?"

"Did you tell Shorty I was making meatballs and green beans with garlic tonight? And that I had plenty and he was welcome to join me?"

"Uh, well I think I mentioned you'd invited me for supper tonight, but I couldn't make it. So I guess I did."

"Child, did you forget that I cook a batch of food on Monday and then eat on it for the rest of the week? That way I only have to cook once."

"Uh yes, Dad, I did remember that. But I just thought since you invited me to supper and I couldn't come, that you might enjoy some company tonight."

"Well, you thought wrong. If I want Shorty at my house eating my food, I'll invite him myself."

"Dad, Shorty's one of your best friends! And besides, you'd already factored in the amount of food I'd eat, right? And you cooked extra so you'd have enough for the week. I really don't see the problem."

Had my father purchased one of those industrial fans that blows air at ninety miles an hour, then aimed it his cell phone? No, he was just exhaling to keep his patience on a leash.

"Evangeline, how many times do I have to tell you? Shorty's a good guy, but he eats a person out of house and home! Now he's going to come over here and eat a pan and a half of my meatballs, and probably all my green beans. Child, you don't just pull those meatballs out of the refrigerator and plop them on the table all ready to eat! No, sir, you don't. Why, I make those meatballs from scratch. You bet I do."

That was the signal. My father was about to give me his recipe step by step. "First, I take a good ten minutes just to season the hamburger meat and mix it all together. Then I have to squish it all into balls. Balls of meat you know. That's another twenty minutes...at least! Next I've got to put all those balls of meat into my two glass baking dishes. And I can't just throw those balls in there—no sir! It takes another seven minutes to place them all side by side. Then there's the cooking time, which is a whole forty-five minutes. And that doesn't even include cooking the green beans."

Please don't tell me about the green beans, please don't! "I've got a busy schedule, Evangeline! Making those meatballs takes a good hour and seventeen minutes out of my day."

Oh, of course...It was time for the busy schedule lecture. "Child, I don't have time to make another batch of meatballs and green beans this week. I've got Bible study on Monday, dominos on Tuesday, church supper and fellowship on Wednesday, and men's coffee on Thursday. Not to mention you've got me running back and forth to Baton Rouge helping you and Shorty solve your case."

Interesting, I thought my father enjoyed working on the case. "Evangeline, what am I going to eat for the rest of the week?"

An answer popped into my brain, something along the lines of *you're a grown man and I'm sure you'll figure it out.* But that was definitely not the right thing to say. "Dad, why don't you come over to my house tomorrow night for supper? I'll fix us two pans of lasagna and a big bowl of salad, and you can take home the leftovers. How does that sound?"

The man didn't miss a beat. "I'd like it better if you called Bonnie and sweet-talked her into making us a big pot of gumbo. I'd like to eat on that all week."

Would I ever leave this house? I bent under my bed, looking for my black ballerina flat, but it was nowhere to be found. Zy stared at me, then began a serious washing of his front paws. He only stopped when we both heard a knock at the front door. I hopped into the hallway and peeked through the window. What was Maggie Wheeler doing on my front porch with two strange men? And why did the forty-something dark haired man have a death grip on the teenage boy beside him?

"Ev, I'm sorry to bother you at home. But I've cracked your fruitcake investigation. Could we come in?"

"Normally, I'd say yes, Maggie. But I'm on my way out the door for Baton Rouge. That is, when I find my left shoe."

The teenager pointed to the floor. "Is that your shoe, by the potted plant?"

How'd that happen? Never mind! The way my life played out, this was probably the most normal event of the day. "Yes, thank you, uh, what was your name?"

Gosh, this kid had amazing eyes the color of Maggie's famous cinnamon dolce latte. Wait! I'd seen those eyes before on the face of...

"Maggie, is this your son?"

My coffee dealer snorted. "How old do you think I am, Ev? I was fourteen when Coy was born. He's my brother Charlie's kid."

The oldest person on my porch offered his right hand to me, his left one firmly clamped on his son's shoulder. Charlie was also gifted with the Landry cinnamon dolce latte eyes. "Nice to meet you, ma'am. I'm real sorry it's under these circumstances, though. We'll make it quick."

Coy stepped forward, his father's hand extending like a tether. "Miss Ev, I was the one who took Miss Pearlie's fruitcakes. You see, I have to perform community service hours for my civics class. And, well, we were getting to the end of the semester and I still needed six hours. I work down at

Graisseville Tires n' More, for Mr. Rabalais, Miss Pearlie's son. And I was telling him I was worried about how I was going to get my six hours..."

Oh my stars, this kid was worse than Shorty at putting stories on extended play! Or was he better than Shorty?

"...so that's how I ended up with Miss Pearlie's fruitcakes in the bed of my truck. Anyway, I'm real sorry."

Huh? Note to self: ask Santa for a longer attention span. Thank goodness Maggie helped me out. "Even Miss Pearlie's own family can't stand her fruitcakes! I guess her son Eli thought stealing the fruitcake would benefit the entire community. I can't believe he distracted his own mother while Coy threw the loaves into the bed of his truck, put a tarp over them, and drove away. Then he took them to our family farm and dumped them in the pond. Can you believe it? Eli even signed off on Coy's community service sheet. It was all fun and games until Miss Pearlie hired you and Shorty to solve the mystery."

Charlie pulled Coy back to stand beside him. "Again, Coy's real sorry for the trouble he's caused. We had a long talk about how it's okay to tell your boss *no* when it goes against your values, even if it means losing your job. We've always taught our kids to respect authority, and he was doing what he thought we'd taught him. This afternoon he came to me, the weight of the world on his shoulders, and confessed what he and Eli had done. We're headed to Miss Pearlie's next, so he can apologize to her too. But Maggie said we needed to let you know, so you could close your investigation."

Was there enough time for Shorty to ask Santa for new truck tires? Somehow, I doubted he'd be getting any from Miss Pearlie. And definitely not from Eli Rabalais either.

"Thank you for letting me know. And thank you, Coy, for finding my shoe. I'll pass this information on to Shorty. I really hate to close a case and run, but I'm late for an appointment."

Maggie and company stepped aside. Charlie spoke up. "Oh, yes ma'am, we don't want you to be late. Please tell Senator Sexy that he's doing a great job and he's got my vote."

Dear Lord, please don't let me kill my caffeine dealer, at least not right before the holidays. I really don't want my Christmas meal to be a baloney sandwich. Amen.

Nate's ringtone filled my Bronco, but I'd spoken to enough people that afternoon. I turned my phone on *silence* and focused on the road. My GPS told me I'd reach Jack's driveway in twenty minutes, and navigation systems don't lie.

"Good evening, Ev! Welcome to my humble home. Why don't you follow me to the courtyard—I've got our steaks on the grill."

Courtyard? Who has a courtyard in their backyard? Or maybe Jack had a courtyard *instead* of a backyard? Is that what rich people did, convert their backyards into courtyards? I was about to find out.

"My late wife Ally fell in love with the house because of this courtyard. And, well, what Ally wants Ally gets. Or she did." Jack's eyes began to water, so I gazed at the brick walls to give him some privacy.

"I just love how the entire house surrounds your backyard! That's what makes it a courtyard, correct?"

"Uh, yes. A courtyard is an uncovered outdoor area surrounded by walls from other buildings. In this case, my home. It's totally private, unlike a backyard. And because there's no cover, we can enjoy the stars at night, and grill out here too."

As Jack turned to inspect the ribeyes, I counted the doors. "I see one, two, three...eight doors! Do all the rooms have an exit out here?"

"Not all of them, Ev. Just the five bedrooms, my office, the family room, and the kitchen. None of the bathrooms or the laundry room have doors to the courtyard."

"Well, of course. You have to draw the line somewhere, I guess. And the fountain is just beautiful."

Jack's eyes shone bright, like the embers of a cooling fire. "That's my favorite part of the house. Ally and I spent many nights out here, staring at the stars and listening to the gurgling fountain. Those were good times."

His eyes darkened, and the fire was gone. "But I don't have to tell you that, do I, Ev? Memories are bittersweet—they warm the heart, until you remember you'll never make another memory with that person again."

My hand found its way to Jack's arm. "It gets better with time. Well, no, it really doesn't get better. But it does get easier to deal with. I've found losing Doug is like losing an arm. I won't ever return to how I was before the loss, but I've learned how to cope with it. And you will too. Are the kids coming home for Christmas?"

Jack's shoulders straightened and his mouth curved into a smile as he relayed his holiday plans. We spent our meal discussing the joys and trials of adult children. "Ev, I have thoroughly enjoyed our evening together. But we need to discuss business. How about we go inside? I've got a Chocolate Ganache cake from The Ambrosia Bakery."

Why did I wear jeans? Why didn't I choose my black leggings with the elastic waistband? "Yes, that sounds lovely. I'll get our plates."

"Oh no, don't bother. My housekeeper's coming in the morning. She'll take care of everything."

But he was too late. I'd already scooped up the plates and glasses and headed inside. "No, Ev, really! My housekeeper can take care of it tomorrow. Please don't..."

He couldn't rein in Muriel Bergeron's lessons on being a guest. I'd already entered the kitchen with my armload of dirty dishes.

"Wow! Jack, you could fit my living room in here, with room to spare! And I just love how you've decorated it, like a French bistro. Why, here's the Eiffel Tower. It's all so charming!"

My fingers brushed the metal statue. I'd always wanted to visit Paris—maybe I'd decorate my kitchen like a bistro too. Jack's wife had impeccable taste. I measured the statue's height with my eyes. Would it fit on that small shelf above my sink? Hmmm, approximately eight inches, give or take. I picked up the statue, touching the top with my index finger. My heart skipped a beat. The square tip was about one inch long. "Gosh, that's funny." I said, suddenly fighting a dry throat, "This Eiffel Tower reminds me of the murder weapon. At least, the description of the murder weapon in the coroner's report. Isn't that..."

Jack's solid frame blocked the kitchen door. "You weren't supposed to come into the kitchen. That's why we ate outside. I had it all planned out. We'd have a marvelous supper outside under the stars. Then we'd come inside for dessert in the family room. You'd sit comfortably on the couch while I got our dessert and coffee. But you've ruined everything, Ev. Why did you do that?"

How does one respond to a question like that? Probably not with the truth, that Jack was the one who ruined everything by murdering Ronald Reynolds. I studied the statue.

"Is this Ronald's blood on the tip? Was that intentional, leaving some of it as a trophy of sorts?"

"Maybe. Probably. I'm not really sure. What are we going to do here, Ev? I'm not sure I can kill you."

"Well, that's a relief! Why don't we start with why? Why did you kill Ronald?"

Was the kitchen the best place to have this discussion? The back of my head that stored short-term memories reminded me of the door to the courtyard to my left. But where would I go from there? Note to self: don't ever buy a home with a courtyard—they're the worst! The only escape from the house was the front door or the garage.

"I met Ronald at the country club, and he impressed me with his knowledge of investments and his MBA from Tulane. I sunk all my money in one of his real estate development schemes. Ally was sick and I hoped to make some quick cash to pay the rising medical bills. Then her doctor declared her terminal."

Jack stepped forward, spreading his hands in the air. "Look at this kitchen! Ally had always wanted to go to Paris, sit at a French bistro and sip coffee and people watch. She wanted to tour the Louvre and go to the top of the Eiffel Tower. But I'd always been too busy campaigning and jetting back and forth between here and DC."

The senator dropped his hands to his side and hung his head. "Ev, I never made time for the only thing my wife wanted to do! So I went to Ronald, explained that I needed at least $20,000 back, so I could give Ally the vacation of her dreams. That fraud bobbed and weaved, dodging all my efforts to get my money."

Jack leaned his back against the counter. "Six months later she died, and nothing mattered anymore. The money or the prestige or the power...none of it held any attraction for me. I'd failed to make my wife's dreams come true. And it was all Ronald's fault."

Could I get past Jack and head toward the door? Unlikely. Not to mention, the keys to my Bronco were in my purse, which was in the family room. Maybe I could run to the neighbor's house? No, this fancy neighborhood boasted the ultimate privacy, with houses thousands of yards apart. Jack was in much better shape and could overtake me without breaking a sweat.

"It was too late for Ally, but I could still get my revenge. I went to the New Horizons office, and parked around the corner. I snuck in the back door and confronted Ronald, I demanded that he cut me into his next scheme. But it was all a distraction, Ev. I'd already planned to kill him using the Eiffel Tower. It was fitting, don't you think?"

Was there any way to get out of the house? It wasn't looking good. Could I appeal to his emotions? "You're right, it was. It's tragic you didn't fulfill Ally's last wish, but that's on Ronald. Jack, you can't forget your children—they still need their father. Turn yourself in, so you can continue to have a relationship with them."

Jack's eyes, slits really, bored into my face. "That's the worst idea I've ever heard! No, my children aren't visiting me in Angola! Ally made me promise to keep the family together, and that's what I'm doing. I told the kids we're spending Christmas overseas, on a beautiful little island with the bluest ocean you'll ever see. An island without an extradition treaty, of course. The kids finished their finals today—I pulled some strings and got permission for them to take exams early. They've left New Orleans and are on their way."

Who kept zip ties in the kitchen? My senator, apparently. "I'm going to tie you up and leave you on the guest bed. Don't worry—my housekeeper will be here in the morning. I'll land on the island just a few hours after the kids, and we'll all meet at the hotel. It will be the merriest Christmas since Ally died, don't you think?"

"Jack, please don't do this. You'll be on the run for the rest of your life! And your children, they're going to be accomplices. Which means they'll be fugitives too! Ally wouldn't want that kind of life for them."

Jack's biceps told me I was no match. But I struggled anyway. As he tightened the zip ties, Jack patted my head. "You should work out more, Ev, if you're going to continue this line of work. The next killer might not be as chivalrous."

He stepped back to admire his handiwork. "As for what my wife would or wouldn't want, you didn't know her. I think she'd be okay with a life on the run, if it involved living on a tropical island with a forty room mansion and servants everywhere. You see, American dollars go a lot farther in undeveloped countries. I never got my money back from Ronald, but what I do have will last long enough. Besides, in the end all we ever really have is family."

G uest rooms should have clocks. Yes, everyone had a cell phone with the time on it. But what if someone was, for example, restrained by zip ties while utilizing a guest room? Lounging comfortably on the guest bed, for example, but prevented from checking the time? Presumably, if this someone had a phone, it wouldn't be accessible. In fact, it probably wouldn't even be in the aforementioned guest room. No, a clock would be quite handy. Want to know what else would be handy? A phone in the guest room. But who had landlines anymore?

What was that muffled sound? Maybe Jack had a change of heart? He'd slung me over his shoulder like Santa's bag of toys, dumping me on the bed. No, it wasn't Jack at the door.

Perhaps my brother? But I couldn't make out his words. Surely he was saying something like, "Ev? Ev, can you hear me? Hey, look! Her car's here, but no one's answering. And her phone just rings and rings. I say we've got enough here to knock down the door. It's a welfare check."

My PI appeared in the doorway. "Whatcha takin' a nap for, Doc? Nate's got the entire parish tryin' t'find ya'. Is that why yer not answerin' yore phone? Cuz yer nappin'?"

Thank You, Lord, that my hands are zip tied behind my back.
"No, Shorty, I'm not napping. Jack Hebert's the killer, and I
figured it out. He tied me up so he could escape."

Shorty pulled out the pocket knife Annabelle had given him
for his birthday. "Yeah, I know. I was jus' teasin' ya'. Not even
you'd go tuh someone's house for supper an' lie down for a
nap."

I rubbed my wrists as Shorty put away his knife. "Where's
my brother? Why hasn't he broken down the door yet? I think
this qualifies as a welfare check."

Already halfway down the hallway, my PI tossed the reply
over his shoulder. "Nah, he an' the officer are too busy arguin'.
They can't agree if this situation really *is* a welfare check.
The cop says yer an adult, an' what ya' do on yore personal
time is yore business. Iffen ya' want t'spend the night with
a man ya' hardly know, that's not illegal. Kinda makes one
question yore morals, but it's still within the lines o'followin'
the law. But Nate's defendin' yore honor, sayin' ya' ain't that
kinda woman, the kind who'd spend a night with a feller jus'
cuz he cooks ya' a ribeye steak. Right now they're jus' standin'
on the front steps arguin' over what kinda morals ya' really
do have. That's when I decided t'come through the side door
into the garage."

I followed Shorty down the hall, still rubbing my wrists.
"Well, I'm glad *someone's* concerned with saving me. Thank
you for that."

Shorty opened the refrigerator and pulled out the Chocolate Ganache. "Don't be too hard on yore brother. *Someone's*
gotta defend yore honor. I mean, it don't look real good,
Doc. Ya' came over tuh the senator's house at six o'clock last
night. It's now one in the mornin', all the lights in the house

are off, an' yore car's still in the driveway. The neighbors are gonna be talkin', that's for sure. An' Graisseville's not too far away—jus' a hop, skip, an' a jump down the road. By the time Moe's domino game starts today your evenin' antics are gonna be all over the village."

"Well, let's save those zip ties, okay? We'll show them to everyone, along with the welts on my wrists and clear my name."

Shorty opened the cabinets, presumably searching for a plate. "That's not a good idea, Doc. Iffen ya' show people zip ties an' welts, well they're jus' gonna think yer into all that kinky stuff ya' see in the movies. Ya' know, like *Twenty Tints o'Black*."

"I think you mean *Fifty Shades of Grey*. But yes, I see what you mean. Let's just throw the zip ties in the trash and we'll come up with something else."

He pulled out a white dinner plate that cost more than my couch. "Hey, do ya' know where the forks are? I thought ya' could save me some time."

"No, but I can tell you where Jack stores the zip ties, if that helps."

Shorty stared at me, opened his mouth, then closed it. "Never mind, I'll keep lookin'. Why don'tcha go out the front door an' let yore brother know yer okay? He's the one who made the stink that got us all headed tuh Baton Rouge in the middle o'the night. He couldn't reach ya' on the phone an' he got worried."

"My brother, worried about me? You don't say!" At least, in this case, I was grateful for his preoccupation with my life and wellbeing. *Thank you, Lord, for little blessings—even if they sometimes come in the form of overbearing siblings.*

The voices of men shouting led me to the front door, a solid oak monstrosity. My heart warmed at the thought of my brother defending my honor so loudly I could hear him through a six inch wooden door. A six inch wooden door difficult to open—how had Jack managed that?

"Gentlemen, you can stop arguing. I'm fine, really I am. And I solved the case! Senator Jack Hebert murdered Ronald Reynolds, and I've got the murder weapon." That is, if Jack didn't dispose of it before fleeing the country. Why didn't I check the kitchen for the statue before declaring my safety and success to my brother?

"Ev, thank goodness you're okay! Now, will you tell Officer Charbonnet that it takes more than a ribeye steak to get your clothes off?"

I shut the door. Hmmm...I'd never gotten a piece of that cake.

"That was quick, Doc. I bet Nate was glad t'see ya'. He'd gotten himself all worked up, worried that the killer had come after ya'."

Nearly three-fourths of the cake was missing from the box, yet less than a quarter of that portion remained on Shorty's plate. "How did you manage to eat almost the entire cake in the two minutes I was gone?"

My PI wiped his mouth with an embroidered white napkin, leaving a trail of chocolate across its once pristine...top? Front? Anyway, Shorty left chocolate all over the white cloth napkin.

"Hey, now! A quarter o'the cake was gone before I got to it. Didn't ya' get a piece before the senator tied you up?"

"No I didn't! And I can't believe my host was that rude! Jack tied me up and *then* had a piece of Chocolate Ganache? I'm not sure which breach of social etiquette is worse: tying me up with plastic zip ties, or eating dessert and not offering me any."

Shorty lifted his fork so it hovered just in front of his mouth. "Well, I ain't no Emily Post, but I'd think it's ruder t'tie up yore supper guest in the spare bedroom than eatin' dessert without her. But ya' might wanna ask yore friend Elizabeth Trahan about that."

I turned to look for a plate, but shifted my focus on the cake box itself. With only a quarter of the cake remaining, why should I get a plate? After all, I'd been tied up in a guest room for...what? Five hours? Six? If anyone deserved to finish off the cake it was me. Shorty handed me a fork.

"I figured ya'd want the rest o'the cake, Doc. An' ya' do deserve it, iffen I do say so myself. Any idea where Jack's off to now?"

It was my turn to poise my fork in front of my mouth. "Not really. Just a beautiful little island with the bluest ocean he'd ever seen, and with no extradition treaty. Oh, and he and his kids will be living in a forty room mansion with servants everywhere."

Shorty polished off his cake while I told the rest of Jack's story. Then he rummaged through the refrigerator again. "Nothin' washes down chocolate cake like milk! Good thing the senator didn't empty his fridge before he fled the country. Otherwise, I'd have t'run down the road for some milk. Mmm...and it's whole milk too, not that hippie skim."

How was skim milk for hippies? Never mind, I didn't want to know. Did hippies still exist? What was a hippie anyway...?

"Doc! Yer daydreamin' again. Are ya' ready t'go? I need a ride back home, cuz I came with Nate. Yore brother might be here all night, defendin' yore honor."

My brother appeared in the doorway. "Actually, we all need to stay awhile, until Detective Barton shows up. But Ev, your honor's not in question anymore. Hey, did you guys eat all the cake?"

Shorty hopped to the freezer. "Yeah, we did. But I found some vanilla ice cream earlier. An' the senator's got a box o'chocolate chip cookies in the pantry. How about that?"

"You don't have to tell me twice! I'll get the cookies. Ev, get the bowls and spoons."

I'd never seen that side of my brother. "Nate, aren't we breaking some kind of law, sitting in a murderer's kitchen eating all his food?"

Nate hesitated half a second. "He's in the wind, right? He's not coming back for this food. And who knows what kinds of evidence we'll find, while we're eating? Let's keep our eyes and ears open."

"Oh!" I spun around and fixed my eyes on the Eiffel Tower. "He did leave it! Look, guys, this is the murder weapon. Jack left it, and it's got some of Ronald's blood on it. I bet Jack's DNA is all over it too. But I wonder..."

I resumed my task of securing bowls and spoons for our evidence search disguised as an eating project. "Jack explained what this tower meant to him. It represented the missed opportunity to take his dying wife to Paris, and fulfill her last wish. But Shorty, you and I had always theorized the murder weapon meant something to both the killer *and* the victim. What did this mean to Ronald?"

I placed the bowls in front of me, along with the Williams-Sonoma scoop I'd found. Shorty brought me the ice cream. As I prepared our dessert (the second one for me and my PI), my brain worked overtime. At 1:30 a.m. that brainpower didn't amount to much.

My younger and more alert brother placed the cookies into the bowls. "Now that you mention it, I heard something about Ronald and Judy taking a romantic trip to Paris just before they got divorced. Or it was supposed to be—romantic, that is. While they were on top of The Eiffel Tower, Judy told Ronald she was divorcing him, and she'd make sure she got half of everything he owned. He'd never see his kids, but he'd cough up plenty of money for child support. She left him at the top of the tower, caught a cab, and canceled all the credit cards on the way to the airport. Of course, she'd already cleaned out their joint accounts, and opened a separate account and credit card in her name only. So, yeah, that Eiffel Tower statue sure had a lot of meaning for Ronald too." Nate licked the last remnants of ice cream off his spoon. "You'd better call Dad and Elizabeth. They've been up for a while worrying about you."

"Yes, as soon as I finish my ice cream."

"Evangeline, are you all right? Now who saved you: Nate or Shorty?"

"I'm fine, Dad. And I guess it was Shorty."

"Dadgummit! Are you sure? Maybe Nate had a hand in saving you?"

"Not really. Nate was outside the house arguing whether..." No, I wasn't going to give the full story to my father. "...uh, arguing whether they had enough evidence to break down the door. Shorty came in through another entrance and cut off my zip ties."

"Are you absolutely positive Nate had nothing to do with rescuing you?"

"Yes, Dad, I'm certain. Why do you keep asking?"

My father grumbled some words I couldn't hear. "What? Dad, what did you say?"

"Oh, nothing. But I guess I owe Shorty twenty bucks. He bet me that he'd save you before Nate could." Why didn't that surprise me? "Oh? You and Shorty took the time to place a bet before he came to rescue me? Did Shorty also stop for a snack? Maybe take a few minutes to shove some money into the slot machines?"

"Evangeline, don't be ridiculous! Shorty called to let me know you hadn't made it home from Baton Rouge. He was on his way to meet Nate at his home. They'd already contacted the Baton Rouge police, and were meeting them at Jack's house. We made the bet before he got to Nate's. And he couldn't have stopped for a snack—it was after midnight. You know the sidewalks roll up in Graisseville after eight o'clock. Even the Gas n' More."

"Oh, thank goodness! Who knows how long it would have taken Shorty to rescue me, if he could have stopped for food? But then you might have won your bet."

"Child, I just don't know about you sometimes. You have a flair for the dramatic, I tell you. And you get that from your mother's side! The Bergerons, we don't have that flair. No sir! We're as calm as cucumbers. Why, I remember one time..."

"Dad, I have to go. I've still got to call Elizabeth. Oh, and I'm sorry you lost your bet." Sorry, not sorry, that is.

My best friend seemed more relieved and less disappointed in my story. "Oh, honey, I'm so glad you're okay. Cliff was ready to drive back home from his brother's tonight, to form a search party for you. We were both down on our knees praying for your safe recovery. Now get a good night's sleep, and when you're all rested and refreshed, you can tell me all about it. Sweet dreams."

Detective Lydia Barton arrived soon after our ice cream party. "Thanks for staying, everyone. I'll try to be quick. Ev, let's start with you."

By my definition, a wrap up of the killer's motive, means, and opportunity in twenty minutes was pretty darn quick. The detective kept her word. "Lydia, I have one question, though. Why did Jack hire me and Shorty to clear his uncle's name? Didn't he worry that we'd figure out he was the killer?"

The thirty year old detective smiled, her face smooth as fresh sheets on the clothesline. Twenty years ago I looked that refreshed rolling out of bed after midnight. Nowadays, I didn't look half that good, even after a full night's sleep.

"I can't say for sure, Ev, but I'd bet Jack felt pretty guilty his uncle was on trial for his crime. Maybe he hoped you'd gather enough reasonable doubt that Sid would go free."

Her eyes locked mine. "Didn't you two go to high school together? Maybe he had an unresolved crush. You know, something that compelled him to spend time with you. Regardless, you solved the case, and kept an innocent man out of jail."

She looked at our bowls with creamy pools of melted goodness. Was that a longing look in her eyes? "Like I said when we met, we all want justice for Ronald Reynolds. I'm glad we got that for him. And is there any ice cream left?"

Could an adjunct professor call in sick to finals? What if said professor had been zip tied and left in Baton Rouge for over five hours? No, best to haul myself to the LSU campus with a tumbler full of Maggie's strongest coffee.

"Bye, Dr. Delafose! See you next semester!"

And just like that, my fall teaching requirements were complete. Well, except for the grading and the posting. And yet, much as I enjoyed my students and they enjoyed me, we were all ready for a break. As I dragged myself to faculty parking, my phone buzzed.

"Mitch, what a nice surprise! Are you calling to check up on me?" How much did the sheriff know about my wild night with the senator?

"Well, you don't sound like someone who's been zip tied and abandoned in a multi million dollar mansion for almost six hours. In fact, you sound like your usual self. How are you feeling?"

"I'm feeling great, although that's probably from the thirty ounces of coffee with five shots of espresso I poured into my body a few hours ago. But it's wearing off—any idea where I could get some more for the ride home?"

"As a matter of fact I do. How about you swing by the station, and I'll treat you to some good coffee, not the motor oil we serve to the employees. What do you say?"

Mitch's voice reminded me of a blackberry cobbler fresh out of the oven, warm and inviting. "Mmm...as tempting as that sounds, I'd prefer hitting a drive thru on my way home to a hot bath and happy bottoms. Any recommendations?"

Disappointment seeped through his voice, but he smoothed over it. "Of course. I'll text you the closest drive thru coffee shop to the campus. But only if you can tell me where to get some...what did you call them? Happy bottoms? Sounds like I need some of those."

"It's a long story—how about I tell you on New Year's Eve?"

The disappointment scurried out the door, and Mitch's voice returned to blackberry cobbler mode. "Oh? So we're still on for New Year's Eve? Any chance I could see you before that?"

"Mmmm, easy now, sheriff. One date at a time. I'll call you when I'm coherent." I ended the call to focus on my drive home. Only thirty minutes to my loving dog and a hot bath. Oh, and a pot of tea sounded amazing, maybe with some of those dark chocolates Bonnie had given me.

My PI's truck jarred my vision of bubbles and chocolate. "Hey Shorty, what're you doing in my driveway?"

He shuffled from one foot to the other, like people did when they delivered bad news. Just like Doug's partner, Brad, when he told me Doug had been shot.

"Uh, we need t'talk. Can I come in?"

Shorty followed me straight into the kitchen, despite Zydeco's nose pushes and whines. He wasn't used to his buddy walking in without doting on him. The news must be pretty bad. But what could it be?

"Would you like an orange soda? Sweet tea maybe?"

Shorty's eyes conducted a staring contest with his shoes. "No thank ya'. Uh, Doc, I'll get right tuh the point."

He swept his prosthetic leg in an arc from right to left. "Ya' may've noticed I've been kinda quiet lately, an' snappin' at things ya' say. I don't know if ya' noticed, mebbe ya' didn't. Cuz yore mind kinda wanders around sometimes, so it's hard t'know what ya' catch an' what ya' miss."

So far our conversation was going well, as usual. "Uh, okay. But now that you mention it, yes I had noticed. I just figured when you were ready to tell me, you would. And I guess you're ready to tell me."

My friend nodded, still hosting the staring contest with his shoes. Was Shorty ending our friendship? What could I have done to make him do that? My chest forced the air in and out of my lungs. It was hard, because of the elephant-sized weight sitting on my ribcage.

"Doc, when I asked yore advice on Annabelle's Christmas present, I kinda thought ya' might tell me...well, I thought ya' would think that...well geez, Doc, don'tcha like Annabelle?"

Oh goodness, where did that come from? "Of course I do, Shorty! I consider her a dear friend, and I just love that you two are together. I think she's wonderful for you, and you make her extremely happy. If I've ever said or done anything to contradict that, I truly apologize."

The staring contest ended, and Shorty's eyes started round two with me. "Then why don'tcha want me t'marry her?"

Like Vanna White revealing those last key letters to solve the puzzle, Shorty divulged that final, most important clue to solving this mystery. Why wasn't I jumping up and down yelling the answer? If Vanna had been standing in my kitchen, she would have shrugged her shoulders.

"Marry her? I'm sorry, Shorty, I had no idea. When have I ever said I don't want you and Annabelle to get married? When have we ever talked about you marrying *anyone*?"

Nope, I wasn't winning the staring contest. Shorty'd had too much practice with his shoes. "Look, I asked ya' what I should get my girlfriend for Christmas. The girlfriend I've been datin' for goin' on...what? Fourteen months now. That's a record for me, Doc! A dadgum record! But the one person I want t'give her blessin' on my marriage proposal...well, she ain't givin' it!"

Vanna, if she were in my kitchen, would have given up and gone back to the studio. But I was starting to catch on. "Oh, I think I understand. When you asked me to suggest a gift for Annabelle, you wanted to see if I'd mention an engagement ring. You reasoned that if I wanted you two to get married, I'd tell you. But since I didn't do that, *you* think I don't want you to marry Annabelle."

That was some convoluted thinking, even for Shorty. And yet, the tears in his eyes confirmed my theory. I'd royally screwed up and hurt my best friend. My other best friend? My second best friend? Okay, this wasn't about me and how I ranked my friendships. But how could I salvage a misunderstanding as big as the Honey Island Swamp? *Lord, what should I do?* Oh yes, start with an apology.

"First of all, I'm sorry. Annabelle is one of my favorite people in the world, and I don't think you could do any better as far as a wife goes. But your dating life isn't my business. Neither is when and if you get married. Those are extremely personal decisions that should be made with much prayer and thought. But if you're asking my opinion, I'll say this: I think you should settle down and marry An..."

Okay, maybe Shorty's patience wasn't improving. And who knew I couldn't breathe when Shorty was hugging me? Had Shorty ever hugged me? Were the lights growing dim...?

"Oh, sorry, Doc! I think ya' almost blacked out there. That's great! Cuz I couldn't do this without yore blessin'. An' while we're talkin' about our feelin's...wouldja be my best man?"

T he glow from Christmas Day wrapped my heart like one of my grandmother's quilts. Was it the gifts from Matty and Ellie, a vanilla scented candle and a chenille lap blanket? Or was it the promise to come home for Spring Break? Or Matty's assurance that no matter where his career took him, he'd always have a space on his couch for me?

No, it was definitely baking cookies on Christmas Eve with my kids while my niece and nephew attempted to help. My father perched himself on a kitchen stool, offering his sage wisdom on baking hacks. Nate and Bonnie? Those two love-birds sat on the couch as LSU played Ole Miss. Nate draped his arm over his sweet wife's shoulders, squeezing her gently as he dozed off. I felt my mother looking down, taking some time from her deep conversations with friends and family members to approve of my special Christmas memory.

My thoughts ran to Miss Pearlie. Maggie told me the week before, over a cup of skinny chai tea, that Miss Pearlie cried during Coy's confession. Her tears dried up faster than a sprinkle of rain during a drought when her son's name came up.

"Oh, that boy! His daddy spoiled him, that's what's wrong with that one. Coy, all is forgiven, honey. And don't you worry—I still own fifty-one percent of Graisseville Tires n' More. Your job's safe as long as I'm around. Now Eli's job, on the other hand..."

Shorty got the best truck tires in Miss Pearlie's store.

I snuggled into my couch, watching Matty and Elly battle it out on some video game they'd attached to my television. I declined to join in, but they'd promised to take me on at Scrabble before bedtime. Where was I? Oh, yes, my cases.

On one hand, I had Sid and his huge sigh of relief at spending Christmas in a red and green plaid vest with matching bowtie. Despite the fashion faux pas, it beat an orange jumpsuit any day. He invited his investigators to his annual New Year's Day brunch, normally reserved for clients and close friends. I considered going, mostly out of curiosity. But Shorty promptly declined.

"Why would I wanna spend the first day uh the new year with a bunch uh fancy pants? Nope, me an' Annabelle are gonna have French toast an' scrambled eggs with her mama, her kids, an' any uh my family that cares tuh show up. C'mon, Doc—don'tcha wanna spend yore New Year's Day with people that love ya', even with all yore problems? Yore daddy's gonna be there, he won't never turn down free food. I bet he'd love t'talk tuh ya' about yore plans for next year."

Hmmm, did I? Did I want to spend my new year with people who knew me? Or did I want to spend it with people who had no idea how flawed and fractured I was? "I'll get back to you on that, Shorty."

Speaking of Shorty, what duties did I have as best man...best woman? Maids and matrons of honor threw bachelorette parties and planned mani/pedi's around the bride's schedule. Maybe Dino from The Dirty Pelican could help me with a bachelor party? Or should I host it at The Cajun Frog? These were the times I missed Doug. And yet...my friendship with Shorty wouldn't be so strong if I was married. Most married women and men didn't hang out together without spouses.

Would Annabelle join our investigation team? Could I spend time alone with Shorty when he was married and I was single? Was that appropriate? Would village tongues wag? Oh, Ev, who were we kidding? Tongues had been wagging the moment I saw my first dead body.

And what was Jack doing on Christmas Day? With forty rooms and an army of servants, I imagined his baby blues and caterpillar eyelashes blinking in bliss as he watched his kids open their mountain of gifts. The man had literally gotten away with murder.

My shoulders twitched and I pulled my blanket closer. Ah, my New Year's date with Mitch! More warm thoughts took over my brain and I closed my eyes. The past year resided on a large shelf of my heart, storing lots of happy memories. But this next year? Yes, for this next three hundred and sixty-five days I'd need even more storage space. This next year promised to be full of fun and excitement. And hopefully more mysteries to solve.

LAGNIAPPE CHAPTER

H ere in Louisiana, a lagniappe is a little something extra, a bonus. An additional donut at the donut shop, an extra play for a season ticket holder, a little something special tucked into your order at the boutique. My lagniappe to you, my dear reader, is this short story about one of my characters. It has nothing to do with the story you just read. Instead, it gives more insight into the character.

"Doc, ya' got a few minutes? I need t'run somethin' past ya.'"

"Sure. Talk to me while I wait for my kettle to boil. That's about ten minutes, give or take."

"Great! Can ya' open the door for me?"

Ah, so that explained why my dog was standing in the hallway wagging his tail. And here I was, just thinking Zy really liked my front door. "Sure, I'll be right there." Of all the tricks Shorty had taught my dog, opening the front door wasn't one of them. How did fetching a ball or barking on command rate higher than opening a door?

"Zydeco, for the millionth time, how can I open the door if you're standing in front of it?" Yes, teaching my dog to open a door needed to be next on Shorty's list. Which brought me back to my original question: why was my PI on my front porch at nine o'clock on Friday morning during my Christmas break?

"I'm sorry t'barge in on yore mornin', Doc, but I waited as long as I could. I know ya' like t'hang out in yore pajamas and drink a pot o'tea. But this is mighty important."

We'd made progress—Shorty's usual greeting mentioned me sleeping until almost noon, even after multiple corrections. Old dogs *could* learn new tricks, it seemed.

"Orange soda is in the fridge, and I was just about to scramble some eggs. How many would you like?"

Despite his prosthetic leg, the guy crossed my kitchen as fast as Zy. "Well, I jus' ate breakfast three hours ago. So make it five eggs. Ya' got any boudin t'go in there? Uh, who'm I kiddin'? Ya' never got any boudin."

He stared at the inside of my refrigerator, studying the contents like he would a police lineup. Which one would he choose?

"Yeah, here's some salsa. I thought I saw that last time I was here. Oh, yeah, here's some shredded cheese, an' some bacon. How about we put all that in the eggs?" Arms full, he rotated before emptying his load onto my island. "Do ya' got an onion, Doc? They're real good for ya', got those cancer fightin' things in 'em, an' those *ox dense* things too."

"I think you mean *antioxidants*, and yes, I have an onion in the pantry. Oh, there goes my kettle."

Once again my two scrambled eggs turned into a dish out of a diner, complete with sides. Shorty hadn't mentioned those yet, but they were coming.

"How about some grits, Doc? Mebbe some biscuits an' gravy too. Yeah, ya' can't have eggs an' bacon without biscuits an' gravy." My PI hopped to the pantry again, presumably to gather ingredients for homemade biscuits and gravy.

"How about I make the biscuits an' gravy, an' you take care o'the eggs an' grits?" He handed me the bag of stone-ground corn.

"Here's the problem with this setup: We both know you won't eat instant grits, and the regular kind will take about an hour to make. The biscuits and gravy aren't fast either, but I'm willing to work with that. Could we skip the grits?"

One might think Shorty had a monumental decision to ponder, something akin to our commander in chief's daily dilemmas. This could take a while—would he have to make a call, bring in an advisor...or two? I snuck a glance at the clock on my microwave.

"Yeah, okay, I guess that'd work. It is my mid mornin' snack, so jus' biscuits an' gravy should be enough." Much as he tried, Shorty couldn't chase the disappointment out of his eyes.

"Don't forget the bacon and eggs too, with cheese and salsa. I think we'll be fine. While we're cooking, could you tell me what's going on? What do you need to run past me?"

Shorty pulled out the mixing bowl and measuring cup. When he made something from scratch, he made it just the way his mother had for decades. Madie Cormier never used an electric mixer, and neither did her son.

"Well, I've been workin' on my marriage proposal. Now this may surprise ya', Doc, but I ain't ever asked a woman t'marry me. Oh, I've been proposed to more times than I got fingers an' toes! But I ain't ever been the one t'do the askin'."

Shorty whisked the dry ingredients. My mother had convinced Madie to try a whisk, and it changed her life. She'd been in a kitchen since before she could walk, and subscribed to the belief that the old ways were the best. But she embraced the whisk with enthusiasm, and had one in every size she could find.

"I'm gonna pack a picnic supper an' drive Annabelle out tuh the pond. Y'know, the one at the back, near Rattlesnake Ridge?"

Shorty's great grandfather claimed he'd spotted a rattlesnake on the back of the property and named the ten acres after his encounter. No one had seen a rattler since, but the new name stuck, mostly because it surpassed the old one. Not to mention, it rolled off the tongue much easier than *the back ten acres that bumps up against Bob Cahill's place.*

"That sounds lovely. Annabelle will love that. What do you need to run by me?"

Next came the butter, then all the wet ingredients. "My words need a little work. Lemme tell ya' what I got, an' ya' tell me what ya' think. Oh, an' get me the wax paper—I gotta knead this biscuit dough."

As Shorty worked his dough, he practiced proposing. "Now, Annabelle, I was raised on country sunshine. My parents raised me right. But I've been looking for love in all the wrong places. But then I met you. Annabelle, sweetheart, I'm a man of means by no means. And I can't never promise you a rose garden. But I fall tuh pieces each time I see ya'. An' I'm crazy for lovin' ya'. An' I thank God that the world's been blessed by a thing called love,..."

"Okay, I'm going to stop you right there. Correct me if I'm wrong, but aren't your words from a handful of your favorite songs?"

Shorty paused his kneading. "Mebbe. But they're good songs, Doc, from good singers. Ya' got Lynn Anderson, Roger Miller, Barbara Mandrell, an' my girl Patsy Cline. An' the two Johnny's—Mr. Lee, an' Mr. Cash. Those are some o'my favorite singers, Annabelle too. It seems fittin' t'quote their songs in my proposal. Can ya' get me yore rollin' pin an' yore biscuit cutter?"

As Shorty rolled out the dough, I crafted my response. "That's a nice sentiment. May I make a suggestion? Why don't you play some of your and Annabelle's favorite songs in the background while you're proposing? And use your own words. Maybe something like, Annabelle, I want to spend the rest of my life with you by my side, listening to our favorite songs."

Shorty dropped the rolling pin. "Hey, yeah, that's great! Hold on, I gotta get a piece of paper. No, wait! I'll jus' record ya'. Start over, Doc, an' don't forget that part about spendin' the rest o'my life."

Our eggs sat cooling on the plates. "No, you've got to do this, Shorty. All by yourself. Because if anyone other than you writes it, then it's from someone else's heart. Not yours. Now eat your eggs before they get cold."

JOIN MY TRIBE!

I'm looking for readers to join my twisty Southern mystery tribe! Would you like to apply and potentially receive free copies of my eBooks in exchange for an honest review? Scan the QR code below and submit your application, or click here and note you want to become a Twisty Tribe member.

Scan me

A Little About Me

J ann Franklin is a faith-based cozy mystery writer attracting readers who enjoy twisty Southern mysteries with a touch of romance and a dose of humor.

Her books offer mysteries in Louisiana with curious clues and characters who exasperate as much as they endear.

These quirky yet charming residents are just like family—sometimes you want to hug them, and sometimes you want to disown them. Immerse yourself in small town culture as you exercise your sleuthing skills and your funny bone.□

Jann lives in the small town of Grand Cane, Louisiana. Over three hundred other people also live in Grand Cane, and many of her chapters came from her weekly visits at the downtown coffee shop.

She and her husband John enjoy Sundays at Grand Cane Baptist Church, dinner with family and friends, and watching the lightning bugs in their backyard. Their kids come to visit, when they aren't too busy living their big-city lives.

www.ingramcontent.com/pod-product-compliance
Lightning Source LLC
Chambersburg PA
CBHW051938220626
47052CB00004B/698